# Praise for *The California Wife*

"This vital, sweeping story is delivered in Harnisch's silky, upscale prose. Much like a fine glass of wine, *The California Wife* is a highbrow indulgence that is tasteful, captivating and heady."
—*The Globe and Mail*

"*The Vintner's Daughter* was an enjoyable romantic saga, and this new entry, which spans 1897 to 1906, is even more involving. Harnisch has hit her stride as a writer . . . The story brings readers deeply into the economics of the wine industry – a unique historical fiction subject . . . Readers will enjoy being whisked back in time to Napa's beginnings as a major wine-producing region, and the stage is set for future adventures with these warm-hearted, ambitious characters."
—*Historical Novels Review*

"It was easy to get lost in the pages of *The California Wife,* Harnisch's compelling new novel. Harnisch is adept at creating determined, complex characters, whose combination of strength and vulnerability make them irresistible. Her admirable ability to bring forth a strong sense of place made every glorious detail of the Napa Valley sparkle: I wanted to reach for a glass of wine as I read. This sweeping tale is a true delight!"
—Linda Holeman, International Bestselling author of *The Linnet Bird* and *The Lost*

"*The California Wife* is not only an accurate and nostalgic account of the early history of our wine industry in California, it's a lovely novel with characters you want join in a harvest, a meal, and a glass of wine. I recommend this book to wine lovers and historical fiction fans alike!"

—Tina Vierra, Associate Publisher, *Wines & Vines*

"… a vivid, fine-tuned novel about two fiercely ambitious and determined people who face obstacles that would bring most of us to our knees. Harnisch's skillful blend of 19th-century societal norms and details about wine-making practices never overwhelm the characters but enrich them, captivating the heart. You'll long remember this beautiful story about redemption, forgiveness, love, and family bonds."

—Ann Weisgarber, author of *The Promise* and *The Personal History of Rachel DuPree*

"A passionate novel set in the beautiful Napa Valley in the early 1900s. You'll cheer for Sarah Lemieux as she tries to balance, love, family, and independence in a time when women were expected to obey. Rich in history, passion, and community, *The California Wife* is a novel that continues to surprise until the very end."

—Marci Nault, author of *The Lake House*

"Fans of historical fiction, heart-pounding romance, and remarkable women look no further. Kristen Harnisch does more than craft a rollicking good tale in intriguing locales; she transports you back in time through engaging dialogue, complex characters, and vivid description. Sara is no shrinking violet, and as she travels from France to the Napa Valley she learns how to channel her passions to build the life she's always dreamed of. An exquisite read from start to finish."

—Alexandria Brown, Napa County Historical Society Research Librarian

"As seasoned wine country travelers, we see the present-day struggles of small, family-owned wineries and know how difficult it is to become successful. Winemakers are constantly at the mercy of unpredictable weather and must work long hours to ensure a good product and profitable wine sales. Kristen Harnisch does a remarkable job of transporting us back 100 years and gives us an authentic feel for what it was like to make wine at that time without the benefit of enology and viticulture programs or the advances of modern-day science. Sara and Philippe's love for each other helps them face hidden family secrets, threats from a rival winemaker and a tragedy that could destroy everything they have."

—Joe and Janella Becerra, *Winecountrygetaways.com*

"Rich with setting and story, Kristen Harnisch pulled me deep into the Napa Valley vineyards and through the streets of San Francisco in her lovely turn-of-the-twentieth century story, *The California Wife*. Harnisch weaves history and family passion together so seamlessly that I had to remind myself I was reading fiction. This is a simply stunning follow-up to *The Vintner's Daughter*. Both enlightening and delightful. Bravo!"

—Carla Stewart, Award-winning author of *Stardust* and *A Flying Affair*

# Praise for *The Vintner's Daughter*

"[A] fast-moving romantic saga about two independent, ambitious people hoping to succeed in winemaking....This relaxing summer read offers an enjoyable armchair voyage to wine country."
—*Historical Novels Review*

"One of the novel's highlights is its rich history of the winemaking process through the eyes of a woman who is passionate and meticulous about each step.... In the beginning, [Sara] endures nonstop pain and loss, but these tragedies transform her from a smart, hardworking girl into an independent, resourceful woman. At its core, *The Vintner's Daughter* is a story of perseverance and transcending one's past."
—*Booklist*

"A young French woman, determined to pursue her dreams, shows resourcefulness and endurance as she journeys from her home to America in a novel set in the late 1800s....the plot is engaging and well-paced. Wine aficionados and fans of romance and historical fiction will drink this in."
—*Kirkus Reviews*

"Lush and evocative, this novel brings the Loire Valley and its glorious vineyards to life in a story that will delight readers everywhere. Enjoy with your favorite glass of Merlot!"
—Adriana Trigiani, bestselling author of *The Shoemaker's Wife*

"A lovely novel with sparkling dialogue, intricate plot and great characters. This tale of a young girl determined to hold onto her beloved father's vineyard in the Loire Valley will invoke inevitable comparisons to *Gone with the Wind*. Sara is a girl with grit and determination, and seizes what she wants from life with both hands, evolving over the course of the novel from an impetuous, headstrong girl to a mature woman. A pleasure."
—Roberta Rich, author of *The Harem Midwife* and *The Midwife of Venice*

# THE CALIFORNIA WIFE

Also by Kristen Harnisch:

*The Vintner's Daughter*

*The*

# CALIFORNIA
# WIFE

A NOVEL

## KRISTEN HARNISCH

SHE WRITES PRESS

Published 2016
Printed in the United States of America
ISBN: 978-1-63152-087-7
Library of Congress Control Number: 2015959392

For information, address:
She Writes Press
1563 Solano Ave #546
Berkeley, CA 94707

She Writes Press is a division of SparkPoint Studio, LLC.

*To my parents, Maryellen and Frank Lacroix,*
*for your kindness, enthusiasm and courage.*
*And in memory of my mother-in-law, Susan Harnisch,*
*who taught us to find joy in life's simple moments.*

# THE CALIFORNIA WIFE

# Part I

# Chapter 1

S ara Thibault had never been this sure—or scared—of anything in her life. Marriage to Philippe Lemieux would be like jumping into the rushing current of a river: thrilling to the senses, adventurous and undoubtedly tumultuous.

When she slid her arms around the man she'd just agreed to marry, his brilliant blue eyes warmed with affection, and his lips formed the crooked smile that never failed to soften Sara's bones. She pressed her cheek to the lapel of his damp wool coat, enjoying the clean smell of the snow that blanketed them on this crisp, gray November morning. Sara was happy—for the first time since she'd fled Saint Martin last year.

Sara recalled the events that had brought them from Eagle's Run, Philippe's California vineyard, back to her family's vineyard here in the heart of the Loire. The tragedy that had forced Sara and her sister, Lydia, to flee France in the first place had taken Sara to California. There, in spite of the tangled history between their two families, Sara and Philippe had formed an unbreakable bond. She shuddered, remembering how close they'd come to being separated forever—all because of one man.

"Are you cold, love?" Philippe asked. "Shall we go inside and share our news?"

"Not quite yet." Sara looked past him to the watchman's shed where her mother, her new husband, Jacques, and Sara's nephew, Luc, waited. Of course she would have to tell them, but what would she say?

"Sara?" Philippe's lips skimmed hers, and she instantly craved more.

She explained shyly, "I want to spend more time with you—alone." The ten hectares of bare, dormant vines and rocky soil beckoned to her, just as they had during the winters of her youth. How could she make him understand? "I want to show you Saint Martin."

His expression relaxed. "And I'd love to see it through your eyes."

Sara's face brightened and she linked an arm through his, tucking her hands into her warm woolen muff. Touring Philippe around Saint Martin was a sensible idea. It would keep her mind off the beautiful planes of his face, his tall, vigorous physique and the simmering need she repressed every time he called her name.

They strolled for nearly an hour. She guided him around the perimeter of the farm, past the watchman's shed to the stables, which held two horses and a wagon. Sara paused at the spot with the clearest view of the Loire's surging waters. Philippe was quiet and contemplative when she pointed out the three hectares, now vacant of vines, that had been ruined by the phylloxera louse two years ago. "When will we replant with American rootstock?" she ventured.

Philippe shook his head. "Not quite yet." What did he mean? Sara grew self-conscious, suddenly aware of how small Saint Martin was in comparison to Philippe's California vineyard. Ten hectares—nearly twenty-five acres of chenin blanc grapes—was no match for the two hundred acres of cabernet, zinfandel and chardonnay grapes at Eagle's Run. Eagle's Run was one of the largest vineyards in Napa, and Philippe was one of the county's most respected *vignerons*—how could she compete? Nevertheless, this small patch of vines in Vouvray had shaped Sara's soul from birth. She'd spent years of her life kneeling on Saint Martin's rocky soil, plucking the thin-skinned chenin blanc grapes from their stems and tasting their juicy flesh. She and Lydia had chased chickens through the vine rows, their girlish laughter playing on the summer breeze. As a young girl, she'd carved her name into the winery's enormous fermenting barrels, staking her secret claim upon her father's legacy. Philippe would never fully understand Sara until he acquainted himself with every meter of Saint Martin—and Sara would never be satisfied until they restored Saint Martin to its former vitality.

She'd gone weak with relief when he'd appeared earlier today, but she couldn't allow herself to blithely, blindly follow him back to America, away from her own aspirations. She would bide her time, but Sara was determined to have her way.

They finally arrived at Sara's favorite part of the vineyard, the area that held the most memories for her: the cave dwellings and the family wine cellar, both hewn from a long ledge of tufa rock that ran along the vineyard's northern border.

"How long ago were these carved?" Philippe asked as he ran his hand along the jagged yellow stone.

"The eleventh century," Sara guessed. "My mother's parents refurbished them." She unlocked the oak doors to the wine cellar and led him inside the dark limestone cave, which was filled with barrels of the Thibault family's 1897 chenin blanc. The scent of oak and sweet wine reminded Sara of Papa.

Sara swallowed her grief and walked over to a pyramid of smaller barrels, stacked five high and extending over fifty meters to the back of the cave. Her hand slid over the smooth barrel staves. "My father taught me how to select the best oak from the different forests in France, and how to ferment and rack the wine." She paused for a moment before adding wistfully, "But Jacques taught me how to press the grapes."

"Using this beauty over here?" Philippe's pleasure was evident as he placed a hand on the new Morineau press Sara had just purchased.

"No!" Sara waved off his assumption. "All we had before was the old basket press, like the Romans used centuries ago," she joked. "We used this one for the first time last month. I'd been pestering Papa to buy a more efficient press for years, but he always believed it wiser to spend the money on the fruit first, equipment second." She sighed. "Papa was right about most things, but not that."

Philippe moved closer. "He'd be so pleased with what you've accomplished," he assured her.

Sara squeezed his hand. "He'd be even more pleased if we replanted the vines we lost," she replied coyly.

"Replanting is expensive, love. I need more time." But time was the problem. Once planted, the new vines wouldn't produce decent wine grapes for three to five years. Rather than press the issue now, Sara led Philippe outside. She jiggled the key, trying to lock the stubborn doors. Philippe circled his thumbs between her shoulder blades, relaxing her. "You've been busy since you've returned," he observed. "I was hoping you'd spent the last five weeks pining away for me, but apparently not."

"I'll never tell," she teased, her playful tone masking a deeper truth. Five weeks ago, they had argued terribly, and Philippe had told her to return to France. She had reluctantly left him, believing that they could never overcome the rift between their families. Sara had missed their days of working together side by side at Eagle's Run, and she'd mourned her long-held hope of uniting their two lives and vineyards. But Philippe had appeared today and convinced her that they could make a new start together, free from the sorrows of the past. Neither one of them, she suspected, could fully live without the other.

Sara stepped back from the cellar door and pointed to the cave dwellings a level above, their doors painted a cheerful robin's-egg blue. "This is where the pickers live during the harvest season, and where I sleep with Luc now." She had been mother to her fifteen-month-old nephew since Lydia had died in childbirth.

Sara turned to the scorched earth behind them. She grew quiet at the sight of the two chimneys and the pile of stones, all that remained of her ancestral home, burned to the ground in one night—the night Sara and Lydia had fled. Her pulse quickened. The fire had destroyed all physical evidence of that night's violence, but not the rush of panic Sara felt every time she passed these ruins.

Philippe squeezed her tightly. She shut her eyes and melted into his chest. His words were tender, but resolute. "Don't you see, Sara? This is why we need to leave France and live our life in California." He was right. Her old life at Saint Martin was gone forever.

And everything was settled. They would finally join their lives and their two vineyards: Eagle's Run in Napa and Saint Martin in Vouvray.

"But we'll still visit, yes?" Sara didn't know how Philippe truly felt about Saint Martin.

"As often as we're able. Your mother and Jacques, God willing, will run the vineyard until Luc is eighteen. What happened here will always be part of us, Sara, but we need to leave it behind."

Sara pressed her hands to his cold cheeks, her heart filling with the same determination she read on his face. "Yes," she agreed.

Philippe pulled his gloves back on. "Have you mustered the courage to tell your mother yet?" he nudged. Sara smiled, lured in part by the thought of the warm hearth. He began to pull her back through the labyrinth of vines toward the small watchhouse where her family waited. While she hurried over the chalky pebbles, struggling to match his stride, her coat snagged on some of the smaller vine branches, disrupting its smooth woolen surface.

Sara paid no mind. She had secured her heart's two desires: to reclaim her beloved Saint Martin, and to spend the rest of her days with Philippe Lemieux. Sara now shared Philippe's ambition: to make Eagle's Run the largest-producing and most profitable vineyard in Napa by 1900. In truth, Saint Martin's survival hinged on Eagle's Run's success. Sara stood to gain everything by marrying him, but she couldn't stop herself from wondering: what might this union with Philippe cost her?

# Chapter 2

Linnette Cross was surely a disappointment to her ancestors. Generations of her kinfolk had worked in respectable professions as cobblers, bakers and laundresses. Then there was Linnette, the harlot. Fortunately, she had no family left to judge her.

Since she could remember, men had always found her attractive, and she liked their attention. When Jimmy Mather had offered her a dollar to stroke her sweets, she was a fourteen-year-old orphan, as thin as Job's turkey. That money had bought bread for two weeks.

Satisfying men's needs afforded Linnette the freedom and money that most women only dreamed of. She was providing a service, like nurses do for their patients, she told herself.

Still, it had its risks. Linnette had managed to not fall in love with any man she'd charmed—until Philippe Lemieux. She'd first approached him over two years ago on the sidewalk in front of the Clinton Street House—the Napa City brothel where she worked. His fair, lean looks and confident stride sparked her interest. She'd guessed that a man like Philippe would never set foot inside a whorehouse, but she also knew how appealing her golden hair, plump breasts and willingness could be to an unmarried, red-blooded male. Within a week, he'd installed her permanently in the Palace Hotel. She owed him a debt of gratitude for plucking her out of the parlor-house. Philippe and Linnette had reached a satisfying business arrangement: she gave pleasure to Philippe alone, and he, in turn, gave her food, clothing and a home at one of the nicest hotels in downtown Napa.

Linnette guessed—when he came to her that April morning earlier this year and told her he'd met someone—that Philippe never suspected how fond she was of him. She'd hidden it well, sassing him about their time together, enjoying a few laughs and one last roll in the hay. When he left, however, she pressed her cheek to the cool, knotty pine floor and cried herself to sleep. How could one of Napa's most admired and successful vineyard owners slip from her grasp?

Then along came Pippa, the baby Linnette had birthed in the bedroom of her San Francisco apartment three mornings ago. Philippa Mary was her daughter's given name. Mary was after Linnette's mother, who died shortly after giving birth to Linnette. Philippa, Linnette thought, was too grand for a five-pound peanut of a baby, so Pippa would do for now. Linnette figured she must have been two months gone with Pippa when Philippe had broken things off. When she discovered her condition, she thought of using a syringe, or hiring the local woman to fix her up, but she couldn't bear the thought of killing Philippe's flesh and blood.

Instead, she caught the ferry from Vallejo to the city, where a friend—from Linnette's days in the Tenderloin's finest parlor—offered her a room. Since Linnette couldn't very well carry on her day job, she agreed to help with her friend's sewing business: hemming clothes and darning socks. Linnette was relieved to escape Napa, to slip undetected through San Francisco's loud and lively streets, to never again see or hear of Philippe and his new girl.

Pippa released a satisfied yawn and drifted off to sleep in her mother's arms. Her pink, wrinkled face reminded Linnette of a little old man, and her hair of a dandelion's soft down. Only a mother could overlook the defect that marred the newborn's face. To her, Pippa's lip simply looked as if God had grown distracted, like a seamstress when her thread snags—she tugs the fabric too hard, causing a tiny rift. The cleft lip had caused others to cringe or brand the baby "the Devil's child," but Linnette knew different. This child needed her more than anyone ever had—to nurture her, to teach her, but most importantly, to protect her. Love swelled and filled Linnette's dormant heart. If she couldn't have Philippe, his daughter was the next best thing.

Only one thing troubled Linnette: when should she tell him?

# Chapter 3

DECEMBER 1897, TOURS, FRANCE

Sara teetered on the edge of the bed, staring at the brass hook on the door. Scarlet floral paper decorated the walls of their hotel room, which was lit by two hand-painted oriental lamps perched atop the bedside tables. She'd released the crimson velvet drapes from their tassels to block all but a sliver of light from the avenue below. The room was small but luxurious. It must have cost Philippe a week's earnings for the night.

He had chosen the hotel in Tours himself. There was no privacy at Saint Martin with her family there. Sara had been relieved when Philippe insisted they spend their wedding night in a new and fashionable hotel. While she waited for him to return from the washroom, she wondered what on earth she was supposed to do.

Heat rushed to her cheeks. Of course she understood the workings of it all, but she didn't know how she was supposed to act, or dare undress in his presence. A moment ago, she had changed into the ivory peignoir her mother had given her. Sara recalled her mother's surprisingly sensible reaction when she'd announced her betrothal to Philippe. She'd expected Maman to object to her marriage to a Lemieux, but Maman wished them only joy, clapping her hands together and proclaiming, "Luc needs a good home, and who better to raise him than his aunt and uncle?"

Sara studied her reflection in the looking glass that hung on the far wall. She had brushed her chestnut-colored hair until it shone, and thick, dark lashes framed her vivid green eyes. The neckline of her gown was trimmed with intricate Amboise lace and tied with an ivory silk ribbon. The cotton draped perfectly from shoulders to ankles, hiding the half-moon scar on her chest but revealing just enough to make Sara shiver from the cold air on her bare skin. Sara had never worn anything so elegant in her life. She sighed, wishing Lydia were here to see it and give her some sisterly advice. Hopefully, Philippe would be too busy admiring her nightdress to notice her shaking hands.

The glass knob turned, and the door creaked open. Sitting on the bed, Sara plucked at the loose threads of the quilt. She drew a deep breath. As he entered the room, she appraised his neatly combed sandy hair, and the column of smooth, unblemished skin that his open shirt now revealed. The butterflies in her stomach danced again.

Warming her cold hands with his, Philippe steered Sara closer to the fire. She inhaled the enticing scent of shaving cream.

"You are stunning," he declared. To hide her embarrassment, Sara trained her eyes on the carpet, which was thick and luxurious. She concentrated on the gold arches along its border and the intricate red and pink floral design. Philippe's thumb smoothed the crinkle above her nose, a playful gesture he often used to relax her. "What are you thinking about?"

Sara gulped. "How happy I am."

"Liar," he whispered as his fingers grazed her jawbone.

Sara cringed at her own ignorance. "You caught me. I was trying to figure out what to do," she said, flushing. "Um, I mean, should I disrobe and slip under the covers?"

"Where's the fun in that?" he asked with a mischievous glint in his eye.

Before Sara could say anything else, he'd already started to untie the ribbon on her gown, as if he were opening an exquisite gift. He slipped the white cotton off her shoulders and brushed his lips over the tender skin of her clavicle. "You've done this before," she guessed. Sara didn't like to think about Philippe with other women, but his confident, easygoing manner soothed her.

"Not with someone I love," he insisted. Then Philippe moved behind Sara before allowing her garment to fall to the floor. He inhaled sharply, and his fingers, as soft as a feather, traced her spine from the nape of her neck to the dimples below her waist. He folded his arms around his bride and buried his face in her hair, murmuring, "So lovely."

Touched that he understood her timidity, Sara turned to reveal what until then had been left to Philippe's imagination. The need to press herself against his warm flesh overwhelmed Sara, yet she stood perfectly still, barely breathing. Philippe gently pulled her down onto the plush layers of sheets and quilts.

As Sara admired the flat muscles of Philippe's chest and the long, graceful lines of his legs, her belly tightened with longing. Philippe's hands explored her skin, and she reveled in the new sensations that charged through her body. But when he ran his hand down the inside of her thigh, Sara's body rebelled and she pushed him away.

"I'm—sorry," she stammered, mortified.

"What is it?" he asked with surprise.

Sara tucked the bedsheet under her chin; she didn't know how to tell him. Was it always going to be like this? Bastien was dead, yet he still divided them. Sara's spine tingled with fear when she thought of her sister's abusive husband—Philippe's brother— and how he'd attacked her the night they'd left France. She could still taste his sour tongue in her mouth, see the perverse pleasure flash in his coal-black eyes and feel the sting of his teeth piercing her delicate skin. The flood of memories paralyzed her.

"Sara," he commanded. "Tell me."

Sara couldn't. Philippe knew the story, but their wedding night was hardly the time to remind him of what his brother had done to her and of Bastien's death—the very reason why Sara and Philippe had parted two months ago.

Propped up against the headboard, Philippe stared at the door. Was he angry with her or with Bastien? She rested a tentative hand on his arm.

"I thought you stopped him," he said, searching her face.

"I did, from doing the worst, but not before he had . . . you know, touched me." Sara shuddered.

"Touched?" he asked skeptically.

"No." She swallowed hard, determined not to think of Bastien's assault on her most intimate parts. This is what Sara had feared: that Bastien would live on as a ghost in their marriage.

Philippe's arms encircled Sara and the two lay locked in healing silence. He was the first to speak. "Do you trust me?" he asked lightly.

"I do."

"Good. Then we'll just start somewhere else," he suggested, lowering his lean body over hers. He carried his weight on his elbows, careful not to crush her. Sara's fingertips glided from his chest to the springy line of hair below his navel. He released a raspy, satisfied sound before his lips began a slow but insistent contemplation of Sara's skin. "Remember what the priest said, my love," he murmured, his blue gaze lifting to meet hers. "And the two shall become one flesh." His smile twisted provocatively. He kissed the scar above her left breast, but did not linger. He moved on, circling her nipples with his thumbs. She gasped when he fastened his mouth on a pink tip and began to suck ever so gently.

This, Sara mused, is heaven on earth.

She was wrong. Heaven was what happened next.


Sara smelled strong coffee and bacon. Silver clanked against a tray, and she strained to pry her eyes open. Philippe sat down next to her, wearing a fresh shirt, vest, tie and trousers. She'd slept so soundly, she hadn't heard him rise.

"Good morning, Wife. Breakfast?" He handed her a small tray. "We have a big day ahead of us."

"Where are we going?" Sara sat up against the stack of feather pillows and settled the tray on her lap. Waking up with a man in her room was a bit startling, and she self-consciously raked her fingers through her tousled hair, trying to smooth out the knots.

Philippe didn't seem to notice. He slathered butter on a croissant and devoured it in three bites.

"Mind your manners!" Sara chided, yanking the knife from his hand. He leaned in to kiss her. The taste of creamy butter on his soft lips reminded Sara of how his body had felt, moving against hers, only hours before. She pulled away from their embrace, and with considerable effort, flipped her mind back to the question at hand.

"Where are you taking me?" Sara bit into a crisp slice of bacon, savoring the sting of salt on her tongue.

"To meet my grandparents."

"Your mother's parents?" In the days before their marriage, Philippe had stayed overnight with his grandparents in Tours.

He slurped her scalding coffee. "Yes, François and Jacqueline LeBlanc."

"Are you sure they *want* to meet me? They didn't come to the wedding." Even though it had been a small affair with only ten people in attendance, it would have been nice to see Philippe's family there. Their first meeting was destined to be awkward.

"Yes, they *do* want to meet you," Philippe assured her. "They didn't come to our wedding because Pépère has an ailing heart. Mémère doesn't like to travel without him, even the short distance from Tours. I promised we'd visit." Philippe's face lit up when he

18

spoke of his grandparents. "When my mother was alive, we visited my grandparents every Sunday afternoon. My grandfather taught us how to thread a worm on a fishhook, how to set mousetraps, even how to ax a chicken from the henhouse for Sunday dinner." Sara winced. Growing up, she'd left that chore to Papa.

Philippe shrugged, laughing. "We had to eat."

Intent on changing the subject, Sara asked, "Have they always lived in town?" Fully satisfied by her meal of coffee, hot milk, bacon and *petit pain*, she set the tray aside.

"No, they moved here two years before I left for America." Philippe hesitated for a moment. "You see, my father forbade us to see them."

"Why?" Sara was appalled.

Philippe's eyes narrowed as he struggled to explain. "It was strange . . . I suppose it was his way of controlling us while Mère was alive. But once she passed, he seemed to blame them for her death. Mémère and Pépère never lost hope. They mailed us letters and gifts on our name days, most of which my father gave away or destroyed."

Sadness swept through Sara when she thought of Philippe's fragmented family. Last night, her fingers had traced the rough ridges that ran the length of Philippe's back.

"Philippe . . . may I ask . . . why did he beat you?"

Philippe released a sigh. "You're referring to my scars?"

Sara nodded.

"On that particular day, my father accused Bastien of stealing money, but he'd only borrowed the ten sous to buy me a fishing pole. My father grabbed the strap, and I told Bastien to run.

He whipped me instead. I was so weak after, I couldn't stand." Philippe's voice didn't falter once.

Sara blinked, trying to conceal her tears.

"Sara, look at me." Philippe handed her the napkin. "Those days are long gone, and I'm a happy man now." He kissed her and sank back onto a pillow. The corners of his mouth curled. Sara shot him a quizzical look.

"Don't worry, I took my revenge. My father used to kick me in the rump, for sassing, for cursing, any reason at all. One day, when he wound up his foot and leveled the blow, I clenched my *cul* so hard that he broke his toe! The old man limped for a week." Sara giggled, and Philippe laughed unabashedly at the thought of Jean Lemieux reaping his comeuppance.

Sara dressed in her woolen walking suit and feathered felt hat, both in a forest green that complemented her eyes. These town clothes were so different from the hand-sewn cotton dress and apron she usually wore on the farm, but Maman had insisted she purchase a costume worthy of her new station as Philippe's wife. Sara felt as primped and pressed as Marie Antoinette herself, but she did want to impress Philippe's grandparents. Maman, for all her motherly fussing, would have been pleased.

After losing Papa and Lydia, Sara understood the fragile nature of earthly bonds. To find a true friend, a lover, in Philippe, was a stunning twist of fate. Sara flushed, recalling the urgency of their couplings the night before. With patient encouragement, Philippe had eventually moved Sara past her pain—over the edge into pure pleasure. Her senses were filled with Philippe now, and she would follow him to the ends of the earth.

On this sunny, cold December day, they strolled arm in arm, treading carefully along the cobbled streets. They admired the half-timbered, gabled houses and the splendor of Cathédrale Saint-Gatien, with its two imposing towers, ornamental façade and grand rose window—a prism of yellow, blue and red glistening in the midday sun.

Tours, named *le jardin de France* by its countrymen, was still the vibrant city Sara remembered from her youth, when she accompanied Papa to town to purchase new oak barrels. Tours was a town of silk merchants, clog-makers, wine merchants and guilds representing tradesmen of all kinds.

Turning left off the rue des Halles, Sara and Philippe walked to the Basilique Saint-Martin, pausing to observe its surviving towers. Despite these scars from the Revolution and the German occupation of 1870, this region of châteaux, vineyards and orchards persevered. Sara enjoyed watching the Tourangeaux bustle about town, delighting in the warmth of the winter sunlight.

Sara and Philippe crossed the nearby square, arriving at a four-story medieval building with hand-carved corbels supporting each of its three overhanging floors. The first floor was occupied by a crêperie, and Sara's mouth watered when she caught a whiff of the freshly grilled pancakes. Philippe pounded on the black lac-quered door to the right of the crêperie entrance.

A slightly stooped man with a shock of gray hair answered the door. "Philippe!" he cried, his arms opening wide to embrace his grandson. When he pulled away, he grasped Philippe's shoulders with his hands, his face glowing with affection. "Ah, my boy. Congratulations!"

Behind him, a slender, elegantly dressed woman scrutinized Sara. Her white, chignoned hair, dark eyes and long nose reminded Sara of a snowy owl. The woman inched forward and pulled Philippe to her. When she broke away after several moments, she waved them into the warmth of the foyer and again shifted a keen eye toward Sara.

"Mémère, Pépère, allow me to present my new wife, Sara Thibault Lemieux. Sara, François and Jacqueline LeBlanc."

Sara opened her mouth to speak, but Madame LeBlanc cut in. "Philippe tells us you killed Bastien, but he still loves you. Why is that?"

"Mémère!" Philippe reproached her. "Must you say such things?" Although Sara felt the familiar sting of regret, she squeezed Philippe's hand to reassure him that she was fine. He wrapped his arm around her waist, drawing her near.

Madame LeBlanc gave a half-shrug. "I'm old and incapable of idle chatter, Philippe. Besides, judging from what you told us, I think your new bride can speak for herself."

Sara figured a straight answer was her best defense. She pressed her shoulders back and replied with the small speech she'd rehearsed. "I had no choice but to defend myself against Bastien's assault. I am sorry for your family's suffering, but I love your grandson and intend for us to be happy."

Madame LeBlanc stared at Sara in silence. Monsieur LeBlanc chimed in, "You and your family have also suffered." He rubbed the deep lines above his brow. "Poor Bastien never had a chance.

Any warmth or compassion our daughter instilled in the boy was beaten out by his barbaric father."

Sara cringed upon glancing at Philippe, whose spirits were obviously deflated. She was about to introduce the happier subject of their thriving adopted son, Luc, when Madame LeBlanc cleared her throat. "Bastien chose his own path," she said, clutching Philippe's hands. "Ah well, my dear boy, I suppose we have to bid adieu to the past so we may embrace the future." Turning to Sara, she motioned toward the narrow staircase behind her. "Madame Lemieux, welcome to our home."

The foursome climbed the dimly lit stairwell and entered the sitting room. Sara was surprised to see expensive furnishings of silk, velvet, and glossy mahogany and cherry. Most striking was the far wall, decorated with shelves of shiny brown, emerald and translucent medicine bottles of all shapes and sizes, some embossed and others smooth. Sara marveled at the curious sight. Philippe must have seen her eyes widen, for he leaned in and murmured, "Pépère was an apothecary for many years. This collection—and growing herbs—are his hobbies now."

Philippe and Sara sat on the gold brocade settee while the LeBlancs sat in the wingback chairs opposite them. A maid appeared with a tray of small sandwiches, brioches, a silver coffee service and four glasses of muscadet.

As Madame LeBlanc poured the coffee into ivory Limoges teacups stenciled with tiny pink roses, Philippe's grandfather sipped his wine, smiling warmly at Sara. "Tell me, madame, how do you enjoy the California vineyards? Are they much different than those of Touraine?"

Sara's thoughts flashed to the verdant landscape of Carneros, where she'd worked with Philippe for seven months. She hesitated, trying to find adequate words to describe the vastness of California in comparison to the Loire. "I find southern Napa's fertile soil, its rolling golden hills and modern cities so beautiful. The conditions for growing grapes in Carneros are very different than here. Carneros grapes grow in a cool climate; the rains fall mostly in winter. The clay soil, the ocean, the Mayacamas Mountains and even the morning fog and afternoon breezes off the San Pablo Bay all lend a unique flavor to the grapes. Wouldn't you agree, Philippe?"

"It's true." He beamed.

"Philippe's first cabernet and zinfandel vintages, bottled this past summer, are exquisite," Sara announced proudly.

"Sara's not taking enough credit. She helped me craft the '96 and '97 vintages."

"So the grafting worked? You're producing a decent yield now?" Philippe's grandfather leaned forward. Observing his fine-pored skin, red silk tie and trimmed nails, Sara noted that he was quite handsome for a man of his age.

"Yes, and we picked 550 tons of grapes this past fall. No mildew, little dry rot and, thankfully, no new phylloxera. Napa yielded a bumper crop this year."

"As you may know, Philippe has secured a contract with the archdiocese to provide most of its sacramental wine. Also, we plan to diversify the farm by expanding the orchard," Sara added. "We want to guard against prohibition."

"Is that still a concern?" Monsieur LeBlanc asked skeptically.

Sara was about to elaborate when Philippe interjected. "The

prohibitionists are losing their hold on the state. Even Lady Somerset, an early champion of the movement, has thrown up the sponge and defected. I'm more concerned about the price war."

"How so?" Monsieur LeBlanc inquired.

"Eastern demand for California wines is growing, but labor costs were sky-high this year. The growers are demanding ten dollars per ton, but the California Wine Association is only offering them five. I'm guessing the average price for a gallon of wine will drop from ten to six cents by next year."

"Why?" his grandfather gasped. "Here in France, a gallon fetches close to twenty cents."

"With the '97 vintage, there's an oversupply of California wine, and the dealers won't pay what the winemakers are asking."

"Where does that leave you?"

Philippe laced his fingers together. "We ship our wines east with Carneros labels, directly to the wine merchants. Sensible people, who don't believe that a French label makes a wine, appreciate fine California table wines." Philippe glanced at Sara and continued, "We hope to fetch ten cents a gallon—not nearly what it should be, but more than the California wine dealers are offering."

"Where are you selling?"

"San Francisco, Los Angeles, Sacramento, Boston, Chicago, New York and hopefully New Orleans. Sara and I were planning a trip to Louisiana on our way home, but it's still gripped by yellow fever. We'll visit Boston instead."

"And what of the Saint Martin property? Didn't it burn to the ground?" Madame LeBlanc stirred her coffee innocently, but

25

Sara knew what she was implying. Sara glanced at her husband, hoping he wouldn't mention that Jacques Chevreau had set fire to Saint Martin to hide the evidence of Sara's crime and obscure what had happened between her and Bastien that awful night.

"Mémère," Philippe said gently, "Sara did not set fire to her ancestral home, if that's what you're asking. The house was destroyed, but the grapes survived."

"We plan to graft the infested vines to a phylloxera-resistant American hybrid rootstock. In three years, those vines should flourish with fruit," Sara added pointedly.

"Ah," Monsieur LeBlanc said, nodding thoughtfully. He turned back to Philippe with a question about the grafting costs.

"Madame," Philippe's grandmother whispered to Sara, "may I show you our winter garden?"

"Oh, do go and admire all the work they've done," Philippe encouraged her, patting her knee. Sara reluctantly left the safety of his side.

Madame LeBlanc guided Sara down a wide hallway to the south-facing side of the apartment. Double doors opened onto a small kitchen. The tang of rosemary and seared beef greeted Sara. She stepped closer to the hot oven, hoping it would chase the chill from her bones.

A wide gleaming bay window lined with potted herbs was centered on the scullery wall. "*Voilà*, our little treasures," she announced. "I like to cook, and François grows these for me in winter. In the south-facing window, we have the plants that require the most sun—sage, basil, oregano and . . . ah, smell that rosemary. Here, in the eastern and western corners, we have bay leaf, chives, thyme and some exotic plants that Philippe's uncle Arnaud brought back from Spain, whose names I can never remember."

She made a considerable effort to sound lighthearted, but the sun streaming through the bay window betrayed her. Years of unspoken anguish creased the delicate skin around her eyes. Sara recognized the stigma of sorrow—it was the same as her own mother's. During the day, when caring for her grandson, Luc, filled the cavern of her heart, Maman's irises sparked with life. When night fell, sorrow brushed her eyes with its blue, merciless shadow. Sara suspected that in the stillness of the gloaming, every bereft mother prays to be released from her consuming ache—and to smell and cradle her lost child once more.

One thing Sara knew for certain: the living need to reminisce about the dead. "Madame LeBlanc, would you tell me about your daughter?"

She clipped some chives into a small glass bowl. "Did you ever meet Adèle?" A shroud seemed to lift as she spoke her daughter's name.

"No, but when I was a child, I saw her in church on Sundays, with Philippe and Bastien. I thought her the loveliest woman I'd ever seen."

Philippe's grandmother smiled for the first time, revealing a string of pearly-white teeth. "She was, my dear. Her hair was spun gold, her eyes the color of the sky on a cloudless day—Philippe has the same. Adèle possessed a charm that drew people, and animals, to her.

"Do you know that she had a parakeet named Trudie? Every morning, when that bird hopped on her shoulder, Adèle would dip her spoon in her café au lait and hold it out for Trudie to sip.

"'Wait, Trudie,' Adèle would caution, 'it's too hot.' She'd make a show of gently blowing the steam off the tiny spoonful, and when she was done, Trudie would lap it up. Each day before I kissed my daughter goodbye, I had to wait for that darn bird to finish her café." She sighed. "One misses the simple, everyday moments."

Sara understood. She still missed the musty smell of Papa's pipe and the bounce of Lydie's tight curls.

Madame LeBlanc interrupted Sara's reverie. "Why did you travel to Eagle's Run in California?" In spite of herself, Sara admired the woman's candor.

"Actually, I stumbled upon Eagle's Run accidentally. I traveled to California with the hope of starting a new life—and running my own vineyard some day. I worked in many Napa vineyards, picking and pruning, but none as magnificent as Eagle's Run."

"So you knew Philippe—when you saw him, that is?"

"Yes, madame, but he didn't remember me."

"Why did you stay? Weren't you afraid?"

Sara faltered, remembering both the terror and fascination she'd felt upon encountering Philippe. "Yes," she answered, matching his grandmother's directness. "But I also wanted Saint Martin back. I never expected that we'd form such a strong attachment."

She studied Sara intently. "You must indeed love my grandson, to marry into the family that fractured yours," she said.

"I do," Sara said firmly. What Sara couldn't share with Philippe's grandmother is how she relished the memory of their wedding night and had craved the touch of his bare skin on hers all day.

"Ah, the romance of youth." Madame LeBlanc gave Sara a knowing look. "Years pass, romance fades . . ." She tugged the brittle, brown leaves off the basil plant and continued, "But loyalty—that is what remains in a good marriage." She held a fresh green stem between her fingers. "See?"

After a luncheon of filet mignon, stuffed potatoes and a full-bodied cabernet, and promising to return soon with Luc, Sara and Philippe began the walk back to their hotel. Storm clouds formed in the afternoon sky. They mirrored the mouse-gray color of the stone streets and buildings of Tours in wintertime. She could hardly discern where the city ended and the sky began.

Sara flipped up her collar to keep out the chill. Her confidence was rattled. Philippe had excluded her from his conversation with his grandfather. She bristled a bit at this but chose to not to mention it. Her silence didn't last.

"You're rather sullen. Did you enjoy your chat with Mémère?" Philippe asked cheerfully.

"I'm not sure your grandmother approves of me."

"Darling, she's just made your acquaintance. She doesn't know you like I do. I think my grandfather took a shine to you." Philippe squeezed Sara's kid-gloved hand, but the gesture only provoked her.

"How could he 'take a shine' to me? I barely finished a sentence."

Philippe stopped short on the rue des Halles. "What?"

"You knew how nervous I was to meet your family, especially under these circumstances, yet you abandoned me."

"Abandoned you? You act like I fed you to the wolves, when I only suggested you walk down the hallway to see my grandparents' herb garden. You're being irrational."

"You were trying to get rid of me."

Philippe thought about that for a moment. "That's true," he conceded.

"You admit it?"

"My grandfather wanted to speak with me privately."

"About me?"

"No, not about you—must you always be so suspicious?"

Sara knew she was being paranoid. She walked past Philippe in a deep sulk. He caught her hand, turning her around to face him. "I'm ridiculous," she pouted.

He squeezed her shoulders. "You're exhausted."

Sara slumped in defeat. Philippe ducked down, seeking her lips. The brims of their hats provided a reassuring canopy of intimacy. When Sara broke away, she remembered where they were: on the street, in broad daylight.

"Philippe, stop!" Sara chided.

"Why? We're married."

"You can't just grope me on the street." Even in America, Sara never would have permitted it.

"I wasn't groping you—although I considered it." Philippe laughed, tugged on her hand and broke into a run.

She giggled and held on tightly to her hat as she navigated the tricky cobblestones in her short heels. "Where are you taking me?"

Philippe winked. "Back to the hotel!"

They burst into the room and Philippe kicked the door shut. Without a word, he slipped his hands beneath her skirts and lifted her from the floor. She wrapped her legs around Philippe's waist and he slid her onto the empty desk.

Sara was surprised by how easily he shimmied off her stockings and peeled off her cotton drawers. He didn't bother to remove anything else.

She pulled his shirt from his trousers and moved her hands upward, relishing the feel of his sinewy chest beneath her hands. As he gave himself over to her, every fear Sara held was stripped away.

Philippe wouldn't dare ignore her now.

They fell upon the bed, mostly clothed, but completely sated. "What did you discuss with your grandfather?" Sara asked, chewing on her lower lip.

"What? Oh, the World's Fair is going to be held in Paris in 1900. Rather exciting, don't you think?"

"Yes," Sara said absently. "Perhaps we should attend, if we have the means."

"And that's the other thing. My grandfather wanted to discuss finances."

"Really?" Sara burned with curiosity.

Philippe laughed. "Go look inside my coat pocket."

Sara reached over, extracted some papers, and unfolded what looked like a bank draft. Her eyes widened with shock.

"Twenty thousand francs? For you?" she exclaimed, reading the document.

"For us. Pépère sold his drugstores three years ago and he saved a portion of the profit for Bastien and me. When Bastien came to collect his share, he was soused, so Pépère told him to return when he cleaned himself up. He never did. Luc's share is included."

"That's four thousand dollars!"

"Don't get too excited; I need to use a portion of ours—almost three thousand francs—to pay back my father."

Sara had been so pleased when Philippe returned, she hadn't asked about some important details. Sara's mother had sold Saint Martin to the Lemieux family after Papa had died, but Philippe had returned the property to Sara just before she left California. He had also persuaded his father to drop the charge against her for the murder of his brother. "What arrangements did you make with your father?"

Philippe shifted on the bed, rubbing his eyes. "All right, I'll tell you, but please don't comment until I'm finished." Sara glared at him, dreading his answer.

"After Bastien died, my father wanted no part of Saint Martin. He didn't want the hassle of rebuilding from the fire and replanting the vines. He deeded the vineyard and dwellings to me, and offered to cover Bastien's debts until I could repay him. Considering the house was burned to the ground and a third of the vines were useless, I thought it a fair bargain. By law, the property would have been half mine and half Luc's upon my father's death anyway. So he signed it over to me and I invited your mother and Jacques to stay and manage it."

Sara's mind scrutinized every detail of Philippe's story, but settled on the one missing link. "Why did your father drop the charges against me?"

"I sent a telegram and explained that if he ever wanted to meet his grandson, he would write to the magistrate at once and explain your innocence—that you killed Bastien in self-defense."

"And he agreed?" Sara was shocked that Jean Lemieux ranked knowing his grandson higher than retaliating against her.

"Yes."

"So you plan to introduce Luc to your father?"

"What choice do I have? Otherwise you might stand trial. I won't have that."

"Does he have to see him more than once?"

"Luc will inherit half of my father's estate some day. It would be beneficial for both of them."

"But Philippe, he's such an awful man," Sara blurted, then drew back.

Philippe didn't even blink. "He's a miserable man, with no wife, no sons who love him, and only rancor in his heart. Sometimes children can be a tonic for such bitterness," he added.

"I don't want Luc to be a 'tonic' for that man."

"I will supervise all the visits." He wasn't asking her permission.

Sara sighed and fell back on her pillow. Philippe propped himself up on his elbow, a solemn vow in his voice. "I won't let anything happen to our son."

A lump rose in Sara's throat. Until that moment, Philippe had never called Luc his son. Sara stroked the stubble on his chin. "And so you are his legal guardian?" Sara recalled that, under

French law, custody of orphans was usually awarded to the paternal grandfather.

"Yes," Philippe confirmed, adding, "We both know my father isn't fit for the job, so I'm the primary guardian in my father's stead. I named you as his secondary guardian."

He'd been so gracious, even in his grief. She could have been so easily cut from the boy's life had Philippe not forgiven her. "Philippe?" she murmured. "I want to help repay some of the money you owe your father."

"No, Sara. This isn't about money." Philippe's expression softened as he cupped her wrist and kissed it. "It's about reparation."

# Chapter 4

Early in the morning, Sara knelt down and ran a wet comb through Luc's hair, trying to flatten his tangled cowlick. The fire roared, heating their cave. It may have dated from the eleventh century, but it was furnished now with the comforts of two straw beds, a table and four chairs.

"We're not going to church yet," Philippe said lightly. Sara flashed him a stern look. Was she still upset that he was bringing Luc to visit his father? Unfortunately, this was part of the deal. Sara's freedom and Philippe's guardianship of Luc depended on the success of this visit, and Philippe would not surrender either.

She kissed Luc on the head and stood up, clad in her gauzy morning gown, her claret-colored shawl draped over her shoulders. Sara's thick, chestnut hair cascaded loosely down her back.

Philippe admired her ripe, pink lips. He could scarcely find the will to leave her, even for a few hours. He pulled her close before she could protest.

"Be nice," he teased, nuzzling her neck, trying to dissolve the frown on her face.

"Don't stay too long," she whispered with a touch of melancholy.

"We'll go for an hour, and after Mass tonight, we'll start packing for our trip home."

"Home . . . to California." Sara smiled. "I like the sound of that."

While he drove the carriage to his father's house with Luc seated upon his lap, Philippe's thoughts ran back to Sara. Her green eyes reminded him of a sunlit meadow, and he couldn't wait for the day when her belly would swell with his child beneath that nightdress.

Luc shrieked with delight when they turned down the dirt road to Jean Lemieux's home. Philippe guided the boy's hands, helping him tug on the reins to slow down the team.

When Philippe knocked, his father did not answer. Entering, Philippe was surprised to see piles of paper scattered about the room and soiled dishes stacked haphazardly. A faint sickly odor hung in the air. Had his father sacked his housekeeper, or had he simply given up?

Père stopped rocking in his chair, looking a bit startled to see Philippe and Luc. Without a handshake or a word, he motioned to the nearby chaise. Philippe hadn't been here in over six years, and now that he was, he couldn't wait to escape to California.

Philippe studied his hunched-over, withered father. Curiously, Philippe felt no anger. Instead, he wondered what the hell had happened to the man. Why had he ever feared him? When his father had cracked the strap, cutting his young skin, did he ever consider the possibility that the cowering child would grow into a strong man, capable of crushing his skull with one hand? Of course not. Jean Lemieux, who enjoyed tormenting the vulnerable, had assumed that his boy would snap under the strain. He hadn't counted on Philippe's resilience.

Examining the cluttered room, Philippe was pleased to see his mother's photograph, framed in pewter, on the mantel. Her sweetness had helped him endure his father's cruelty so many times.

Philippe sat on the edge of the sofa while Luc clung to his knee. Père ran his trembling hands through his thinning hair. "You are well?" he asked gruffly.

"Very, thank you. This is your grandson, Luc Lemieux," Philippe said evenly, trying to soothe his father's obvious agitation.

A forlorn smile lit his father's face for a moment. "He's like Bastien, isn't he?"

"Yes, he does resemble Bastien. Let's hope we raise him better, though." Philippe regretted saying it, though it was the truth. He didn't want to argue; he just wanted to fulfill his obligation and leave. Intent on changing the subject, Philippe pulled an ivory envelope from his bag. "Here's the money I owe you. We're settled now, yes?"

Père stretched forward, snatching the money from his hand. "I'm glad to be rid of that headache."

"You'll be happy to know that Saint Martin will be Luc's one day."

His father drummed his fingers on the chair arm. "May I say hello to him?"

"Of course."

"May he have a chocolate? He looks like he's got a full set of teeth, although I can't say I have the same." The old man chuckled, revealing a row of crooked, tobacco-stained teeth.

Philippe was surprised. He didn't remember Père ever offering anyone sweets. "Yes, a chocolate would be fine."

Luc took the chocolate, chomping and grinning. His grandfather's face beamed, but then suddenly clouded with concern. His eyes darted to the kitchen door, and he wagged a finger at Philippe. "Don't go telling Mère. She doesn't like you boys to eat candy before dinner."

Philippe stared at his father.

"Oh, and I bought Bastien a gift." His father handed Luc a box of wooden ninepins, which the boy jiggled until the pins all dropped onto the floor.

"You mean you bought *Luc* a gift?"

"Yes, yes." He pointed at the pins. "I used to play as a boy. I was the champion nine-pinner at school. You're young, but you'll learn."

While Luc sat cross-legged, rolling the ball and knocking the pins over, Philippe watched the man in the rumpled shirt and tatty shoes who was now a stranger. When his father grew excited, his left cheek twitched. Something was very wrong.

Père flinched, observing Philippe with unblinking eyes. "How's the California vineyard? Any phylloxera? Prohibitionists?"

Maybe the man was starved for conversation. "Thankfully, the vineyard is thriving, and California's 1897 vintage was a huge crop. I don't anticipate we'll see one of its size in the next five years." What Philippe didn't tell his father, and had not told Sara, was that he stood to lose half of his annual income every year the price war continued. If prices remained low, he wouldn't be able to cover his expenses.

His father persisted. "I keep reading about those pesky prohibs in America."

"Their campaign is gaining followers, but nothing to be concerned about yet. Although they recently fell victim to a convincing prank."

"Really?"

"A rumor circulated that the California winemakers were going to install a Niagara Falls–like exhibit at the Paris Exposition, one that would feature a hundred thousand gallons of wine instead of water, surrounded by beautiful gardens and places for young men and women to drink their fill without payment." Philippe smiled at the absurdity of the image.

His father rubbed his palms together expectantly. "That must have whipped those prohibs into a proselytizing frenzy!"

"Indeed. The temperance union traveled door-to-door, collecting thousands of signatures to protest. The poor gents at the exposition headquarters sifted through piles of letters expressing outrage at something that was never proposed."

"And I bet the prohibs still think it's a government conspiracy, right?" Rather than waiting for Philippe's response, Père began picking at his shirtsleeves and mumbling under his breath.

Philippe rose abruptly. His father's bizarre behavior unnerved him. One minute he can't remember his grandson's name, and the next he's talking lucidly about the prohibitionists? Philippe thought of his wife, waiting for them at Saint Martin while he was here offering up Bastien's son to the man who'd never cared for them. What was he thinking?

"It's almost Luc's naptime, Père, so we'll go now."

He stood and clasped Philippe's forearm. "I've given you all you asked for. Bring Bastien back to see me on your next visit to France, yes?" he croaked.

Bastien again. Philippe felt sick. He gripped his father's arm in an effort to steady him. "Père, are you ill?"

His father ignored the question. "You promise me you'll bring him here?" he asked frantically.

Philippe sighed, giving in to his frail father, knowing Sara would be livid. "All right."


The rest of the day, Sara didn't ask about their visit, and Philippe didn't volunteer details. They spoke only about Christmas and the trip home to California.

After Mass at Cathédrale Saint-Gatien and dinner with Philippe's grandparents in Tours, Sara, Philippe, Maman, and Jacques returned with Luc to Saint Martin to discuss how they would manage two vineyards on separate continents. Thank God for Jacques Chevreau, thought Philippe, for Saint Martin would not have survived without his expertise and willingness to help. The new winemaker Jacques had hired last year would stay on, and Jacques would oversee the general management of the vineyard. He had worked there for so many years that he knew Saint Martin like no one else—and was further tied to the land by his marriage to Sara's mother. They both missed Sara's father but seemed to have settled into a new life together.

"I propose we save half of Luc's ten thousand francs for him, and use the other half to build a new, smaller house. After all, Saint Martin will be Luc's home someday," Philippe said, scribbling more estimates down on paper. Surely Sara would agree that a new house for Marguerite and Jacques was more important than replanting the vines.

"But that could cost nearly fifteen thousand francs!" Marguerite fretted.

Jacques patted her hand and replied, "I'll hire masons to salvage the stones and reuse them. Three bedrooms, a parlor, dining room, scullery and water closet should suffice. I'll oversee the construction myself," he added excitedly. "Don't worry, my dear, we'll find the money."

Sara folded her hands and asked brightly, "Philippe, couldn't we contribute something to help finish the house?" He found it hard to resist those emerald eyes and sweeping dark lashes, but with wine prices falling, they couldn't afford it.

"Unfortunately, I need the money for Eagle's Run, but we could allocate Saint Martin's profits over the next few years to pay for the project." He felt like a heel, dashing Sara's hopes right in front of her mother.

Jacques agreed, "That's a sensible idea."

Marguerite clapped her hands together enthusiastically, but Sara just shrugged. "I suppose so."

The day after Christmas, Philippe slid their three steamer trunks onto the wagon, and they bid adieu to Marguerite and

Jacques. With tears streaming down her cheeks, Marguerite embraced her only living child. Her desolation reminded Philippe that Sara and Luc were her only kin left in the world—and he was taking them away. He could hardly conceive, although he supposed it was possible, that his own father felt just as forlorn about the departure of his only son and grandson.

# Chapter 5

Once the ship cleared the protection of the Saint-Nazaire harbor, the sea breezes picked up, slapping the waves steadily against the ship's hull and whipping the wind against Luc's raw cheeks. Fortunately, they found a spot in the lee of the ship to shield them from the weather. They huddled together for warmth, watching Europe fade over the horizon.

The ship had a unique rhythm. The crew worked in shifts around the clock to make sure the engines produced enough steam to turn the propellers and drive the vessel through the water. The cook and stewards prepared and served meals on a strict schedule, and the seamen performed myriad duties, from laundering to repairing mechanical failures and cleaning and checking equipment. No sailor on the ship was idle for long.

During the first few days of their journey to New York, Philippe, Sara and Luc found it pleasant to stroll around the main deck. Their first morning, seagulls squawked above, flying in lazy figure eights. Luc squealed with amusement to see the dolphins jumping in and out of the ship's rippling wake, as if they were escorting it to America. Even though he'd made this crossing before, Philippe was awed by the brilliant sunsets over the western horizon and the smallness of their ship relative to the endless Atlantic Ocean.

On the third day, Philippe spied thin, ominous-looking clouds forming off the starboard side. The passengers were instructed to rig their cabins and stow their belongings to prepare for the rocking, climbing and falling of the ship over the coming waves. Out here, with no land for hundreds of miles, Mother Nature—not man—ruled.

Soon, the cutting winds blew fiercely and the upper deck was off limits. Sara, Luc and Philippe were confined to their cabin. The absence of windows and clocks below disoriented Philippe. To keep his mind engaged, he consumed the trade papers and scribbled calculations in his journal—itemized costs, grape yields, expected profits—attempting to draft a year's plan for each vineyard. He planned carefully, but there were so many unknowns.

When, if ever, would prices increase? How much of the '97 vintage should he keep to blend with the '98? How could he ensure the archdiocese would renew its contract with Eagle's Run for sacramental wine? If he lost the business, they would be sunk. Philippe recalled how his critics had jeered when he first purchased Eagle's Run: "What's the quickest way to become a millionaire? Invest a billion dollars in a vineyard!" Judging from the pit in his stomach, he had to admit that they may have been right.

There would be bad years—this was the nature of farming. Yet Philippe had spent nearly five years uprooting dead vines, planting robust ones and then waiting until he could finally harvest enough grapes to press his first vintage. Each year since, anxiety gripped him when he feared they'd picked too soon, and fatigue stripped him bare by the end of each harvest, but the exhilaration of smelling and then tasting the wine for the first time was indescribable. He was creating something from nothing. He would continue to make the finest wines, shipping and selling them across the globe—for as long as he could afford to.

He considered sharing his worries with Sara, but something held him back. Sara had worked by his side, but he was still the owner of Eagle's Run—shouldn't he be the one to devise a solution? Besides, Sara was preoccupied caring for Luc, who had developed a rattling cough two days before their arrival. He cried most of the night, and Philippe did not want to add to her anxieties. They were both relieved when the ship docked in New York.

"Do you think Marie might have something to cure him?" Sara asked as she rocked Luc on her lap, pressing a wet cloth to his forehead. The boy's cheeks flushed red while he sucked his thumb.

"I'm certain she will," Philippe said with confidence, ruffling the boy's hair and attempting to soothe him. Marie Chevreau— Jacques Chevreau's niece and one of the sharpest women Philippe had ever met—was knowledgeable in many areas of medicine. Her life had been entwined with the Lemieux and Thibault families for years, and she had been the truest of friends to both Philippe and

Sara. Seven years ago, Marie had been seduced and abandoned by Bastien. Philippe had rescued the eighteen-year-old girl and taken her to New York. There, Marie had given birth to Adeline and subsequently established herself as a successful midwife. Marie had been Sara and Lydia's only friend in New York when they had arrived in May 1896, escaping their own tragic scandal. The convent where Marie and Adeline lived had been their first home in America.

Just as Philippe expected, Marie was quick to help them once they reached her small apartment located behind the convent on the Lower East Side of Manhattan. She slipped Sara beneath the bed quilts for a nap and coaxed Luc into drinking a few teaspoons of warm honey, and then slathered eucalyptus oil on his chest. Within a half hour, his cough had eased. Two hours later, Sara rose looking rested and energized, more like the girl Philippe had married.

Although he'd seen Adeline just a month earlier, Philippe was certain she'd grown two inches in his absence. Now seven years old, she excelled in her studies at the convent, but was shy of answering Philippe's questions. However, she perked up when he asked her to entertain Luc.

"How old is he now?" Adeline asked, playing patty-cake with Luc upon her lap.

"Almost seventeen months, can you believe it?" Sara smiled proudly.

Luc tugged on Adeline's curls, which hung in dark ringlets, framing her sweet face and chocolate eyes.

"Maman, look how sweet he is," Adeline said, beaming with satisfaction.

Marie offered Sara a glass of brandy. "Adeline's right. It's such a pleasure to see you three together, as you should be."

"Thank you, Marie. We'll always be grateful to you," Philippe declared, thinking of her many kindnesses toward Sara and Lydia during their stay at the convent.

"Now, what about you? How are your classes going?" Sara asked. Marie was studying midwifery at the Women's Medical College.

"Quite well. I've witnessed several new cesarean techniques and, in all but one case, the mother survived." Marie continued excitedly, "Do you know that medicine men in Uganda have been performing successful operations like these for hundreds of years? One group of healers uses banana wine to intoxicate the mother, and to cleanse her abdomen before they perform the operation. Then they make the incision and pull the baby out. They cauterize the wound to stop the bleeding, pin the skin together with iron needles, and then apply a salve made from plant roots. In most cases, the mother lives."

Sara's color faded. Philippe might need to grab the smelling salts if Marie shared any more of her stories. Marie, enraptured with her own tale, didn't seem to notice. "I'm only training in midwifery, not surgery, but wouldn't it be something if I could one day perform these operations myself—and save women's lives?"

"It would indeed," Philippe agreed, placing a reassuring hand over Sara's, "and you obviously have the mind for it, Marie." He needed to change the subject. "And what of Adeline?" Philippe asked cheerfully. "Does she stay here with the nuns during the day?"

"Yes. I have classes and clinical observations four days a week. On the fifth day, she usually comes with me to visit my patients. The sisters are kind enough to teach Adeline her reading, writing and arithmetic. I think they love having a child around the place."

"Forgive me, Marie," Philippe said, lowering his voice to prevent Adeline from overhearing, "but isn't it a bit lonely for her, shut up in the convent, with no friends?" He knew he was skating on thin ice, but after watching Adeline cuddle and stack blocks with Luc, it seemed obvious that his niece was starved for youthful companionship.

Marie swept invisible particles of lint off her skirt. "It might be lonely, Philippe, but it is the safest place for a girl her age in this city. I have to work every day, and we're very lucky to have the protection of the convent."

He'd overstepped. "Of course, Marie, and you do an excellent job." He watched Adeline hitch Luc to her hip and dance him gently around the room. "I was just hoping that you might consider moving west, closer to us. You and Adeline could live in wider spaces, with fresh air, in a town with children her own age."

"Oh, we would love for you to come to California!" Sara echoed.

Marie's shoulders relaxed a bit. Perhaps he'd smoothed things over for the time being.

"Can we, Maman, please?" Adeline chimed in.

Marie rolled her eyes. Philippe offered one more enticement. "You know, I hear that Cooper Medical College in San Francisco is one of the finest in the country," he persisted, smiling. "I'll send you the enrollment forms." He winked.

48

"Very well." Marie smiled and held up her palms in surrender. "I still have a year and a half of studies left to complete, but after that I suppose we could visit."

In Boston, Philippe called on six wine merchants in one day. Fortunately, he was staying at the Parker House, centrally located near the foot of Beacon Hill, Boston Common, Quincy Market and Faneuil Hall. Philippe was able to return at midday to refill his carrying case with more bottles of Saint Martin's chenin blanc, which Sara insisted he offer as a gift to his potential buyers. He had to commend his wife's instincts: she had a knack for identifying every possible sales opportunity. So far, he'd secured one order for ten cases of Eagle's Run 1896 Chardonnay, and another order for twenty cases of the French chenin blanc. Not what he'd hoped, but it was a promising start.

His last call this afternoon would be on Heath and Strong, the premier Boston wine merchants, whom he'd supplied with twenty thousand gallons of wine from Carneros last fall. Despite Philippe's letters and telegrams, they still hadn't paid him the balance due on that shipment—nearly $1,250. Of that amount, Philippe would receive $350, but the rest was owed to his fellow winemaker and friend George Lamont. To make matters worse, Heath and Strong had been Philippe's biggest sale in Boston, and he doubted Lamont would trust him to sell his wine again if the firm didn't come through with the rest of the money.

Unable to secure a hackney to drive him over to Walnut Street, Philippe trudged through snow drifts down School Street. The brisk air smelled clean. He turned left onto Beacon Street, slogging past the white calm of Boston Common and the idle trolleys lining the roadside. Philippe could barely see the fountains or frozen ponds beneath the pearly snow, only the paths cut by children dragging sleds and chasing each other until they tumbled in the light powder. Otherwise, the city was tranquil, for the snow kept many indoors and muffled the noise of the few horses and pedestrians who ventured out.

When Philippe arrived at the office of Heath and Strong, a red sign announced that the merchants were closed for business—permanently. A tattered notice of eviction hung on the green wooden door. Lowering his bag to the ground, Philippe looked up and down the vacant street, hoping to find someone who might know what had happened. He saw no one.

Why hadn't he heard of this sooner? He hadn't seen an announcement in the trade papers, and had never received any correspondence from the owners. How would he recover his money?

Philippe's feet were frozen and his mood dark when he passed through the glass door of the hotel into the warm lobby. He faltered when he spied Sara waiting for him on a lush blue velvet chaise. She was studying a piece of paper clasped in her hand, and speaking in soft tones to Luc, who sat next to her. Her cheeks were flushed a dewy pink, and her hair pulled back into a relaxed knot. She was wearing the simple red dress he'd bought her in Tours, but with her regal posture, she was easily the most elegant woman in the room. As he approached her, he found himself tongue-tied.

Sara spoke first, running a finger down the piece of paper in her hand. "Do you realize that there are only two California wines offered on this list? A claret and a white wine." She pursed her lips.

Philippe held up a hand to interrupt her. "Sara—"

"Oh, and naturally, the hotel offers Krug's Champagne, but that's the only one listed by its proper name," she huffed.

Philippe sat down beside her. "Sara," he began to explain when she lifted her eyes.

"They're bankrupt," Sara announced.

"What?"

"Heath and Strong. Bankrupt. Six months ago."

"How . . . ?"

Sara threaded her arm through Philippe's and lowered her voice. "While you were gone, I struck up a conversation with the sommelier. I mentioned we made wine and that you were, at that very moment, meeting with Heath and Strong. When I mentioned the name"—Sara sighed—"he said he regretted to inform me that Heath and Strong had gone bankrupt in June, without warning, leaving over fifty thousand dollars in unpaid debts. Their assets will be sold off, and the money will be divided between their debtors." Sara winced. "It could take years, Philippe."

Philippe slumped. "So that's it? We have no recourse?"

"You can contact your attorney and have him place a lien on your behalf. You'll recover something—eventually."

"How will I pay Lamont the nine hundred I owe him?" Philippe muttered, staring at the opulent blue carpet that ran the length of the lobby. Who was he fooling, staying in such a lavish place? He was bleeding money.

"You'll reimburse him half, but he'll have to absorb the rest," Sara replied sensibly. "That's the risk of doing business." Yet her eyes twinkled.

"Wait a minute. What did you do?" he asked warily.

Sara raised her chin and clasped her hands together, nearly bursting with excitement.

"I offered a taste of our chenin blanc to Monsieur Clisson, the sommelier," she announced. "Did I tell you he's from Montlouis-sur-Loire, right across the river? He knows Saint Martin, of course. I gave him your card and told him to telegraph with his order, if he wished." Sara smiled mischievously.

"And?"

"He ordered twenty cases on the spot. I suggested he try your Eagle's Run Chardonnay, which is a bit drier, and he ordered two sample cases."

"You brokered the deal without me?" Philippe didn't know if he was impressed or insulted.

Sara rolled her eyes. "What else was I to do? Wait for my husband's approval? I would have looked ridiculous."

"On what terms?"

"Half now, half on delivery."

"Are you sure he's good for it?"

"The Parker is one of the most prestigious hotels in Boston, darling. Now you're just paranoid." Sara frowned.

"Those aren't my usual terms." Philippe raised an eyebrow.

"No, but I added a condition."

"Which is?"

"That the hotel lists our wines as 'Saint Martin Chenin Blanc' and 'Eagle's Run Chardonnay,' so people will know exactly what they're drinking."

Philippe stared, astonished. He had underestimated her again.

Philippe was itching to return to Eagle's Run. With several hours left on their journey, he looked forward to a nice long stretch and a steaming bath. While Luc happily played with Philippe's leather wallet, Philippe watched Sara intently. She sat opposite him, looking out the window at the cows and sheep that dotted the blurred California landscape north of Los Angeles. She was content, and Philippe aimed to keep her that way.

"Sara, we should discuss the vineyard."

"Yes?" Sara's eyes widened with such allure that Philippe's heart skipped a beat. Incapable of remembering anything, he just blinked at her. "What?" she asked, laughing.

Philippe's throat thickened. "You . . ." He couldn't find the words.

Sara bent forward and kissed him, teasing his lips with her velvety tongue. When she finally retreated, Philippe swallowed hard, battling for control over his emotions.

"Aurora sent a telegram. The Wine Makers' Corporation is hosting a meeting in February. They're going town to town, trying to convince growers to sell them their wine. They want to control eighty-five percent of the wine in California, so they can drive prices higher."

"Would we still be able to sell directly to our buyers?"

"I don't know."

"We should listen to their proposal."

Philippe squinted at the orange sun melting behind the western foothills. "Yes, I suppose we should." He didn't like the idea. Herd mentality was dangerous; he had watched many a sheep drown by blindly following others.

"The new cellar man is working out well," he said cautiously. "I'm eager for you to meet him—a quiet, efficient sort of fellow." Philippe had hired Mac right after Sara's departure, but he hadn't been able to bring himself to hire a foreman or winemaker in her stead. Those had been Sara's jobs, and it would have been like admitting she was never coming back.

"You definitely needed one."

"I was thinking," Philippe ventured, "now that we're a family, and the new vines will bear a record tonnage of fruit this season, we may need help . . . you know, managing the harvest."

"Oh, so now you're hiring someone to replace me?"

Philippe placed a reassuring hand on her knee. "Settle down, no one's trying to replace you."

"Some women love to cook and embroider cushions—I'm not one of them. I thought you understood that," Sara replied.

He laughed. "Of course I do."

"Growing grapes and making wine, that's what I love to do."

"Don't underestimate yourself, Sara. You've done a fine job with Luc, and you had no experience with babies."

"I'm a vintner first, a wife and mother second."

"You're all those things. You're my Sara. No need to make grand proclamations."

"I just think that you sometimes forget. I want to make my own wines," she said feistily. "Don't think that's changed just because I married you."

"Heaven forbid," he said, resigned to a compromise. "So you'll continue to oversee the grape growing and assist me with the winemaking—but I'm hiring more laborers to help with the vineyard work. Mac Cuddy claims he can secure high-quality Italian workers for cheap wages."

Sara shrugged, but her mouth twitched into a smug smile. "Suit yourself."

# Chapter 6

Sara wandered between the vines, through the shin-high, bright-yellow mustard flowers just beginning to bloom. She inhaled the cool, crisp air into her lungs. After nearly a month in the hot belly of a ship and the cramped coach of a train, Sara was overjoyed to be back home in California.

Sara had been unsettled by their conversation on the train. Why would Philippe even think of hiring another winemaker? Did he really expect her to abandon her passion for winemaking to serve solely as wife and mother? Female vintners were rare, but not unheard of. If she didn't fight for her place in the family business, she feared that the demands of married life might, over time, eclipse her own ambition.

She rambled down the southernmost slope of the vineyard to the last bare vine and turned her attention to the breathtaking view. The edge of Carneros, where Carneros Creek met the Napa River, felt like the edge of the world. In the distance, the saltwater marshes shimmered in the winter sun, and the rivulets twisted like a maze, winding their way to San Pablo Bay. She could see the shadow of Richmond's skyline, and to her right, the smooth curves of Mount Tamalpais, the Sleeping Princess. From spring to autumn, the small southern wharves bustled with commerce. Scows laden with hay, oats, barley, apricots, prunes and other crops prepared to set sail for the port of San Francisco.

On this particular winter afternoon, all was quiet; the vines were sleeping. After nine months of hard labor, they had earned three months of slumber. Sara scooped a handful of the clay loam and squeezed it. The small clumps of dry soil did not crumble between her fingers. She loved their rough, rocky texture, so porous, so perfect for growing grapes.

Sara ran her hand along the delicate vine, over the bulge where it had been grafted and up to the eight-inch-long cane, cut back for the winter months but left long enough to prevent bacteria from reaching the vine. In five weeks' time, the buds would break, starting the new growth season. Ninety days after, in the heat of summer, veraison would begin. The grapes would color, soften and develop their flavors and sugar. Ninety days later, the harvest would begin.

Now was the time to prepare. They would prune the vines and repair the owl boxes. After budbreak, when they counted the buds and estimated the crop, they would order new bottles and barrels.

Sara felt a surge of hope, and a tinge of trepidation, in anticipation of a new, bountiful growing season.

The hurly-burly crowd of Napans clamored to be heard over one another. They hoisted their fists, pounded on benches and bickered with gusto—and the meeting hadn't even started yet. The leaders of the California Wine Makers' Corporation gathered onstage in the refurbished barn. Everyone was eager to hear what Henry Crocker, the president, along with Hotchkiss and Crabb, some of the most influential wine men in the state, had to say about the mess they were in.

Philippe and Sara took their seats near the back door just as the gavel pounded, calling the room to order. Fifty-three Napa Valley vintners had been invited to St. Helena so the corporation leaders could persuade the winemakers to turn over their wines to them. The corporation, in turn, would manage the supply and sale of California wines to the rest of the country.

With nineteen million gallons of good, sellable wine from the '97 harvest, and another ten million gallons of older wines still in supply, California had produced enough wine to easily meet demand for two years. With the oversupply, prices had plummeted from an average of nineteen cents per gallon to ten this year—and they were still falling. The corporation argued that if it controlled eighty-five percent of the wine supply, it could bring the price back up to eighteen cents.

Philippe had his doubts. He and other vintners had started negotiating their own contracts because the corporation had failed in the past to strike a fair price with the shippers. However, given the increase in the rail freight tariff, which made it more costly to distribute Carneros wines to the East Coast himself, he'd promised his fellow Carneros winemakers that he'd attend the meeting and hear what Hotchkiss, Crocker and Crabb—and the other Napa vintners—had to say.

Sara stared ahead, silently stewing beside him. He had unwisely suggested she remain quiet. Sara was one of only three women at this meeting of men, already a target for criticism, and he didn't want to invite unnecessary trouble.

Hotchkiss laid out his argument, insisting that the wine producers of California band together and sign the contract. "Give us a greater percentage of the wine, and we'll be able to set a better price," he promised the grumbling crowd.

His remarks sparked a whirlwind of opposition. Philippe listened to his fellow Napans raise every fathomable objection. "I need the money now, not six months from now!" "If we sign, then we lose control of our own wine, and our livelihoods!" "You already control seventy percent of the crop—and prices have still fallen, even though you promised eighteen cents this year. Why would we give you more control?"

Some cheered in agreement with this. Others, presumably those siding with the corporation, jeered at the dissenters. The room plunged into chaos, and none of the corporation's leaders could be heard. Philippe jumped to his feet and marched down the center aisle toward them, waving his hands in the air, shifting the attention again to the front of the room.

"Gentleman and ladies!" he boomed several times. Once the gavel pounded again, the room quieted. Philippe introduced himself to the crowd. "Let's give Mr. Hotchkiss and Mr. Crabb the opportunity to respond. I, like most of you, engage in private trade with merchants around the country—"

"And you snapped up the church's business for yerself, quick as a fox!" someone shouted. Philippe spied Sara's face in the back of the room, pinched with anger as she scanned the crowd, looking for the culprit.

"That's un-American!" a stout corporation sympathizer hollered from underneath his bushy moustache.

"Un-American? On the contrary, competition—with the best wines offered to the public, or the church, at the best prices—is a very American virtue," Philippe shouted over the naysayers. He didn't believe he had a monopoly; other small vineyards had been providing sacramental wine for years. But Eagle's Run had received the largest share of the church's business last year, and that vexed his neighbors.

"Now, I'm sure the corporation has no intention of restricting all of our private trade. Their argument is that they need eighty-five percent control over the California wine supply to boost wine prices. Let's allow them to answer. Gentlemen?"

Crabb acknowledged Philippe, and immediately assured the vintners that they would receive a three-cent advance on the wine provided to the corporation, and the rest once the wines were sold. That calmed some of them. He said that if the vintners present handed over the wine in their possession, then the corporation could guarantee a minimum price of seventeen cents per gallon, by slowing the supply of wine to the market. Lastly, the winegrowers were free to participate in some private trade as long as it was not in the state of California, or in competition with the corporation.

Half of the vintners signed on the spot. The other half, including Philippe, refused. They wanted time to make the calculations and consider the risk. Philippe wanted to consult Sara.

He handed her into their wagon and slid in beside her. She clasped her hands and stayed as silent as the grave. Not a promising sign, he wagered. "So, what did you think?"

Sara flashed him a sharp look. "Oh, was I to *think*?" she clucked. "I'm never quite sure when it's expected of me." Philippe had anticipated the cold shoulder. He'd insisted she remain quiet during the meeting to protect her from ridicule, but Sara was a more capable vintner than most of the men there.

"I'd be most obliged if you would share your opinion of the corporation's proposal," Philippe offered in his most conciliatory tone.

"Fine. From what I understand, the '93 crop was also sizable, but was followed by a medium-sized crop and two smaller ones. If we assume that because the '97 crop was large, the '98, '99 and 1900 crops will be medium to small-sized, then we should store the wine to meet demand in the upcoming years, when the crops fall short. We can do this ourselves, or hand some of the wine over to the corporation."

"Yes, we should hold some back. If we hand it off directly to the merchants, they won't store it. They'll force unaged wines on the market, which could damage the reputation of California wines," Philippe agreed.

"But I don't trust the corporation. How can they promise seventeen cents? They haven't been able to deliver fair prices in the past," Sara continued.

"It's too bad we won't know the archdiocese's decision until after the harvest. If I knew we had a contract with them for this year, I wouldn't feel the pressure to sell to the corporation."

"However, if we sign and sell them some of our wine, we could temporarily tie the tongues of the gentlemen who are envious of our business with the church," Sara said.

"You're probably right about that. Did you see who yelled out?"

"Didn't you? Boone Sumter. He produces a measly twenty-five thousand gallons a year and he's throwing his weight around as if he were Niebaum himself."

"He's just madder than a hornet that I beat him to it, just like I beat him to Eagle's Run. Apparently, he had his eye on the land before I bought it."

Sara squinted with skepticism. "Do you really think he would have replanted the largest vineyard in Carneros—over two hundred acres—like you did? He's far too lazy."

Philippe laughed. "You've got a scorpion's bite, my dear. Maybe I should let you handle ol' Sumter—"

"What are you two spouting off about?" A man's voice bellowed behind them. Philippe spun around to see Boone Sumter strutting toward their wagon.

"We were just discussing your outburst in the meeting, nothing more," Philippe said calmly.

Sumter planted his legs wide, flipped open his pocketknife and used the tip to clean his fingernails. "You're a swindler, stealing the church's business before the rest of us had a chance."

Sara tried to interject. "Don't," Philippe warned. For some reason, she listened to him. He stepped down from the wagon. Sumter stood shorter but wider than Philippe, with considerably more heft, so Philippe raised his palms and reminded him politely, "I never stopped anyone from negotiating with the church."

Sumter looked from left to right. Philippe's friends, Lamont and Gautier, walked over to join them. Sumter waved the blade in the air. "And now yer puttin' on airs, refusing to sign over yer wine to the corporation? That's not very neighborly, is it?" His lip curled. "Yer pissin' against the wind, Lemieux."

Seeing his Carneros friends filled Philippe with renewed confidence in his decision to hold off on signing. "I'll take my chances," he retorted.

Sumter spit tobacco juice at Philippe's feet and walked away. Lamont, who'd moved quickly, ready to defend his friend if needed, now rested a hand on Philippe's shoulder. "Word is he lost half his vines to phylloxera. He's like a caged grizzly. I'd sleep with one eye open," Lamont said. Philippe shook hands with his friends, thanking them.

"Just returning the favor," Gautier tipped his hat. Philippe had brokered contracts for Lamont, Gautier and other Carneros wine men with merchants throughout the Midwest and the East Coast. Their loyalty ran deep, and in this tumultuous time of price wars and phylloxera, they had to band together.

# Chapter 7

Linnette wrapped a woolen shawl around her shoulders and another around her head, and swaddled Pippa in a freshly laundered quilt from the mending basket for their journey down Lombard Street.

She'd paid five dollars for a physician to perform a cursory examination of her daughter's ears, nose and throat. He'd scribbled two remedies on his prescription paper and insisted she visit the local drugstore.

The doctor had warned that infants with a cleft lip like Pippa's were susceptible to ear infections. The best remedy was a drop of tea tree oil in each ear, twice a day. Pressing a warm hessian bag of salt against her ear before she slept would help soothe her, he promised. Linnette hoped so. For the last two nights, Pippa had whimpered inconsolably until Linnette nestled her into the softness of her chest, so the two could sleep, bolstered by feather pillows, for five hours straight.

On this blustery winter's day, as Linnette walked from the corner of Scott and Lombard toward Pacific, she was short on sleep, sanity and money. She had fallen behind in the mending, and Tildy was pressuring her to cough up her share of the rent. Linnette knew how to earn money quickly, but it meant breaking a promise she'd made to herself only three months ago, when Pippa was born.

In any decent Tenderloin parlor-house, she could entertain two suitors in the course of an hour and earn twenty dollars. If Tildy would care for Pippa one evening a week, a girl with Linnette's pretty face and ripe bosom could perform at the Midway Plaisance, entertaining a visitor or two between acts in the thick-curtained booths on the mezzanine floor.

But now that she had Pippa, the idea of whoring herself made her stomach churn. Her heart was true to Philippe and she couldn't bear the thought of degrading herself with other men.

At the drugstore, the oil was far more expensive than she'd expected, and the apothecary less welcoming. When Pippa's covering slipped, revealing her cleft, the man pinched his eyebrows together. "What in tarnation? What *is* that?" Linnette drew Pippa closer and covered her face. The apothecary pushed Linnette's items toward the edge of the counter. Coins clattered as he dropped her change. "Kindly take your medicine, miss, and don't return."

Heaviness seeped into Linnette's chest; her limbs lost their vigor. She glared at the apothecary for a few moments, wanting him to feel shame for treating her child like a leper. He broke away to restock his shelves.

Back on the street, the wind moaned and the dirt swirled, pelting Linnette's face. She ducked her head, still holding Pippa tightly, anxious to rush her home to a warm fire.

The doctor had said there was a surgery that could heal Pippa, but it cost over two hundred dollars. In her heart, she knew Pippa would be shunned if she didn't have the operation. But right now, Linnette was more worried about affording their rent, food and medicine. There were only two ways Linnette could make more money: beg Philippe for it, or earn it.

However, Linnette was too afraid of what Philippe would say to ask. He might reject them altogether, now that he had a new woman. Her heart sank with the realization that her best option for quick, uncomplicated money was the parlor-house.

# Chapter 8

At seven o'clock in the morning, Philippe appeared in the winery. "Sara," he barked, poking his head into the manhole of a cask, "will you please let the cellar man do his job?" Sara stood inside, clad in Philippe's work boots and rain slicker, scrubbing the staves with soda and hot water. Philippe shot Mac an apologetic glance, but Sara worked on unperturbed.

Mac Cuddy had grown up running scows from Cuttings Wharf to San Francisco, until he began working at Los Hermanos with the Beringer brothers, where he'd served as cellar man for the last ten years. He knew all the special requirements for making sacramental wine, and had been looking for work south of Napa

City—closer to his sister in Vallejo. His reference from Jacob Beringer had been excellent, Philippe told her. Sara chuckled, remembering Mac's surprise when she introduced herself as Philippe's winemaker. She rather enjoyed shocking people.

"I'm just showing Mac how we take extra care to scrub our equipment as clean as a whistle." Sara smiled at the cellar hands, who regarded her strangely. Luckily, Mac Cuddy didn't seem threatened by a woman with ideas. He was the youngest of an Irish Catholic family, with five older sisters and a widowed matriarch who reportedly ruled the household with an iron fist and a blue-ribbon soda bread. He had a sense of humor about things, and Sara liked that. "Hose it down, Mac. Cold water until it runs clean."

"You're taking the day off, so Mac here can get some work done," Philippe teased as he handed her out of the barrel. "Aurora is taking you to town, where you'll buy a new dress and shoes, and then you're off to the milliner's. Tomorrow, you and I are going to a picnic."

"Where?" The affair must be quite elaborate if Philippe was encouraging her to purchase new attire. Their neighbor, Aurora, would make a delightful shopping companion. She had been a surrogate mother to Sara since her arrival in Napa. Aurora was a widow, a professor of husbandry and a suffragette—born with an extra helping of gumption. Sara couldn't admire anyone more.

"We've been invited to the festival of the Italian Swiss Colony in Asti. We take the ten o'clock train tomorrow, and we'll return home late in the evening."

"Oh—will there be a lot of people there?"

"Over two hundred winemakers, bankers, Supreme Court justices, millionaires . . ."

Sara rolled her eyes, mostly in an effort to hide her nervousness about attending such a grand party.

In town that afternoon, Aurora was bursting with opinions. She helped Sara choose a summer silk-and-cotton dress, with a parasol to match. Sara objected to the generous frills at the cuffs, but Aurora insisted that if she wanted to blend in with the San Francisco socialites, and appear as guest rather than servant, she couldn't dress like a farmer's wife. Sara decided this was good advice, and that she could justify the purchase because she now had one elegant summer costume in addition to her handsome winter walking suit, with matching shoes for both. She required no more.

"What have you done with my wife?" Philippe mused, eyeing every detail of Sara's ensemble later, back at home. He made a twirling motion with his hand, and Sara spun around. Aurora beamed, bobbing her head with satisfaction, which whipped her springy auburn curls into a frenzy.

"You like it?" Sara felt silly, all done up with puckered lace at the collar. Thankfully, sleeves and skirts had slimmed in the last few months, and, with help from her S-curve corset, she looked slender, if more curvaceous.

"I think you're far too fashionable a creature to be *my* wife."


The train chugged along, whistling its high pitch before every stop. The highfalutin San Francisco socialites had boarded earlier, and now Sara and Philippe watched their Sonoma and Santa Rosa neighbors pile in, not nearly as stylish as the city-dwellers, but far more interesting.

At the station, a string of carriages lined up to take guests to the Colony, home to Italian and Swiss families for whom cultivating their two thousand acres of fruit was more than just making wine. The Colony was recreating the feel, the smell and the taste of Italy and Switzerland—right here in California. How ironic, Sara thought, that she had more of an opportunity to immerse herself in other European cultures while living in America than she'd had in Europe!

Once they arrived at the vineyard, Sara took Philippe's arm, and the pair followed the crowd through a row of sweet-smelling lilac bushes and into the immense winery buildings. On their tour, Sara marveled at the gigantic fermenting room, which housed eighty tanks, three times the height of any man, and the vast cellars, where barrels were stacked five-high.

"Wait until you see what's next," Philippe whispered.

In her wildest dreams, Sara couldn't have imagined it. The crowd advanced toward the broad concrete structure, which looked like the lower portion of an Egyptian pyramid. A reverent hush fell over the crowd; only an occasional "ooh" or "aah" could be heard.

Philippe explained softly, "One thousand barrels of cement and six thousand barrels of sand and gravel from the Russian River bed were used. Fifty men spent fifty days and nights building it. Once the 500,000 gallons of wine are steam-pumped inside, the hold on top is hermetically sealed. They emptied it in March."

Sara's jaw fell open. "How do you know all this?"

"The men I hired to bench graft the vines at Eagle's Run all live here. When I met some in town last week, they told me all about it and invited us to their fête. Are you impressed?"

"Goodness, yes—it's the eighth wonder of the world," Sara gushed.

Philippe laughed. "Indeed, but the best is yet to come." Philippe was cut short by the line of Italians standing on the edge of the cistern roof, clapping their hands to gain the crowd's attention. The president of the chamber of commerce waved his hands and began speaking.

After thanking the leaders of the Italian Swiss Colony and the dignitaries present, he invited the guests inside. The crowd exploded with a huge cheer, and everyone lined up to climb the concrete stairs to the cistern roof. The flat roof was decorated with a potted tulip garden and six stone walkways leading, like sunbeams, from the arched fountain in its center out to its edges. Underneath the center fountain, from which no liquid flowed, was a hole three feet in diameter, which was the entrance to this immense wine cistern. From here, the guests descended down to the floor of the reservoir via a twenty-four-foot spiral staircase.

What a treat to escape the midday heat and enter the cool, damp reservoir! The glazed walls were stained a bishop's purple from the Chianti that had rested inside for five months. Once every last guest was inside, a jovial Italian man stood atop a small ladder and announced, "*Buongiorno!*" *Buongiorno*s echoed around the reservoir walls for over a minute before petering out, and the crowd applauded the trick of acoustics.

Next on their journey of pleasure was a quarter-mile walk across the viridian lawn through the vibrant pinks, yellows and whites of the rose garden to the banqueting grove, where they dined under a lush canopy of trees and trellises. The waiters were all teenagers from the Italian Swiss Colony, in native costume, serving the elegant fare with the grace of quadrille dancers. The diners sat at white-linen tables, drank local Chablis and Chianti from crystal glasses, and speared their cold mutton with silver flatware. Sara took in the scene: over two hundred guests, ten to a table, silver clinking, faces shining, laughter and celebration on the breeze. She was in a new country, with new friends and her new husband—could any day be more glorious?

After numerous toasts and introductions, Philippe excused them from the table, guiding Sara to the orchard. She was relieved to escape the hammock-tossing, chair-pulling antics that had started once the diners were properly crocked.

"Are you enjoying yourself, Mrs. Lemieux?"

"I've never enjoyed myself more."

"Never?" Philippe winked.

Sara swatted him. "Not in polite company!" Truthfully, she was pleased with his attention. Philippe was always near her today, with his arm threaded through hers, his palm resting on the small of her back or his fingers wrapped reassuringly around hers as she descended the stairs. He understood her from the inside out.

Philippe led her deep into the orchard, choosing an obliging pear tree for their resting spot. He tossed his straw boater on the grass, spread his jacket beneath the tree branches, and seated Sara upon it. When he lay down, placing his head in her lap, she tensed.

With eyes shut, Philippe reassured her. "There's no one here to see, love. Besides, we're married."

"You seem to think marriage entitles you to all kinds of liberties," Sara teased.

Philippe grinned lazily. "I'm just allowing the wine to soak in. You should try it."

Sara examined his face, in awe of his sandy hair and cinnamon lashes resting above high cheekbones and a square jaw. He looked as though God had hewn him from marble. Sara swept a few strands off his forehead and exhaled. Reclining against the tree, she felt its rough bark chafe her skin through the thin cotton of her dress. The day smelled of lilac, fresh-clipped grass and Chianti.

Sara awoke to coquettish giggling and panting—and it was coming closer.

Out of the grove of apple trees only twenty paces away burst a young woman with a scarf of loose, golden hair flying behind her as she zigzagged. In rapid pursuit was a young man, calling out, "Isla!" Neither was a guest, Sara surmised, for he was wearing a server's livery and she a plain skirt, her hands and apron dusted with flour. When he finally caught her by the waist, he tipped her back and planted a lingering kiss on her lips. She didn't resist.

Before Sara knew what was happening, Philippe was on his feet. "Giuseppe!"

The man stopped and turned. "Filippo? Ah, Filippo!" He didn't seem the least bit embarrassed, but instead took the girl by the hand and pulled her over to meet Philippe.

Although Sara understood none of the introductions, she managed to croak out a *buongiorno* and a few *grazie*s. Philippe seemed quite at ease, conversing alternately in Italian and English with Giuseppe. Giuseppe's girl whispered something in his ear, lowered her eyes and curtsied, then dashed back toward the banqueting tables.

Feeling a bit woozy in the afternoon heat, Sara sank down on Philippe's jacket and fanned herself with his hat. The two men chattered for another twenty minutes, pausing only to gesture toward the banqueting grove.

The blaring of a trumpet ended their exchange. Giuseppe shook Philippe's hand, bowed his head toward Sara, and then inquired, "*Noi danziamo, va bene?*"

"*Si!*" Philippe responded with gusto. He turned to a bewildered Sara and, taking her hand, hoisted her up.

"What's happening?" Sara smoothed her wrinkled skirt.

"The party's in full swing. Come with me—I'll show you."

Philippe guided Sara back toward the enormous wine cistern.

"What were you two talking about?"

"I'm sorry, I didn't mean to exclude you. Giuseppe was speaking so quickly, I couldn't take the time to translate. I just wanted to remember everything he said."

"About?"

"Giuseppe, who was very skilled at grafting my vines, has also been planting apple, pear and olive trees since he was eight years old. His father is the orchardist for the Colony."

"No!" Sara said in amazement. "Between his knowledge and Aurora's, we'll be set!" she said excitedly, but then caught herself. "But why would we plant an orchard at Eagle's Run before we replant the grapevines at Saint Martin?"

"Because, Sara," Philippe paused, pressing his shoulder

against a tree, "planting fruit trees is less expensive and requires less labor. We can do it ourselves, on a small scale."

Sara sighed with frustration. "Perhaps, but it will take years for them to produce fruit, just like the grapes," she cautioned, turning away. Philippe clasped her hand, pulling her back to face him. "You're never going to honor your promise to me, are you?" she accused. "We only need three hectares of new vines at Saint Martin. Surely that won't bankrupt us!"

"Keep your voice down!" Philippe's grip tightened. "You don't understand, Sara." His voice faltered when he uttered her name. "We've lost forty percent—over ten thousand dollars—of our income this year because of this damned price war. We must use some of my grandfather's money for the orchard. We can't waste our time planting more grapes now. We need apples, pears, anything that costs less money to harvest."

Sara stumbled back, shocked that he'd kept these details from her. No wonder he'd been so secretive about their finances. Eagle's Run was teetering on the edge of insolvency. A thousand questions leapt to mind, but Sara forced them aside for the moment. Bewildered, she asked, "So, what's our plan?"

Philippe inhaled deeply and explained, "We need to dig five-foot holes, ten paces apart, clustering trees of the same fruit together. We'll plant on the slopes of the foothills, not too high or too low. And they should be planted straight, but then pushed to lean slightly in the direction of the prevailing wind.

"Giuseppe also said something about bacteria." Philippe began to weave between the trees, running his hand down one tree's smooth bark, examining the leaves of another. "Yes, he said we should come up here to Asti and find the very best specimen of each tree we've planted. We should take soil from the Asti trees to use for ours. He says it never fails."

"How many trees?"

"I'm not sure. A hundred?"

"Hmm. Very well," Sara acquiesced. "And Saint Martin?"

Philippe placed a hand on her shoulder. "Patience, my love."

Two more glasses of wine blunted Sara's irritation. She joined Philippe and the other revelers inside the cool wine cistern, enjoying the Strauss waltzes and two-steps. Sara danced like she hadn't since Papa was alive, especially when Philippe demonstrated the cakewalk for her to mimic. Such silliness! He swept her up and spun her across the floor until it was time for the last train home.

Sara and Philippe lifted bucket after bucket from the wagon. They had brought a total of twenty, filled with soil taken from the colony's orchards and marked with the type of fruit that flourished in them.

They had planted twenty-five each of apple, pear and apricot trees on the southern foothills of Eagle's Run, just north of the intersection of the Napa River and Carneros Creek. Luc loved plunging his hands into the buckets, sprinkling soil around each tree and patting it down to make sure the nutrients seeped in to feed the roots.

Sara had underestimated the time and strength it took to plant an orchard: before the grape harvest, they only had time to plant seventy-five trees. In three years, they would bear fruit. But what could they do to earn money now?

# Chapter 9

Linnette had three hours to earn thirty dollars. The money would sustain her and Pippa for two months, if she scrimped.

Her roommate, Tildy, who had offered to watch Pippa tonight in the hopes she'd receive her rent money tomorrow, tightened the stays of Linnette's corset while Linnette hoisted up her breasts as far as gravity would permit. She slipped a peach silk dress over her head. The garment hung loosely off her shoulders, and it was a tad outdated, but Linnette was certain that her coiffure would make up for what the dress lacked.

Tildy, who had quick fingers and a keen eye, arranged Linnette's hair in loose waves, with a soft pompadour at the front and a fluff at the neck. Three horizontal puffs were arranged at the back, held in place by two tortoiseshell combs on the sides and an elegant ivory silk rose on top. Linnette sprayed herself with Coudray's violet scent, which, ironically, Philippe had purchased for her.

Madame Beaumont had promised to give her a go. Linnette had lied, insisting she was twenty rather than twenty-four. Most of the girls who worked there were ten to twenty years old— Linnette hadn't started till fourteen.

She deliberately arrived fifteen minutes late so she could make an entrance and catch the eye of a wealthy gentleman. The parlor room at the front of the Italianate house was small, hot and populated with smartly dressed johns petting gussied-up girls. Bodies sprawled across the expensive furnishings, some drowsy with opium, others chewing on chicken legs and sipping red wine. Linnette's stomach somersaulted at the mingled odors of sickly sweet perfume and gamy chicken fat. She was far too sober to be in this company. Still, she intended to proceed with her plan, so her darling Pippa would never have to debase herself like this.

Linnette knew she was still vibrant and beautiful and that any man in this room would be lucky to touch her. She walked over to the sideboard and poured wine to the goblet's rim. After three sips, she felt its warmth spread through her chest and her muscles begin to relax.

Madame Beaumont walked to the center of the room. "Gentlemen, we have a stunner for you this evening. Mademoiselle Cross, who has been independently employed for several years, is available for your entertainment. She is quite talented and therefore comes at a premium this evening of five extra dollars."

Linnette nodded to thank her and smiled without sincerity at several men who had put down their goblets and pipes to gawk. She could tell by their desperate leering that none were accomplished lovers. Still smiling, she walked over to an empty wingback and sat down next to a middle-aged businessman. Linnette leaned in, dramatically revealing the full heft of her cleavage, and murmured, "I hope you find the weather to your liking tonight, sir."

He did.

He was not attractive, with a gut hanging over his belt and an unruly black beard, but he was dressed to the height of fashion. Linnette allowed him to guide her to an upstairs chamber, where he began to undress her. His clumsy fingers floundered—he was unable to free the buttons on her dress. She finished the task herself, and then stripped down to her corset and drawers. He watched her with glassy eyes. When she sat beside him on the bed, he began to paw at her chest. His hot breath smelled of boiled onions, and his hands were still soiled with grease from the chicken thigh he'd been gnawing earlier.

He really is a beast, Linnette thought, trying to hide her distaste by humming her favorite ditty, "San Francisco Sadie," while she unfastened his red silk waistcoat. She needed to finish this quickly so she could return to Pippa. Suddenly, he swayed from side to side, and then his eyes rolled. He fell back onto the bed with a light thump and began to snore.

Linnette wasted no time. She peeled off every last stitch of his clothing and covered him with the quilt. She tangled the bed-sheets on the other side of him and used the heel of her hand to make a head-sized dent in the adjacent pillow. She winced as she plucked three strands of hair from her head and arranged them on the white pillowcase, along with the silk rosette from her hair—a souvenir for the dreadful dolt.

Linnette dressed and sifted through his belongings. She pulled fifty dollars from his pocket, dropped twenty in the till downstairs for Madame Beaumont and sauntered out the front door.

# Chapter 10

P hilippe and Mac were loading the second batch of grapes into the crusher when Monsignor O'Brien arrived, wearing his thirty-three-button cassock and black cappello and carrying a leather satchel and walking stick. He looked cheerful, with lively brown eyes, a fleshy pockmarked nose and a ruddy complexion. Standing in the doorway of the winery, he doffed his hat, dropped his bag and rubbed his palms together. "This looks like great fun!"

Philippe shook the cleric's meaty hand. "Welcome to Eagle's Run, monsignor." Philippe exhaled the breath he'd been holding for weeks, anticipating the arrival of the priest. His contract with the archdiocese hinged on satisfying O'Brien that the sacramental wine was produced to the standards of canon law. His approval was the only judgment that mattered.

"Will the *curé* be joining us today?" Philippe was surprised by his absence, for Father Price, their new Napa priest, had never been one to pass up the opportunity to lick the boots of his superiors.

"He intended to come. However, when I made it clear that I would be laboring in the vineyard, up to my elbows in grape sludge, he demurred. Apparently he has to work up Sunday's sermon." O'Brien added slyly, "One wouldn't want to disappoint."

Philippe stifled a laugh. They would get along just fine.

Getting down to business, Philippe regarded the monsignor's cassock. "If you're serious about helping, Père, you'd best change into some work clothes."

O'Brien clapped his hands together excitedly. "Show me the way, kind sir."

After he had changed and washed his hands at the pump, Philippe led him back to the winery. "Have you inspected many wineries?"

O'Brien smiled wryly and replied, "I've inspected many wines, but this is my first assignment for the archbishop. I was a parish priest in Monterey for the last two years."

This could work to Philippe's advantage. He would tell O'Brien what he needed to know. Beyond that, the priest probably wouldn't know enough to ask.

Philippe brought O'Brien to the edge of the third-floor door and pointed to the horses and lift below. "This is what we call gravity-flow. The grapes are lifted up here and poured into this crusher, which moves the grapes through a set of corrugated rollers, breaking the skins but keeping the seeds intact. Then they move through this de-stemming machine." Philippe pointed to the chutes in the floor. "The pulp flows down to the next level into the fermenting tanks. This way, we don't need to use pumps, like they do in the single-level wineries."

"Brilliant," O'Brien replied, peering down a chute to the tank below.

Philippe led him down to the second level. He pointed to a vat of crushed grapes sitting between the fermenting tanks. "Cabernet grapes with the skins, to give them a robust red color. They've started fermenting. Press down on the cap with your hand."

O'Brien lit up like a child with a new toy, and placed his hand gingerly on the skins resting at the top. Philippe demonstrated, pushing his hand down and releasing it. O'Brien followed suit and laughed. "Bouncy! Like sponge cake, isn't it?"

"Yes, I suppose it is." Philippe continued, "About six inches of skins are forced to the top by the carbon dioxide that's released when the grapes are fermenting. We punch down the cap four or five times a day so all the flavors, color and tannins are released out of the skins and into the juice. Cabernet grapes have the thickest skins, but they produce the most vivid reds."

O'Brien's face lit with understanding. "Just like our Savior's blood," he whispered with reverence.

"Indeed." Philippe was a believer, though he still harbored doubts.

"And no yeast is added?"

"No, the wild yeast that grows on the grape skins ferments the grapes naturally."

"Fascinating. Just like the Old Testament. And what happens to all the stems?"

"We use them as fertilizer for the vines." Philippe gestured out the window to a patch of purple-stained dirt adjacent to the vine rows. "That's a compost of skins and stems from the red grapes."

"Excellent use for them." The priest's enthusiasm for learning was infectious. "So how many bottles will this harvest yield?"

"Depends," Philippe said. He didn't want to offer too high a number, for he knew the price would drop accordingly. "One ton of grapes usually yields about seven hundred bottles. Nearly three pounds of grapes are pressed to make each bottle."

"And how many tons per acre?"

"About five, for a total of a thousand tons this year, we hope." Philippe looked at him quizzically. "Do you want a journal to write this down?"

O'Brien tapped his temple with his forefinger. "I have the memory of an elephant."

Last, Philippe showed him the cellar, filled with barrels of sacramental and non-sacramental red wines. A burst of cool air and the heavy aroma of oak greeted them.

"My goodness, I didn't realize the size of your operation."

"And, with any luck, we'll continue to grow. See these barrels?" Philippe pointed at the pyramid against the cellar's northern wall. "All American oak, from various forests, all reused four or five times, but only for the sacramental reds."

"So, upstairs the juice is drawn off the pulp and flows down here, where it's stored in these barrels?" O'Brien was a quick study.

"Exactly, but the work doesn't end there. Every four months, we drain off the wine from the sediment and move it to a new, clean barrel. Then we top it off with more wine, to make up for the angels' share."

"Angels' share?"

"The barrel loses some wine to evaporation, and that's what we call it."

"How charming. I'll take care to remember that one." O'Brien looked up to the heavens and smiled.

Although Rose, their housekeeper and cook, had set the dining room table for supper, O'Brien asked to eat with the vineyard workers outdoors. "Lately I find myself dining with the archbishop in very formal surroundings. I enjoy a hard day of work ending with a glorious sunset," he said.

Sara and Rose threw a tablecloth over the picnic table out back, and set out the jugs of wine and plates of ham, cheddar, bread and piccalilli.

Sara poured two glasses of wine, a zinfandel and a chardonnay, for their guest.

"Now tell me, Mrs. Lemieux, what's the best way to taste wine? Aren't I supposed to swirl it?"

Sara laughed and obliged him. "Yes, you swirl it, sniff it and sip it, but don't swallow. You want to breathe a little air into your mouth, slurp it a bit, to feel its texture. Once you swallow it, wait for the finishing taste."

"Ah," O'Brien closed his eyes, relishing the flavor. Everyone at the table watched, hoping for his approval.

"What do you taste? Berries?" Sara guessed.

"Yes. Blackberry, maybe even a bit of cinnamon?" The priest smacked his lips.

"Could be. The cinnamon taste comes from the inside of the barrel. The staves are toasted to give it that flavor."

"Really?" O'Brien released a satisfied sigh. "Delicious."

Halfway through the meal, their guest dropped his cutlery with a loud clank, startling everyone. He exclaimed, "I haven't tasted a piccalilli that good since my Aunt Maeve's back in Brooklyn. Where did you find this?"

"I made it," Sara replied proudly. "It's the only thing I make, besides wine. It was my mother's recipe."

"Saints preserve us! I've not tasted its rival."

Sara puffed with pride. "Then you must take some jars back with you."

O'Brien glowed with appreciation. "I'd be most obliged to you, ma'am."


Monsignor O'Brien spent the rest of his week in the field picking grapes and in the winery punching down the fermenting grape caps with a wooden paddle. Whenever Philippe encountered him, he was wholly engaged in the task at hand and seemed without a care in the world. Rather than slowing down the harvest, his presence revitalized the workers. He prayed with them, ate with them and worked alongside them. Each man gathered in an average of two tons per day, working ten hours a day, from the evening into the early morning hours, to pick the grapes at their coldest. Philippe rather wished O'Brien would stay on as their mascot.

Philippe was surprised when the priest, on the last day of his visit, divulged his other reason for coming. He sat at the kitchen table and slid a letter over to Philippe. Ten Napa vintners had scrawled their names at the bottom.

"We received this several months ago. They're all parishioners, and they're protesting your position as the major supplier of wine to the archdiocese. They say it's risky and unfair for us to purchase the bulk of our wine from one winery." O'Brien opened his palms. "They do have a point."

Philippe recoiled. "How is it risky? Eagle's Run has reconstituted rootstock, virtually immune to the threat of the phylloxera. Can these growers say that?" Philippe tapped his finger on the list of signatures.

"Probably not. I'm going to visit each of them over the next two months before I make a recommendation to the archbishop. Here's the rub. Over the past year, you've served us well. You do a credible job, and I will recommend that we keep you as our largest supplier. However, as an archdiocese committed to supporting the plight of the laborers, we need to spread our business around. We can't play favorites." O'Brien took a deep breath and blurted, "We're cutting back your contract by fourteen thousand gallons a year, and we're asking for a price reduction of two cents per gallon."

"But that's half of what we provide you now, and we're already at twelve cents!"

"These winemakers are offering ten."

Philippe's revenue would drop by nearly two thousand dollars until he found replacement buyers. He knew delivering the wine locally was cheaper, but keeping the sacramental wine business was critical in case a prohibition of alcohol was passed.

"Agreed," he said, before deciding to push him further. "Monsignor?"

"Yes?"

"As the archdiocese expands, will you consider Eagle's Run first if you need to increase your supply of wine?"

O'Brien hesitated for a moment.

"Perhaps on your next visit, you should try your hand at making your own wine, and take a few cases home with you," Philippe said, trying to tempt him.

O'Brien smiled broadly. "Agreed."

Philippe blotted his damp forehead. Every wine man for himself, he thought bitterly. Because he hadn't sold the bulk of his wine to the Wine Makers' Corporation, his fellow Napa winemakers had retaliated against him. Boone Sumter, along with a handful of other vintners who were too lazy to go out and make merchant contacts of their own, was more than eager to steal Philippe's ideas.

# Chapter 11

Aurora burst into the kitchen, breathless, waving a thick book in the air. "My dears, you must write at once."

Sara and Philippe stared at her as if she'd lost her mind. "What is it?"

"I borrowed it from Berkeley. Hot off the press. The instructions on how to apply to exhibit in Paris!"

"You want us to showcase Eagle's Run wines at the World's Fair in Paris? Against French wines?" Philippe asked.

"Yes!" She plunked the book down on the table, and flipped the pages. "Group Seven, Class Sixty, right here on page sixty-one: 'Wines and Brandies.' We'll send your application and bottles of your best wines, along with my recommendation."

Aurora looked from Sara to Philippe, her eyebrows arched in anticipation. Sara was surprised at Philippe's reluctance. She thought it was a grand idea. Philippe could check on Saint Martin if he went to Paris, and if Sara wasn't needed here, perhaps she could even go with him.

Philippe lowered himself into a chair. "Do you honestly think, Aurora, that we can compete against French wines in an internationally judged competition? Do you think we can *win*?" Philippe had a point. If they entered their wines in the World's Fair, and came back without so much as an honorable mention, they would suffer universal humiliation.

Aurora hands flew to her hips. "Would I be standing in your kitchen waving this book around like a madwoman if I didn't?"

"If they accept us into the competition, merchants across the globe will hear about Eagle's Run wines. But if we win," Sara added with a smile, "then they'll actually buy them."

The threesome took the next month to complete the commissioner's application and taste all the vintages, finally selecting the '97 cabernet and chardonnay. They packed up three bottles of each, along with recommendations from Aurora Thierry, world-renowned expert in grape varietals and professor of husbandry at the prestigious Ladies' Seminary, and from Monsignor O'Brien of the Archdiocese of San Francisco, who confirmed the archdiocese's business arrangement with Eagle's Run and vouched for Philippe's character. On top of the application and recommendations, they placed the four blue ribbons Eagle's Run had been awarded in the last two county fairs. With an Our Father and three Hail Marys, they mailed it to the commissioner's Chicago office and waited on pins and needles.

# Chapter 12

MAY 1899

Luc raced through the tunnel of towering eucalyptus trees that lined the roadside. It was nearly suppertime, and after a grueling day of weeding, Sara wanted nothing more than to sit on the grass and enjoy the soothing, menthol scent of the eucalyptus oil floating through the air. Luc finally slowed and stayed close by, peeling the long strips of gray bark from the tree trunks and humming softly.

When they returned to the house, Sara pecked Philippe on the cheek and excused herself from supper. Her back felt as though someone had clubbed her from behind, her head throbbed and she couldn't stay awake a moment longer.

Lacking the strength to even change into her nightgown, Sara drifted off to sleep. In her dream, she was holding a child—a girl—

with dark hair and lashes, perhaps a year old. She was rocking her to sleep in the black lacquered chair Philippe had given her. She was singing Brahms's lullaby—*Bright angels beside my darling abide*—when a man wearing a priest's robes appeared and ripped the child from Sara's arms.

Sara awoke with a start, heart thudding. Her shirt was soaked with perspiration, and the hair framing her face was matted with moisture. She sat up, wondering if she were still asleep. Philippe's reassuring hand squeezed her shoulder, bringing her back.

"Sara?" he touched her forehead. "Sara, you're feverish."

"No, it was just a dream."

"A nightmare. You screamed just now. I'm surprised Luc didn't wake up."

Sara remembered the girl, the feeling of serenity, and then the evil man with black robes and no face. An iron weight of sorrow pressed upon her chest.

"Should I fetch the doctor?"

The moonlight shining through the bedroom window cast a glow on the bedside table. Sara picked up Philippe's pocket watch, straining to see the time. Two o'clock.

"No, that's silly. Once I change, I'll be fine."

"I'll fetch him in the morning."

Sara peeled off her damp clothes, slipped on a cotton night-dress and ducked out of the room. She opened the front door and stepped out onto the porch. She could barely see the front garden, but could easily view the glowing moon and stars, and wondered if Lydia and Papa could see her gazing up at them in the heavens.

Sara sat on the top step of the porch stairs and hugged her knees to her chest. The night air chilled her skin, and she liked the quiet, with only the chirping of the crickets to keep her company. Sitting still, without the daily demands of Luc and the vineyard to distract her, she realized she felt different.

Her fatigue consumed her, but it wasn't harvest time. She felt twinges of pain in her breasts, and instead of her monthly curse, she'd only spotted blood for a few days. Her corset made her nauseous, so she only wore it to church and social outings. Sara's mind whirled like a prize wheel at a carnival, and then finally clicked into place.

Might she be pregnant?

If she were, Sara didn't want Philippe to know yet. She loved children, but after what she'd witnessed Lydia and so many others suffer, she had trouble forgetting the screams, the blood and the mortal danger of childbed. Nothing frightened her more. She'd even considered asking Philippe to wear something to prevent pregnancy. However, she hadn't done it, knowing it would put her soul in jeopardy and that Philippe would never agree to it.

No, she wouldn't tell him until she was ready.


The next morning, Sara wouldn't hear of Philippe fetching the doctor. Instead, she suggested that he drop her off at the doctor's office on his way to the general store. He reluctantly agreed.

Dr. Pratt conducted a short physical examination and declared Sara to be expecting in late December. Sara's spirits soared to learn that Philippe's child lived inside her, but her fear quickly stomped out her happiness.

Sara remained quiet during the ride home. She had begged the doctor not to tell Philippe, or anyone, until she had time to think. "What's there to think about?" he'd replied. "It's what every newly married woman dreams of."

Philippe, now sitting next to her in the wagon, threw her a concerned look. "So, what did the doctor say?"

Sara clutched his arm. "Why don't you stop for a moment?"

Philippe guided the horses over to a grassy patch under a maple tree and set the brake. "What's wrong?"

"Nothing at all." Sara looked in his expectant eyes and rallied as much enthusiasm as she could. "We're going to have a baby." Her tone fell a little short. She shouldn't have said anything; she wasn't ready.

Philippe's face glowed with happiness. He grasped her shoulders and pulled her near, kissing her. "When?"

"The doctor thinks December."

"A Christmas baby," Philippe declared. "What a surprise!" When she didn't reply, he asked, "Aren't you happy?"

"Of course I am," Sara said tentatively. "Just a little nervous."

Philippe squeezed her hand. "Everything will be fine, you'll see."

For you, thought Sara. You're not the one who has to birth it.


The late July rains endangered the fruit. Fearing mildew and the dilution of the grapes' flavor, Philippe sent the men into the field to cut back leaves and drop some clusters to the ground, allowing the remaining fruit to soak in more sunlight. But both Philippe and Sara knew full well that if the sun blazed during the week before the harvest, it might wither the grapes. This risky dance always set Sara's teeth on edge.

During the last week of August, the red hawks circled high overhead, squawking and scaring off the rodents, orioles and starlings that used their sharp beaks to puncture the nearly ripe grapes and pilfer their juice. Luc, wary of the hawks' cries, stayed indoors until the owls took over at night. They emerged from their boxes—hand-built by Sara and Philippe—to hunt mice and other grape thieves.

The men worked through the night, harvesting the grapes at their coolest, loading the boxes into the wagons and then tossing the clusters into the crusher. After Sara guided each wagonload into the machine and down the chute to the floor below, she rested on the wooden stool until the next batch came. Her stomach was a small mound now, and the child moved like fairy wings inside her. On days when her back ached more than usual, she would eat lunch quickly and settle in for a long nap with Luc on their bed.

By the time the fruit ripened, grapes on the southern slopes had withered in the sun, and they'd lost close to nineteen hundred bottles. On the last day of the harvest, when the pickers combed through the vines searching for last clusters, Rose approached Sara in a panic.

Luc was burning up.

∽

After three days of sweating through his sheets and waking during the night, Luc was resting peacefully. His fever had finally subsided.

Sara was relieved. Even Aurora's elderberry tea hadn't helped this time. Exhausted from carrying Luc to the creek several times a day to bathe him in the cool running water, Sara ached to her bones. She sat down in her ebony rocking chair and shoved a pillow behind her lower back. This was more than muscular fatigue—the soreness in her joints wouldn't relent.

She soon retired to bed, and after a fitful sleep, Sara awoke to find Philippe's side vacant. As was his normal routine these days, he would quietly slip out for a cup of coffee and toast before he started working in the vineyard. He insisted Sara sleep as long as possible, for the health of the child. Sleep was elusive these days, especially with the deep ache in her knees and hip joints. She would ask Aurora if she could mix up some root concoction to ease her pain.

Luc bounded up to her bedside, giggling and flashing a toothy grin. His cheeks were bright red, as if he'd been slapped. She worried the fever had returned, but his forehead was as cool as a bay breeze. When she lifted his nightshirt, she noticed his mottled skin. A rash covered his trunk and arms, forming a pattern that reminded Sara of Amboise lace. If he spiked a fever again, or started scratching, she'd call the doctor. Otherwise, she had a house and vineyard full of work to be done.

Rose was in the kitchen, frying eggs and buttering toast. Sara sipped the steaming black coffee Rose had just poured for her. "G'morning, Rose. Thank you, I'm starving."

"Yer most welcome, missus," Rose replied cheerfully. "And you're a live wire this morning, aren't you, my little one?" She ruffled Luc's hair and strapped him in his chair. Sara was about to sit down with him when Rose's expression filled with fright. "Missus!" Rose pointed to the floor beneath Sara, and then her hand flew to cover her mouth.

Sara glanced down. A small puddle of blood pooled between her feet. She jumped back, lifted her skirts and observed a thin but steady stream of blood running down between her calves. "Rose, call Philippe." Sara reached for the chair. "Send for the doctor at once."

She walked slowly back to her bedroom, her heart pounding. She leaned on the wall, then gripped the bedpost and finally lowered herself onto the bed. She felt a wave of nausea overpower her.

Within an hour, Sara was doubled over, knees to chest, lying on her side. This knifelike pain was even worse than when she'd dislocated her shoulder in the earthquake two years ago. Philippe stood over her, rubbing her back and holding a cool, wet cloth to her forehead. Neither spoke. Dr. Pratt came at ten o'clock and instructed Philippe to leave the room. Near ten-thirty, with a burst of pain and a rush of blood, Sara expelled their baby onto the yellow flowered sheets of their bed.

The doctor wrapped the baby in a white cloth before Sara could see it. He placed the bundle at the bottom of the bed. He examined Sara and told her she'd be fine and able to have more children. Was this proclamation supposed to cheer her?

After whispering something to Philippe outside, Dr. Pratt ushered him into the room. Sara didn't have the time or the inclination to clean herself. Instead, she pulled the quilt to her neck and turned over to face the wall.

She felt Philippe's hands massaging her shoulders tenderly. "Oh, Sara." His voice quivered.

She had failed him, and their child. Her shoulders started shaking. She could see nothing through her tears, but she heard Philippe muttering something to the doctor. If she didn't pull herself together, they would take charge of her situation. Sara wiped her tears with her sleeve, rolled over and propped herself up on the pillows.

"Is it a boy or a girl?"

"It was a girl, Mrs. Lemieux," the doctor said softly.

"I want to hold her," Sara demanded, her voice breaking.

The doctor frowned, then hesitated before saying somberly, "Mrs. Lemieux, I believe that would be unwise." He paused, and then continued, "The best thing you could do now is to heal, and then try to have another baby as soon as possible."

Another baby. Her little girl's body was barely cold, swaddled in a blanket at the foot of her bed, and he wanted her to think about *another* baby. Sara sat up in bed and glared at the physician. "Hand me my child."

Philippe laid a hand on Sara's shoulder, perhaps to calm her, but she batted it away. "Sara, the doctor thinks that's not healthy for you."

"Mrs. Lemieux," Dr. Pratt said softly, "your baby's heart failed and . . . her body is rather swollen."

Sara's gaze remained fixed on the rolled-up wad of cloth. "Get out," she said, glancing sharply at Philippe. "Out!" she shrieked.

Philippe left the room, and the doctor followed him out.

Sara's hands quivered when she reached out to gather the soft, weightless bundle into her arms. She sucked air between her teeth spasmodically, trying to calm down. She peeled back the top layer of flannel. A tiny gray face appeared, with closed eyes, puffy cheeks, sweet rosebud lips and small buds for ears. She looked serene, as if she'd simply drifted back into God's arms. Sorrow stabbed Sara through.

She unfolded the blanket, revealing the baby's bloated limbs. Despite the swelling, she looked even more fragile than Sara had expected. She thought of the unused bowl of water Philippe had boiled an hour ago at the doctor's behest. With her child tucked into the crook of her arm, Sara walked over to it, dipped a finger in and decided the lukewarm water would suffice.

She made the sign of the cross on her daughter's forehead and anointed her without naming her. "I baptize you in the name of the Father, the Son, and the Holy Ghost. Amen." This baptism was so different from Luc's in the convent. No shining faces filled with joy; no hope for what this child would one day become.

Sara plunged the soft cloth into the water and wrung it out. Carefully, she sponged the blood and pasty white coating from the creases of her baby girl's skin. Preparing her child's body was the only thing she could do now. Just as she had done for Lydie, just as Maman had done for Papa.

When she finished, she swaddled her in a fresh towel. She pressed her lips to her daughter's forehead. The skin was supple, like a ripe peach. No matter how intently she gazed upon her baby girl's face, she couldn't coax her little eyelids to open.

Sara's lip trembled, and her shoulders began to heave. She rocked the child that would never be, tearfully murmuring her goodbyes.

Sara awoke to tapping at the door. She must have fallen asleep, supported by pillows and holding her baby. Philippe came in, closing the door behind him. He stopped short when he saw his wife and child. His expression was ravaged with grief. "Sara, Father Price is here. I spoke with him about arrangements for the baby."

Sara blinked. What arrangements?

Philippe placed a warm hand on her arm. "The baby will be buried here, at Eagle's Run. We'll find a nice spot for her, where we can . . . spend time with her." Philippe barely choked out the words before his large hand cradled their daughter's head.

Sara was confused. "Why? Why wouldn't she be buried at Tulocay Cemetery?"

"Because that's sanctified ground."

"She has been baptized—I baptized her. Her soul is in heaven, with God."

Philippe hesitated. An uncomfortable silence divided them. Taking Sara's hand, he called to Father Price. When the priest entered, Philippe backed away, allowing the priest to take the chair beside the bed.

Sara scrutinized the pastor, dressed in a spotless soutane, smelling like fresh leather and shoe polish. Beneath the quilt, her thighs were still caked with sticky blood.

"Mrs. Lemieux, you have my deepest—" Shock registered on Father Price's face as he regarded the small, blanketed creature Sara held in her arms.

"Father, my wife baptized our child. Surely that changes things?" Philippe's voice was tinged with desperation. Sara glanced at him. What did he mean?

The priest pulled out a handkerchief, wiped the droplets of sweat from his brow, and then tucked the folded square back in his pocket. "Mrs. Lemieux, I'm deeply sorry for your loss. However, it is incumbent upon me as your pastor to explain that because the child was not baptized while living, and therefore did not receive the sanctifying grace necessary to remove original sin, her soul cannot live with God. It will be assigned to limbo."

Sara had heard of limbo, of course. Limbo bordered heaven. It was where the souls of the good, unbaptized people lived. Limbo wasn't hell, for the souls in hell knew they were denied the beatific vision of God, which made their eternal sentence more horrifying. No, the souls in limbo didn't know about God. And the souls in limbo could never cross over to meet the souls in heaven.

Was there no hope? Would she be separated from her daughter forever?

"My wife baptized her. She will be buried in holy ground," Philippe asserted.

"I understand you are grieving, Mr. Lemieux, but your wife baptized the baby *after* she died, not in time to save her soul. The church, the pope himself, won't allow it."

Sara glared at the priest and wondered how he, or the pope, knew whether or not God had saved her daughter's soul. It was hogwash, all of it. She was about to tell him this when Philippe abruptly escorted Father Price from the room. Her husband knew she was about to say something they'd regret—something that might jeopardize their contract with the archdiocese. Sara couldn't think about that now. She kissed her first child for the last time, determined to etch her daughter's perfect face in her memory.

Sara sat at the foot of her daughter's grave. She flinched each time Philippe's spade crunched the dirt, gouging a deep, narrow hole. When he finally stopped his frantic digging, he dropped the spade, shuffled over to Sara and wordlessly attempted to take the child from her arms. Sara could not release her, or look at him. She removed the muslin shroud and pressed her face against her daughter's cold cheek.

She heard Philippe's breath catch again and again. Sara bowed her head when she lifted the child, for she could not bear to see his expression. When he walked away, Sara stole a glance. Philippe nestled his daughter in his arms, dropped to his knees and laid her gently in the grave. He sprinkled soil over her swaddled remains.

They had decided to bury her at the edge of the vineyard, in a quiet, lush, green patch of earth, where they would plant a pear tree. Without thinking, Philippe had suggested an apple tree, but Sara had refused. She would not allow the symbol of Adam and Eve's fall—the reason why her daughter could not live in heaven— to be a marker for her daughter's grave.

Sara collected ten pale stones the size of her fist and placed them in a circle around the grave. Philippe secured a small cross at its head. He'd spent the afternoon meticulously sawing and sanding two old barrel boards that he'd nailed together.

They recited the Hail Mary and Our Father. Sara knelt down, pushing her fingers into the cool mound of dirt until her nails began to bleed. After half an hour, Philippe lifted her limp body and carried her into the house.

Weeks passed before Sara regained her strength. To stop her breasts from aching for the child who would never suckle, Aurora wrapped her chest in cotton beneath her corset. Sara refused to stay in bed, as the doctor had insisted. When she was alone, in the wrenching silence, all she remembered was her daughter's precious pearl-like face, the eyes that would never open and the tiny fingers that would never grasp her own.

She tried to sleep in the downstairs bedroom, but it was too noisy and her nerves too frayed. Instead, she rocked for hours in the black chair, hoping to numb her mind with the tedious repetition. At times she succeeded, while at other times she felt as though she might suffocate from the pain that pressed upon her chest. She had suffered loss before. Why was this so different? Because this was her child—and her fault.

Sara feared she might lose her mind.

The next time Aurora stopped by it was with a picnic basket, a jug of wine and a bouquet of flowers from her hothouse. "Something to lift your spirits." She smiled as she handed the zinnias to Sara.

"Did Philippe send you?" Sara snapped. She hadn't spoken to him about their daughter. He went about his daily chores, occupying himself with the business of fermenting and barreling wine. His touch was cautious—his hands on her shoulders, a sympathetic peck on the cheek—but nothing more. She was a china doll, too fragile to hold. For now, her desire for him remained hidden beneath a heavy cloak of grief, if it existed at all.

"What if he did? He's worried about you. You've lost the blush in your cheek, and," Aurora said with a disapproving look, "you look like something the cat dragged in."

Sara couldn't have cared less. "Thank you, Aurora," she said flatly, "but I have to finish the housework and then stir the fermenting vats."

"Oh no you don't, missus," Rose interrupted loudly. "You go with madame. I'll tend to Luc and the cleaning. The wine will keep."

Aurora nodded and steered Sara gently by the elbow toward the door. "Come now, you have to eat. Why don't we go sit under that big oak down by the stream?" Unwilling to argue, Sara shrugged and fell into step with her.

They picked a shady spot and spread out an old quilt. Aurora dunked the jug in the stream, wedging it between two jutting rocks to keep it cold. They unpacked without speaking and before long were eating a luncheon of apples, freshly baked bread, smoked picnic ham, Monterey jack and two butter cakes. The salty ham and smooth, rich cheese, along with a few sips of cold white table wine, relaxed Sara.

The sweet candy fragrance of magnolia wafting through the warm air, and the sound of the breeze rustling through the leaves, beckoned Sara to lay down her head and close her eyes. She tried to slow her spinning mind by concentrating on the sound of the lapping water and the hardness of the earth beneath her.

Sara had no idea how long she'd slept. When she awoke, she swept a few ladybugs off her skirt, sat up and groggily looked around. Aurora was down at the stream, casting her enormous net, trying to catch fish and crabs for supper, no doubt. She looked content, her small, robust figure blithely bouncing barefooted from rock to rock across the shallow water, as though there was nowhere on earth she'd rather be. Sara wondered how Aurora did it, after losing both her son and husband so many years ago. How did one snap back after such crushing loss?

"Whoa, whoa, whaa!" Aurora shrieked, as she slipped off a rock and fell with a splash into the stream. Her skirts were soaked, and she guffawed, her generous bosom shaking with amusement.

Sara rushed down the slope to offer Aurora a hand.

"Thank you, my dear. Oh," she cried, smoothing her wet, matted coiffure, "that was great fun."

"We'd best head back so you can change."

"Come now, don't fuss," Aurora said soothingly. "The heat will dry my dress, and I don't mind sitting like this for a while." She lowered herself onto the soft grass, a few loose auburn curls falling to her shoulders.

"Sorry you didn't catch anything. I didn't know you fished," Sara said, forcing herself to start a conversation, something she rarely felt like doing these days.

"Not with a pole and line, but yes. I'd just netted a ten-inch trout when I slipped and he made his getaway! I suppose I'll just finish the ham tonight." Aurora squeezed out her waterlogged skirt. She looked up with pink, watery eyes. "I'm terribly upset over your loss. I do know how you suffer."

"It's not the same as your son, René, I know. My daughter never drew breath in the outside world."

"No, but with her died all that you hoped for her," Aurora said with such conviction that Sara's heart ached anew, knowing her friend had endured the same agony. Sara's mind filled with the memory of her tiny daughter, and her face crumpled. The truth was, she hadn't wished for Philippe's child, hadn't wanted her. Yet now, she'd do anything to have her, alive and fluttering inside her again.

Aurora patted Sara's knee. "I've lost a spouse and a child. Losing a child is worse."

"Why is that, do you think?" Sara sniffled.

"Because we're supposed to protect them, and it doesn't matter if they're stillborn, two years old or thirty-five years old with a family of their own. They're our own flesh, forever bound to us—like your daughter is bound to you."

Sara hung her head. "I was afraid, Aurora. After watching my sister die giving birth to Luc, I didn't want a baby." Sara picked at the threads on the quilt. She confided softly, "I didn't want to die."

Aurora leaned in. "And so you think it's your fault? Oh, my dear, the baby most likely died because of the illness Luc contracted, and then passed to you. There was nothing to be done."

Sara's mouth formed an *O* but no sound emerged. Even if this were true, it still didn't change the fact that now she and her daughter would be apart forever. The familiar feeling of nausea washed over her.

"The priest said—"

"I know what the darn priest said." Aurora peered over her shoulder, then whispered, "That priest doesn't know his head from his arse! Limbo is something invented by the pope to scare the living daylights out of folks, so they'll have their children baptized. Matthew 19:14, 'Jesus said, suffer little children, and forbid them not, to come unto me: for of such is the kingdom of heaven.'" Aurora bobbed her head defiantly in conclusion.

Sara ran her fingers over the thick, braided grapevines of the picnic basket. Her head throbbed, her back ached and goose bumps sprang up. Death had crossed their threshold four times in the last four years—what was to prevent it from crossing a fifth?

Aurora stretched out on the grass, her hands behind her head, and closed her eyes. She spoke softly to Sara. "I know what it's like to be afraid, anticipating every disaster that might lurk around the corner—your heart palpitating, palms perspiring, waiting for the other shoe to drop." Her eyes opened, and she squinted at the cumulus clouds rolling like balls of cotton above them. "Strange enough, the day I decided to stop fearing death was the same day I stopped fearing life."

Later that afternoon, when a stranger rapped loudly at the front door, Sara practically jumped out of her skin. "Mr. W.H. McNeill of San Francisco at your service, ma'am," the visitor announced. He was short and wore a suit and bowler hat. He proffered a business card and asked, "Is Mr. Philippe Lemieux at home?"

Sara turned the card over, running her fingertips over the black embossed lettering—very fancy. "Yes, he's in the winery." She untied her apron and moved to the door. "I'll take you to him."

The man trailed two steps behind her. "This is a fine operation you have here. How long have you been growing grapes?"

"This will be our third substantial vintage."

"You're kidding, really?"

"My husband and I take our business very seriously, sir. I suppose you sell equipment? I think you'll be disappointed. We've already installed modern machinery in the winery, and don't require any more."

"No, ma'am, I'm here for a much more important reason."

Sara twirled around to face him, hands on hips, at the entrance to the winery. "What may that be?"

"To extend an invitation."

Probably another Wine Makers' Corporation function. "Oh, very well," she muttered, unimpressed, as she ushered him to the cellar door.

"Philippe," she called down. "Mr. McNeill of San Francisco is here to see you."

Philippe's head popped around the corner. He bolted up the stairs and extended his hand. "Mr. McNeill, it's an honor," he said deferentially. Sara was stunned; he must know the man.

"The honor is mine." Reaching into his bag, he slid out an ivory envelope and handed it to Philippe. "You have been selected to represent the United States of America at the Exposition Universelle in Paris this spring. I've come to collect your wines."

# Chapter 13

Linnette sat on the edge of the bed, absentmindedly chewing the cap of her fountain pen and holding a single sheet of paper. If she wrote him, he would either ignore her or respond. She didn't know which would be worse: the sting of another rejection from Philippe, or the pain of seeing him again, not as her lover, but as her daughter's father.

She must write, for Pippa's sake.

Taking care not to give any details that might alarm his wife if she happened to read the letter, Linnette penned every word as if her life depended upon his reply.

*Dear Mr. Lemieux:*

*I have in my possession something that belongs to you. Kindly visit me between the morning hours of ten and twelve o'clock on the 29th or 30th of November.*

*Mr. L. Cross*

*2390 Lombard Street, San Francisco*

# Chapter 14

Philippe hopped off the crowded omnibus five blocks from Scott Street. He wanted to walk down the rest of Lombard Street, to clear his head before meeting Linnette. He felt like a cad, sneaking out to see his former mistress. Perhaps he should have told Sara, but she was so depressed after losing the baby, he didn't want to worry her. Or at least that's what he told himself.

What could Linnette possibly want? Her note was cryptic, probably for his benefit. *Something that belongs to you* could mean only one thing: Linnette was in love with him and wanted to revive their liaison. She had been a lovely distraction during his bachelor days, but Sara and Luc were his world now.

Linnette answered the door, as beautiful as ever, with shining blond hair and opal skin, although she looked a vast deal thinner. Dark circles underscored her eyes, which shimmered with relief when she saw Philippe.

"You came! I knew you would." She extended her hand, as if to touch his sleeve, but quickly recoiled.

"Your letter was unexpected." Philippe entered the foyer at her invitation. His heart sank when he saw the peeling paint, sparse furnishings and dusty wood floors.

"I know, but I wouldn't have written if it wasn't urgent."

"What is it, Linnette?" Philippe was worried now.

She hesitated, glancing furtively at the closed door at the hallway's end. Finally, she spoke. "I've no wish to unsettle your life. I tried everything, Philippe, before writing you."

"Yes?" he asked warily.

There was a scratching at the door, then a muffled sound. "Mommy?" The pronunciation was garbled. "Mommy?" Linnette walked down the hall, opened the door and swept a small, straw-haired girl up in her arms. She was no more than two years of age. Her appearance startled Philippe: she possessed a split lip, and his own bright blue eyes.

Linnette pecked the child's cheek. Philippe froze. "This is Philippa, or Pippa, as I call her." She searched Philippe's face, and then confirmed his worst fear. "She is your daughter."

Her words were a punch to the stomach. How could this be? He studied the child with the dark, thick lashes, and the abrupt cut of her mouth—as though God had nicked her upper lip with his paring knife. She was tender, patting her mother's face affectionately, blissfully unaware that her appearance was anything out of the ordinary.

Philippe suddenly felt hot and dizzy. He'd always assumed his first daughter would be a beautiful miniature of Sara. Never in his wildest imaginings did he consider that she would be the deformed child of his ex-mistress.

Linnette watched him stare at the child, waiting for him to say something, no doubt. When he looked at her, he felt as if he were seeing the true Linnette for the first time. In the past, he'd always viewed her as an amusement, a plaything. She was a mother now—stripped of her silk finery, her flirtatiously coiffed curls and her violet-scented skin—clinging to her daughter. The heat of shame spread through his chest. This was not the man he'd intended to be.

Linnette offered him a seat. He must have looked as ill as he felt. She sat across from him, releasing Pippa to toddle around the room while they spoke.

"Pippa was born on December 9, 1897." Philippe was stunned. That was days before he had married Sara. "When you came to see me that April, I didn't know I was with child. I found out weeks later, but decided to keep quiet. You had made your choice," Linnette said. She examined her clasped hands, no longer adorned with silver bracelets and gold rings. "I didn't want to burden you." Philippe felt like a heel.

"We did well for awhile, but Pippa's cleft lip causes ear infections, which require medicine. Some days, it's medicine instead of food." Linnette shrugged. "I tried other ways to make money," she added, shifting her eyes to the window, "but I can't carry on like I used to, now that I have a daughter. That's when I decided to ask you to . . . to pay for her care," she said squarely.

"Can she . . . may I talk to her?" Philippe leaned forward, watching Pippa intently.

"Yes, but you may not understand her. She can't form all her words properly. It takes some getting used to." Linnette smiled feebly.

As Philippe sat on the floor opposite the child, she handed him a threadbare cloth doll, then snatched it right back with a laugh that bubbled up from her belly. "What? Now you're taking it away?" Philippe asked playfully. The child had a twinkle in her eyes that drew him right in. "May I shake your hand, miss?" Pippa obliged him immediately, and he was surprised that she understood him. Her hand was a ball of warm, soft dough, and he marveled at the daintiness of her fingers between his. He thought of Luc and his lost daughter. Guilt washed over him anew.

"Is she healthy? What does the doctor say?"

"She's normal in every way, except for the ear infections, and the slurring of words caused by her cleft. She's smart as a whip," Linnette said proudly.

"Of course she is. You've done a fine job with her, Linnette." He and Linnette had always had frank discussions in the past. "Is there any way to repair her lip?"

Philippe had never seen Linnette tear up before. "Yes, but the operation will cost hundreds of dollars, the doctor said."

Philippe didn't have hundreds of dollars to spare. He had used most of his savings to plant the orchard, hire Mac and pay Lamont the money he owed. And he needed to pay for the journey to Paris. "So it can be done?"

Linnette nodded. At least there was hope for the girl, Philippe thought.

"I can't afford the surgery right now, but I'll send you what I can afford each month."

"Thank you, Philippe."

"Linnette," he said staunchly, "you know I love my wife."

"I know," she replied softly.

"Things are complicated right now."

"Have you told her about me?" Linnette fussed with the moth-eaten pillow next to her.

"Yes, before we were married."

That didn't seem to satisfy her. "She doesn't know you're here?"

*She. Her. My wife.* Why couldn't he name Sara to Linnette? Because they were from two separate times in his life, and he could never introduce them. Linnette was his past, but Sara was his present and future.

He sprung up and hovered near the window, glancing down to the alley below. A white-haired old man sat on a bench, puffing a cigarette and scratching his short beard. When the man met Philippe's eyes for just a moment, Philippe inhaled sharply and turned back toward Linnette. The man had his father's blue eyes and critical gaze.

"Philippe?"

He focused on Linnette. She looked small and tired. He knew he had to explain things properly to her, so she would understand.

"My wife is in a very fragile state right now."

"We're all in a fragile state, Philippe," Linnette persisted.

Was she threatening him? Philippe was firm. "We just lost our daughter—a stillbirth. I will tell her about Pippa, but not yet." His voice softened. "You understand, don't you? Why I need your cooperation in this?"

Linnette shifted as though she were sitting on pins. "I suppose so."

Pippa tugged on her mother's skirt, and Linnette pulled her onto her lap and hummed a melody in her ear. Looking at the two of them—his other family—Philippe was touched by their happiness, but disgusted with himself. He would tell Sara this happened before they met, before they married. But nothing would soothe the sting when Sara discovered that he had a living daughter, born of another woman.

He could not tell her.

Philippe was absent overnight. Sara had asked to accompany him to San Francisco for the day, hoping to buy Luc a new pair of black leather shoes with blue buttons, and a new suit for Sunday best. Philippe had refused. Without further explanation, he'd just saddled Lady and galloped off into the dissipating fog.

At noon the next day, Sara heard the stable door slam. Lady's whickers and snorts confirmed his arrival. She ran out to greet him. "Where were you?" Sara had pictured him dead in a ditch.

Philippe removed his hat and raked his hands through his disheveled hair. "I'm sorry, Sara." He kissed her forehead absentmindedly. "I should have sent word that I'd be away overnight. It was thoughtless of me." The whites of his tired eyes were pink, and his irises shone with intensity. Whatever business he'd conducted in the city hadn't gone well.

Sara tightened her arms around her weary husband, who smelled of sweat mixed with dust from the road. Resting her head on his chest, she felt his heart thudding. He stroked her hair and sighed, "Sara."

Though her body craved his warmth, she pulled away, fearful that she might not be ready. Touching a hand to his scruffy cheek, she chided, "You need a bath, and a shave."

"Yes."

"Wait here." Sara swung open the kitchen door and called to Rose to fill the tin tub. After doing so, Rose discreetly disappeared with Luc for some cool fall air and exercise.

In the kitchen, the stove heated the room, but the bathwater remained so tepid, Philippe bathed for only five minutes. With her back to him, Sara spied Rose and Luc out the window, skipping between the vine rows.

After he toweled off and pulled on clean breeches, Sara seated him at the kitchen table. She expertly honed his steel razor blade on the stone, just as Maman had done for Papa, ten times in each direction. She stropped the razor on the leather twenty times, until it could split a mouse hair. She dropped a dollop of shaving cream into the mug and worked it into a fine lather by swirling the wet brush. The clean, fresh smell of the soap relaxed her.

When she looked up, Philippe was watching her. "Come here," he said hoarsely.

With the mug and brush in one hand, and the sharpened razor in the other, Sara settled herself between Philippe's legs.

Philippe placed his hands on her hips. She ignored the bare need in his eyes, and instead brushed lather over his beard. She held the razor at a slight angle, and her strokes were light and even. She pulled his skin taut, shaving in the direction of the day's growth.

"Hold still," she bid him. She knew the skin under his chin was especially prone to cuts, and she wanted a smooth finish, not a smattering of red bumps. When she was done, Sara dipped a towel in the hot water basin. She gently wiped the remaining slivers of shaving cream away and admired her work.

"There," Sara said, satisfied that she'd been able to complete a task.

Without a word of thanks, Philippe pulled her down onto his lap. His moist lips teased her neck, while his fingers moved like a silk scarf up the back of her thigh. He moved carefully, handling Sara like a glass figurine. For months she'd drifted, disconnected from her body, but with each caress, he coaxed her back to life.

She stroked his shoulders, built to bear so many burdens, and allowed her lips to linger on his, reacquainting herself with his taste, his feel, his scent. When she edged away, breathless, he touched his palms to her cheeks, forcing her to look at him. In that excruciating moment, Sara confronted everything she feared: his torment, love, even his guilt—all laid bare. Consumed with her own grief, she'd hardly recognized his. Sara resolved to bridge the chasm between their souls, furrowed by months of sorrow.

Desperate to meld her body to his, Sara unbuttoned his breeches and lifted her layers of skirts. She closed her eyes and relaxed. She moved slowly at first, concentrating on his sighs of pleasure and the stir of his breath in her hair. It was not long before she arched her back and her muscles tightened, seeking to contain the shattering sensation. Philippe surrendered moments later—and they were bound together once more, as one flesh.

Exhausted with emotion, Sara nestled her head on Philippe's chest. She was so relieved to have him back, but her spirits flagged, remembering how she'd failed him. "I'm sorry," she murmured.

His fingertips massaged her neck. "Don't. *You* haven't done anything wrong." Sara found his emphasis odd. He was not the culpable one. She still had so much to learn about him.

Remembering that Rose and Luc would return soon, Sara stood up and straightened her dress. Philippe followed suit, donning a fresh shirt from the laundry basket. His face held the expression of a boy who'd just stolen his first kiss. "Come with me to Paris," he blurted. "We'll bring Luc. He'll stay with your Maman and Jacques while we attend the exposition."

"Don't you need me here to tend the vineyard?"

"No, I need you beside me. Mac and Aurora can oversee things." Sara's heart rejoiced at the mere mention of Paris. To stroll through exotic exhibits, and have the chance to showcase Eagle's Run wines to representatives from around the globe—how could she refuse?

Sara's thoughts turned to the long journey. What if Luc became ill on the train or the ship? What if they made it to New York, but one of them couldn't make the crossing? What if? Her heart raced with anxiety, but she suddenly remembered Aurora's words: *when I stopped fearing death, I stopped fearing life.*

"Yes, yes!" Sara kissed Philippe hard on the lips, and he hugged her tightly. When she pulled away, she was smiling for the first time in months. She felt like her old self, charging back into life.

# Part II

# Chapter 15

The city of Paris was a kaleidoscope of color, delighting visitors with its shifting shapes and stunning pageantry. Even its night sky was draped in deep indigo for the exposition, studded with stars sparkling like gemstones and lit by moving electric spotlights. The air was chilly, with an occasional burst of warmth rushing from the food wagons, carrying the sweet scent of freshly baked cinnamon cakes and exotic spiced meats. Paris was a marvel.

Sara and Philippe pressed close together amidst a throng of visitors from all over the world as they walked through the vast entrance, the Porte de la Concorde. Its three-legged dome and minarets were bedecked with colored lights, reminding Sara of a frosted cake decorated with button candy.

Once inside the gate, they stood speechless, absorbing the carnival that played out before them. Algerian and Egyptian dancers, draped in gold and silver dresses, swayed tantalizingly to the rhythms of harps, lyres and lutes. Devil dancers hid behind long painted masks with bulging eyes, and Spanish dancers twirled, clicking their castanets in time with the thumping of the drums. Their primitive movements, the sheer abandon of their dance, mesmerized Sara. The vibrations spread from their instruments to the ground beneath her feet, and traveled through the core of her body. She tightened her grip on Philippe's arm, pressing her thigh to his. When he answered with a seductive smirk, Sara blushed. Had they not been in the company of half the world, she might have ravished him right then and there.

The pavilions, or "palaces," of the countries represented at the exposition rose along the edges of the Seine River, each with its own uniquely designed façade, and each with its own treasure trove of creations stashed inside. As they walked through the fairgrounds, down the Champs-Elysées to the Hôtel des Invalides, Sara was struck by the magnitude of the exhibits and the tiny part that they and Eagle's Run would play. Every country seemed to be here, although the displays of French art, agriculture, technology and architecture dominated the fair. They'd never see it all before they returned to California.

Sara scanned the exhibition map. The fairgrounds encompassed a large area of Paris on both sides of the Seine. They first visited the Grand Palais, with its immense leaded glass dome and winding wrought-iron staircase. Sara was drawn to the collection of modern sculpture they found there. The smooth musculature

124

and lifelike rendering of these men, women, birds and animals, carved from marble or fashioned from bronze, fascinated her. The time and care it took to shape these intricate figures must be an inconceivable challenge for the artist, but the result was pure joy for the beholder. How did they choose the stone? What tools did they use? Sara could have spent all day examining the curves, faces and blank eyes of each sculpture, imagining a story for each one. Philippe, on the contrary, was eager to view the U.S. pavilion, across the Seine on the south bank.

As they approached, Sara and Philippe craned their necks to see the U.S. pavilion's immense white dome. An eagle was affixed high atop the structure, and its archway depicted a group of muscular men and women attempting to rein in the four wild horses that pulled the chariot of Progress. Inside the chariot, the triumphant goddess of Liberty glowed. Clearly, the Americans had spared no expense.

"It looks like a Greek pantheon, doesn't it?" Sara tilted her head, trying to decide if she liked the design. She admired the detailed planning that must have gone into it.

"Yes," Philippe agreed, "but don't you think that a Manhattan skyscraper would have been more symbolic of American progress?"

When they entered, Sara was disappointed to see that the American pavilion was rather banal on the interior, with linoleum floors and unadorned walls. The four stories, which one could navigate easily using elevators and stairways, offered its visitors recreation rooms, waiting rooms, writing desks and general information bureaux.

Of course, it was mid-June, and the exhibits were not yet complete. Sara followed the exquisite melody of a string quartet down a wood-paneled hallway. She stopped suddenly at the open doorway of a grand salon, holding out her hand to prevent Philippe from bumping into her while his nose was wedged between the pages of her guidebook.

The windows of the salon were draped in ivory silk, and the walls were adorned with crystal sconces, but the most brilliant decorations were the diamonds, pearls and turquoise dangling from the necks, wrists and earlobes of the American women inside. Such wealth in one room! As Sara stood awestruck, she couldn't help but stare at their costumes. The silver-gilt, golden satin damask and sapphire silk gowns amazed Sara, and she stood mesmerized by a woman fluttering a folding fan made of painted silk, feathers and mother-of-pearl.

Philippe tried to hurry Sara along, but she wouldn't budge. This was the closest to American royalty that she'd ever come. With steamship prices as high as they were, most of the women attending from America would be either wealthy, or exhibitors like her, here on their own pinched dime.

Sara hushed Philippe, dragging him behind a tall potted fern to better conceal them as they watched the fine crowd. He rolled his eyes and made a beeline to the bar further down the hall. Sara didn't care a whit. When would she ever have this opportunity to observe wealthy, wine-drinking women in their element? Sara counted the number of women who held goblets of wine, and made a mental game of deciphering their ages, whether they drank red or white, and even how fast they drank it—all just part of her ongoing effort to understand the appetites of potential customers.

∾

Sara and Philippe must have walked four miles that evening, and they had not even seen half of what the fair's one hundred forty hectares had to offer. Tomorrow, they would begin to create their display and wander over to the Champs de Mars to visit the theatres, restaurants and carnival rides on the river's edge.

The pair fell into bed at one o'clock in the morning, and slept until ten. They never slept past five-thirty at home. To Sara, it felt like being on their honeymoon again.

Sara was certain that Luc was enjoying his long visit with Maman and Jacques at Saint Martin. Her only reservation in leaving him was the concern that Jean Lemieux would arrive and demand a visit with his grandson. But this morning, she shook off her anxiety, and reminded herself that she was supposed to be sightseeing in Paris.

After consuming a pot of coffee, steaming milk, rolls and butter in their room, they paid a cab driver to take them from the Hôtel Le Meurice, in the rue de Rivoli, to the U.S. exposition commissioner's office. Philippe greeted the clerk there in English. He just yawned, pushed his glasses up and tapped the form Philippe was to complete and sign. After Philippe scribbled down their information, the clerk handed him their exhibitor credentials. Sara squeezed her husband's arm covertly, and he winked in return. Her heart was beating so fast, she thought it might burst out of her chest. They would submit the Eagle's Run 1897 cabernet and chardonnay to the tasting tables next week—for the world to judge.

Sara and Philippe's driver dropped them off at the Palais d'Agriculture, where Sara was determined to design the most attractive booth at the Fair. Sara clutched her satchel, which contained the exquisite lace tablecloth Maman had insisted she borrow, along with the elegant leather book Sara had created to describe the Eagle's Run vineyard, its history and wines. Under her right arm, she pressed a silver tray, polished to a mirror shine, and in her hand, she held her *Guide de l'Exposition Universelle* as if it were her Bible. Philippe carried the toolbox he'd borrowed from Jacques.

They entered the 4,500-square-meter annex and walked between the rows of displays, past the cotton, hemp and wool, and through the impressive agricultural machinery, until they finally spied the displays of the Beringer Brothers and the California Wine Association. Eagle's Run, they found, would occupy one of the tables between them. Sara and Philippe would also have to contend with Boone Sumter, whom they discovered would be their neighbor for the duration of the exposition.

"Of all the rotten luck," Philippe whispered to Sara after reading the name plaque.

"Yes, but aren't you the one who says it's better to keep your enemies closer than your friends?"

"Not at the next table," he grumbled.

Sara chuckled. "With any luck, we'll continue to miss him. Besides, the Beringers are a vast deal more entertaining." The two brothers, Jacob and Frederick, had sailed from Mainz, Germany, and purchased Los Hermanos in 1875. The vineyard in St. Helena was one of the first in the Napa Valley, and Sara considered them to be winemaking pioneers.

Sara and Philippe worked through the afternoon. They had shipped crates of their finest wines, and goblets, and found that they'd arrived intact. They were lucky—others' wines had congealed en route aboard the steamships and trains and were declared unfit for competition.

The red sign displaying the Eagle's Run name and the names of their wines, painted in gold, had arrived in one piece but was scratched on its lower edge. Sara would have to find supplies and repaint it tomorrow. Philippe hammered it onto the side of the French oak barrel they'd brought from Saint Martin.

They straightened the lace tablecloth, placed four goblets and a wine opener on the tray, and assembled the bottles in a crescent shape around them. Sara placed the beautifully bound black book on the table next to the tray. She scribbled tomorrow's to-do list on the inside cover of her guidebook: buy flowers, a guest book, a fine-tipped pen and red paint.

A smartly dressed woman stopped Sara to ask if she could take a photograph. Sara and Philippe posed beside their newly decorated table as she snapped her Kodak. The moment would be etched in Sara's mind forever.

Sara stepped away from the table to borrow some twine and scissors from another vintner. When she returned, Philippe was chatting with a gentleman she didn't recognize right away, whose back was turned toward her. At first, Philippe was smiling and nodding, but then a shadow passed over his face. Was it something the man had said?

As Sara neared, she heard them speaking French. The short, gray-haired man looked over his shoulder, directly at Sara, with squinched eyes. She recognized him immediately—it was Bastien Lemieux's old friend and fellow debaucher, Gilles Bellamy. He owned a vineyard near Tours. Knowing it was too late to slink away, Sara stood tall and marched forward.

Philippe's tone sounded a warning to Bellamy. "Allow me to introduce my wife, Sara Lemieux."

Bellamy glared at her, then at Philippe, his face contorted with disgust. "What the hell were you thinking?" Bellamy's words slurred and he grabbed Philippe's arm. "For Christ's sake, man, she *murdered* your brother!" he shouted.

Ashamed, Sara stepped back, fearing his next move.

Philippe slid between Sara and Bellamy. "You're drunk, Bellamy. Why don't you go sleep it off." Philippe put an arm around his shoulders, trying to guide him in a straight line toward the door. Bellamy would not be thwarted. He swung around, stumbling.

"I bet she's a tasty bite of tart, ain't she, Lemieux?" he spat.

"Don't, Bellamy."

"Oh, I see," he emitted a wheezy laugh, "you two were in cahoots all along, weren't you? Now that Bastien's dead and gone, you get Saint Martin too!"

Sara reeled as her husband smashed a right hook into Bellamy's jaw, sending him spinning to the floor. When he landed with a thud, Philippe yanked him up by his right arm, twisted it behind his back, and escorted him out into the street, where he dropped Bellamy on the gutter cobbles. Philippe straightened his waistcoat, smoothed his hair and walked back to Sara.

Sara's eyes darted from left to right. Everyone, including Boone Sumter, was staring.

Her cheeks burned, and her eyes stung. She wondered if the onlookers had heard all of Bellamy's accusations, or worse, if they believed them.

"You all right?" Philippe said softly.

"Fine," she lied. "You?"

Philippe massaged his knuckles. "Better now," he said, flashing a wide grin. She laughed nervously at his bravado and gratefully took the arm he offered her.

Philippe tipped his hat to the bystanders, who stood agog with disbelief, and led Sara out the door. Both took great care to step around Bellamy's rumpled mess, still lying in the street.

Exhausted and famished from the day's drama, Sara and Philippe sank into their chairs at the Restaurant de la Terrasse on the boulevard Montmartre. They shared a supper of filet of beef, potatoes, *haricots verts*, cheese and cake, for four francs each. They skipped the claret, opting instead for bottles of Saint Galmier, the safest water in Paris.

Philippe was unusually quiet. Sara tried to lighten his mood, feigning a calm she did not feel. "So, what's left to do?" she asked lightly, awaiting his answer while nibbling on her chocolate cake. The rush of sugar revived her.

"You tell me. I saw you recording every little detail." Philippe smiled brightly, but as he stabbed the last morsel of cake off her plate, he looked tired.

"Paint, flowers, and a guest book and pen."

"Are you going to ask them to record their addresses?"

"Of course. What's the point in having them record their names if we don't know how to reach them? Everyone who passes by is a potential customer, even if they purchase our wines in a restaurant. People are more likely to purchase a bottle if they've met us personally, don't you think?"

"Absolutely." His response was hollow. Philippe was saying all the right things, but his mind was elsewhere. Sara sipped her coffee, considering whether she should ask him plainly. These doubts, if left unanswered, would build a barrier between them.

"Philippe?"

He clanked his cup down on its saucer. "Hmm?"

Sara's voice was whisper-soft. "What were you thinking when you punched Bellamy?"

Philippe raised an eyebrow. "I can't say what I was thinking, but he had it coming."

"Because of what he said about me?"

"Because of what he said about *us*." Philippe laced his fingers through Sara's. "Our marriage is not wrong. It's the holiest of unions. It was born out of forgiveness and grit . . . yours and mine. Our union was hard-won, and it's forever."

A long speech for Philippe. Sara raised her other palm to touch his cheek. He pressed her cold fingers against his heated skin. "Tomorrow morning, we'll finish things up, but before sunset, I want to take you somewhere special."

"Where?"

"Have you ever climbed the Eiffel Tower?"


The sky over Paris was sunny and cloudless as Sara and Philippe climbed to the third and highest platform of the Eiffel Tower on Tuesday afternoon. They sacrificed dinner for a view that cost them five francs each, but Sara managed to smuggle up a demi-baguette, a wedge of Brie and a butter knife in her satchel. Philippe, for his part, concealed in his jacket a pocket flask of the finest Beringer brandy, bartered from his friends.

When the crowd thinned, Sara and Philippe stood at the southeastern end of the platform, looking down the Champs de Mars to the Grand Waterfall. The waterfall, constructed especially for the fair, was an immense grotto with electrified fountains. They could see for thirty miles. Paris was breathtaking.

Philippe broke the spell, offering Sara a nip. She sipped the brandy sparingly, feeling the liquid warmth wash down her throat. Looking around, they discovered they were the only people left in their corner of the platform. Sara sat on her shawl, secured the baguette on her lap, and smeared it with the soft cheese. Handing it to Philippe, she sighed and said, "You asked me if I'd ever visited the Eiffel Tower, but I never answered you."

"No, you didn't," he answered, watching her face.

"My father brought me here when I was ten years old. The tower was newly built for the 1889 fair. We couldn't afford tickets to walk up, but when I stood underneath it and stared up at its enormous spire, I remember wobbling on my feet and falling backwards. Papa caught me, laughing." Sara smiled at the memory of Papa's deep chortle. "It was a wonderful day."

"He was a good man."

"The best of men," Sara corrected him, struggling to remember Papa's chocolate-brown eyes.

"I'm glad we could come here together." Philippe grinned,

and tucked a flyaway tendril behind Sara's ear. She ripped off a bite of bread. She missed the simple things from her former life: the soft, earthy chèvre from the Vouvray creamery, the scratch of Papa's evening stubble and her sister's round, rosy cheeks.

"The wind is picking up," Sara said, sniffling as she faced the easterly breeze. A cool blast of air nudged the teardrops from the corners of her eyes, unfurling them like streamers down her face. Philippe draped a sympathetic arm around her shoulder.

"Sometimes I forget how much you've lost," he said, giving her a handkerchief.

Sara dabbed her cheeks with the soft cotton square. "I've gained a lot, too."

"We both have," he replied with conviction. They looked down at the throngs of tourists milling around the exhibition grounds. "We're going home with a medal, Sara—I know it."

She admired his self-assurance. "Maybe, but the competition is fierce. Thirty-six thousand wines represented, I'm told."

"Yes, but probably only a hundred well-crafted ones," he answered as he bit into a chunk of bread. "You've got to have faith, Mrs. Lemieux," he teased her.

Sara kissed him lightly. "Faith in you." Sadness flashed in his eyes—or was it regret?

The white beams spotlighting the Eiffel Tower brightened the evening sky. The colored lights of the Grand Waterfall danced on the sheets of water cascading from its crest to the basin below. The pair stood up to take in the glory of it all.

"Beautiful," Sara murmured, leaning against the iron lattice.

"Sara," Philippe entreated, "never lose faith in me."

Struck by the urgency in his voice, she reached for his hands, locked securely around her waist. "Never."


The wine-tasting competition had begun in the testing room of the Entrepôt Saint-Bernard, opposite the Place Jussieu. From nine to twelve each morning, twenty groups of five judges moved from table to table, swishing and spitting wine, and scribbling notes in brown leather journals. Their judgment would not be announced until every one of the thirty-six thousand samples had been tasted, probably several months from now. Then the prizes would be awarded: a grand prix, or a gold, silver or bronze medal. Most vintners would go home empty-handed.

Sara felt exhilaration and trepidation at the thought of presenting their wines to an international jury. Of the 101 jurors and alternates, 77 represented France and only 24 represented foreign countries. Sara knew Philippe was already worried about the bias most Europeans, and especially the French, held against American wines. He and the other winemakers were so concerned that they strove to make their bottles appealing to the foreign contingency, dressing their labels with European designs and listing the French name of the grapes used to make each wine. Luckily, the British and Canadian judges discerned wine quality as well as the French, but without the century-old bias of the Europeans.

On the nineteenth of June, Sara and Philippe were on hand with several other American vintners to watch as the American wines were prepared for tasting. Just as the last bottles were produced from the cellar, a messenger arrived with a summons for all the judges present to report to the jury room.

Philippe refused to step out for lunch before the men returned, fearing he might miss the news. When the tasting officials finally emerged late that afternoon, the face of Dr. Wiley, the only jury member Philippe and Sara had met, was livid.

"Is there trouble?" Philippe asked.

"The president of the exhibition has advised the jury to disqualify the majority of American wines from competition," Wiley replied despondently.

"On what grounds?"

"They're accusing us of exhibiting under false pretenses. They charge that the names we've chosen to use—Sauternes, Champagne, Burgundy, Chablis—denote the European origin of the grapes, and therefore deceive drinkers into thinking they are drinking European wines."

Sara was appalled. "But each label clearly states the origin of the grapes, the name of the vintner and his address. It's obvious to anyone who can read that these wines were made in America."

Dr. Wiley shrugged, his face registering shock. "I explained all this, but I'm the only American on the jury. My voice was silenced by the majority."

"We must protest this!" Philippe cried. The rapt crowd of Americans cheered in agreement.

Wiley raised his voice to be heard over the ruckus. "I plan to do just that, gentlemen. Now, if you'll excuse me, I have a formal complaint to lodge with the commissioner."

# Chapter 16

Desperate for a distraction, Sara and Philippe took the train south to Tours and hired a hackney to drive them to Saint Martin. Over the past two and a half years, Maman and Jacques had rebuilt a smaller version of the original Saint Martin home, one section at a time. The salvageable stones had been used to construct a small kitchen, located at the eastern side of the house, and they had purchased new stones and lumber to complete a dining room, parlor and water closet, and three upstairs bedrooms. Maman had sewn thick cotton draperies to keep out the cold drafts in winter, and crocheted down-filled cushions to soften the hard maple chairs. Layers of blankets, donated by her church's quilting circle, warmed the beds at night.

Maman and Jacques were overjoyed to see Sara and Philippe earlier than expected. Luc, however, balled his fists and stamped his feet, retreating to the kitchen. "Don't worry, dears, he's fine," Maman said to Sara and Philippe in the adjacent parlor. "Just upset that he wasn't invited to accompany you on your grand adventure."

"He's three. How does he know the difference?" Philippe teased.

"Four in August, and he's hurt that you left him, that's all," Maman explained patiently.

"Surely he's enjoying his stay with you, Maman. Besides," Sara said loudly, "if my dearest Luc won't greet his maman with a kiss, then how am I going to show him the colored postcards I brought him?"

When Sara spied a quick flash of his head and an inquiring eye from behind the doorjamb, she knew she'd piqued his curiosity. She rummaged through her satchel for the small bag of cards, crinkling the wax paper with her fingers, making it impossible for the boy to resist.

"Look what I have here: postcards from the Eiffel Tower. Do you know anyone who might like these?" She fanned them out. Luc ran to Sara, nearly knocking her over with the force of his embrace. Sara covered him with kisses. She hadn't realized how much she'd missed him.

"May I see?" Luc's cheeks were like two perfectly round apples, each with a dimple, accenting his grin. He clutched a postcard in each fist, waving them in the air.

Philippe pointed to the pictures. "This is the Eiffel Tower, almost as high as the summer sun, and this one here is the Palace of Engineering, chock-full of the newest and most fashionable automobiles." He released Luc to stand on the floor, and then retrieved a beribboned box from his case. "For you."

Luc unceremoniously yanked off the bow and opened the box. His nose crinkled with delight. Philippe knelt down and pulled out the treasure. "It's a Mercedes thirty-five horsepower, the newest automobile! See, you drive it." Philippe squatted down, rolling the tin car on the parlor floor. Luc's face lit up when the moving wheels squeaked. The boy turned over the model in his hands, absorbing every detail.

"Papa?"

"Hmm?" Philippe was showing Luc how the hood lifted and the steering wheel rotated.

Luc's brow furrowed and his head tilted. "Where's the horse?"

They all laughed. Philippe tapped a finger on the glossy, hand-painted metal. "They shrunk the horse, and hid him right here, under the hood. Go on, see if you can find him."

Before supper, Maman and Jacques peppered them with questions about the fair. When Philippe explained the disqualification to Jacques, he was incensed. "I'm ashamed that an international jury, composed mostly of our countrymen, would do such a thing, just to prevent the Americans from taking some medals from them this year. In a backwards way, I suppose it's quite a compliment to you and the American winemakers." Jacques waved his finger. "You've got 'em quakin' in their boots! Maybe you actually have a chance."

Philippe rolled his eyes. "Thanks for the vote of confidence, Jacques."

Jacques cackled and slapped Philippe on the back good-naturedly.

"To have traveled all this way, and incurred all this expense, for nothing? We're a mob of muttonheads, aren't we?" Philippe put his head in his hands and rubbed his eyes.

Sara added, "Jacques, we can't afford to stay in Paris much longer. We're leaving next Sunday, whether or not the jury has decided to include our wines in the competition. Who knows how long this could go on? The jurors could continue tasting for the next two months."

"Hell's bells! Two months?" Jacques's chair creaked as he reclined.

"That's extreme, isn't it?" Maman spooned a thick vegetable stew into bowls, and set them on the table with chunks of crusty baguette.

"Yes. We want you to return with us for a few days, so you can see the sights. It's the trip of a lifetime, to be able to experience all these innovations and cultures in one giant carnival."

Jacques speared a hunk of meat and began chewing, before they'd even said grace. "Where would we stay?" he asked.

"We've already reserved you a room next to ours."

Maman slid into the chair opposite Sara and smoothed her napkin over her lap. "We never did have a proper honeymoon, Jacques."

Jacques answered with a wink and a playful smile.

"We'd love to come!" Maman replied enthusiastically.

Sara realized they must be desperate for fun. Maman and Jacques were already acting like schoolchildren at the picnic races. Luc was underwhelmed, having fallen asleep on the chaise, clutching his new toy car.


Seeing the labyrinth of exhibits meant walking several miles each day as they toured the fair, so they often rode the new *trottoir roulant*, a raised electric moving sidewalk, to travel from one end of the exposition to the other. Philippe, Sara and Luc preferred the stomach-churning Ferris wheel. Sara had worried that Luc would be frightened of its tremendous height and spinning motion, but Philippe insisted that he try it. They were rewarded with Luc's shrieks of glee, which proved contagious.

Luc especially loved the ship made of chocolate and life-sized cows sculpted from butter. Sara, for her part, was mesmerized by the five-meter-tall bottle of Moët et Chandon, decorated with gold-leaf foil. When it lit up, seven dancing girls emerged—one from out of the cork!

Philippe and Jacques, with Luc sitting high on Philippe's shoulders, visited the Canadian lumber and mineral exhibits, while Sara and Maman meandered through the educational exhibit. Perhaps because she felt a kinship with the underdogs of society, Sara spent time learning about the advances in education for handicapped children. With their adoption of special accommodations for wheelchairs, and innovations in feeding implements and physical strengthening exercises, the Canadians seemed committed to creating opportunities for all of their country's citizens. She could only hope that America would soon follow suit.

The women discovered a futuristic world at the Palace of Electricity. Someday Luc might be able to simply pick up the telephone receiver and talk to her from halfway around the world. He'd also be driving a car rather than a horse and buggy! All this had been inconceivable to Sara until now.

Maman was enamored with Vieux Paris, with its actors in medieval dress milling about the streets, speaking to the crowds as though they were truly from that time. When the family visited the Russian exhibit, Luc was entranced by their "ride" on the Trans-Siberian Railroad. As they sat in a replica carriage, scenes of wild Siberia rolled by the windows on a long painted canvas. Actors posed as natives in Siberian and Chinese vignettes. At the end of the "trip," a Chinese attendant walked through the cars serving tea and shouting, "Last stop, Beijing!"

Two days before they planned to leave Paris for Saint Martin, the international wine jury amended its decision. The headline was splashed across newspapers worldwide: American wines would be included in the Paris competition.

After searching the length of the warehouse, Philippe found Dr. Wiley and shook his hand vigorously. Sara, too, beamed with relief. "How did you manage it?" Philippe asked.

"We wrote a formal letter to the French commissioner-general, expressing our outrage at the snub. We reminded him that at the Paris Exposition of 1889, the very same wines bearing the same labels were not only examined, but awarded many medals. The jury's decision was inconsistent with past precedent. The French had no choice but to capitulate."

"I'll be damned. Wiley, I'm sending you a case of red, as soon as we return home."

Wiley nudged him. "You mean your prize-winning red, eh?"

As hard as it was to leave France, Sara and Philippe had to head back to California if they were to arrive in time to make the most critical decision of a vintner's year: when to harvest the grapes.

Back at Saint Martin, with two days left until their departure for New York, Sara hung socks by the fire, preparing to pack their belongings. The vineyard at sunset was empty of workers, the house was quiet, and she could smell the savory aroma of roast turkey and currant buns cooking in the new oven. She'd just stepped into the kitchen to ask if Maman needed help when two shots erupted outside.

Sara ran to her mother and pulled her to the ground. "Stay down!" she hissed. Philippe had taken Luc for a walk behind the house, where Luc loved to dash through the honeycomb caves, his voice echoing through the warm summer air. Sara listened but could not detect any sounds through the open windows in the back of the house. She had crawled to the front door when she heard a man's strangled shriek outside.

Just as she slid the bolt into place, Jacques came bounding down the stairs behind her, clutching a loaded Colt. "It's Lemieux. Damnation!" Jacques ducked beneath the foyer window.

Jean Lemieux's cry echoed off the cave walls fifty meters away. "Bastien! Bastien!" The old man's keening for his dead son was steeped in pain. Sara peeked out the window and watched as Philippe's father, gripping an old Enfield, sank to his knees. "Where's my son?" he wailed, arms flailing.

Jacques murmured, "Poor bastard thinks Luc is Bastien."

Sara stared at Jacques in horror. "What?" Jean Lemieux was the man Sara held responsible for her father's death, and now he was a gun-wielding madman hunting for her son. She swallowed hard. "Are you going to shoot him?"

"Before he shoots me? Yes."

Lemieux's head jerked to the right. His eyes were fixed on something near the corner of the house, hidden from Sara's view. Her chest tightened when Philippe stepped into her sightline, holding Luc and walking straight toward his father. Jean Lemieux lifted his firearm with trembling hands, and pointed the gun at Philippe and Luc.

What was Philippe thinking? She would have to throw herself between Luc and Jean Lemieux. Sara lunged for the door, but Jacques tugged her back. She tried to twist free, but Jacques stopped her.

"If Lemieux sees you, he'll kill you. You killed his son, and he doesn't care about why, understand? Philippe knows what he's doing, so you calm down and stay put," Jacques ordered. Against every instinct she possessed, Sara heeded his advice. Jacques released her and raised his Colt, aiming to fire out the half-shuttered window.

Peering out again, Sara was shocked to see Philippe gingerly remove the rifle from his father's hands. Philippe must have pacified

144

the old man somehow. Jean Lemieux's face crumpled, his whole body heaving with sobs as he now embraced his grandson.

Maman rushed from the kitchen to Sara's side. Jacques signaled to them to stay indoors, secured his Colt in his belt and slipped out the front door. He walked cautiously toward Philippe and took the rifle from his hands, leaving him free to rescue Luc from Jean Lemieux's grasp. The boy bounded into Jacques's arms and Philippe's father fell to the earth, clutching his head with talon-like fingers.

Back at Jean Lemieux's home, Philippe studied his father as he helped him into bed. He'd thinned since Philippe had last visited with Luc, two and a half years ago now. His blue eyes were dim, his hair sparse and white, his skin a sickly gray. But his forehead was smooth, his face peaceful, if only in sleep.

Had Bastien's death been the tipping point for his father, or had he always been a bit mad? Perhaps he'd hidden it better when he was younger. Maybe the beatings, the anger, even his egocentricity and the tight control he wielded over all of them had been signs of a deep-seated malaise.

While his father slept, Philippe emptied the gun closet of three rifles and four revolvers, storing them beneath the woolen blanket in his wagon. In his childhood home, old papers, empty wine bottles, dirty dishes and clothing covered the tables, chairs and floor. Apparently, no one had given the place a thorough cleaning since he last visited. Philippe sighed. His father had his faults, but he was ailing, and Philippe had shirked his responsibility to care for him.

The stench in the small parlor was so potent that Philippe opened all the windows to let in the cool summer breeze. He inhaled the fresh air deeply, trying to summon the courage to organize his father's affairs and decide what should be done.

He started making piles of laundry and garbage. Once the floors and tables were cleared and items stacked, Philippe rummaged through the kitchen for cleaning supplies. He found olive oil, lemon, and soda cleanser, a mop and some old rags. He began to scrub the sticky, soiled kitchen table, but even though he scoured until his fingers were raw, he couldn't remove all the decades-old stains that tainted its surface.

Once he'd finished washing and drying the dishes in the kitchen, Philippe warily eyed the laundry. He would have to hire a washerwoman, for the dirty clothing was piled waist-high. In his father's study, he was surprised to see columns of paper piled against the bookshelves that housed his father's simple collection. Philippe saw the candles on the desk and shuddered at the thought of an open flame in this firetrap. Too tired to think anymore, Philippe sank into the threadbare wingback in the parlor. His chin dropped, and he dozed off.

At the sound of his father's screams, his eyes flew open and his body tensed. He rushed toward the bedroom door, but before he reached it, the shot rang out, pulsating in his ears like a blast of dynamite and halting him in his tracks.

With his heart pounding and lungs clamoring for air, Philippe threw open the hallway window, and took several long breaths. The sting of the night air jarred his memory: he'd forgotten to take his father's loaded handgun from beneath the mattress.

Philippe flattened his hand against the wall for support, his skin crawling with dread. He trembled as he pushed the bedroom door open. His father was lying on the floor on the far side of the bed, but Philippe could only see his stocking feet. Philippe ventured closer, his legs dragging as if shackled by iron bands. He collapsed on his hands and knees at the sight before him.

There was more blood than he could have ever imagined. His father's hands were curled inward, and smoke curled from the gun by his side. His eyes stared vacantly ahead. But it was the sharp smell of gunpowder invading his nostrils, and the shards of bone and bits of blood-soaked hair on the braided rug that forced Philippe to vomit. He turned from his father's lifeless body and rocked on the edge of the bed, trying to wrest control of his thoughts. He retreated deep inside himself, cowering like a child.

Jean Lemieux was buried a few days later. At the graveside, Philippe's thoughts raced. If only he'd stayed by his father's side that evening, if only he'd remembered the gun under the mattress, if only—Philippe stopped himself. As tortured as his death was, Jean Lemieux had brought it upon himself. In life he'd driven away his wife and sons. He'd abused Bastien, turning him into the kind of man who gambled and caroused and attacked Sara. And now, instead of making amends, his father had committed this last horrid act.

Had his father loved them, or just the thrill of dominating them? Philippe would never have the answers, no matter how hard he tried to understand the man whom he'd spent his entire adult life trying to forget.

# Chapter 17

Linnette's fever would not break. Her skin itched and her throat burned. Pippa nestled beside her, as she had for the past two days, pacified by her mother's warmth.

When Linnette's neck swelled and her heart misfired, she'd sent Tildy for the doctor. That was hours ago, and now Linnette labored to catch each breath. Her fingers and toes tingled with numbness, and it frightened her. She couldn't move her neck to look down at Pippa, but she could smell her daughter's soap-washed hair and feel her little heart, fluttering as fast as the wings of a hummingbird against her ribs.

Linnette stared at the curling paint on the ceiling above her bed, sucking in a thin stream of air as her throat constricted. With rising panic, she closed her eyes and listened to Pippa babble and sing, unaware of her mother's struggle. Pippa's contented sigh rolled over Linnette like a calming wave.

She'd sinned for seven years, but for the past two she had loved this child fiercely. Linnette had never feared death, but she was terrified of abandoning Pippa. The room grew smaller, darkness closing in from the corners to the center, until the pinprick of light vanished. Linnette could no longer feel Pippa's heat against her ribs, could not see her face. Yet she could hear her feathery whisper. "Mommy?"

*Pippa.*

# Chapter 18

P hilippe stabbed the toe of his boot into the clay loam. The pebbles of porous rock crunched under his thick sole, dry again after a week of rain. After touring Eagle's Run with Sara, he wanted to kick himself. If only they'd returned a week earlier. A week of heavy rains in mid-July had soaked the grapes, placing them at risk for mildew.

Mac, after consulting with Aurora, had decided to prune back the leaves to allow more sun to reach the grapes. But the crew had over-pruned the vines on the southernmost hill, which received the most sunlight. As Mac sheepishly walked his employer through the vine rows, Philippe's concern mounted. He flipped over a few clusters and cringed: the grapes had withered from overexposure.

Many Napa vineyardists had reacted just like Mac, but Philippe wouldn't have made this mistake. They would lose ten tons, by his estimate.

Sara and Philippe broke open a sampling of grapes: some that received morning sun, and others that basked in the afternoon sunlight. Their skins were soft, their pulp was white and their seeds were brown. The juice was sugary and delicious. They both agreed: they must harvest the grapes at once.

Late that evening, after Sara and Luc had settled into bed, Philippe sat at the kitchen table, flipping though the pile of mail Sara had left for him. At the bottom, he discovered the envelope he'd mailed to Linnette before he left for Paris. It had been returned—unopened.

Philippe ripped it open. The fifty dollars in tens he'd sent her fell onto the table. Had Linnette moved? Why hadn't she written?

Sara ran through the vines faster than a streak of greased lightning, as giddy as a schoolgirl, waving a newspaper in the air like a banner. She was out of breath when she reached him, but it didn't matter. He guessed why she was so happy: they'd won a medal.

The article was just below the photograph of Sara and Philippe standing next to their display table in the annex of the Palais d'Agriculture. Philippe read every word aloud. The decisions of the international jury at the Paris Exposition had been announced. California wines had won nine gold, seven silver and twelve bronze medals. The grand prix medal had gone to a

French vintner, but Eagle's Run Cabernet Sauvignon had won gold!

Every muscle in his body relaxed with relief. He'd been holding his breath since they'd returned—hoping, and praying. His bravado had been an act. He knew the vintage was superb, but he didn't know how it would fare against over thirty thousand other wines. He picked up Sara and twirled her around, bursting with pride. She laughed, and her soft lips smacked his robustly. God, he loved this woman. Her mile-wide grin, her tenacity, her trust in him made him believe he could do anything.

"I must tell Aurora. You coming?"

"No, you go ahead. She'll be dying to know, if she hasn't already bribed the paper boy to deliver an advance copy." Philippe was grateful to Aurora for pushing him to enter the wines in competition.

Sara kissed him again, lifted her skirt hem and skipped off as though she were filled with a renewed zest for life. He wished it could last, but he knew he'd eventually have to tell her about Linnette and Pippa.

Once they had harvested the grapes and filled the fermenting tanks with 150,000 gallons of juice, he was able to break free from the vineyard and take the ferry to the city. He'd received no correspondence from Linnette, and the silence worried him.

Tildy, whom Philippe had met on his previous visit, answered the door. "Philippe—oh, come in," she said, obviously startled.

"Is Linnette at home?"

Tildy's quivering fingers covered her mouth. "I didn't know how to reach you," she blurted. "Linnette . . . well, she died . . . of diphtheria." He stared blankly at her. Why hadn't he suspected something like this? Because Linnette was young, strong and seemingly healthy.

"When?" His voice cracked.

"July." Tildy didn't blink, or shed a tear.

"In *July*?" He felt a surge of pity for Linnette and Pippa. Pippa! He pushed past Tildy into the hallway, looking, listening for any sound. "Where's the child?"

"Family Services took her."

"Where?"

"She's probably at one of the city's orphanages."

Philippe wanted to throttle the woman. "My daughter's in an orphanage because you didn't have the decency, or sense, to figure out where I lived?"

Tildy grimaced. "I gave your name to the women there. I thought they'd find you."

"Where is the Family Services office?" he asked. Tildy shrugged, her expression blank.

Philippe was disgusted. He turned to leave, but she grabbed his arm. "There's the small matter of Linnette's back rent," she said in a syrupy voice. "She owes me twenty-five dollars."

Philippe gripped her fat wrist until she winced. "Linnette doesn't owe you anything," he exploded. "She's dead." He slammed the door behind him.

～

Philippe was certain about one thing: he must find Pippa. He was frantic to rescue his child from the misery of the city's orphanage system. He didn't have time to enlist Sara's help—or Aurora's—to locate the girl. He would have to stay in the city and search himself, until he found her.

Philippe telegraphed Sara only to say he'd be delayed. Then he rode the omnibus to the new Ferry Building. There, he waited until a throng of disembarking passengers strolled past him. He asked twenty people if they knew where Family Services or the local orphanages were located. A young woman finally directed him to the Protestant orphanage asylum, bound by Haight, Buchanan, Hermann and Laguna streets.

Philippe rode to the outskirts of town. The orphanage was a four-story stone mansion, with wide gables and sharp spires that pierced the afternoon's yellow light. It was a formidable structure, and one that would scare the living daylights out of any arriving youngster. However, as he came closer, he witnessed a surprising sight: laughing children of all shapes and sizes, running up and rolling down a grassy knoll. They looked healthy, even happy.

Philippe examined their faces, hoping for a glimpse of Pippa. He did not see her. Perhaps she was inside, or perhaps she'd fallen ill and died, like her mother—alone. Fear gripped his heart. He could not lose two daughters in a year—he would not.

Philippe entered the foyer, where a middle-aged matron greeted him. "May I help you, sir?" She had a pleasant, motherly demeanor and sounded as though she might be hosting a garden party, not caring for dozens of unruly children.

"I'm looking for a girl—my daughter. Her name is Pippa. She's nearly three years old."

The woman's face brightened and she regarded him curiously. "Forgive me, but it's rare that children like Pippa are ever claimed."

"She's here?" He dared to hope.

"Yes, she's here. However, I'll need to see your identification, and I'll need you to describe your daughter."

Philippe pulled out his citizenship papers, which he always carried with him while traveling. "I'm Philippe Lemieux." He pointed to his written name and continued, "And her mother was Linnette Cross. From what I've been told, Linnette died of diphtheria this summer. The last time I saw Pippa was almost a year ago. I've been in France. That's why I didn't know. Pippa has beautiful blue eyes, straw-colored pixie hair and a cleft lip."

The matron extended her hand to shake Philippe's. "I'm Katherine Miller. Follow me."

She led him to a dormitory where three toddlers lay on cots. A young woman, presumably one of the nurses, sat reading a book by the window in the fading daylight. Philippe froze when he saw Pippa. A tousle of blond hair covered her face. She was snug in bed under a light blanket, with a stuffed doll wedged beneath her chin. She looked delicate, and Philippe felt the fatherly urge to hold her, to shield her from all of life's difficulties. But they would not allow him to take her. Matron Miller insisted that a thorough investigation into Philippe's financial situation and living arrangements was compulsory.

She explained that Pippa had had a difficult time when she first came to live at the orphanage. Obviously, she missed her mother, but she was also isolated from the other children—quarantined to make certain she didn't carry diphtheria.

When Pippa awoke, Philippe was pleased to see she had grown a few inches, and her cheeks blushed a healthy, rosy hue. She blinked, twisted her lips into a half-smile, and returned to playing with her toys. She didn't remember him.

Truth be told, Sara was happy to have some time alone while Philippe was in San Francisco. Since the harvest, he had continued working night and day, sleeping only in fits. Sara often awoke near midnight to Philippe's absence. Spying the unruffled quilt on his side of the bed, she would tread quietly downstairs to find him scribbling numbers in his journal. He seemed so distracted that Sara hesitated to ask him what he was calculating. Perhaps the visit to the city would do him good.

Today was a Saturday, and she planned to spend the day indoors, rummaging through old boxes, organizing closets and, with Rose's help, dusting and polishing the furniture to a high shine. Sara despised housekeeping and preferred to be outdoors, but now that Luc trailed a mess of toys, dirt, grasshoppers and sticks through the house each day, nothing made her happier than the scent of Rose's olive oil and lemon polish.

Sara started with Philippe's closet. She laid out all his hanging clothes on the bed and lined up his black leather high-button shoes and muddy work boots to clean later.

She dragged out two boxes filled with old office items and papers. Sara was about to sweep the closet floor when she spied a torn-open brown envelope in the corner. She threw it on top of the box behind her and finished her sweeping. When she turned around, a stack of ten-dollar bills lay on the floor. Sara gingerly picked up the envelope, which was addressed to an L. Cross at a post office box in San Francisco, but had been returned to sender. The sender had been her husband.

Sara picked up the money, and fingered the loose cord around it. Then she remembered sorting the envelope into Philippe's pile of mail. She'd assumed L. Cross was a merchant or a friend of Philippe's in San Francisco. She had placed it with the rest of Philippe's mail on the desk in his study without thinking anything of it.

He was hiding something. Did he owe Mr. Cross this money? There was only one person she could think of who might know. She would march over to Aurora's farm at once and ask.

It was a balmy late-summer day, so she packed up a basket with chicken, cheese and bread and headed to Aurora's house. Luc ran ahead of her through the vines and a small meadow. Although only four years old, he was sturdy and energetic, and could easily run the distance.

Aurora was standing on her tiptoes with her pruning shears, cutting back her azalea bush until it looked like a tight green box, reminding Sara of the hedges in the Versailles gardens. For a moment, she was a tourist in France again, her arm in Philippe's as they wandered through the Orangerie, down its gravel path, past the Bacchus fountain and through a smattering of small trees. The citrus scent had been heavenly.

Luc squeaked upon recognizing Aurora. "Tante Rora!"

Aurora squatted down, and opened her arms. "My sweet boy Luc!"

"Join us for a picnic," Sara urged her gaily. "Have you eaten?"

"I'd love to!" Aurora smoothed Luc's hair, washed her hands at the pump and dried them on her apron. They sat down under a dwarf apple tree in Aurora's backyard and ate their fill. Luc dangled from the lowest branches of the tree. Sara thought it dangerous, but Philippe always chided her, "Boys need to explore." She reluctantly allowed Luc up, but kept a watchful eye.

"Philippe's in the city this weekend, so we're on our own."

"What's he doing? Visiting the archdiocese?"

"I don't think so." Sara broke the chunk of bread in her hand. The crust flaked and fell on her napkin. "I think he's visiting a gentleman by the name of Cross. Ring a bell?"

Aurora shrugged and nibbled on her chicken leg. "No, I can't say it does."

"Oh, I just thought you two had so many common connections, you might know the gentleman's trade."

Aurora poured them each another half-glass of chardonnay. "No, I can't say that I do."

"First initial is L—L. Cross," Sara persisted.

Aurora's eyes shifted from Sara to the basket. "Any cakes? Luc, your Tante Aurora can never pass up a sweet."

"Aurora?" Sara pressed.

"Are you sure Philippe is visiting an L. Cross?"

"No, but he's had some communication with him recently. I found an envelope addressed to him that had been returned to Philippe. It was full of money, Aurora."

"Oh, my." Aurora's voluminous chest heaved with a deep sigh. "Now don't jump to conclusions, but . . . L. Cross is Linnette Cross."

Sara looked expectantly at Aurora. Who was Linnette Cross?

"You don't know?"

"About . . . ?"

"Jesus, Mary and Joseph, he could have told you," she muttered. "Linnette was the one before you."

"His mistress?" Sara blurted. The words sent her mind into a tailspin. Was this money part of a business transaction, or was he seeing this woman romantically again? The thought made her sick. She dropped her plate.

"I'm sorry to have to tell you her name. If Philippe's corresponding with her, then you'd best confront him about it." Aurora shook her head and clucked her tongue. "Believe you me, there's never a good explanation for cavorting with a known strumpet when you're a married man."

Philippe's telegram, delivered on Monday, had said that he'd been delayed. But now it was Tuesday afternoon. Sara was pacing the kitchen floor wringing her hands, imagining him with *her*, considering what she'd accuse him of when he returned.

A voice called through the screen door, "Mrs. Lemieux?"

Startled, Sara nodded, and a boy swung open the door, presenting her with another telegram. He would be home on Thursday. He was bringing a guest for an early supper and asked that she invite Aurora. That was all. Not a word of apology or explanation.

Sara scrunched the paper into a tight ball. She tried to tell herself that the guest could be anyone, but all she could think was, How dare he bring that woman into their home!

Sara hurried to the door when she heard the carriage. Philippe dismounted his horse, opened the door of the black phaeton and handed down a tidy, dark-haired woman. She wore spectacles perched atop the bridge of her nose, and carried a small case and folded parasol.

Sara felt very attractive in comparison. This couldn't possibly be Linnette, could it? The woman was old enough to be Philippe's mother.

"Sara, so sorry for my delay," he said, as he pecked her on the cheek and turned to his companion. "Miss Carmichael, this is my wife, Sara. Sara, Miss Carmichael from San Francisco."

"Nice to have you with us, ma'am," Sara said politely, even though she felt like screaming.

"Yes, thank you. Mind if I walk around a bit? I need to stretch after the long ride."

"Of course," Philippe smiled warmly, "there's a path over there down to the creek." Miss Carmichael nodded and wandered in the direction of the walkway. He took Sara's hand, pulling her into the kitchen. He had a strange energy about him—nervous and excited at the same time.

"Philippe, who is that woman?" Sara asked sharply.

"She's one of the teachers at the Protestant orphanage in San Francisco."

"Orphanage?"

Philippe pulled out a chair, and Sara lowered herself into it.

He remained standing, pacing the kitchen. He always thought best on his feet, she recalled. "I have some news, Sara."

Well, she thought, I have news, too. "Is it about Linnette Cross, your mistress?" she seethed.

Philippe stopped short and whirled around to face her, clearly shocked. "Yes, it involves her, in a way." Sara stiffened her spine, bracing herself for the blow. His voice was tender, but his words hit hard. "You know I ended my relationship with Linnette when I first met you. I didn't know she was pregnant at the time. For two years, she didn't tell me about the child. Last November, when she found herself unable to pay for her daughter's medicine and food, she contacted me. I met the girl, and gave them some money."

Last fall? Last fall was . . . when Sara had lost the baby. Her head felt light. She shut her eyes and pressed her palms flat on the table.

Philippe knelt down beside her and clasped her hands. "Sara, I didn't tell you because you were so upset about our child. I didn't want to rub salt in your wounds. I thought that if I told you, you might never recover from your depression."

She reviewed the clues in her mind. His preoccupation, the envelope of money she found in his closet. The lies were bad enough, but the fact that he'd fathered a child with his mistress was inexcusable. Humiliation lodged like a stone in her throat. As she stood up, the chair legs scraped the wood floor. She stumbled away from Philippe to the other side of the room, but he followed her.

She pushed him away, scrambling for words. "Why did you want Aurora here? To keep me calm, to keep me from spitting in your face like you deserve?"

Philippe looked at her like she was insane. "Get a hold of yourself, Sara." He clutched her arms and began to explain. "Linnette died while we were in Paris. The child, a girl named Pippa, was placed in the orphan asylum. I found her on Saturday. I'm bringing her home to live with us." He pointed to the door and continued, "That woman, Miss Carmichael, is here to ensure that our living arrangements are suitable. I invited Aurora to supper to serve as a character witness for us."

She stared at him, confused. So he hadn't taken up with Linnette again, but this . . . this child—she was just another thorn on the same branch of betrayal.

Miss Carmichael called from the front porch. "Mr. and Mrs. Lemieux?"

Philippe planted a warning kiss on Sara's forehead, whispering, "Please do this." Without waiting for her response, he strolled over and opened the door.

"Come in," he said cordially. "I'll show you around."

Sara's feet remained rooted to the kitchen floor. Ten minutes later, when she spied Aurora coming up the front walkway, she ducked into the water closet. Sara couldn't face her friend. She knew she'd burst into tears. Let *him* explain it to Aurora. Her own husband was forcing his bastard child upon her. It was unforgivable—so why was he so delighted?

~

Philippe, Aurora and Miss Carmichael settled down to supper in the dining room. Sara busied herself with feeding Luc in the kitchen, so she didn't have to sit across from her insufferable husband and pretend that she agreed with his preposterous scheme. Philippe was particularly charming, and Aurora played the part of the supportive, approving friend. Sara, on the other hand, barely ate, flitting between the kitchen and dining room as if she were treading on hot coals. She shuttled dishes to and from the table, but managed to avoid the conversation, including the discussion of the little girl.

Miss Carmichael cornered Sara on her way out. "Mrs. Lemieux? Might I have a word?" Sara directed her out onto the porch. "From what Mr. Lemieux has told me, this must be a shock to you. Pippa will be three in December and requires extra care, as I'm sure your husband has mentioned. Before we finalize her release, I need to know that you agree to care for Pippa to the best of your ability, as if she were your own child."

*As if she were your own child.* But she wasn't Sara's child. Sara's thoughts drifted to her baby girl, and her eyes sought the tree grove, where she could see the ring of white stones glistening in the late afternoon sun.

She choked back the bile in her mouth. "I'll discuss it with my husband."

"Do let us know, Mrs. Lemieux."

Sara walked back into the house, took Luc by the hand and marched upstairs without glancing at Philippe or Aurora. While Philippe escorted Miss Carmichael to a hotel in town, Sara read Luc his favorite book of verses, *Penny Whistles*, and tucked him in.

Her head throbbed, and her shoulders felt like she'd been strung up on a meat hook. How could Philippe do this to her?

Why couldn't the girl stay at the orphanage? They could send money for her care. Was that so terrible? They already had the vineyards and their own family to worry about.

She slipped her cotton nightdress over her head and brushed the knots out of her hair. Two hours later, she heard the kitchen door slam and the bolt slide. Philippe was in for the evening.

Sara loosely braided her hair, brushed her teeth and slid under the sheets, facing the wall. She would pretend to sleep so she wouldn't have to talk to him. Philippe creaked down the hallway, pausing as he normally did to check on Luc. When he came into their room, he placed the lamp on the dressing table and hiked his shirt over his head. Sara couldn't resist a peek.

His torso was lean, and his arms looked toned in the glow of the half-light. Desire stirred deep in her belly. That was the moment when it hit her. Linnette's child was born the same month they were married. She bit her lip and squeezed her eyes shut. If he'd kept this from her, what else was he concealing?

Philippe slid into bed beside her. Sara hoped she'd fooled him, but he called her bluff. "Sara?" His hand grazed her hip. She continued to glare at the wall. "Why don't you tell me why you're so unsettled?" He made it sound like she was overreacting. He had some nerve.

"I know I sprang this on you, but it couldn't be helped. Pippa needs a home." It sounded like he was trying to convince both of them. "Is it because I fathered a child, or because I'm bringing her here?" He tugged on her shoulder, forcing her to face him.

"Both—all of it," she answered.

"You brought up Luc as your own son. How is this different?"

"It's completely different. She's a bastard, Philippe, born of your whore." As soon as the hurtful words escaped her lips, she regretted them.

Philippe sat bolt upright. His palms slapped his thighs. "You're right, of course. Let's blame the child for the sins of her mother and father! That's the Christian thing to do."

"How do you even know she's yours?"

"I know, and you will too, once you see her." The blade sliced deeper. "After everything we've been through, after I forgave you for my brother, can't you do this for me? She's my *daughter*, Sara."

Sara looked into his pleading eyes, and felt a hardness creep into hers. "No."

Philippe ignored Sara's refusal and arranged for Pippa to arrive on the following Wednesday. Sara wondered if Pippa remembered her mother; she wondered if Linnette had loved Pippa like Sara loved Luc and the unnamed daughter who was buried beneath the pear tree.

When she heard the carriage outside, Sara stepped out onto the front porch, leaving Luc at the kitchen table. He was driving his wooden truck to the edge, dropping it and cheering as it crashed to the ground. Despite her reservations, Sara would take care not to overwhelm the girl. She was even younger than Luc and none of this was her fault.

Pippa squirmed from Philippe's arms as they approached the front door, never taking her eyes off Sara. Philippe had forewarned her about the girl's appearance. Her face was startling, but not horrifying, Sara thought. Pippa's fair, fine hair framed her rosy cheeks and bright blue eyes—Philippe's eyes. Sara's heart dropped. Would their daughter have looked similar? Pippa was a scrap of a girl, all skin and bones. She reminded Sara of a monarch butterfly with a clipped wing—vibrant but vulnerable. Rose would need to fatten her up with crisp bacon and warm buttered biscuits.

Feeling Pippa's curious eyes upon her, Sara gave her a welcoming smile. The girl's face brightened and she released a deep sigh.

Sara was stunned when Pippa ran toward her and wrapped her arms around Sara's legs, burying her face in Sara's skirts. She tepidly touched the girl's hair with her fingers, feeling a strange mixture of pity and shame. Sara's eyes flashed to Philippe's, now pink with emotion. He tenderly mouthed the words "Thank you."

For the next two weeks, Pippa would not leave Sara's side. When she fed the horses, Pippa held on to her skirt with one hand and fed Lady an apple with the other. She giggled when Lady bent her head down, tickling the child's palm with her rough tongue. As Sara picked the first apples of the season, Pippa was her field hand, collecting fallen fruit and gently placing it in the basket. When Sara used the water closet, Pippa stood outside the door, jiggling its handle, babbling in a dialect Sara couldn't yet decipher.

Though Sara tried to remain detached, each day Pippa found a way, with a sigh, or the gentle flutter of her dark lashes over her soulful blue eyes, to wind her way closer to Sara's heart.

A week after Pippa's arrival, in a gesture obviously intended to make amends, Philippe handed Sara an envelope. "This is yours.

Use it however you like," he said. He watched her expectantly. "Go on, open it."

Sara gasped. She counted nearly seven hundred dollars in cash inside. "It's not much," Philippe explained with a shrug, "but it's all that remains of my father's estate."

As tempted as she was, Sara handed the envelope back to him. "No, Philippe. I don't require anything."

"Please, Sara," he pleaded. "Ease my conscience."

She wasn't sure if he meant his guilt about Pippa, or about the pain his family had caused hers. Either way, his tortured expression compelled her to do as he wished. "Thank you," she whispered.

Sara felt both sadness for Philippe and rising excitement at the prospect of helping Maman and Jacques. This wasn't enough money to replant Saint Martin, but it was a start. Sara would deposit the funds in the bank. This spring, she would collect thousands of phylloxera-resistant vine cuttings, encase them in airtight paraffin paper bags, pack them in moist sawdust and send them by fast express to Tours. Jacques and Maman could hire expert grafters and use the cuttings to replant the vines. She would write them at once.

# Chapter 19

The new bedtime routine was a success. After a week of cajoling, threatening and bribing Pippa, Sara had thrown up her hands in defeat and allowed Pippa to sleep on a cot in Luc's room. Luc was not thrilled with the prospect of his new shadow sleeping in the same room with him, but he generally regarded Pippa with the polite, detached interest a vaudeville performer shows his audience. This suited Pippa just fine.

Tonight, Sara checked on them one last time before retiring. Pippa was curled up against Luc's back, the two of them locked in deep slumber. The piece of Sara's heart that remained cold to the girl thawed at the sight of them together. Pippa was her child—just as Luc was. Sara couldn't believe that, at age twenty-two, she was responsible for two adopted children.

Sara shut the door to her room and gratefully climbed into bed. Hours later, she awoke to Philippe tugging violently on her shoulder. "Sara! Sara! Get up—fire!" He threw on his breeches and flew down the stairs. Sara heard him ringing the fire bell with force: *clang-clang, clang-clang,* a pause, then one final *clang-clang.* He repeated the Eagle's Run signal three times. Amidst the clamor, the horses neighed, dogs barked and bells began to toll throughout the lower county, rising up in a frantic answer to Philippe's call for help.

Sara could only see the orange light from the fire reflecting off her bedroom window. She ran to the children's room. From their window, Sara saw flames jutting from the winery's first floor. A shadow darted past her sightline, and crawled up the ladder to the second floor. What was Philippe thinking, running into a burning building?

Glancing at the children's beds, she saw Pippa was missing. Sara yelled the girl's name, but she didn't answer. Luc, roused by the commotion, rubbed his eyes and began to wail. Rose bounded up the stairs to comfort him while Sara charged out the front door, screaming Pippa's name. She stumbled in her tracks. The block of vineyard closest to the winery, planted with cabernet grapes, was engulfed in flames, too.

There was only one reason why Philippe would climb to the second floor of the winery. She rushed into the barn, and noticing two axes were already gone, grabbed the small pickax and a saw, and ran toward the winery. Choking on smoke, she scanned the winery's perimeter and the field nearby for some sign of the girl. Surely Pippa would have enough sense to stay clear of the fire's heat, but where could she be?

Just then, she heard Philippe scream from the window. "Sara!"

Sara threaded the pickax through her dressing gown sash, and held the saw's handle tightly in her left hand as she maneuvered up the ladder, the flames nipping at her feet. The pungent smell of fermenting grapes hit her, and when she crawled through the second floor door, her feet plunged into a river of cool wine. Over the roar of the flames, Sara heard the boom and creak of Philippe's ax smashing the vast fermenting tanks, releasing thousands of gallons of wine to flow across the floorboards, down the chutes and stairwell, to douse the fire below. Philippe was a madman, his face distorted with exertion as he chopped wildly through the thick redwood of the second tank, wading in wine up to his shins. Sara sprang to his side and raised her pickax, driving the pick into the wood, straining to pull the staves toward her. She was too weak to break the wood, and grew frustrated. She was relieved when Mac arrived to take over—she was desperate to search for Pippa and fight the vineyard fire.

While the men battled the fire inside the winery, Sara sprinted for the stables. Her eyes swept over the inside of the stalls. There was no sign of the girl. Sara hitched the horses to the spring wagon, already loaded with water barrels and gunnysacks, and they burst through the stable doors. She drove the horses at a reckless pace where they did not want to go: toward the burning vines. All the while, Sara's eyes scanned the ground. What if Pippa were out here in the dark? What if Sara accidentally struck her with the wagon?

Smoke billowed into the indigo sky, consuming the great oak and choking Sara as she drove closer. The fifty-foot flames that had shot up from the winery had now diminished. Philippe's plan to extinguish the fire with a year's worth of wine was working.

Sara stopped the horses in the vineyard, a safe distance from the fire's edge, leapt to the back of the wagon and doused the burlap sacks with water. She jumped down with one in each hand, and began to beat the flames back. Within moments, she saw Philippe's form back by the winery, dark against the orange swell of fire. Sara blinked back tears—he was safe, for now.

Just then, she spied a long line of wagons racing up the road, gas lamps careening and horsewhips cracking. She knew each neighbor's wagon, like hers, was fitted with three barrels of water and a dozen burlap sacks, as was the county fire plan. As they moved closer, Sara was shocked to see Boone Sumter leading the charge. His face did not register his usual hostility, but rather distress.

Sumter waved his arms, directing the neighbors to roll their barrels to the right and left of the fire, and motioning for others to place a ladder on the oak tree and climb up to swat the flames out from above. The men opened the barrels and soaked the gunnysacks with water. In less than two minutes, they'd surrounded the spreading pyre and begun beating it back with a vengeance.

The smoke stung Sara's eyes. Wiping the moisture away, she scanned the base of the fire, and the wagon wheels, hoping to find Pippa. She saw nothing. A moment later, Sumter's shout cut through the uproar, and he ran out of the smoke cradling a listless child. A wail escaped Sara's throat, and she stumbled to reach them. She snatched the girl from his arms and ran her back down to the house. The fire was still far enough away, but it was spreading fast. With God's grace, it would not reach the house.

Inside, Rose sat at the kitchen table, rocking Luc, who had fallen back to sleep. Aurora, still in her dressing gown and coat, rushed in to Sara's aid. "What should I do?" Sara's voice cracked with desperation.

"Bring her in here," Aurora urged her, ushering them down the hall to the back bedroom. "Sit her up on the pillows. Close all the windows and cover any vents to the outdoors with wet towels." Sara ran out to Rose and gave her the instructions. She couldn't leave Pippa's side for too long.

When she returned to the child, Pippa's eyes opened and she gasped for air. The rattle in her chest frightened Sara. The girl couldn't speak, or even choke out a cry. "There, there, my love," Sara soothed, kissing her blackened cheek. She patted her scraped knees and whispered, "You'll be all right. Just stay calm. Tante Rora is going to make you some special medicine." Sara forced a wobbly smile.

Pippa struggled to catch her breath. Aurora pressed her ear between Pippa's shoulder blades and listened. "She's wheezing hard. Get some soap and water. Sponge off the soot. Start with her face, hair and hands. I'm going to the kitchen to mix a tincture and some tea."

Sara did as instructed. Meanwhile, Rose arrived with a glass of cool water, which she held to Pippa's lips. The child guzzled it down so fast, half of it dribbled down her chin.

Aurora returned within minutes. As she stirred the tea, Pippa watched with cautious eyes. "Aren't you clever. Do you know what this is?" The child nodded between coughing jags. She seemed more alert.

"Peach and mulberry-leaf tea, with a teaspoon of honey to make you even sweeter." Aurora smiled, but Pippa sniffed it twice and then turned up her nose. "The feistiness is a good sign," Aurora whispered to Sara. "The tea will reduce the inflammation in her lungs and relax her chest, so she can breathe easier."

"Come now, Pippa," Sara begged. "You must drink."

"Let me try," Aurora interjected. "The inside of your chest is black with soot, but this tea will wash it away and make it shine. Don't you want your insides to be sparkling?"

Pippa squinted, but she took the spoonful offered by Aurora. Two cups later, Pippa drifted back to sleep. Aurora rubbed her leg soothingly. "I'll stay with her and clean her up—you go to Philippe," she insisted.

Sara was eager to return to him. She grabbed the copper stockpot from the kitchen and burst out the front door. She gagged on the air, heavy with smoke and flyaway particles of ash. How stupid! She hadn't thought to cover her face. Sara grabbed the kerchief off her head, wet it under the pump, and tied it to cover her nose and mouth. She then filled the pot to the brim and scrambled up the hill as fast as she could.

When she crested the hill, Sara was unprepared for the sight before her. More men and women had joined the fight, forming a bucket brigade from the creek to the fire's border, which was now creeping westward. In its path was a grove of tall eucalyptus trees only fifty yards away. God save us, Sara thought. The eucalyptus oil was so flammable that if the fire came any closer to the trees, their crowns would burst into rings of fire.

Over the next hour, the roar and crackle of the winery fire quieted to a hiss, and curling gray smoke replaced the orange flames that had illuminated its now melted windows. Sara, Philippe and their neighbors continued to beat back the vineyard fire while it snapped at their feet. She was stunned by its sheer power, the way the flames climbed trees and crawled over vines and rocks. Sara continued to throw water over dry gunnysacks, passing them out to her neighbors. Adrenaline coursed through her veins, and the scorching heat stung her eyes.

Hours later, Sara's spirits flagged as she took in the scene of destruction before her. The damage to the winery was irreparable. They had used nearly a hundred thousand gallons of premium wine to drench and extinguish the fire inside. The rest of the wine in the cellar was tainted by smoke—unsellable. An entire year's work lost. The nine-year-old cabernet vines that were now burning had been at the peak of their production, yielding over six tons per acre this year. Sara's hands hung uselessly at her sides. These vines that had produced gold-medal and sacramental wine—the cornerstones of their business—were turning to ash before her eyes.

The instant Sara turned away, she heard the pit-a-pat of a steady rain. The crowd murmured in astonishment, and Sara lifted her face to the sky, overjoyed to feel the refreshing drops on her soot-streaked skin. She heaved with relief: the downpour would help snuff out the rest of the fire.

A few women lifted their voices in a chorus of "Blessed Assurance." Slowly the anthem gained volume and strength, until the impromptu choir sounded as powerful as a host of angels. Over a hundred men and women encircled the pyre, swatting it with fervor for two more hours, watching it diminish before their eyes. Their voices rang out in thanksgiving—all but one.

Sara found Philippe kneeling on the ground with his soot-darkened hands pressed to his thighs. He was coughing so hard he could barely draw breath. How badly was he hurt? When she threw her arm around him, he pulled her tight, squeezing her so hard, she felt ashamed that she'd ever doubted his devotion. "Sara, Sara," he gasped, his chest convulsing.

Yellow light from the morning sun ascended like a halo in the eastern sky. The fire had died, but to be safe, every man selected one section of the charred, blackened acreage to canvass for embers. They stomped their boot heels into the smoldering remains to ensure the fire was completely extinguished. After checking the last acre, Sara and Philippe shook the hand of each man and woman who had come to their aid. Words, at this moment, failed them.

Sara assumed that Aurora had fallen asleep with Pippa, but was anxious to return and check on her. Too tired to think, she turned toward the house. Philippe caught her hand. "Are you hurt?"

Sara shook her head, blinking back tears.

"The children?"

Sara glanced at the tree where they'd found Pippa. Philippe's face crumbled. "Sara?"

"Luc is fine. He's with Rose. Pippa . . ." Sara's fatigue made it hard to form the words. "Pippa was out *here*. Sumter found her unconscious, up near the tree. She inhaled a lot of smoke. She's wheezing. Aurora is with her."

Philippe squeezed his eyes shut. "What the devil was she doing out here?"

"I don't know. Sleepwalking? Did you bolt the door last night?"

"I—I don't know." Philippe erupted in a coughing jag.

Sara laid a hand on his chest, still hot and dark with ash. "It doesn't matter. Lord willing, she'll recover. What about you?" Spying the blistered skin on Philippe's left hand, she reached for his arm and gingerly examined the wounds. The welts were red, and the skin had melted off in parts. "Philippe!"

He flinched. "Aurora will have something for it." He draped his wounded arm over Sara's shoulders as she helped him back to the house. When he glanced back at the scorched earth and mangled shell of a winery, his face twisted with anguish. Sara pressed her palm to Philippe's chest, steadying him. What on earth would they do now?

Aurora wouldn't allow Philippe through the door. "No sir, you are not coming in here wearing all that grime. Pippa's lungs are very fragile right now."

"Is she going to recover?" he asked, panicking.

Aurora moved closer, whispering, "Too soon to tell, but she's breathing easier now."

Philippe exhaled with relief. He was blocking the doorway, so Sara peered around his shoulder, asking, "Aurora, what should I put on that?" Aurora followed Sara's eyes to the blisters on his hand. "Good Lord! Sara, you wash off and sit with Pippa. I'll dress his wound."

Even with Aurora's salve and bandage, Philippe's hand still hurt like hell. He slept in fits, coughing up dark phlegm, rolling from side to side, too dazed and pained to find comfort. Had he left the door unlocked? Why had Pippa left the house? Could she have started the fire somehow? Philippe's mind tossed in turmoil.

He walked downstairs, carefully sidestepping each of the floorboards he knew would creak. Aurora slept sitting up in the rocking chair, while Sara snored softly next to Pippa. His wife's long dark lashes could not cover the deep purple smudges of weariness under her eyes. Philippe stroked her hair, still braided down the back, but disheveled from a long night of work and worry.

Sara's hand encircled Pippa's delicate wrist. The girl's head was elevated on two pillows, and her breathing was shallow. Here, in deep slumber, when she wasn't contorting her lips, working so hard to form words with a mouth that betrayed her, her face was serene.

Philippe had never been one for deep prayer, but he muttered a Hail Mary before quietly slipping out of the house. He walked into the vineyard and kicked the black earth. The smell of burnt leaves and wet cinder overwhelmed him. As he picked up a gnarled vine, it disintegrated in his hand, falling like snow to the ground.

He'd worked tirelessly to make Eagle's Run the most productive and profitable vineyard in Napa, and he'd come within a hair's breadth of succeeding. He'd been too proud, too certain his luck would continue. In one night, all his hopes had been dashed, and now his child lay fighting for her life. How had this happened? There was no open flame, no lightning strike. Losing the entire vintage and ten acres of vines was torture enough, but watching Pippa fight for the shallowest breath had gutted him.

Philippe walked toward his once beautiful winery. The fire had burned the wood interior of the first floor, though most of its stone exterior was still intact. Flames had consumed the entire second floor, causing it to collapse, pulling the third floor and all its equipment down with it. Thousands of dollars of machinery, redwood tanks and oak barrels were destroyed. The unbottled wine in the cellar would be undrinkable. The empty bottles were now pools of glass melted into the floorboards.

Philippe stared at the shattered fermenting tanks. The entire 1900 vintage—chardonnay, cabernet and zinfandel—had been wiped out. To make matters worse, wine prices had just reached twenty cents per gallon, and he'd just renegotiated his contract with the archdiocese for fifteen cents per gallon. Instead of raking in the cash this year, Philippe had just lost fifteen thousand dollars of future profits in one night.

With his uninjured hand, he picked up the ax lying near his foot and raised it over his head. He struck with all his might, again and again, attacking the chunks of barrel that remained, hacking the staves into splinters, spewing profanities like a possessed man. When his limbs finally lost all strength, Philippe sank down on an overturned bucket. Thirty thousand gallons of the 1900 cabernet had already been ordered for delivery next fall—14,000 for the archdiocese and another 16,000 for shipment to local and eastern merchants. How would he fill the orders now?

The sun cast macabre shadows over the piles of debris. A silver gleam caught Philippe's eye. As he moved closer, he realized the object was a blade's edge, glinting in the light. He picked up the pocketknife and wiped it off. Barlows were a dime a dozen in these parts. Mac must have dropped it last night. Philippe turned the haft in his hand. The letters *B. SUMTER* were carved into the handle.

His first thought was that he ought to return it to Boone Sumter, and personally thank the man for saving Pippa. Yet, even in his sleep-deprived state, through the haze of bewilderment, Philippe sensed something was amiss. Why would Sumter's knife be in the winery ruins, where only he, Sara and Mac had fought the fire?

# Chapter 20

Pippa's color returned and her chest cleared. Father Price rode out on Sunday to offer Mass for the Lemieux family and their neighbors, entreating God to spare them from further trials. He baptized Pippa, sprinkling holy water over her head three times and anointing her forehead with chrism oil. In front of all their neighbors, he signed the cross above the cleft lip that frightened so many. His compassion surprised Sara.

Since the fire early Tuesday morning, the larder and icebox had been filled to the brim with breads, cheeses and meats from their neighbors. They had so much food that Sara and Philippe invited everyone to a stay for picnic after Mass. A crowd gathered around the old cart laden with fruit-filled crates, meat pies and bread. Sara approached some women sitting at the picnic table, intending to thank them. Before she reached their circle, she heard one of them whisper, "Devil's child, fer sure," and another, "Born of a strumpet, a city streetwalker."

"The child conjured up that fire with her dark magic," a shriveled, graying woman mumbled snidely. They didn't seem to notice Sara standing ten paces from them, or if they did, they didn't care. She bit her lip and darted toward the other side of the house. She pushed her spine into the wall, trembling with anger.

Maybe it was her fault. She'd been so busy with the farm and the children that she hadn't had any time to attend the suffrage meetings where Napa's women gathered and socialized. Perhaps she appeared aloof, or unapproachable.

When Sara returned, she hoped no one would notice her red, puffy eyes, but Philippe appeared beside her. "What is it?" he asked, touching her elbow gently.

"I'm fine, it's nothing," Sara replied. "Just some old crows cackling about Pippa—about how she's somehow responsible for the fire."

"Who said such things?" he fumed.

She sighed in defeat. "It doesn't matter, Philippe. They all think them."

Philippe looked ready to explode. In a hushed tone, he replied, "Their tongues have been wagging, that's for certain. Father Price pulled me aside. The archdiocese is canceling our contract because my illegitimate child 'presents a moral conundrum for the archbishop.' Can you believe it? What about all the priests who've sired children? Hypocrites."

Sara held up a hand. She couldn't believe O'Brien had double-crossed them. "Are you sure about this? Wouldn't Monsignor O'Brien have sent you a letter or paid a visit?"

"Perhaps he's just as pigeon-hearted as the rest of them," Philippe said with disgust.

~

Sara left Pippa and Luc with Rose for the day. Philippe had left early for Napa Junction with barrels and cases of the 1899 Eagle's Run Zinfandel, ready for shipping to his eastern merchants. Sara anticipated he'd be running errands in town until supper, which would give her and Aurora ample time to travel to the city and return without raising his suspicions.

When Sara and Aurora stepped off the omnibus near the archdiocese's Chancery Office on Franklin Street, Sara looked up at the imposing stone structure and thought about turning back. Thinking about the archdiocese's action against them, and the thousands of dollars they'd be losing, her heart raced and her palms began to sweat. Such injustice required a bold response.

Sara and Aurora stacked the boxes they were carrying on the front steps. Sara pounded on the door. A slender, aging priest soon answered it. He looked vaguely annoyed by their presence.

"Father, I am Mrs. Philippe Lemieux, this is Mrs. Aurora Thierry, and we were hoping for a brief word with Monsignor O'Brien, if he's in."

"And what is your business with the monsignor? There are no females allowed within the sanctum of the chancery," he added.

Sara bristled, but was determined to remain pleasant. She shot Aurora a quick glance, trying to convince her to do the same. Passivity wasn't their strong suit.

"I am aware, Father. My business with the monsignor is of a personal nature. My husband and I are acquaintances of Monsignor O'Brien."

"He is a very busy man." The priest stared at her—as if he were willing her to disappear.

Sara considered how she could convince him. "It's an urgent matter, regarding the purity of the sacramental wine provided to the archdiocese," she fibbed.

"Wait one moment."

The priest did not return. Within a few minutes, Monsignor O'Brien appeared in the doorway. "Mrs. Lemieux! What a pleasure to see you again," he declared, as he stepped out onto the stairs, introducing himself to Aurora. "Pleasure," he repeated. "What brings you here?" Sara was surprised that he didn't know.

"Father Price, the curate of our parish, told us that the archdiocese is terminating its contract with our winery because of some past behavior of my husband's—immorality and infidelity, we were told."

"Glory be to God! I knew nothing of it." O'Brien scratched his chin. "Tell me, did he give you specifics?"

Sara resented having to explain her husband's indiscretions to others. "Before we were married, my husband had a liaison with a woman and she gave birth to a child. Neither he nor I knew of it until she died recently, and the child was placed in our care."

"Illegitimate, I presume."

Sara nodded, her throat dry. At least he hadn't used the word "bastard."

"Very grave, indeed," he said. "Someone must have reported this, but since I handle the wine contracts, I'm surprised I knew nothing of it."

"Tell him, Sara," Aurora nudged.

"My husband doesn't know I'm here. Three weeks ago our vineyard caught fire, and we lost ten acres." She hesitated. She couldn't tell him they'd lost the entire 1900 vintage of sacramental wine. "Losing your business now would truly jeopardize us."

"Dear Lord, how awful," O'Brien said.

Sara sighed with frustration. "We were only trying to do the right thing."

"Which was?"

"To take in a two-year-old child, who is orphaned and deformed, and give her a proper home."

O'Brien rocked back on his heels and scratched his head. "What would you have me do?"

"Monsignor, if I can bear to raise a girl whose mere existence is a daily reminder of my husband's transgression, then surely the archdiocese can overlook it. In the spirit of our Christian faith, wouldn't it be unjust to punish us, when we are only trying to right a wrong?"

Aurora proclaimed, "'Let ye without sin cast the first stone.'" She always proffered her biblical guidance at the worst times.

Fortunately, O'Brien's brown eyes warmed with understanding. "Wait here."

Aurora paced back and forth on the street, while Sara sat on the top stair and tapped her shoes upon the brick step. Twenty minutes later, O'Brien returned. His expression was unreadable.

"Your contract was canceled, but without my knowledge," he announced solemnly. "An additional complaint was lodged, but it seems outlandish, if you ask me."

Sara's heart thumped in double time. "What is it?" She glanced at Aurora uneasily.

O'Brien cleared his throat. "That you killed a man, your husband's brother. The letter reprimands the archdiocese for allowing 'a murderess' to touch sacramental wine." There was a question in his voice.

Then it dawned on Sara. Boone Sumter had overheard Gilles Bellamy's accusations at the Paris Exposition. Sara's anger rose from the pit in her belly, and would have spewed from her mouth had Aurora not clutched Sara's arm.

"Monsignor," Aurora spoke up, "my friend was attacked by the man you mention. She defended herself when he tried to rape her, and accidentally killed him. Her husband knew this before he married her."

O'Brien might have been knocked over with a feather, he looked so stunned. Sara squeezed Aurora's hand in thanks; she didn't know if she could bear to explain it herself. However, she did want to assure the priest of one other thing. "Monsignor," she said contritely, "you should know that I have confessed, and received absolution."

She studied him, trying to discern whether he was upset or sympathetic. "Monsignor?" she asked cautiously.

He waved his hands, dismissing her anxiety. "My dear, if your story is accurate, you committed no sin. I see no reason why I can't reinstate our agreement." Sara's lower lip began to tremble with relief. O'Brien quickly added, "You have suffered a great deal in your young life. I'm going to treat this little exchange as I would a confession. I shan't utter a word."

Sara shifted nervously. What if Philippe found out? "Even to—"

"I shan't utter a word to *anyone*." O'Brien smiled. Aurora exhaled, clasping her hands together in gratitude.

"Thank you, Monsignor. You are a true Christian," Sara said, choking out the words.

She gestured toward the boxes. "The piccalilli we promised you, as a token of our appreciation."

"A bribe?" O'Brien winked.

Sara exhaled loudly. "Luckily, it didn't come to that."

On Saturday, Pippa sat on the front steps with her favorite toy ball tucked beside her. She studied Philippe as he knelt on the clay ground, showing Luc how to shoot marbles. When Pippa began one of her coughing jags, Philippe rushed to the pump for a cup of water and held it to her lips, catching the drizzle of spillover with his handkerchief. Before he returned to Luc, he placed a pebble-sized cat's eye in her palm, for good luck. Her mouth curled into her unique version of a smile, and her face lit with excitement.

Every time he lost a marble to a crack in the ground, Philippe crossed his eyes and stuck his tongue out, causing Luc and Pippa to erupt in a fit of giggles. When Luc grew frustrated with marbles, Philippe pulled him near, and rested Pippa on his knee. Then Philippe swatted an imaginary mosquito on his leg.

"Did I ever tell you about the mosquito man?"

"Ew! No!" they chimed.

"You see, young Forrester fancied himself one of the smartest lads in the county. He and his pa knew all the tricks for rooting out mosquitoes. They even covered their pond with a thin coat of oil, just to keep 'em from breeding baby skeeters. One season, a swarm of 'em was growing in numbers, buzzing through the county, stinging everyone. But these were no ordinary skeeters." Philippe held up a clenched hand. "They were the size of Forrester's fist. When he saw the black cloud of insects headed his way, guess what he did? He ran into the barn, locked the door and grabbed his pa's hammer. There he hid—waiting, and listening.

"The buzzing came closer, and got louder, but he thought he'd outsmarted them. Then they started to sting the door! Stinger after stinger pushed through, and young Forrester pounded them down, one by one." Philippe wagged his index finger. "But he didn't count on the skeeters being smarter.

"After he'd nailed their stingers down, they summoned all the strength they had, beating their wings feverishly"—Philippe flapped his arms wildly—"and pulled the door right off its hinges! Our young Forrester was taking hot baths and swabbing with alcohol for weeks after."

Luc's mouth hung open. "Is that true, Papa?"

"What do you think?" Philippe jabbed him gently in the ribs.

"Naw, it can't be!" Luc said, and started to laugh. Pippa giggled with skittish relief.

Boone Sumter clattered up in his wagon with his gangly fifteen-year-old son, Jess, packing more foodstuffs from the neighbors. Philippe thought it was uncharacteristically kind of him to have organized the delivery.

Philippe greeted Sumter and Jess, and in reply, Sumter tipped his hat. Jess stacked the food by the kitchen door, but then walked back to the wagon without a word. He didn't greet the children, or even glance at them as they played ball. Maybe he'd heard the gossip about Pippa and decided to steer clear. Philippe sighed. He knew most children would never accept her. Each rejection his daughter faced chipped away at his hope for her future.

Sumter tipped his hat again, and headed back toward the wagon. Luc kicked Pippa's ball and it flew down the front path, bouncing right on Sumter's heels. Pippa ran after it, but froze when she neared the wagon. Without fetching the ball, she whirled around and ran back to Philippe. Her eyes were as wide as saucers, and her mouth slack with terror.

Philippe knelt down. "What is it, Pippa?"

She choked and sobbed, rubbing her eyes with her fists. She grabbed Philippe's hand and whispered, "I-yah boy."

"What?"

"I-yah boy!" Pippa's eyes darted to Jess, then back to Philippe. The color drained from the boy's face.

Jess pointed at Pippa, trembling. "Don't come near me, witch!"

Sumter slapped the boy hard, and ordered him to apologize.

"Wait." Philippe held up his palm, incredulous. Could Pippa be right? Did he understand her correctly? He clenched the knife in his pocket and asked softly, "Did you see this boy set the fire?"

Pippa was trembling when she nodded. She tightened her grip on Philippe's leg and buried her face.

"You can't blame my boy when she was the one I found that night, right in the thick of things. How d'ya know she didn't do it herself?" Sumter objected.

Philippe pulled the Barlow from his pocket and handed the knife to its owner. An expression of alarm flashed across

Sumter's face. Beneath the weight of his father's accusing stare, Jess broke down.

"Pa, I didn't mean for anyone to get hurt!"

Sumter slumped, deflated. Clearly he hadn't an inkling of his son's crime. "What in tarnation?" he demanded.

"They stole the church business from us!"

Sumter's face twisted into a strange mixture of sorrow and rage. "So you burned their winery? You could have destroyed half the county!"

By then, Luc had wandered up to see what all the hubbub was about. Philippe whispered, "Take your sister in to Maman, and you two stay inside, understand?" Luc's lower lip quivered, but he obeyed his father.

When the children were out of earshot, Philippe walked up to Jess. This snot-nosed kid had had the nerve to set fire to Philippe's property, destroying a five-thousand-dollar building and a year's worth of profit, and placing his family in harm's way? When Philippe came face-to-face with Jess, Sumter did nothing to interfere. "Arson is a crime, punishable by imprisonment," Philippe threatened, the words souring his tongue.

"Yessir." Jess was cowering now, waiting for a blow that did not come.

"Do you know what life's like in the Napa County lockup? Crowded. Jailer Behr doesn't separate the murderers from the thieves and arsonists. You'll spend the rest of your life in a tiny cell, or flushing the city sewers with the chain gang."

Sumter wrung his hat in his hands mournfully. "Have mercy, Lemieux," he implored. "Half our vines were ruined by the phylloxera. The boy overheard me spouting to his ma about it;

189

how we'd be all right if we just had more of the church business." Sumter hung his head. "The boy got himself carried away with things."

Philippe stepped back and exhaled, raking his hand through his hair. He startled when he heard a high-pitched shriek behind him. His wife, eyes blazing, ran toward them at full speed. Sara barreled into the teenager, shoving him into the side of the wagon. Jess crumpled to the ground. Before Philippe understood what was happening, he heard the crack of Sara's palm hitting Boone Sumter's face. Philippe lurched forward, taking hold of Sara's arms, while her body contorted with rage. "You bastard!" she spat at Sumter. "Your son almost killed my daughter, destroyed our vineyard and you—you go off telling the church that I'm a murderer, when you don't even know the truth!" She tried to wriggle free, but Philippe locked his arm around her waist. While he didn't comprehend what she was saying about the archdiocese, he shared her fury. He would have done the same thing if he hadn't felt a pang of sympathy for Jess.

Sumter rubbed his cheek, looking dazed. The boy stayed near the ground, his arms shielding his head. Philippe wanted to mash this kid's face to a pulp for what he'd done to Pippa. But he remembered what he'd been like at fifteen—hot-blooded and fast-tempered with no understanding of restraint. He had to think this through, because he faced a bigger problem than Jess Sumter. Philippe needed to fix the mess Jess had left in his wake.

He pulled Sara tight as she heaved with sobs. "Shhh, my love. You're exhausted. Let me walk you inside." He was surprised when she leaned on him for support. He held her up as they walked back toward the kitchen. But when she turned to go inside, she was still spitting sparks. "Don't you disappoint me, Philippe. You give 'em what they have coming."

He held her face in his hands, wiping her tears away with his thumbs. "Do you trust me?" he asked gently. Sara nodded, still shaking with anger. "I will fix this—and I'll punish Jess Sumter. But you have to let me do this my way." Sara's gaze met his for one long moment. She said nothing, but he could tell she wasn't sure. Unwilling to compromise, he kissed her hair, which smelled of sun and soap, and headed back to Sumter and his son.

When he reached them, he announced calmly, "I'm not going to press charges." Philippe glanced at Jess. "Locking you up doesn't help anyone, least of all me. Here's what you're going to do." He pointed at the boy. "Every day after school, you come here and work till suppertime. You're going to repair the damage you've done." Philippe gestured to the charred, mangled vines in the western field. "And you'll help replant the vines." Philippe looked from Sumter to his son. "In summertime, you'll arrive at sunrise and work till sunset. In the spring, you'll dig holes for the new orchard trees. Your father's going to give you up for two years, in servitude to me, as repayment for your crime."

"Yessir," Jess replied feebly. Sumter was silent, waiting.

"This will cost your parents money. I expect you to help them around the house when you're not here." Philippe rubbed his forehead, trying to ease the splitting ache there. He was certain this was the right course. "Boone, I'll thank you not to thrash the boy. I need him well-rested and in working shape tomorrow."

Sumter flashed his son a withering glance, but reluctantly agreed.

"I'm not finished," he said gruffly. "You'll apologize to Pippa for calling her names. She almost died from the smoke. You're going to treat her as you would your sister. She's your new best friend, and you're her guardian, understand?"

Jess nodded, shoved his hands in his pockets, his shoulders shaking. Philippe was glad to see the boy had a heart.

"Did you see my daughter that night? Do you know how she got out there?"

Jess looked up, wiping his nose with his sleeve. "No, sir. After I . . . when I ran away, I didn't see anyone."

"How'd you light it?"

"Kerosene lamp and some rags." He shrugged. "With no rain for weeks, it spread quick."

"Which fire did you light first?"

The boy shifted his gaze down. "The winery," Jess whispered.

Philippe shoved his clenched fists into his pockets to keep from thrashing the kid. "It was stupid and dangerous."

"Yessir," Jess mumbled.

"Be here at six o'clock sharp tomorrow morning," Philippe commanded.

Jess scrambled into the wagon. Too choked with emotion to speak, Boone Sumter tipped his hat in gratitude.

"Boone, there's one more thing," Philippe added. "Your boy cost me an entire year's profits, and burned down my winery. Your winery hasn't been at full capacity for a while. I want free use of the building, all the equipment, and your spare storage capacity for every year I'm unable to rebuild. Agreed?"

Sumter's frown was apparent beneath his scraggly blond beard. "Fair enough."

"I want it in writing," Philippe persisted.

Sumter glanced back. "You'll have it." As he rode away with his son, Philippe realized he probably should have asked Sumter about Sara's allegation, but he decided to take it up with Sara. Boone Sumter had enough trouble to deal with for today.

The next morning, Jess arrived five minutes early. Philippe sipped his steaming coffee, watching the boy from the kitchen window. Jess circled the water pump, head bowed, kicking the dirt and raising a cloud of dust. Philippe took one long last sip, pushed his hat down and set out to teach Jess Sumter a thing or two about life.

The boy was stone quiet all the way into town, arms locked over his ribs. He was not the sniveling, cowardly boy Philippe had confronted yesterday. He wasn't sure how he was going to pull it off, but he knew that he'd have to break Jess Sumter down before he could build him up right.

"Where are you taking me?" Jess's face paled when Philippe stopped the wagon right in front of the Napa County jailhouse. Philippe didn't answer. He wanted Jess to sweat it out a while longer.

At eight o'clock, the Napa County jailhouse was dimly lit and half-empty and smelled like a strange mixture of tobacco, shit, sweat and onions. Four men were cramped in one of three iron-barred cells, lying on their bunks, choking on a haze of smoke. Jailer Behr came out from behind his desk, obviously surprised to see anyone at this hour of the morning.

"Visiting hours are Sunday afternoons only," he snapped.

Philippe introduced himself, asking where the other inmates were. Behr gave Jess the once-over. "Why, thinking of signing up your son for hard time?" He laughed wheezily before breaking into a coughing spasm. "Just kiddin'. They're on the chain gang today, working in back of the courthouse."

Perfect, Philippe thought. Before leaving, he asked only one more question. "What are they doing time for?" His eyes flashed to the men in the cell.

"We got ourselves quite a variety: murderers and thieves, mostly."

"Any fire starters?" Philippe flashed a sideways glance at Jess, who'd started to tremble.

Behr caught on instantly. "Arsonists? No, not lately. Last one hung himself with a belt back in '98."

Philippe tipped his hat in thanks, and directed a silent Jess back out to the wagon. Within minutes, they arrived at the courthouse. When they circled around back, they found the chain gang, supervised by the deputy jailer, clearing rocks from the land in the yard. As Philippe moved closer, with Jess a step behind, he could see the men were pale as ghosts, their fingernails crusted with dirt. Flies buzzed around their beards, which glimmered with grease, and their eyes darted around like minnows.

"Pick up the pace, girls," the jailer called, resting his hand on his billy club.

Philippe shook the jailer's hand. "No shackles?" he asked.

"Naw, slows them down. We need to clear this field by night-fall, judge says."

A shout interrupted their exchange. Two of the men were dashing toward the street. The jailer pulled his revolver from its holster and charged across the field after the escapees. When he'd closed the gap to twenty yards, he stopped, aimed and fired. Though he missed the first man, he shot the second clean through the back. He dropped to the ground.

Philippe learned the next day that the other man was captured trying to board a Southern Pacific rail car at Napa Depot. He was hauled back in chains.

After their trip into town, Philippe had no more trouble from Jess Sumter. In fact, the boy turned out to be a decent worker. He milked the cows, fed the horses, mucked out the stables, cleaned out the root cellar in preparation for winter and helped Philippe take down the blistered winery walls, board by board, stone after stone.

In late October, when they were finally done stacking useable stones and discarding burned materials, Jess wiped his sweaty, soiled face with his sleeve and stood tall before Philippe. "I want to thank you, sir," he gulped, "for sparing me."

Philippe looked into the boy's eyes for a long moment, and seeing sincerity there, replied grimly, "You're welcome."

"Sir," Jess faltered for a moment. "Why did you do it?"

Philippe pulled his neckerchief off and wiped the perspiration from his brow. "Let's just say you remind me of someone. I don't want you to end up like him."

# Chapter 21

Sara reclined on the cool grass next to Pippa and Luc, who were already spread out like two eagles, pondering the beryl sky above. They traced the clouds with their fingers. "A cat! An elephant! Papa's chapeau!" they howled with delight.

October had come and gone without its usual fanfare. With no new vintage to rack, Sara, Philippe, Jess and Mac spent their days cleaning up the debris from the fire, counting their barrel and bottle inventory in the two adobe cellars, and packing cases of the 1899 cabernet, zinfandel and chardonnay for shipment.

Philippe's mood had been so dark since the fire that no one, not even Sara, dared to ask about his plans to rebuild. Instead of allowing his depression to drag her down, Sara retreated with the children to the orchard. Usually they worked hard, harvesting the apples and pears from the mature trees, but today they were taking a break. Sara could not have hoped for a greater friendship between her two children. Luc behaved like any four-year-old brother should. He sometimes pinched his face in irritation when Pippa trailed him like an over-eager puppy, but he also taught her how to balance on the concrete slab to use the water pump, showed her how to capture fireflies in glass jars, and warned her about the dangers of the creek. He taught her how to pick worms off the apples and place the fruit gently in the basket, taking care not to bruise the skin.

Sara refused to dwell on the recent events that had been so devastating to her family. She had explained to Philippe how Sumter had tried to destroy her reputation with the archdiocese, and she had accepted Jess as part of their daily lives, so long as he kept his head down and did his chores. He helped Philippe with everything from planting cover crops between the vine rows to delivering demijohns of wine to their city customers. Over the course of a month, her bitterness slowly eased into a tolerance of the boy. He'd endeared himself to all of them by teaching Luc and Pippa to shoot marbles with their thumbs, to jump rope, even to thread a worm on a fishing hook. But Jess still avoided looking at Sara, or speaking to her unless she approached him directly. One day, when he became a father, he'd understand why she'd lost her temper and lunged at him.

Pippa chased Luc between the nearby vines, brushing past their gold and crimson leaves and stumbling over thick patches of dried grass. Pippa's wispy blond hair framed her face so sweetly that Sara's motherly eyes hardly noticed her cleft lip anymore. Pippa's beige melton coat complemented her peachy complexion and brought out the blue in her striking eyes. How could their neighbors be so cruel? How could the same women who shared Holy Communion with them at Mass call Pippa a witch? If they could see her now, running and laughing just like their own children, would they stop spreading rumors about her?

Sara's thoughts turned back to Philippe. It had been so long since he'd smiled flirtatiously at her, or followed her into the barn for a midday romp.

Perhaps all he needed was time. His father's death and the fire had shaken them to the core. With a little cleverness and a lot of effort, they could replant and thrive again, but it could take years.

Sara refused to wallow. Just as she'd done with Bastien's attack, Papa and Lydia's deaths, and Linnette's existence, she placed the trauma of the fire in her mind's cupboard and locked it away.

She was the heart of this family, and it was a responsibility she took seriously. They needed something to build—together. Not something to repair, like the burned-out winery, which would take years of savings to complete, even with the proceeds from the insurance. That kind of work was necessary, but disheartening. Sara wanted to earn money, and quickly. A year from now, with no 1900 vintage to sell, they would have little income. Luc would be in school, needing books, pencils, shoes and clothes. Sara had thought for years of a stand at Napa Junction, where city folk headed to Aetna Springs or Napa Soda Springs could stop to purchase refreshments of wine, lemonade, fruit and whatever else she could sell them. Perhaps now was the right time. Regrettably, this meant she would have to reduce the number of vine cuttings she planned to ship to Saint Martin. Instead, she would use a portion of the money Philippe had given her to finance her new business.

Sara resolved to start selling her wares at Napa Junction this coming spring. The children could help her organize the fruit, wine bottles and sundries to sell. She would display their blue ribbons from the county fairs and their gold medal from Paris as proof of their wine's high quality.

Pippa and Luc, who'd been chasing each other in circles around Sara, tumbled into her lap, knocking her over onto the soft grass. She embraced them tightly. She couldn't wait to start!

# Chapter 22

T hank God for Mac Cuddy, Philippe marveled. They were standing amidst the ten acres of vineyard that had been destroyed by the fire in September. The land had been cleared of debris in October, and by November, Mac and his crew had plowed the soil to a depth of sixteen inches, and then loosened it again with a Deere sub-soil stirrer he'd rented in town. With no cellar left to manage, Mac had immediately shifted roles from cellar man to vineyardist, sharing the expertise he'd gained working with the Beringer brothers for so many years. They would replant in April, and Philippe was riveted as Mac animatedly revealed his plan to train the new vines along trellises. It was an innovation that allowed grapes to be grown at a much higher volume per acre.

Mac finished explaining his idea and scratched the day-old growth on his chin. "What d'ya think?"

"So we'll use posts instead of stakes?" Philippe wanted to make sure he understood the science behind trellis training.

"Yes, sir," Mac replied, "one seven-foot post every thirty feet, set two feet deep, with a stake placed between the posts to help steady the vines."

"And we'll connect them with wire?"

"Yup. Number twelve amalgamated wire is strong enough. The first wire is stretched between the posts a foot above the ground. The second is stretched a foot higher, and the third, two feet above that."

"And this will allow for more shading of the fruit?" Philippe's question hinted at last year's calamity, when Mac had cut the leaves back too far, allowing the rain-drenched fruit to wither quickly.

"It will," Mac said confidently. He knelt down, outlining an invisible trellis with his hands. "You see, the vines grow freely the first year, and by the second year, we'll be able to start trellising. Eventually, we'll fasten the bearing canes to the two lower wires in a fan shape extending to both sides. We'll tie the young canes in the middle and train them along the top wire. That way, the air can circulate among the vines, and the fruit is better shaded by the young growth above."

"Hmm." Philippe tilted his head in concentration. "That should also protect the trunk, cordon and canes from high winds and help the fruit ripen more evenly, right?"

"Absolutely," Mac said. He sprang to his feet, his wiry frame as straight as a lightning rod.

"And you're sure this'll work?"

"Yes, sir."

"Who else has tried it?"

"George Husmann writes about his success with trellis training, and they've been using it in Missouri and other Midwestern states for years." If Husmann, the region's premier grape-growing authority, recommended it, Philippe might as well give it a try. Besides, the area would hold only a small percentage of his vines, and if they could produce more grapes, he could help pioneer this new growing technique in these parts.

"What do you figure for cost?"

"We'll need posts, wire, staples and labor. I'll work up an estimate."

Where would they find the money? Philippe had already ordered the costly new vines. He didn't want to mortgage the farm or dig into Luc's inheritance. Only one solution came to mind: he'd have to borrow the money he'd given Sara.

Having made up his mind, Philippe asked, "So we'll plow and harrow the soil again in March?"

"Yup, then we'll plant in April."

Nothing excited Philippe more than innovative ideas. He clutched Mac's bony shoulder and shot him a look of gratitude. "April it is, my friend."


Sara hadn't told a soul. She couldn't be more than two months along now, but the signs were obvious. This time she wasn't taking any chances. She would eat well and sleep late. She wasn't going to jinx herself by visiting the doctor either. Winter was the perfect time to hide her condition under bulky clothing—at least until Philippe noticed her thickening waistline. Things would progress normally, or they wouldn't. Worrying about it wouldn't make this baby any healthier than the first.

Sara resolved instead to keep her mind busy with planning her new venture. At nine o'clock in the evening, the house was quiet, except for the popping of embers in the stove's firebox. Sara wrapped her shawl snugly around her shoulders and sipped her piping hot toddy, burning the tip of her tongue. The aroma of honey and cloves invigorated her, and the shot of bourbon warmed and relaxed her. Philippe retired earlier than usual on these winter nights, but she didn't mind, for it allowed her two hours to dream, uninterrupted.

Sara had spent the last month jotting down her ideas for a wine wagon at the Napa Junction. She would sell their lighter wines—bottles of chardonnay and zinfandel—the few remaining cases of their award-winning 1897 cabernet, cold lemonade, paper-wrapped cheese sandwiches and piccalilli to passengers on their way north to Aetna Springs to take the waters. She would take along a sampling of apples, peaches, plums and pies to sell. Sara even considered the young mothers traveling aboard the train with their babies. She would have fresh milk, flannels, pins and canned applesauce at the ready. She had listed the items, what each would cost to make or buy, and the price she'd ask.

Sara doodled on her blank page. Now she needed to find the perfect vehicle for her endeavor. A harvest wagon wouldn't work—its sides were too tall. Besides, Philippe would be using all of theirs in the spring to deliver their wines to buyers in Napa City and San Francisco.

Sara considered the smaller pushcarts she'd seen crowding the streets of New York. The ice-cream man, the sandwich man, even the hot-potato man did a booming trade in the summer months. The tenement housewives had flocked to the fruit and vegetable carts two, sometimes three times a day to purchase what they needed for the day's meals. The carts served as an extension of their home kitchens. However, for Sara's scheme, a pushcart was simply too small.

She began to sketch exactly what she envisioned: a new one-horse, wood-wheeled wagon, with a short-sided bed painted brick red, the same color as the sign she'd made for their exhibit at the World's Fair. She would organize her items in sections. Shoppers could peer into the wagon bed to find what they needed quickly, purchase it and board their train north for the Springs.

A new wagon would cost anywhere from thirty to seventy-five dollars, she reckoned. What would Philippe say? She didn't plan on asking him, simply because he'd been so preoccupied with replanting those ten acres of vines this spring. That's all he seemed to care about: zinfandel or pinot grapes? Trellis or head-trained vines? He chattered incessantly about Mac's brilliant idea.

Satisfied with her plan, Sara slid her pencil inside the notebook and tucked both behind the potato basket in the larder. She pulled the bed warmer from its place beside the stove and filled it with embers from the firebox. After checking in on Pippa and Luc, she warmed her side of the bed, and then slid under the covers. She curled her knees up behind Philippe's and slipped her cold feet between his warm calves. He sighed, cupped her hand in his and pulled her arm around his waist.

She wondered if he could feel her heart fluttering with excitement. Since she'd been a girl, she'd never been solely responsible for any moneymaking endeavor. She'd either worked with her father or Jacques at Saint Martin, or with Philippe at Eagle's Run. Even now, she still co-managed Saint Martin with Philippe. But this enterprise at the train station would be hers alone, to manage as she saw fit, to succeed or fail on her own merit.

Either way, Sara was sure of one thing. With the baby coming, she must write Marie and persuade her to move to California, now that her midwifery studies were behind her. Since Lydia's death over four years ago, Sara had missed the camaraderie of women her own age. Aurora, though she was Sara's dearest friend, was more like a favorite doting aunt.

The next morning, Sara flipped through the pamphlet and application piled on the table. Cooper Medical College was still accepting applicants to its surgical program for the fall semester. Perhaps Marie just needed prodding from a friend. Sara wrote her a quick note and placed it in an envelope along with the application. The stage line was expected tomorrow. Sara would make sure her package topped the stack of outgoing mail.

Sara glared at Philippe, pushing her fists into her hips. "What are you asking?"

Philippe rested his hands on her shoulders and reiterated his demand. "I need the money to buy materials and pay the vine-dressers." Clearly, he didn't intend for this to be a negotiation.

Sara pushed him away. "You *need* the money? The money you gave me 'to use however I like'?"

Philippe stepped back. "Yes, but it's still family money."

"No, it's not. It was a gift from you to me."

"It's family money, and the family is in dire need of it. If I want the money, Sara, all I have to do is walk into the Napa County Savings Bank and withdraw it. The manager wouldn't bat an eyelash."

Sara held up her palm to silence him. "If this is the part where you tell me that a husband has rights to his wife's money, save it," she retorted. "We're not in France anymore!"

Furious, she clenched her teeth, grabbed her coat and stormed out the kitchen door. Its springs squeaked in protest as she slammed it behind her. What nerve! Sara hurried toward the stables. She felt the sudden urge to ride into town and shop for a brand-new, top-of-the-line farm wagon.

As she clucked at Red, easing him out of his stall and preparing to saddle him, she heard Philippe behind her, closing the stable door. He caught her hand in his and began to playfully nibble her fingers. She yanked it away, angrier than a wild boar.

When he started kissing her neck, she spun around, aroused but incensed. How could he trivialize her feelings? "Don't," she warned.

"Will you hear me out? I'll reimburse you," he promised. She wouldn't allow his silky words and smooth lips to distract her. She was all too familiar with his tricks.

"No." Her voice softened, but her eyes were filled with determination.

"Sara, it's for the replanting—something that will benefit us all," he said in a tight voice.

"Eagle's Run only lost ten acres out of two hundred. Saint Martin is missing a *third* of its vines!"

"Sara—"

"Why can't you use the money your grandfather gave you?"

"Because I used it to build a new house for your mother and Jacques."

He was misrepresenting the facts—again. "No, we used Luc's money for that. Half of *your* share was used to plant the orchard. And, of course, you saved the other half." She tapped her foot expectantly.

Philippe released her hand and squeezed the bridge of his nose between his forefinger and thumb. He exhaled loudly before explaining. "Yes, but when Heath and Strong didn't pay me, I had to reimburse Lamont for what they owed him: nine hundred dollars, nearly five thousand francs."

Sara was dumbstruck. He'd been far too generous with Lamont and careless with their savings. Nonpayment was one of the risks of doing business, and Lamont should have shouldered at least half of the unrecovered sum. "What about our other savings?"

Philippe thrust his hands in his pockets. "We've been living off it—how do you think we paid for Paris?" He continued, "It's a timing issue. We're still waiting to receive the insurance money and the balance of payments from the 1899 vintages. Once the money's in, I'll be able to repay you."

"When?"

"By August."

But August was too late. She planned to ship the vine cuttings to Saint Martin this spring. And, if she were going to start her new business by April, she had to purchase a wagon, umbrellas and a permit right now. Sara stroked Red gently on his withers, resting her cheek against the bay's soft neck.

"Not soon enough," she stated flatly.

"What do you mean?" he asked with an undertone of disgust. "You know it's cheaper and more practical to replant ten acres of vines here than three hectares in France. The shipping alone will be exorbitant!"

Sara begrudgingly understood his point. She set her jaw and declared, "I will let you borrow five hundred dollars, but I'm keeping two hundred. I have need of it." She stabbed a finger at him. "I want every penny back by August, understand?"

Philippe's heavy hands rested on her waist. He nuzzled his face into her hair and murmured, "Yes, ma'am."

She pushed him away. "I have to go shopping."

"No, you don't," he persisted, tugging her toward him, parting her lips with his tongue.

She felt a familiar burn deep within, but wouldn't give in. Her heart raced with indignation. "You owe me an apology."

He stepped back, but held her hands. A tempest of desire and desperation clouded his expression. "I do. I was thoughtless. I hadn't considered that you'd been secretly plotting," he said. "Although Lord knows I should have."

Sara gazed at him a moment longer, trying to discern whether or not he was patronizing her. "Surely, you'll forgive me," he whispered, moving closer to glide his nose up her neck, tickling her earlobe. Sara's knees buckled. When he slid his hands down her outer thighs, she knew she couldn't resist him any longer. Her kiss was a combination of hunger and fury. Despite her anger, she missed his touch, their shared affection.

"Where are the children?" Philippe asked, unbuttoning her collar.

Sara's mind muddled when he brushed his fingers across her collarbone. "Um, they went to the hatchery to buy eggs."

"With Rose?"

"Mm-hmm. And Jess."

"So we're alone?" His breath warmed her ear.

Sara smiled. "Not completely."

"Red and Lady don't count," he chuckled.

Sara placed her hands on her belly and whispered, "I wasn't referring to the horses."

Philippe froze. "You're pregnant? Truly?"

"About three months along, I'd guess."

He swept her up in his arms and planted a hearty kiss on her lips. "A baby is exactly what we need around here!" She couldn't remember when she'd last seen him so happily animated.

Philippe swiftly closed the stall door, locking Red safely back inside. "What is this new scheme of yours?" he asked. "I don't want you to over-exert yourself, with a baby coming."

He pulled his cotton work shirt from his pants and kissed the inside of her wrist. She struggled to hold on to her train of thought. "It's a secret," she smirked, tracing her fingers down his throat to the light thatch of hair on his chest. The stable air was chilled, but dust motes swirled in the afternoon sun that filtered in through a crack in the door. Jess had cleaned the stables this morning, so they smelled fresh—a mixture of dried grass, leather and musky horse.

"You, my dear, are a sphinx," Philippe teased, leading Sara over to the small bales of hay stacked in the corner. On this lazy Friday afternoon, his lips gently meandered over Sara's body. When the mutual surrender of their lovemaking ended, Sara sat up and straightened her skirts. She was still angry with him, but even more upset by her own weakness. Despite their genuine, shared joy over her pregnancy, Philippe had played her like a fiddle. She couldn't let it happen again.

Sara was so elated, she could hardly steer the wagon straight on the road. Lady yawed left, and Sara bit her lip with anticipation as they took the turn toward Eagle's Run.

Philippe would have to admit she was a beauty: a 1901 Rushford one-horse farm wagon, straight from Hooker and Company in San Francisco. The glossy red paint on the wagon bed was stenciled with yellow lettering: *Lemieux Family Wines*. With its matching yellow wheels and skeins, Sara felt like Queen Victoria high atop her throne as she drove into Eagle's Run. Upon hearing the clatter, Philippe, Luc, Pippa and even Rose ran out to greet her.

Sara set the brake and searched Philippe's face. He stared, shaking his head. Pippa and Luc, on the other hand, clambered up onto the seat next to Sara. "Maman, did you buy this for us? Can we keep it?" Luc cried with glee.

"It's for Maman's new business," Sara explained.

"Is booeyful," Pippa slurred adorably as she bounced up and down in the seat, testing its springs.

Philippe ran a hand along the centerboard, tugged on the axle beneath, and then stepped back to examine the paint job.

"Lemieux Family Wines?" He squinted.

Sara shoulders fell. "Don't you like it?"

"It's very colorful. Where on earth do you plan to drive it?"

Sara straightened her back. "All around town, of course, but I plan to park it at the Napa Junction from ten o'clock to five o'clock every Friday and Saturday this spring, when I start selling Eagle's Run *and* Saint Martin wines out of it," she said proudly.

Philippe rested his hands on his hips and gawked. "Unbelievable," he finally said, pronouncing each syllable slowly. "*You* did all this?"

"Aurora helped me find the most suitable wagon, and I used the money you gave me," Sara replied.

"You could have at least asked me," he said.

Sara's chest tightened. The children grew quiet. "I . . . I wanted to surprise you," she said.

As Philippe circled the wagon again, his expression soured. "Well," he blustered, throwing his hands up, "you sure shocked the hell out of me, Mrs. Lemieux!" He muttered something under his breath and walked back into the house. Sara sank back down onto the seat.

While Pippa fiddled with the reins, oblivious to the tension in the air, Luc cuddled up to Sara's side. "I think it's the smartest wagon I've ever seen, Maman," he whispered.

Sara sniffed and smiled. She didn't need Philippe's approval. This was her dream, and she would make him regret ever doubting her.


In mid-April, Philippe admired his cabernet vines, which Mac had planted using premium-grade St. George rootstock. They fanned out in diagonal lines six feet apart, over the ten acres that had been destroyed by the fire.

Planting these vines was the practical way to spend their money. Spending hundreds of dollars on a flashy wagon and a sketchy scheme when they were near financial ruin? *That* was pure folly.

Still irritated by his wife's audacity, he shifted his thoughts to the winery. He'd just received the insurance check, which would cover most of the rebuilding costs. He would use the money he had coming in August for their living expenses and to save for new equipment and barrels, which would cost thousands of dollars. He'd thought of applying for a bank loan, but with the phylloxera afoot, grape farming was considered risky. Interest rates on farm loans ran sky-high. After weighing his options carefully, Philippe had decided to wait and pinch pennies until they could recoup enough money to afford new equipment and cooperage.

Luckily, Saint Martin was thriving. In November, Jacques had reported to Philippe that production had hit an all-time high— 19,000 gallons were aging. Philippe had written letters to his merchant contacts in Chicago, Boston, St. Louis and Los Angeles to explain their temporary lack of inventory and ask them to consider swapping the Eagle's Run Chardonnay they'd ordered for bottles of the 1900 Saint Martin Chenin Blanc.

While he waited to hear back, he consulted with Monsignor O'Brien, and brokered a deal with his neighbors to supply the archdiocese with the 144,000 bottles of sacramental wine Eagle's Run wasn't able to provide from mid-1901 to mid-1902. They would receive twelve cents per gallon; he'd receive three. That seventy-two dollars each month would cover Mac's salary and Rose's stipend. But would it be enough? Could they stay afloat?

$\sim$

Sara's stomach fluttered with a mixture of fear and excitement. She stepped down from the wagon carefully. Her ample belly set her off-kilter. Before she could unbridle Lady and tie her up, the stationmaster appeared outside the one-room depot, and ambled, bow-legged, down the wooden ramp.

"Bill of lading, ma'am?" he asked. The tall, white-bearded man was wearing a dark blue waistcoat and tie, and a pillbox hat with *SPR* embroidered in gilt wire. She'd seen him before. Jacobs was his name.

"No, sir, I'm setting up to sell wine and food out of my wagon."

He popped open the pocket watch chained to his vest. "You're early. Permit?"

Sara retrieved the paper from her bag. She'd hoped he would overlook the fact that she was setting up a half hour before the ten o'clock train rolled in, but she'd wanted to tidy up the rows of wine, jams, piccalilli and sandwiches she was selling, and set up the umbrellas to keep them cool. Sara handed the permit to the stationmaster. She'd paid the Southern Pacific Railroad an annual fee of thirty dollars for that paper, half of what her wagon cost! Yet she'd only be able to sell her goods on Friday and Saturday, in the high season, from the end of April to early October.

While he studied the permit, she added, "My name is Sara Lemieux, and I live just northwest of here, at Eagle's Run."

"Ah, Philippe Lemieux's bride, are you?"

Sara smiled. "Yes, I am."

"He was just here last week, loading up shipments for Chicago. Fine businessman he is. Where is he now?"

"In the vineyard. I'm sure you heard about the fire. We just replanted, and he's tending the new vines," she prattled on. "This wagon here is my new business."

He walked over to the wagon and examined the contents. "No bottle openers in there, I hope."

"No sir, the railroad wouldn't allow it."

"More likely Niebaum wouldn't allow it," he chuckled. "He wouldn't want any other vintner to interfere with the sale of his Inglenook on the Southern Pacific."

"Indeed. It's a bit of a monopoly, isn't it?" Sara tested.

"Yes," he frowned and tipped his hat. "Just keep your distance. We need room for the shippers to move their handbarrows up the ramp and onto the platform," he said, and disappeared into the small depot building.

Eight trains stopped at the station over the next six hours. Sara sold only two bottles of chardonnay and five jars of jam, but every last one of the sandwiches Rose had made that morning was gone. She hadn't anticipated that her best customers could be the vintners themselves, who craved a hearty lunch after loading their wine shipments onto the freight trains. They drained her five gallons of lemonade down to the last drop.

Each week, Sara returned with a greater number of sandwiches and more lemonade, and each afternoon she sold out. Once she began offering a wooden fork with every jar of piccalilli, the men bought up those too, eating the tomato and pepper relish on the spot. Revenues were increasing, but even at this rate, Sara was making barely enough to cover her expenses.

One Saturday morning in early June, two women in a surrey pulled up to the station, and as the driver pulled their trunks down, they opened their parasols. The next train was scheduled to arrive in fifteen minutes, and with nothing to look at aside from the depot and a huddle of ten passengers waiting for the train, what else were two wealthy women on holiday to do?

Standing beside the wagon with her apron stretched over her rounded belly, Sara grew self-conscious as they approached. For her weekends at the station, she always dressed in her nicest linen frock and a spotless apron adorned only with her gold suffragette button. These women, however, wore embroidered silk, cotton and lace dresses, in pale peach and white. Their wide-brimmed straw hats were decorated with white feathers, and they accessorized their ensembles with pearl-drop earrings and fluttering, hand-painted oriental fans. Sara was speechless. They were simply the most elegant women she'd ever seen. When they moved closer, Sara could see they shared the same blue eyes and strawberry-blond hair—they looked like mother and daughter.

Sara recalled the high-society Americans she'd observed at the World's Fair last year. She figured these two women must also be a part of America's elite. She knew exactly how to approach them.

"Good morning, ladies. Might I tempt you with a bottle of our family's refreshing chardonnay, or perhaps our award-winning cabernet, to bring home?"

They whispered like sisters, but when they addressed Sara, they displayed exquisite manners. "Award-winning!" the mother's eyes flew wide open. "May I?" she asked. Sara slid a bottle into her gloved palm.

"Goodness, Laura," she exclaimed, turning to her daughter, "this is one of the wines we served at your debutante ball. Charles, the sommelier at the Palace, highly recommended it. See here," she tapped the last line on the label, "the 1897 vintage won a gold medal at the World's Fair in Paris."

Sara beamed. "Oh, yes, ma'am, my husband and I were in Paris and were delighted to receive such recognition. You know, we deliver regularly to the Palace Hotel and many private residences in the city. If you live in San Francisco, or nearby, we'd be happy to deliver monthly to your home."

The mother pressed her gloved finger to her lips. "How much for a case?"

"Twelve bottles is five dollars, ma'am," Sara replied.

The woman switched to flawless French. "You are French-born and make your wine from California grapes?"

Sara smiled, shifting into her native language. "Yes, my husband and I come from the Loire. Our vineyard is a few miles up the road. We make cabernet, a nice dry chardonnay and a zinfandel that pairs nicely with cold meat in summertime. We also own my family's vineyard in France. Saint Martin Chenin Blanc is sold in some of the finest restaurants in Paris," she added, stretching the truth.

A train whistle shrieked in the distance. "Mother," the daughter fretted, "we should move to the platform."

The woman waved away her daughter's suggestion and narrowed her eyes. "What a smart wagon, so colorful and attractive. And what an enterprising young woman you are." She extended her hand to shake Sara's. "Bridget Donnelly, and this is my daughter, Laura."

"A pleasure. I'm Sara Lemieux." Sara took their fingertips delicately, just like she'd seen the rich American women in Paris do.

"Here's my card, Mrs. Lemieux. We'd like a case of the cabernet delivered monthly to the back entrance. Clifton, our butler, will make sure you receive payment."

Sara glanced at the card, surprised to read that their home was in St. Helena. "Is next Thursday agreeable?" She remembered Philippe was making deliveries north of Napa City that day.

"Perfect, thank you."

"Mrs. Donnelly, please accept this bottle of our chardonnay with my compliments," Sara offered, rolling the bottle in burlap and cinching it with a piece of twine at both ends. "If you like French chardonnay, you'll love ours."

Bridget Donnelly tucked her fan back in her dress pocket, closed her parasol and reached for the wine. "I'd be delighted, Mrs. Lemieux, thank you," she replied warmly. Sara's offering looked rather drab next to Mrs. Donnelly's china-white skin and the peach lace that ruffled at the bottom of her quarter-length sleeve. Sara suddenly found herself wishing she had a more elegant wrapping for their wines. But perhaps they'd find the burlap rustic and charming. These wealthy women often appreciated quaint souvenirs of farm life, she'd heard.

When the Donnellys walked away, Sara felt a burst of exhilaration. Her first customers of the day and she'd already sold a case!

# Chapter 23

Sara reread the note resting on her swollen belly. Marie and Adeline would be here at the end of July, a month before Sara was due. The child could be born right in the middle of the harvest, the doctor had warned. Well then, Sara mused, she'd just do what the Chinese women did: birth the baby in the field and get on with it, metaphorically speaking.

Marie had graduated two years ago from the midwifery course at the Women's Medical College. And now she was the first woman accepted into Cooper Medical College's surgical program. Her classes would begin in San Francisco in August.

Sara admired Marie's pluck. A woman could become a doctor and attend the same surgical program as the men? What a modern example for three-year-old Pippa and ten-year-old Adeline. She smiled, tucked the letter away in her apron pocket and hoisted herself up from the kitchen chair.

As Sara made her way toward the barn to find Philippe, she cradled her massive belly. A hearty kick greeted her. He, or she, was strong and feisty, a life force within her. Sara felt curiously vigorous these days, even when her lower back hurt. Her skin was smooth and glowing, her hair was thick, her muscles strong and her feet steady.

Luc was doing his chores. He was a beautiful child, with Philippe's facial features in miniature but Bastien's dark mahogany eyes and hair. Luckily, he seemed to possess Lydia's personality: he was kind and high-spirited, and he excelled at his alphabet and arithmetic.

Luc wiped his brow with his shirtsleeve, and continued mucking out one of the stalls with a small rake and shovel. His nose crinkled, and Sara sympathized—the odor was even fouler to her sense of smell than usual. Luc had always preferred picking and crushing grapes to his barn chores. Sara hovered in the doorway, feeling a bit sorry for him.

"How's it going?" Sara hid a smile. When he saw her, Luc's face lit up. Two deeply set dimples punctuated his cheeks. "Don't forget to wash your hands with soap when you finish. I left a brick by the pump."

"Yes, Maman."

"And when you've washed up, you're welcome to a slice of the warm cinnamon bread I just took out of the oven. Butter's in the larder."

"Oh, thank you!" Luc shoveled twice as fast.

"Where's your father?"

"Out back."

Sara waited in front of the barn for Philippe to return from the privy. She disliked it and preferred he use the indoor water closet, but he wouldn't during the day. He didn't want to muddy her floors with his boots, and besides, he told her, the workers would think him uppity if they didn't use the same john.

He grinned as he made his way over to the pump, scrubbed his hands and rinsed them, then splashed his face with cool water. Sara slipped the letter out of her pocket and offered him a corner of her apron to towel off. "Thanks, love." He placed a hand on each side of her belly. "How's the pumpkin today?"

"Heavy," she groaned and waved the letter. "Guess who's coming to stay?"

On a steamy Friday in mid-July, a cadre of prohibitionists marched toward Sara's wagon, led by Francine Mason. Sara had instantly disliked the tight-bunned, purse-lipped woman when she'd met her at a suffragette meeting last month. Today, she appeared downright militant, clutching a Bible in her left hand and the pure white flag of the Women's Christian Temperance Union in the other. The group—wives and daughters of prune, apricot and olive growers—shuffled past Sara as she glared. They encircled her wagon and knelt shoulder to shoulder, forming a barricade that made it impossible for any customer to approach.

Sara seethed. What right did they have to interfere with her livelihood? She wasn't serving alcohol; she was merely selling it. Why couldn't they stick to picketing the saloons or the brandy and whiskey sellers? Why target her?

She wasn't going to tolerate it. "Stand up, Francine!" Sara commanded the pious old woman, but Francine's twisted arthritic fingers clutched the flag as if it were a talisman against the fires of hell. Her brown eyes hardened when she looked up. Sara had never seen such a mean old face. Rather than standing, Francine stared straight ahead and chanted loudly, leading her WCTU colleagues in prayer for the souls of Sara's customers. After each singsongy chant, the group responded flatly, "Lord save them."

If Sara walked away from the wagon, they might destroy her inventory. They'd been known to take a hatchet to saloons and throw rocks to break the bottles behind bars. But figuring she had no choice, she hurried up the platform ramp, past a whispering group of waiting passengers, and into the depot. Stationmaster Jacobs was flipping through the *Napa Register*, a mustard-stained napkin tucked into his collar, and eating one of her ham sandwiches.

Sara cleared her throat when he didn't immediately acknowledge her. He finally peered over his spectacles. "Yes, Mrs. Lemieux?" he asked, looking as if he wanted to return to his reading.

"Do you know what's going on out there?" Sara's heart thumped so hard, she had to sit down on a nearby bench and grip its arm to steady herself. Somehow, the fact that she was a pregnant woman being picketed for selling alcohol made the ordeal even worse.

"I can't stop them unless they start destroying your property or railroad property."

"They're interfering with commerce," Sara countered.

Jacobs shrugged. "Liberty of speech, I'm afraid."

Sara spotted a flask on the windowsill behind the station-master. It hadn't been opened—yet. "And what's that drink *you're* enjoying?" She flicked her head. Sara thought she saw his cheeks redden. Then again, maybe he'd already taken a few swigs.

"Vodka, but only after work hours," he added unconvincingly. "I don't go for that sissy wine you're peddling, no offense, ma'am. I like a nip of something a little stronger." Hardly a nip, Sara thought. There must be more than a pint of liquor in that flask.

She pulled her hanky from her apron pocket and blotted her perspiring brow. "I think the police should decide whether or not they're breaking the law." Her eyes darted to the telephone on the wall. She tapped her foot impatiently when he didn't move a muscle. "Well?"

He sighed, reluctantly folded his newspaper and asked the operator to connect him. He looked out the window, studying the prohibs while he described their activity to the police. His tone was flat and, Sara felt, devoid of any urgency.

Jacobs dropped the earpiece back in its holder. "They'll be here when they can. In the meantime, Mrs. Lemieux, I suggest you get back out there and guard your stock." He pointed out the window to where the white-gowned prohibs were now picking through her wagon's wares.

Two women lifted up the oranges, peaches and sandwiches, obviously searching for something beneath. One woman fingered the precious gold medal that Sara usually draped around her neck. She'd been so startled by their arrival, she'd forgotten to bring it with her.

Rooting around in a proprietor's wares without permission had to be illegal. But what could she do until the police arrived? Then Sara spied the jugs of lemonade she'd made earlier that morning. A smile crept over her face.

"Thank you, Mr. Jacobs." She peered out the window, and her hand flew to her forehead. "Good gracious, look at what they're doing now!" Sara stepped aside as the stationmaster rushed to the window.

"What is it, Mrs. Lemieux?" He adjusted his glasses. Sara turned and slid his heavy flask into her wide apron pocket. "I could have sworn one of them was drinking out of a wine bottle," she said over her shoulder. Then she added, with a confused look, "But I don't have a corkscrew in the wagon. How on earth could they get it open?"

After leaving the stationmaster with a perplexed look on his face, Sara strolled back toward her wagon, pretending she hadn't a care in the world. When they saw her coming, the women knelt down again and began to pray.

Sara stepped between two of the protesters to reach the back of her wagon. She squatted down. From beneath the wagon, she could see that while they chanted, the women's eyes were either closed in concentration or shielded by their straw hats. Now was the time.

She opened the smaller jug of lemonade, cooling in a bucket of cold creek water under the wagon, and emptied the contents of Jacobs's flask into it. She lifted the jug, shook it, and resubmerged it in the cool water. When she was certain no one was looking, she shoved the empty flask under a box of apples.

By one o'clock, Sara had endured plenty of stares and whispers from the loitering rail passengers, though she hadn't done business with a single customer. But if these prohibs thought she'd just pack up and leave in defeat, they were mistaken.

The women began to wilt in the oppressive heat. Some fanned themselves with their hats, while others were sweating through their linen dresses.

Sara sat down on her barrel, her perch when she wasn't waiting on customers. She poured herself some lemonade from the large jug and noisily unwrapped an egg sandwich from its paper wrapper. She took two bites plus a swig of lemonade, and let out a satisfied sigh.

Sara walked around the perimeter of the wagon, eating her sandwich and sipping her cold lemonade. She named the women she knew as she passed them. "Francine, Mabel, Susan," she said in a syrupy voice. "This prohibitionist business is such difficult work. You ladies must be parched. Some of this nice cool lemonade, perhaps?" Sara took a sip from her cup. Many of them gulped in response.

Susan immediately rose. "I would. Thank you," she said, while Francine shot her a nasty look. As Sara poured lemonade into a tin cup, Susan added, "It's nothing personal, Sara. We just feel we need to protect the innocent. Men who drink beat their wives, they commit adultery, they . . ." She had tears in her eyes.

"I completely understand," Sara lied sympathetically.

She passed around the tin cups of lemonade, and her unlikely patrons drank the small jug empty. Sara counted. They'd had at least two glasses each—some three. All except that battle-ax, Francine Mason.

Within a half hour, some of the women had fallen asleep against the wagon wheels, and others hooked their elbows over the wagon bed to keep from falling over. Francine tried to rouse them from their stupor, but they swatted her away, slurring their objections. Her eyes narrowed, and her words spit venom. "You"—she stabbed a crooked finger at Sara—"You drugged them!"

"I did no such thing, Francine," Sara said calmly. "They drank lemonade, just like me," she asserted. "I think the heat's overwhelmed them. You should take better care of your supporters," Sara admonished. *And you should know better than to declare war on an expectant mother.*

Before Francine could form a response, the police arrived. Sara, and a confused Stationmaster Jacobs, greeted them. Francine herded her lackeys back into formation.

"These women don't look like they're causing trouble," the officer said. The prohibs were chatting and linking arms, presumably in an attempt to remain upright during the long walk home.

"They were handling my property without permission, and interfering with my business."

"I can't arrest them for that. There's no proof they did any harm. It would be your word against theirs."

"They must be charged with something!" Sara argued.

"What charge would you have me bring against them, ma'am?" The officer tilted his head.

Sara bit her lip, eyes twinkling. "Public inebriation?"

"It's hotter 'n the hinges of hell today," Aurora exclaimed, wiping her brow with her hanky before hopping down from the wagon. "What have you gone and done now?" she demanded with a smirk. "Oh yes, Philippe told me. He was laughing so hard, he could barely spit the words out."

Sara placed a finger to her lips to silence Aurora. The windows were open and Sara didn't want her guests to overhear.

Aurora shot her a befuddled look while hitching her horse to the post. "They'll be back, missy, and with more fire and brimstone than Moses himself!"

Sara rolled her eyes. "I don't think so, Aurora."

Aurora folded her arms. "And why not?"

Sara guided her friend down the gravel walk to the front door. "Because I have a plan," she whispered, flicking her head toward the house. "Just follow my lead."

Once inside, Sara presented Aurora to the five women seated around her dining room table—two of Aurora's suffragette sisters and three of the prohibs who had protested Sara's wagon on Friday. Ida Sumter, Boone's mousy, sweet wife, had agreed to meet with Sara and dragged her cousin, Mary Pitt, along. Sara had cornered the three prohibs after church yesterday and implied that it would be in their best interests to call on her at three o'clock this afternoon. They wouldn't want word to get out that they were intoxicated while protesting the drink, would they?

Sara and Aurora sat down. Rose served water, lemonade and ham and egg finger sandwiches. Some of the women shifted around uncomfortably, while others clenched their hands together. Ida, looking bright-eyed and happy to be there, spoke first. "Thank you so much for inviting us today, Sara," she said quietly.

"Thank you for coming, ladies," Sara replied. She glanced at each of their faces and smiled. "Please, do help yourselves," she said, gesturing toward the trays of food. "I invited you all here because I have a business proposal for you."

All five heads snapped up in surprise. "What kind?" Mabel asked suspiciously. She poured a glass of lemonade and sniffed it. Sara bit the flesh of her cheek to keep from snickering.

"Each one of you has a specific talent, and each one of you, if I'm not mistaken, could use some extra pocket money." She had chosen the group carefully. Ida and Boone Sumter had lost half of their vines to the phylloxera bug and had yet to replant. Ida's cousin, Mary, was widowed with two small children. The rest of the women around the table had sickly husbands or dying crops. Sara hoped to help them—and herself.

"As you know, I sell produce and wine at the train station every Friday and Saturday during the spring and summer months. I'd like to offer you a chance to sell your jams, pies, breads and honey there as well."

"And what's your take?" Mabel asked warily.

"Nothing. You'll receive all the profits from your sales."

"You want us to believe you're doing this out of the kindness of your heart?"

"I make wine and piccalilli, ladies. I'm not a baker or bee-keeper. And yes, I want to help you, if only a little." Sara smoothed a hand over her large belly. "Besides, come August, I'm not going to be able to stand out in the blazing heat all day. I thought we could work in shifts."

Dottie, Mabel's prohibitionist friend, leaned in. "She wants us on her side to prevent another protest at the train station," she said smugly.

"That's one of the benefits," Sara conceded, "but I don't think the temperance union will be returning to picket me anytime soon.

They wouldn't want what happened on Friday to become public knowledge." She locked eyes with each of the three women whom she'd witnessed intoxicated that day.

"What happened?" Ida perked up.

"It was a trick!" Mabel's face reddened.

"Nothing of great importance, Ida," Aurora interrupted, throwing Sara a warning glance. "I think the local WCTU has decided that it has bigger fish to fry. The prohibs will most likely shift their efforts to halting the sale of brandies and whiskeys, which have the highest alcohol content and are the real threat to families. For goodness' sake," Aurora said, flapping a hand toward Sara, "the Lemieux family makes most of their wines for the church, *your* church." She glared pointedly. "They aren't a threat to families."

"And besides," Sara added, "I don't serve any alcohol at the station. I don't even carry a corkscrew with me."

Dottie pushed back her chair and stood up. She had a gourd for a nose and her dark hair was slicked back from her face, tied in a severe knot. She reminded Sara of a black crow. She might actually frighten customers away.

"I've heard enough!" Dottie threw up her hands. "This is more of your trickery, Sara, and you should be ashamed. I will not sell my honey alongside your intoxicants, and neither would any true prohibitionist." She scowled. "And I'll see you removed from the Napa branch of suffragettes if it's the last thing I do!"

"You will not, Dorothy," Aurora interjected. "Sara and I resign from your branch of the suffrage association. We are leaving to form our own women's club, which will be more aligned with interests of working women."

Sara perked up and raised her chin in a show of solidarity, even though she had no idea what Aurora was talking about.

Dottie sputtered, "You wouldn't—you can't—"

"I just did." Aurora linked her arm through Sara's. "And our new club will throw its full support behind the labor unions, not the temperance union."

"That's preposterous," Dottie sputtered, glaring expectantly at Mabel and Ida, who hadn't budged an inch. "Ladies?"

Mabel cleared her throat and said meekly, "I think it's generous of Sara to offer us a chance to make some money." She glanced down at the table. "I'm not in a position to turn it away. I've got a family to feed."

Ida added, "Sara Lemieux is a Christian woman, and Mary and I would love to help her." Ida's grateful expression nearly melted Sara's heart. That woman had been through so much with the loss of half her crop and the embarrassment of her son having set fire to the Lemieux farm. Sara was happy she could help.

"Susan?" Dottie addressed the other prohib, who hadn't yet mumbled a word.

Susan rose slowly, shifting her eyes from Dottie's to Sara's. "Thank you for the sandwiches."

"I'll see you ladies out," Sara offered politely.

Dottie raced out the front door, and Sara heard the gravel crunching beneath her feet before she could even thank her for listening. "Come along, Susan," Dottie snapped over her shoulder.

Susan shot Sara a conciliatory smile. Sara said lightly, "Perhaps we could find a way for you to join us—later."

"Perhaps," Susan replied noncommittally.

Sara returned to her dining room to find Ida, Mary and Mabel huddled together and speaking excitedly to Aurora. Aurora grinned in answer to Sara's bewildered expression. "Our own club? What are you thinking?" Sara asked.

"Oh, it's a brilliant scheme, Sara! Wait until Aurora tells you! We all want to help," Ida gushed, and her friends followed suit.

Aurora started in enthusiastically. "We could model our club after the California Club of San Francisco."

"The California Club of Napa?" Mary suggested.

"Perfect, Mary!" Aurora replied. "Why do you think the '96 suffrage ballot was shot down? Because the San Francisco suffrage association was run by a group of temperance advocates. The liquor lobby had no choice but to throw all their support into defeating it. If we form a club of working-class women, concerned with equality for women, then we can really stir things up, while continuing to campaign for the vote."

Sara was warming to Aurora's idea. "So you mean we'd partner with the female unionists to demand things like fair wages?"

"We wouldn't stop there. Community property rights, shared guardianship of children—the possibilities are limitless!"

Mabel spoke up. "We'd have to form a very large club for all that, wouldn't we?"

Sara and Aurora exchanged a knowing look. Sara left the room and soon reappeared with a stack of stationery and pens. "We'd best get started then, don't you think?"

∾

By the fourth week of July, everything was running smoothly. Ida and Mary were selling thirty blueberry pies daily, and Mabel was contributing jars of honey and bushels of peaches and apricots. Come the end of August, she'd promised to bring baskets of mottled purple and yellow French prunes, which would sell quickly alongside Rose's sandwiches.

Sara was grateful to have their help and some company. She'd never carried a baby to term before, so she was constantly questioning the backaches, the number of times she had to slink off into the woods to urinate, and the sheer weight of the baby, which she found to be cumbersome in the summer heat. Between waves of customers, the ladies planned their club activities, including marching down Napa's Main Street in October with other women's clubs from neighboring cities.

Late one morning, Aurora appeared with fifteen jars each of strawberry-rhubarb and blackberry jam. She refused to let Sara lift a thing. Sara stood back, with folded arms, surprised. Evidently, Aurora had a hidden talent. "Where do you find the time to can fruit?"

Aurora laughed. "This here's a sampling from Susan Pritchard. I persuaded her to give it a try, although I wasn't able to convince her to show her face. That'll come, once she's making decent money." Sara clapped her hands together. One by one, she'd win them over.

Sara's wagon had become the social gathering place for waiting train passengers. She'd recouped the hundred dollars she'd spent on the wagon and supplies by the end of June, and cleared a thirty-dollar profit in the first week of July. With the additional five hundred dollars she expected from Philippe in August, she planned to buy a horse and another wagon to set up shop at Napa Depot in town, or maybe at Buchli Station when it opened next year. Her plan was working.

# Part III

# Chapter 24

**M**arie Chevreau had experienced her share of blood, bile and birthing babies, but this was something new. She stood behind the wall of tall aspiring surgeons, trying to wedge a shoulder in between them so she could properly view today's instruction. She had already received enough withering glances to know she was not welcome here. She didn't care.

Marie shoved her way in, causing a ripple in the huddle. To her great embarrassment, Dr. Burns, their instructor, glared at her. "Yes, do join us, Miss Chevreau."

Marie decided to ignore him, and her fellow classmates, and just focus on the lesson at hand: the forty-five-year-old male cadaver on the table.

Dr. Burns pulled the sheet down, revealing the man's head, neck and chest, and proceeded to wave a hand over the body, pointing out the location of each vital organ. He invited the students to line up and feel for the tip of the liver, glands and Adam's apple. Touching a corpse was a bit strange, but Marie thought instead about all the lives she'd save with this knowledge. Wouldn't it be intriguing when they finally sliced him open and took a gander? She could hardly wait to see.

Just then, she heard a loud thump behind her. One of her classmates had dropped to the floor.

The other students scoffed and returned their attention to the cadaver. Marie also assumed he'd fainted, but then his limbs began to quiver.

She knelt down beside him, instinctively supporting his head to prevent him from smashing it on the floor. Dr. Burns said, "Miss Chevreau, don't fuss over him. The man has no stomach for this sort of thing." He waved her back to the table. "Leave him be. You'll embarrass him when he comes to."

What a horse's arse, Marie thought. "Doctor, he's having a seizure, possibly brought on by epilepsy." The man's legs kicked violently, and his arms flailed. To prevent him from swallowing his tongue, Marie pressed it down with her pencil. Two other students rushed to help her, but she cautioned them not to hold him down, lest they break a bone.

Dr. Burns whispered something to one of the students, who dashed out of the room. In a minute, he returned, followed by two orderlies carrying a stretcher, and the tallest, most striking man Marie had ever laid eyes on. He had wavy light brown hair and was wearing a white coat and carrying a stethoscope. His presence instantly calmed everyone in the room, especially Marie.

When the convulsions subsided, he addressed Marie. "Help me turn him on his side to drain the secretions." His blue-green gaze held hers a moment too long before he leaned over the patient, checking his pulse. She watched as the doctor's elegant hands glided over the man, checking ears, eyes, nose and throat. When he'd finished his examination, he asked the orderlies to load the student onto the stretcher. Before leaving, the doctor glanced at Marie and said, loud enough for all to hear, "Well done, Miss Chevreau." Marie blinked, speechless. How did he know her name?

Marie opened the hospital room door, just a crack, to see if the young man was conscious. Thad Holmes, who seemed to have recovered from his seizure, was sitting up and eating some hospital sludge—and looking rather down in the mouth.

Marie knocked shyly on the door. He beamed when he saw her. "My angel!" He stretched his arms wide to welcome her.

Marie laughed, "Come now, stop." She swatted away his praise as she would a hovering fly. "Feeling better?"

"Much, thank you."

"Anything hurt?"

"Only my pride," he confided.

"No, it could have happened to anyone," Marie lied, and quickly changed the subject. "I came to thank you."

"Thank *me*?"

"Yes, for stealing all the attention." Marie plopped down in the bedside chair. "The scrutiny has been unbearable."

Thad smiled. "Happy to be of service, miss. Or is it missus?"

"Miss, but please call me Marie." Marie hoped she wasn't giving him the wrong idea. She was here to study to become a surgeon—nothing else.

"Marie, from what Dr. Donnelly tells me, you were the only one who realized I was having a seizure, not just fainting because I'm afraid of corpses." So *he* was Matthew Donnelly, the surgeon she'd heard so much about.

"I thought I'd give you the benefit of the doubt." Marie smiled.

"Well done. Would you . . . would you join me for a cup of coffee when I get out of here?"

Marie hesitated for a moment. She didn't want to raise his hopes, but then again, he'd had a trying day. Perhaps he needed a boost. "Sure, sounds good."

Thad Holmes grinned widely. She'd have to let him down easy.

Marie was already drowning, and this was only her second week. With the exception of Thad, the other students ignored her. She had anticipated that the young men would be put off by the presence of a woman in their midst, but she hadn't expected hostility from them. She would have to ask more questions, and know more answers, to excel here.

From her second-floor apartment, Marie navigated down the narrow stairs carrying three heavy books, her satchel and a small jug of water. She rented a two-room flat in a three-story walk-up on Sacramento, just blocks away from the college and several cable car lines. When she stepped out of the doorway, a burst of cool morning air greeted her. She loved this time of morning, when the street was quiet, save for the squeaky wheels of the milk wagon stopping every twenty feet to make a doorstep delivery. Her stomach rumbled at the sight. For breakfast, she'd eaten a roll topped with strawberry jam, the cheapest she could buy, and sipped a cup of black coffee. Milk would have been nice, but she was saving every dime.

This afternoon she'd hop the ferry to Vallejo and take the train to Napa Junction for the weekend to visit Adeline, who was staying with Sara and Philippe. Marie knew she'd be holed up in her bedroom studying most of Saturday, but she couldn't wait to share breakfast with family again.

Marie arrived at the college and looked up, intimidated by a building that towered five stories above her, with the pointed arches and tall spires of a gothic cathedral. Built by Levi Cooper Lane, the current president at the school and a prominent professor of surgery, the college was located at the corner of Sacramento and Webster. A new addition housed a lecture hall and laboratories, the hallmarks of a premier medical institution. Adjacent to the medical school was the two-hundred-bed Lane Hospital, where Marie hoped to work one day. For now, however, she felt fortunate that they'd chosen her and that she'd saved enough money to attend for four years before moving on to the required year-long internship. She inhaled deeply. She could hardly believe she was here.

Marie climbed the stairs to the second floor. Students bustled about, and one or two threw her a smug glance. Other faces were set with nervous frowns. She understood that sentiment, for she too had her toughest class this morning: chemistry.

Marie selected a seat in the center of the classroom. She didn't want to seem too eager by sitting in the front, or too meek by sitting in the back. Smack in the middle, they would be forced to reckon with her.

Her twenty-four classmates were buzzing like bees in a hive. How funny. She'd spent the last eleven years in a nunnery and couldn't fathom that a group of men could cluck like a brood of hens. From what Marie could overhear, Matthew Donnelly had replaced their former teacher.

Dr. Donnelly was one of three professors of surgery who taught classes gratis at the college while managing his own robust practice. He had a reputation for precision and surgical innovation. He was highly educated, liked by the faculty and feared by the students. He was hard-boiled, and had a reputation for throwing unprepared students out of his classroom.

The bell rang, and everyone took their seats. A few students who had been loitering in the hallway rushed to their chairs. Matthew Donnelly walked purposefully into the classroom, his hands in his pockets. He carried nothing and wore a suit, tie and a stern look upon his face. He was good-looking in a fair-skinned, Irish sort of way. Marie judged him to be between thirty and thirty-five. When she began to wonder whether there might be a Mrs. Donnelly, she scolded herself silently. If she were to become a surgeon, she had no time for distractions.

Dr. Donnelly cleared his throat. "I'm a professor of surgery, not chemistry. However, given that Dr. Wenzell is temporarily out

of the country, you'll have to contend with me for the semester."
He smiled, revealing a row of straight white teeth. He probably
intended to put them at ease, but Marie found his expression a
bit menacing.

"Mr. Deaver," he said, approaching a student at the front of
the class. "Tell me, what is the difference between a mixture and
a compound?"

Larry Deaver flipped through his notes, attempting to hunt
down the answer. Donnelly sighed and moved on. "Mr. Schmidt?"

"The parts of a mixture can be separated by mechanical or
physical means, but the parts of a compound must be separated
chemically."

"Thank you, Mr. Schmidt."

"Miss Chevreau," Donnelly called out, clasping his hands
behind his back and pacing across the front of the classroom.
"What constituents are found in the compound of air?"

Marie's head popped up. She heard sniggering behind her
and hesitated for a moment. "The question is flawed. Air is a mixture, not a compound. Liquid air can be distilled to separate the
more volatile nitrogen from the less volatile oxygen and argon."
The room grew quiet.

"Very well, then," Donnelly replied. He leveled the full weight
of his gaze on her. "What are the percentages?"

Marie glanced downward, trying to retrieve the information
from her overloaded brain. "Seventy-eight percent nitrogen,
twenty-one percent oxygen and one percent of argon mixed with
carbon dioxide and other trace gases." When she looked up,
Donnelly had moved on to his next victim.

Marie exhaled. She'd passed the first test, and he'd treated her like any other student.

After spending some time in the library, Marie returned home to pack up her bag. She caught the Sacramento–Clay line to the Ferry Building and stepped onto the four o'clock ferry to Vallejo. Less than two hours later she disembarked at Napa Junction and was greeted by a smiling Philippe and her own dear daughter, Adeline.

She could swear that girl had grown an inch and gained five pounds in the last two weeks. Adeline was blossoming in the fresh air of the farm. She looked healthy and happy.

Philippe took Marie's bag, feigning that he couldn't lift it. "Heaven's sakes, Marie, what do you carry in here?"

"About fifty pounds of books—but hardly a stitch of clothing." She laughed.

Adeline was bouncing on her toes and swinging her arms, but the excitement in her expression was from more than just seeing her mother.

"Go on," Philippe urged, "you tell her."

Adeline threw her arms out and announced, "I helped birth Tante Sara's baby, Maman!"

"A healthy, feisty baby boy, born yesterday morning," Philippe said proudly. He looked tired, but thrilled.

This was a surprise. The doctor had said the baby wouldn't come for another two weeks, and Marie had secretly hoped she'd be there to help. "How wonderful! Congratulations, Philippe! And you, Miss Adeline, birthing a baby at only ten years old." Marie was astonished. "You'll make a fine doctor one day."

"Thank you, Maman," Adeline replied softly. Her timidity had returned, but Marie had seen the fire flash in her eyes when she spoke about the baby. Perhaps she did have a calling for healing.

Marie peppered Philippe with questions all the way home. Was it a normal birth or breech? How long was the labor? Did the doctor give her anything for the pain? How were Sara's spirits?

"See for yourself, Marie," Philippe said as he pulled up to the house. As the wagon dust settled, Marie sighed deeply. The beauty of the vineyard at harvest time, with its gentle slopes and lush vines, left her speechless. She could smell the eucalyptus trees and the sweet, earthy scent of freshly picked grapes wafting from the wagons. Pippa and Luc came running from the pump, where they'd been scrubbing up, to greet the carriage. Marie hopped down, and Pippa hugged her skirts. Luc scrambled into the wagon, eager to help his father unload, while Adeline followed her mother to the house.

Sara met them at the front door, holding a little white bundle. Her hair hung in silky waves, her cheeks glowed and her striking green eyes positively danced. Marie was so happy that Sara, who'd endured so much, now had this great joy in her life. She kissed her friend and admired the baby. His paper-thin eyelids were closed, his delicate hands folded together and his little lips were pursed in a bow. He was sleeping soundly.

"How are you feeling?" Marie asked, stepping into the kitchen. "You're radiant."

"I feel a bit tired, but so very happy!"

Marie pulled down the blanket to see more of him. "And what is the little prince named?"

"Ah, you two kept the secret?" Sara asked Adeline and Philippe, who'd just dropped the bags in the hallway. The two of them exchanged merry glances. Sara announced, "His name is Jean-Marie."

Although Marie rarely cried, a few drops welled in the corners of her eyes at this. "Oh, Sara. You didn't have to do that."

"We wanted to. If it hadn't been for you, I never would have survived New York or made it to California to eventually meet Philippe."

Marie was overwhelmed by the gesture, but all she could muster was a heartfelt "Thank you."

"What smells so good?" Adeline piped up.

"Rose is baking ham and biscuits," Sara announced. Just then Rose bustled back into the kitchen. She maneuvered around the crowd to the stove, donned an oven mitt and handed Adeline the spatula. She nodded to Marie. "Welcome, Miss Marie. We'll have dinner fixed in no time if you'd all shoo outdoors." She smiled at Adeline. "Miss A., will you help me serve?"

Marie was impressed. During her stay here, Adeline had milked a cow, baked biscuits, harvested grapes and, apparently, birthed a baby. Not too shabby for a city girl.


Adeline sat with Pippa on the bench in back of the house, patiently braiding a cornflower-blue silk ribbon through the toddler's straight, blond hair. Sara, washing clothes nearby, had noticed that Adeline was most content when her hands were engaged—kneading bread, cleaning out the larder or planting peas in the garden. "Where'd you find that ribbon, Adeline?"

Adeline blushed, but her eyes stayed fixed on her fingers. "I had a pair of old stockings that Maman wanted me to throw away, but instead I pulled out the ribbons from the tops, and saved the stockings for hand puppets. Something fun for Luc and Pippa, maybe," she said meekly. Her eyes flitted to Sara's and back again. "Do you think Maman will be cross?"

Sara stopped plunging and scrubbing the shirt in her hands. "I think your maman would be impressed by your resourcefulness."

"There, all done," Adeline announced with satisfaction. "You look like a princess!"

Pippa dashed up the stairs, turning just before she opened the door. "Looking glass, Maman?" She slurred, but Sara couldn't recall when Pippa had appeared more beautiful.

She felt a lump rise in her throat. "You go right ahead, dearest," she encouraged.

Sara watched Adeline carefully roll up the remaining blue ribbons and slip the small scissors into her dress pocket. "That was very kind of you, Adeline."

Adeline shrugged. "I want her to think she's pretty."

"Because of her lip?"

"No, that'll be fixed in time," Adeline said sagely. "I mean because her mother died."

"Oh." Sara was surprised and moved by Adeline's understanding. She didn't know how much Marie had told her daughter about Pippa's circumstances.

"You and Uncle Philippe take good care of her, Tante Sara. I just know what it feels like. She doesn't remember her real mother, and I don't remember my father." Adeline stared at her shoes for a moment before tucking her legs beneath her skirt. "Did you know my father, Tante Sara?"

Sara sucked in a sharp breath. "A little," she replied, wondering how much the girl knew.

"What did he look like? Maman doesn't have a photograph, and when I ask about him, she changes the subject."

As much as Sara abhorred thinking about Bastien Lemieux, she owed it to his child to answer her questions. "He was tall and thin, with jet-black hair, an aristocratic nose and eyes very similar in shade to yours."

She perked up. "So he was handsome?"

"Very," Sara confirmed.

"He died in a fire. He never married my mother. He married Luc's mother instead, but I don't blame Luc," Adeline said sweetly. "Maman said my father didn't want us, so that's why Uncle Philippe brought us to America." Her tone was matter-of-fact. Did she understand that Luc was not only Philippe's nephew, but Sara's too, born of her sister, Lydia? That Luc was her half-brother? Sara doubted Adeline remembered their stay at the Manhattan convent, over five years ago now.

"You are a very fortunate young lady to have such a considerate uncle and a mother who loves you dearly."

"I am. A lot luckier than other kids," Adeline agreed, her angelic face scrunched in contemplation. "How did you meet Uncle Philippe?" she asked. Sara could see Adeline struggling to piece the puzzle together in her mind.

Sara slid two clothespins off her belt and fastened a shirt to the line. "I knew Philippe and your father a long time ago in France, when I was a child. We lived in the same village of Vouvray, very close to Tours, where your mother's family still lives. But I met him again here in California four years ago, quite by accident, while I was pruning the vines here at Eagle's Run."

Adeline picked through the laundry bin, handing Sara a pair of soiled breeches to wash. "Did you always know you loved him?"

"What do you mean?"

"I mean, when you saw him again, did your heart know that you had loved him all those years ago?"

Sara marveled at the child's perceptive nature. "You know Adeline, I think I did. But it wasn't a woman's love then. When I was nine, it was a childish love. I think I loved his kindness, his protectiveness toward me at the time. But he was nine years older than I was, so I couldn't possibly have captured his attention then." She winked.

Adeline's chocolate-brown eyes filled with hope. "But when the time was right, Tante Sara, you scooped him up, didn't you?"

Sara laughed. "I think we scooped each other up. We have our difficulties, but in the end, I believe we are supposed to be together," she added wistfully, hoping her words were true.

Just then, Jess emerged from the stables. Adeline stared at him and sighed. He broke into a smile and waved. Sara watched the girl's face turn pink. Oh Lordy, she thought, Adeline Chevreau is sweet on Jess Sumter. Why on earth hadn't she seen this coming?

# Chapter 25

OCTOBER 1901

"Y ou will do no such thing!" Philippe roared. Sara placed a finger to her lips, trying to hush him. She'd just laid Johnny in his bassinet for his morning nap. But Philippe wouldn't let it go. He followed Sara from their bedroom down the stairs and into the foyer.

She whirled around, determined to fight. "We're marching for better pay and working conditions for the shopgirls and factory workers in Napa. The march—and the boycott—are the only ways to persuade these business owners to do the right thing," she countered passionately. She turned toward the kitchen, but Philippe caught her arm.

"If the shopgirls and factory workers don't like their wages, they can work elsewhere. Besides, good men like Jed Miller and Paul LeRoy aren't breaking any laws." He released her arm and pleaded, "These men are our customers, Sara. They're my friends."

Rubbing her aching arm, Sara replied stonily, "Your friends are wrong, Philippe."

He threw up his hands in exasperation. "What's next, Sara? Are you going to drag your club women over here and start picketing the vineyard demanding—oh, I don't know—better meals for the pickers?" The sharp look of disgust on his face stabbed her to the core. She stood frozen, bewildered by the stranger before her.

"You take an eager interest in the concerns of others," he persisted. "What about our vineyards? Our family?"

"I'm doing this for the girls—for their future. I'd hoped you'd be happy that Aurora and I formed this new club to distance ourselves from the temperance fanatics."

He exhaled loudly. "That's all well and good, and you know I think sensible women like you should be allowed to vote. But most women, if given the chance, will vote in favor of prohibition. You can't take sides against the family business!"

Philippe was right about prohibition, but Sara felt like she had no other choice. Standing up for Adeline and Pippa's rights was too important. She turned and walked into the kitchen.

Rose stood at the stove, humming to herself while frying up a skilletful of chicken. Sara felt a twinge of embarrassment upon realizing that Rose might have overheard their disagreement, but she hoped the sizzle of the oil in the pan and the clanking of crockery had obscured their voices in the hallway. "Children should be home any minute," Rose called, glancing at the clock that hung over the carefully set kitchen table. Sara brightened. Every weekday she looked forward to sharing lunch with them and hearing all the news from school. Her cheer faded when Philippe trailed her into the room. Rose quickly exited the kitchen, muttering about fetching more butter from the larder.

Sara would not back down. "Rose has Friday off. The two older ones will be in school, but I need you to watch Pippa and Johnny." She tilted her chin defiantly, although inside she was shaking like a leaf.

Philippe crossed his arms. "I will not allow you to make a public spectacle of yourself. I forbid it."

"You forbid it?" she exclaimed. "You don't own me."

He reached out, gripping her shoulders with his hands. She could see this was hard for him. "No. No, I don't. But if you do this, Sara, you'll be choosing these women and their political agenda over your own family." He released her and stomped outside, slamming the door shut behind him. Sara sank into a chair, shocked by her modern husband's outdated views. How could they see things so differently?

Thad Holmes had become extremely attentive. He settled their coffee cups and cake plates into the small areas of tabletop left around their open medical texts. They'd been studying in the hallway outside the crowded library for three hours now, and Marie had looked forward to this ten-minute break. "Lump of sugar?" Thad asked.

"No, thanks. This is fine," she murmured. He was a little too eager to please; Marie worried he might be smitten. She blew on her scalding coffee. He was nice-looking, with warm, brown eyes and wavy blond hair. But Marie thought of him more like a brother, and less like a romantic pursuit.

Thad sighed. "I have some disappointing news, Marie." His shoulders slumped and his face drooped into the sullen expression of a basset hound.

"What is it, Thad?" She hated to see her friend looking so defeated.

"I'm leaving the surgical program." He held up his hands, examining them with disgust. "I've had another seizure, and they can't allow an epileptic to be a surgeon—too risky for the patients."

"What a shame," Marie said sympathetically. "What will you do?" She was concerned Thad would give up entirely. He was the only friend she had here.

"I'll still pursue my medical degree, but in a less exciting field. Perhaps I'll become a family doctor who specializes in pumicing corns and treating rashes," he joked.

Marie laughed. "It's not that bad," she encouraged him. "You'll make a wonderful physician because you have an easy way with people. You make them feel comfortable. Even the prickly ones, like me."

"You're not prickly, you're just"—he paused—"careful."

"That's a good trait to have as a surgeon, no?"

"Absolutely," he replied, absentmindedly stirring his coffee. "Are you coming to the reception at Dr. Lane's house tomorrow night?"

Tomorrow was Friday. Usually Marie took the ferry to see Adeline on Fridays. "I don't think so."

Thad lowered his voice. "May I offer some advice, as your friend, Marie?"

Marie folded her hands on the table. "Of course."

"All the faculty and students are attending. If you don't make an appearance, even for an hour or so, you'll just give those cads more reason to talk about you behind your back."

"They still talk about me?" She was startled.

"Yes," Thad said, his eyes flashing to the huddle of students down the hall before returning to Marie's face.

"What do they say?" she whispered.

Thad shifted in his seat. "That you leave early every Friday and are never here studying on the weekends because you . . ."

"Because I?"

"Because . . . you have a lover." Thad's ears reddened.

Marie burst out laughing. "If only." What a preposterous accusation. "What else?" She wanted to hear it all.

"That he's a medical doctor, and he used his connections to get you into Cooper."

"That's insane!" Marie argued. "None of it's true, you know." But she had no intention of sharing the truth—that she had an illegitimate daughter living in Napa with family.

Thad looked relieved. "Of course not. All I'm saying is that the more standoffish you are, the more reason they have to concoct these outlandish stories and tarnish your reputation before you graduate."

Marie released an exasperated sigh. "I suppose you're right,

Thad. But just for the record," she said softly, "I'm not interested in any romance at this point in my life. I need to focus on my studies."

Thad leaned in and whispered, "It's a reception, Marie. Not a proposal."

She laughed, embarrassed, but reassured all the same. "I'll stop by for an hour. And you'll be there?" Marie might be able to endure the reception if he were.

"Right by your side."


Adeline was acting strangely. The last few days, she'd skipped off to school as usual in the morning but hardly said two words to Sara when she returned. After finishing her chores, she completed her homework in silence. At the dinner table, she picked at her food, eating only a few bites before claiming she was full. She answered Philippe's questions about school politely, but the light had vanished from her pretty face, replaced by shifty glances directed at Sara.

Tonight, when Adeline was washing the dishes, Sara placed an arm around her shoulders. "Are you well, Adeline?" The girl flinched, knocking Sara's arm away with her shoulder. "I'm fine. Excuse me, Tante Sara," she replied, fetching a stack of soiled bowls from the table.

Sara wondered if she was imagining things, but Adeline truly did seem uncharacteristically hostile toward her. Sara would bide her time until Marie arrived this weekend. Perhaps the child would talk to her mother.

~

Johnny began to stir in his bassinet at six o'clock Friday morning. Sara stretched her arm across the other side of the bed, hoping Philippe would curl his fingers around hers and pull her close, but all she felt was the soft sheets, still warm from his body. They hadn't spoken much since they'd argued on Wednesday, but Sara still naively hoped he'd change his mind. She couldn't have been more wrong—he was already gone.

Sara fed the children breakfast and then guided Adeline and Luc by mule to their school in Huichica, just across the creek. By the time she arrived in downtown Napa, she was thirty minutes late.

Sara was flabbergasted at the sheer size of the crowd assembled at the corner of First and Main. Women, shopgirls, tannery workers, laundresses—from Napa, Sonoma, St. Helena, Asti, San Rafael and Mill Valley—flooded the streets of Napa to support the unionists' plight. Their presence created an energetic whir, electrifying the air. She tucked Johnny in his sling and nestled him against her chest. Tightening her grip on Pippa's hand, she uttered a few words of reassurance, and followed Aurora deep into the sea of friends and strangers to take her place at the front of the parade behind their club's banner. Sara's palms began to sweat.

The protest started out calmly as the women and girls, heads held high, paraded down the dusty street. The day was uncommonly cool, a relief for the throngs of marchers packed like sardines in a can. After a quarter-mile or so, they fell into step with a beating drum near the back of the procession and the fervor of their chanting began to build. "Fair pay!" The crowd pushed forward, carrying Sara and the children along as though they were in a rowboat atop the crest of a powerful wave. Sara glanced down at Pippa. The girl's malformed lip quivered, and she clutched her mother's skirt. Sara edged away from Aurora and her friends toward the fringe of the crowd, but rows of men lined the sidewalks, hooting and hollering profanities. The policemen seemed to be encouraging their jeering, though the women's chanting eventually overpowered the men's shouts.

Sara's heartbeat quickened. If she continued with the march, and a riot erupted, Pippa could be crushed. If she stepped onto the sidewalk, the police might arrest her, or the dissenters might swarm her.

A boot smashed against Sara's shin, stopping her short. Just before she tripped and tumbled, she spied a pair of penetrating blue eyes. Philippe! He had appeared out of nowhere and moved quickly to hustle them out of harm's way, scooping up Pippa in one arm and catching Sara's waist with the other. He extracted them from the crowd in seconds and deposited them in a narrow alley between buildings, safe from view. Sara pressed her back against the brick wall, trying to recover her breath.

"Are you hurt?" Philippe asked in a husky voice. Sara shook her head. He squatted, tugged down her stocking, and lightly touched her leg. She winced.

Johnny's shrill cry startled them both. Philippe removed the baby from his sling and kissed his red, wrinkled forehead. "There, there, you're just a little knocked about, Johnny boy."

Then Philippe knelt down and wiped Pippa's tears away with his thumb. She buried her face in his neck. "Papa," she sighed with a relief Sara shared. Philippe flashed Sara a sharp, disapproving glance.

255

Sara's mind flipped back to the page in their shared history when he'd saved her from Saul Mittier, the town bully, back in Vouvray. She had been nine, he eighteen. Philippe was the same boy who'd picked Sara up from the dirt that day, and she was the same girl who'd smiled and feigned bravery. Perhaps they simply wanted different things now.

The butler guided Marie into the grand hall of Dr. Lane's mansion in Nob Hill. About forty students and professors were here, she guessed, grouped in tight-knit circles, drinking aperitifs and chatting amicably. Marie's gaze floated up to the high, coffered ceiling and the wide, winding mahogany staircase that served as the room's centerpiece. Windows rose from floor to ceiling, framed with striking green velvet damask draperies tied back with gold tassels. Marie was impressed but uneasy.

Dr. Lane's wife, whose first name she missed, greeted her with outstretched hands and a warm smile. Marie guessed she was in her early seventies, like her husband. Dr. Lane, one of the preeminent surgeons in the region and the founder of the college, stood across the room, surrounded by students.

"Do come in, Miss Chevreau!" she trilled. "Levi and I were so delighted you accepted the invitation to study at Cooper. You were his first choice, you know, from over thirty female applicants."

"I was?" Marie was so startled by Mrs. Lane's candor that she didn't know what else to say.

"Oh yes, he was very impressed with your medical experience in the field of midwifery, and that you'd already completed studies at the Women's Medical College." Marie was surprised Mrs. Lane was familiar with her résumé. "Shows you have gumption, my dear, and that you're serious about becoming a surgeon."

"I've never been more serious about anything."

Mrs. Lane rested a white-gloved hand on Marie's arm. "I believe you," she said lightly, "and I'm sure you'll get along famously, but for tonight, just relax and mingle." She gestured to the crowd of students gathering around a long table laden with platters of sandwiches and meat, cookies, cakes and punch. Mrs. Lane then stepped away to rejoin her husband, who was speaking to a rapt audience of doctors and students.

As bold as she was in the classroom or on the streets of New York, Marie was entirely uncomfortable in these surroundings. She moved to the edge of the crowd, hoping no one would notice her. Although she spoke French, Italian, English and a little Spanish, she'd never been skilled at small talk. She scanned the room, desperate to find a kind face.

The other women present were dressed simply but elegantly, in cotton, silk and lace evening dresses and gloves, with most wearing their hair up in Gibson tucks or topknots. Marie had chosen her best daywear: a navy and powder-blue striped dress, probably more suitable for a seashore outing than an evening reception. What did it matter anyhow what she wore tonight, when she'd soon be boarding a ferry bound for Napa? Just the thought of its rolling hills and abundant sunshine made Marie consider bolting for the door.

She was about to thank her hostess and quietly excuse herself when she spied Thad speaking with people whom she didn't know. When they finished their conversation, Marie drifted over to his side.

257

"You made it!" He beamed at her. "I thought you might chicken out."

"I was just about to." She grimaced.

Thad ignored her and turned to the three men next to him. "Tom Reynolds, Jim O'Hare and Reggie Miller, I'd like you to meet Marie Chevreau. She's a first-year, with me."

Marie assumed they must be second- or third-year students. She extended her hand, and Tom took it. "Welcome, Marie. Have they scared you off medicine yet?" he asked good-naturedly.

Marie shook his hand, and Thad chimed in again. "Not at all. In fact, it's Marie who's scaring the other first-years. She's had more experience than the lot of us."

"Really? How so?" Reggie asked, popping a cucumber sandwich in his mouth. He had curly orange hair, a freckled face and smooth, wide lips.

"Midwifery," she replied, waiting for their reaction.

"Is that so? How many babies have you delivered—on your own?" Tom seemed skeptical.

"Nine hundred fifty-two."

They could not have looked more stunned. Jim was the first to recover. "And how many of them survived, if I may ask?"

"Eight hundred thirty-five babies and nine hundred six mothers survived."

"That's quite good, statistically speaking, isn't it?" Jim looked to his friends, who were nodding in confirmation.

"Not good enough. That's why I'm here. To learn the latest cesarean section techniques so I can save more lives."

"An admirable goal," Thad encouraged.

"Indeed," Jim agreed, though to Marie he sounded half-hearted. "And speaking of such, did you see the article about Donnelly in the *Cooper Medical Review*?"

"They all think he's mad. Heart surgery on a patient with a bullet wound," Tom said.

"On a beating heart?" Thad lowered his voice, engrossed.

"So the patient is still alive?" Marie couldn't believe it. This type of surgery was unprecedented.

"No, the man died in surgery."

"That's sad, but chances are he would have died anyway," she declared. "Why not operate, if you can learn something from it?"

Her four fellow students stared at her. Marie filled a glass with water, waiting for the awkward silence to pass. Thad eventually cleared his throat and attempted to reignite the conversation with humor. "Of course, and when we're done experimenting with the live ones, we can dismember the cadavers to construct a Frankenstein of our own."

The men laughed, and although Marie joined in, her cheeks burned. Desperate for air, she excused herself politely. She was worried Thad would follow her, so she was relieved to find herself alone in the alcove beneath the cascading stairs. She stood by the open window, inhaling the crisp fall air and sipping her water. She peered beyond the velvet curtains, down Clay Street. The city was in full swing, with deliverymen, hackneys and evening paperboys scuttling about. The bustle reminded her of New York, but made her long for the wide streets and sun-drenched smell of Napa. She wanted to run there now, to cuddle Adeline in her arms and fall asleep to the chirping of crickets and the soft hoots of owls.

The clapping of hands and clinking of crystal pulled Marie out of her reverie. As everyone converged near her, Marie remained where she was, now eye-level with Dr. Lane's shoes as he stood on the stairs, welcoming his guests warmly. She almost spilled her water when a deep voice startled her.

"You shouldn't try so hard," Matthew Donnelly said, looking toward Dr. Lane.

"Excuse me?" Marie asked quietly, unsure if she'd heard correctly.

His voice was low, but his turquoise eyes locked with hers. "To force their acceptance," he said, flicking his head toward the medical students nearby, all hanging on Dr. Lane's every word.

Marie was tongue-tied. He lowered his head and explained, "This isn't a popularity contest, Miss Chevreau. It's survival of the fittest."

The crowd erupted in applause, and Marie and Donnelly followed suit to be polite. She hadn't heard a word Dr. Lane had said, but she was too distracted by Matthew Donnelly to care. He moved closer to her, as if eager to hear her response. When the guests finally dispersed and the din quieted, Marie replied coldly, "I'm well aware of that, Doctor."

"Are you?" His brow furrowed. "Because earlier, it looked like you were campaigning for class president at the punch bowl," he quipped. Marie blushed with embarrassment. She felt like a simpleton, not the smart, studious young woman she imagined herself to be.

She decided to end their conversation before she became the subject of more ridicule. When she glanced back up at him, he arched a brow. Did he enjoy badgering his students? And why had he even noticed her at the punch bowl? Perhaps this was another test. If she walked away now, without knocking him down a peg or two, he'd probably lose respect for her.

She smiled without humor and retorted, "Perhaps, but the talk at the punch bowl was more amusing than holding up the wall with my back, a feat you seemed to have mastered this evening."

He chuckled, his white Irish skin reddening. "You noticed?" When his face was animated like this, she thought she caught a glimpse of the soul behind the surgeon. He was whip-smart, and he intimidated Marie, but at least he was human. And he was handsome. Marie shoved that thought right out of her head. Desperate for distraction, she pulled her watch from her dress pocket. Five-thirty. The last ferry would leave in a half hour, and Marie still needed to collect her suitcase from her apartment a few blocks away.

"I have to go," she announced.

"Where?" he asked. Marie was surprised he cared.

"To catch the last ferry," she said slowly. She wasn't going to give him any more details about her life.

"Oh, yes," Donnelly said pleasantly, rocking back on his heels. Marie wondered if he'd already heard—or worse, believed—those rumors. "Enjoy your weekend," he said evenly.

"You as well." Marie smiled, unwilling to allow him to think their conversation had disquieted her. She turned to find her hosts. Even as she shook hands and thanked Dr. and Mrs. Lane, Marie felt Donnelly's eyes following her. She wasn't sure she liked the attention.

~

Marie heard the patter of small shoes in the hallway. Her door creaked open. "Maman?" Adeline poked her head into the bedroom where Marie was studying for her chemistry exam. She placed a mug of coffee atop a folded napkin, next to the stack of textbooks.

Marie stroked Adeline's long, dark hair absentmindedly. "Yes?" Adeline gazed for a moment out the window above the desk. Her eyelids were puffy from crying.

Sara had mentioned Adeline was upset about something, but when Marie had arrived a few hours ago, Adeline had behaved normally enough. "What is it, darling?" Marie rubbed her daughter's hands soothingly. Adeline started to shake and cry. "Are you hurt?"

Adeline took sharp, short breaths between sobs. "Jess told me something—a secret about Tante Sara. I told him it was a lie, that it never happened, but he overheard his ma and pa talking about her."

Marie couldn't imagine what this could be. "Out with it, child. What did he say?"

Adeline whispered, "He said Tante Sara killed Uncle Philippe's brother—my father!" Marie's heart dropped. She pressed her lips tight and closed her eyes. This was the day she'd always dreaded, but she thought she'd be the one to tell Adeline, not some loose-lipped farm boy. How the hell did he know anyway?

"Breathe deeply, Adeline. We'll talk when you're calm again." Marie pulled her near.

"So it's true?" The girl asked in a panicky voice.

How would Marie explain things so that she could understand? She took a deep breath. "She killed him accidentally while defending herself."

"From what?" How could Adeline know what her mother was implying?

"Your father was not a kind man. He was married to Sara's sister, Lydia, and he treated her badly. One night he hurt Tante Sara, and he would have done worse, if she hadn't stopped him."

"That's not what Jess said!"

"What makes you think Jess and his father know anything?" Marie was livid. "They may have heard some half-truths about our past, and now they're filling your head with nonsense rumors about your Tante Sara!"

"But she *killed* him, Maman." Marie realized the poor child feared for her own safety.

"Your father attacked Sara and hurt her very badly, just like he did her sister, Luc's mother. She had to stop him, or he might have killed her."

"But you told me he died in a fire," Adeline accused her.

Marie placed a hand on her knee. "There was a fire after. I thought you were too young to know everything that happened."

"Were you ever going to tell me?"

"Yes. Philippe, Sara and I all agreed we'd tell you and Luc together—when you were both older."

"So Uncle Philippe knows?" Her eyes grew large.

"He does, and he knows that Tante Sara had no choice. He loves her in spite of it."

"You can't leave me here with her!" Adeline pleaded.

"Darling," Marie soothed, kissing her small hands. "Sara

loves you. She's not a threat to anyone. She was the victim, not your father. I hate to say it, Adeline, but your father brought it upon himself."

"Because of her, I'll never know him!"

"Because of her, your half-brother Luc is still alive."

"But—"

Marie squeezed her daughter's hands. "Your father refused to marry me, and cast us both off." Her words were harsh to a child's ears, she knew, but this was the truth, and Adeline would have to face it. She squeezed her shoulders gently. "You're a beautiful, smart, kind girl who deserves more. You deserve to be loved dearly, like we all love you. Your father wasn't capable of loving anyone."

At this, Adeline's face shattered into a million emotions. Marie rocked her heartbroken daughter, and they slipped down onto the floor, holding each other in silence.

The next morning, Sara pressed fresh hay into the bottom of the wagon bed. Adeline handed her bottles of chardonnay and zinfandel, and jars of jam, which Sara nestled into the cushion of hay. After giving Sara four demijohns of lemonade, Adeline finally spoke up. "Maman tells me that you killed my father."

Marie had warned Sara this was coming. She replied softly, "Yes. It was an accident, Adeline, and I'm very sorry for it."

"Why are you sorry? Maman said he hurt you and your sister."

"He did, but I'm sorry that I had to . . . use such force to stop him." Sara looked tentatively at Adeline.

"Did your father die, too?"

Sara was taken aback. "Yes, in a mudslide when I was seventeen years old."

"You were young," Adeline said in a sweet, compassionate voice.

"I was, and it made me very sad. So I understand if you're sad, too."

Adeline hoisted herself up into the wagon seat and placed the last of the boxed pies on her lap. "You're not going to hurt me, are you, Tante Sara?"

Sara felt ill. "No," she replied hoarsely. She hugged Adeline and stroked her dark curls. "I love you like my own daughter. We will always be family."

Sara confronted Jess early the next morning while he was filling the horses' mangers with hay. When he saw her, he stabbed the pitchfork into the bale at his feet. "Ma'am?"

"What were you thinking, telling half-truths to a ten-year-old girl and scaring her senseless?" Sara demanded.

Jess held up his palms. "I only told Adeline what I heard from my father," he protested.

Sara fumed. She had to set the record straight, even if her past was none of his business. She stared the teenager down. "Philippe's brother was a brutal man who beat and raped my sister, and tried to rape me. When I fought him off, I accidentally killed him." She moved a step closer to Jess and hissed, "If you'd rather spend your days here than in the Napa County jail, then I'd suggest you stop spreading rumors and frightening little girls, understand?"

Jess flinched. "Yes, ma'am. Sorry, Mrs. Lemieux," he said, flustered. Just then, Philippe appeared at the door.

"How's it going in here?" He looked from Sara to Jess.

"Oh fine," Sara said breezily. "Jess was confused about a few things, but we've straightened everything out, haven't we?" She glanced back at the taciturn teenager, hoping Jess was convinced that her husband would lock him up if he ever crossed her again.

"Yes ma'am," he mumbled, swallowing loudly.

Though Sara and Philippe's relationship was strained at the moment, she knew he would back her on this. She squeezed his arm as she passed outside.

# Chapter 26

DECEMBER 1901

Marie had scored high marks on most of her midterm exams, but her fingers trembled as she scanned the list of her final grades: all mid-nineties, except for Donnelly's chemistry class. How could he justify giving her a measly eighty percent? Before she hopped the ferry to Napa for the Christmas break, she was determined to find out why he'd withheld the grade she knew she deserved. That Friday afternoon, she arrived at Donnelly's door during the last five minutes of his office hours and knocked.

There was no answer. Marie pounded again. "Dr. Donnelly?" she called.

Then, from down the hallway, she heard a voice summoning her. "Miss Chevreau?" It was Donnelly, holding a pocket watch. "This way, if you please." He vanished into the stairwell.

She followed him down two flights. He paused to hold the door for her, and she stepped outside, demanding, "Where are you taking me?"

"You're here about your grade, aren't you?"

He was exasperating. "Yes, but—"

"Follow me," he repeated and began to cross the street toward the hospital.

Marie clutched her books to her chest, rushing to keep up with him, like a puppy scampering after its master. She hated herself for it. Inside the hospital, Donnelly guided her to the operating amphitheater. As they took their places among the hundred other surgeons and students watching, he whispered, "Gangrene has set in, and he's going to make the cut right above the knee. Watch this." Marie bit her lip as the doctor sharpened his knives.

Unlike most of the other surgeons Marie had observed over the course of her first semester, this one spoke clearly and confidently during the entire operation, leading the observers on a captivating journey. He detailed his plans for anesthesia, for the guillotine amputation, for the patient's recovery. Marie was riveted.

The entire procedure lasted two hours. "Why is he bandaging the leg before he finishes closing?" Marie whispered, as the surgeon wrapped the patient's stump with a bulky dressing.

Donnelly replied, "They'll finish closing in a few days, when they're certain the tissue is free of infection."

Marie realized he was studying her. She shot him a sideways glance, frowning. "What is it, Doctor?"

He nodded toward the spectacle before them. "You love this, don't you?"

Marie flushed. He must think her an eccentric woman, an unfeminine freak to enjoy such a display. The truth was, she found it fascinating—and exhilarating. "It's all I want to do," she said, surprised by her own honesty.

The room was emptying, and she rose to leave. "Stay," he said gently. The nurses were tossing heaps of sheets and surgical gowns into the laundry bins. Then they scrubbed down the steel table and mopped the floor beneath it, paying no mind to the pair high up in the stands.

Donnelly fixed his eyes on Marie. "If I'd graded you solely on your written results, you would have earned ninety points. But, Miss Chevreau, if you're going to be a successful surgeon—able to explain your observations and decisions to a roomful of male surgeons like Dr. James did today—then you have to start speaking up in class, and outside of it."

Marie sat back, stunned. "I've answered all the questions you've asked."

"Yes, but I sense that you often disagree with your classmates, or with me. You need to speak up, even if you end up being wrong."

Marie stood abruptly. "I'm a woman, Dr. Donnelly. I can't afford to be wrong," she said flatly. "Thank you for your time," she added, before turning to leave.

Donnelly stood up as she left, calling after her. "Miss Chevreau, if you want a higher grade, I need to hear what you *think*, not just what you know."

Marie just kept walking, limbs shaking, madder than a wet hen.

For three days, Marie stewed over Donnelly's words. Only at Christmas Eve dinner was she able to quiet her frustration and take part in the family celebration. After saying grace, Marie studied the faces around the table. A wave of gratitude rushed over her. How lucky she and Adeline were to have a family like this, after so many years on their own with only the nuns in the Mott Street convent for company.

Sara held Johnny in her arms while Adeline spooned dabs of mashed potatoes into his mouth. Marie was startled by how grown-up her daughter appeared. Adeline's dark hair was tied back loosely in a red ribbon, and her cheeks flushed with warmth from the fire. She was no longer the awkward child Marie remembered. Since she'd arrived at Eagle's Run, her days had been filled with school, chores and playtime with Luc and Pippa. It seemed Adeline liked to be active and busy.

The dining room was lit with candles, and the savory scent of roasted turkey, toasted pine kernels and thistles wafted from the kitchen, reminding Marie of her childhood home at Christmastime. She hadn't seen her parents or siblings in over ten years, and they'd never even met Adeline. She felt a twinge of sadness. She received letters from them each month, but she missed her mother's tight embrace and her sweet smell of rosewater and mint.

Before dinner they'd finished trimming the tree with glass ornaments and electric lights, which Marie and Adeline had never seen before. The bulbs sparkled in shades of green, red and gold, giving the usually sparse parlor a festive air.

Pippa, who'd recently celebrated her fourth birthday, wriggled her way onto Aurora's lap. The child resembled one of the blond tree fairies from Adeline's books: she was spirited and petite, but sharp as a tack. Once they repaired her lip, Pippa would be able to express herself as eloquently as Adeline, and then they'd be in big trouble.

Aurora placed the maple-sugared sweet potatoes next to Marie, but Luc grabbed the spoon before she could take it. While Marie heaped potatoes, green beans, a bread roll and a stuffed tomato onto her plate, she watched Philippe carve the turkey. He'd always been a striking man. His hand had been badly scarred by fire last year, but that hadn't slowed him down. Today, however, his eyes were pink with exhaustion.

During her visits, Marie often spied him walking alone in the vineyard or standing on the plot of land where his winery had once been. His preoccupation, Marie suspected, was related to finances. Sara had confided to her that they'd just scraped together enough money this Christmas to make a small raisin layer cake and purchase one toy for each child. They were saving every spare dime to eventually rebuild.

Marie was about to inquire delicately about Philippe's plans when Aurora beat her to it. "So, Philippe, when are you going to rebuild the winery?" she asked boldly.

He was piling turkey slices high on a platter. "I thought you'd

271

at least wait until I sat down before interrogating me," he said with a laugh.

Sara shot Aurora a sharp glance, but the older woman ignored her. "We're all family here, Philippe," she said as she scooped beans onto her plate. "I'd just love to hear your ideas. In fact, I have a few of my own."

"That's no surprise to anyone, Aurora," Sara replied good-naturedly.

A wide grin lit Philippe's face. "Now that you mention it, well . . . I plan to break ground next summer on our new winery and tasting room!" he announced brightly.

Marie was surprised, and, judging by the dazed look on Sara's face, so was she. The children bobbed up and down in their seats and Aurora clapped her hands together, proclaiming, "I knew it! Brilliant!"

Amidst the excitement, Sara remained quietly rigid in her chair. Once the mouths around the table were filled again, and the chatter ceased, Sara turned to Philippe. "When," she asked deliberately, "did you decide all this?"

Rather than answering her, Philippe addressed everyone. "There's still a lot of planning to do, and we can't start until we've received deposits for the 1901 vintage. Because Sara has had such success with her wine wagon, I thought that instead of bringing the wine to the masses, we might bring the masses to the winery."

"How will you get them here? What design do you have in mind?" Aurora sopped her turkey in gravy. Marie continued to study Sara, hoping she'd be pleased with Philippe's compliment.

But Sara just stabbed at her potatoes with her fork, mashing them into smaller and smaller lumps.

"We'll probably hire a coach to drive visitors from Napa Junction, and the other local train stations, when the tasting room opens. We'll use the gravity-flow design for the winery. We'll crush on the third floor, ferment on the second and age the wines on the first floor and in the cellar, similar to the old winery."

Sara blanched. Aurora, who seemed oblivious of her discomfort, persisted. "With a tasting room on the first floor?"

"Enough to hold fifty comfortably," Philippe replied excitedly.

When Aurora and Philippe finally drew breath, Sara asked, "And why was I not consulted?"

Philippe stopped carving and smacked the knife down on the table. "Probably because you were too busy campaigning for the tannery workers, or the shopgirls, so they could have a longer lunch break—or whatever." His voice was dismissive, but anger lurked beneath his tone.

A hush fell over the table. Aurora was the first to risk speaking. "Oh, come now, Philippe. This is a joyous occasion," she reminded him. "Besides, it's my fault, not Sara's, that so much of her time is spent working for these causes." Aurora wriggled in her chair, and smoothed her napkin over her lap. "You know how I can be once I set my mind to a thing." She glanced apologetically at Sara.

Johnny's squirming and fussing broke the excruciating silence that followed. Sara hastened to her feet, bouncing the baby in her arms. "Please excuse me," she said with strained politeness. "I've no appetite."

~

After knocking on Sara's bedroom door, Marie entered. "Where's Johnny?" she asked her friend. Despite Sara's tall frame, she looked fragile right now, with her long legs dangling over the edge of the bed.

"Asleep." Sara shrugged.

Marie creaked the door shut behind her. "Aren't men the most infuriating creatures?" She sat down beside Sara, wrapping an arm around her shoulders.

Sara let out a short, mirthless laugh. "Yes, I believe they are," she sniffed, blotting her damp face with her dress sleeve.

Marie squeezed Sara's knotted shoulder. Her friend had endured so much, and at the young age of twenty-three, threw herself wholeheartedly into everything she did. It hurt to see her like this—and on Christmas Eve, no less.

"I can't manage this anymore, Marie." Sara's voice sounded panicked. "The children, the winemaking, the wagon, the club— what more does he want from me? He's so damn controlling about every aspect of the vineyard, he works all the time and he didn't even discuss this with me!"

"I know," Marie said comfortingly, "Philippe is headstrong, and hard-working and principled. But dearest," she murmured, "So are you."

"Maybe," Sara bristled. "But he doesn't understand my work with the women's club. What will life be for our daughters if they can't vote, or earn a fair wage? They'll be helpless—just like my mother."

"Not with you as their example. You're fearless, Sara," Marie said with admiration.

Sara smirked. "I think 'obstinate' is the word Philippe prefers." She clasped Marie's hand. "You're so kind, Marie, but would you mind terribly if I spent a few moments alone?"

Sara hadn't looked so forlorn since Lydia's death, over five years ago. No, not forlorn, Marie corrected herself. Sara was heartbroken. Marie patted her friend's knee, insisting, "After everything you two have been through, it's no wonder you're both on edge. I'm sure you'll work things out." Before she slipped out of the room, she glanced back, unable to hide her worry. "You simply must."

Sara pulled Maman's Christmas letter from her dress pocket and ran her fingers over the delicate handwriting. Her mother had posed a simple question—one that Philippe continually refused to answer.

*When might we replant the stricken vines?*

August had come and gone, and Philippe still owed Sara the money that was intended for Saint Martin. Maman and Jacques had used the lion's share of Saint Martin's profits to rebuild the main house. Now, understandably, they hoped to restore Saint Martin's damaged vines. Sara was frustrated by Philippe's evasiveness. If he had enough money to rebuild the Eagle's Run winery, then why couldn't Saint Martin receive the care and attention it needed, too?

Sara paced the room, tapping the wooden cross of her necklace against her lips, calmed by the repetition. The necklace reminded her of Jacques, who had carved the charm for Sara years ago. She thought back to her childhood days at Saint Martin. Sara remembered the flutter in her belly before she bit into the season's first grapes, anticipating sweetness, and fearing overripeness. The pebbles of Saint Martin's soil, even through layers of skirts, always roughened her knees as she pruned the vines and picked the fruit. She could still call to mind the smell of honeyed wine and French oak that greeted her when she opened the cellar door. With a familiar surge of longing, Sara recalled chasing Lydie through the sunflower field and the beauty of her sister's springy, tight curls.

Sara's heartbeat faltered, and she sealed her eyes shut, summoning the feel of Papa's hands on her waist as he lifted and twirled her around the makeshift dance floor they made in their parlor for parties. He always smelled of tobacco and spearmint, and his whiskers rasped her cheek when he kissed her goodnight. Sara gripped the bedpost, suddenly unsteadied. The bedroom blurred, but she blinked her tears away. As the objects around her sharpened again, so did Sara's resolve. Saint Martin was Papa, and she'd be damned if she'd turn her back on his legacy.

Sara sank to the floor and groped for the suitcase beneath the bed. She slid it out, dropped it on the bed quilt, and began to rifle through her chest of drawers, seizing garments and haphazardly heaping them into her suitcase. She was almost giddy: she had made her decision.

The sound of heavy footsteps on the stairs startled her. *Philippe.* Sara peeked in the looking glass. She couldn't help her ruddy cheeks and wild eyes, but at least her hair remained neatly pinned—

some semblance of composure. She inhaled deeply, clenched her hands and waited.

Sara didn't respond to his knocks at the door. When he stepped inside the room, he wore a sheepish expression. Until he caught sight of Sara's overflowing valise.

He closed the space between them in two strides and gripped her upper arms. "Where are you going?" he barked.

"Home to Saint Martin." Sara spoke forcefully, trying to hide the tremor in her voice.

Philippe was burning like a brazier now. "You're leaving me? And the children, too?" His fingers stabbed at the tender undersides of her arms. Sara was alarmed by his strength—he'd clearly restrained himself until that moment. "It's . . . only temporary," she stammered. "While I help them replant the vines," she finished, head held high.

Philippe let her go with a shove, and she stumbled back. Her calves hit the bed, forcing her to sit on the soft mattress. Bending over her, Philippe planted his hands beside her hips, driving Sara's weight back onto her elbows. His shoulders were so wide beneath the thin linen of his shirt. As he loomed over her, his shinbones pressed against hers, causing her to wince.

His face was so close now that she could smell the sweet sherry on his breath. Part of her wanted to slap him, but another irrational, yet equally forceful, part of her wanted to bite his lip, to seduce and torment him with her touch until he begged for mercy. He must have read her conflicting thoughts, for his expression softened, and he shifted his legs to straddle hers. Sara remained motionless. It seemed like an eternity before he gained enough mastery over his emotions to speak.

"Why the sudden urge to visit Saint Martin?" he asked evenly. "I told you we'd replant the vines—"

"It's been four years, Philippe! Four years since you promised to replant at Saint Martin, and now even Maman is losing patience!" Sara waved the letter in front of him. "You can't wait to rebuild the winery here, but did you ever intend to invest money in Saint Martin or repay me? No—because you don't care about anything except Eagle's Run!" she shouted, thrusting her hands against Philippe's chest, making just enough space to wriggle free of him and escape to the opposite side of the room.

Philippe edged toward her like a large, graceful cat. He stretched out a palm, as if trying to soothe her rage. Sara pressed her back against the wall.

"Sara, Eagle's Run is the primary source of our family's income, and for that reason alone, the winery and vines here take precedence. You know this—we built Eagle's Run together. I will instruct Jacques to replant at Saint Martin as soon as we start making a profit again."

Sara avoided his gaze. Was he telling her the truth?

Philippe shifted tack. "Tonight at dinner, I was trying to surprise you, not exclude you, but when you attacked me for not telling you about the winery earlier, I just . . . well, I lashed out."

Sara couldn't believe it. He'd humiliated her, in front of her children and her friends! Her eyes widened. "I'm never going to stop fighting, or campaigning, for the girls' rights!"

Philippe gave Sara an incredulous look. "And I'll never support your involvement with the suffrage movement, which you know could result in a prohibition and endanger everything I've worked for!" he thundered back. Down the hallway, Johnny began to wail.

"Everything *you've* worked for?" she hollered. "What do you think I've been doing all day? While you were out spending money on the vines here, who was *making* money down at the depot, pregnant, in the blistering heat? Me! I was the only one supporting this family!"

Philippe slammed his palm into the plaster wall near her head. White particles exploded into the air and showered onto the pine floorboards. Sara ducked to the right, flushed and scared, but Philippe hooked her waist with one powerful arm. "Damn it, Sara!" He pinned her shoulders to the wall. "You're not going anywhere until we talk this through!"

"Talk! Ha! You don't care what I think! You want to dictate what I do, when I do it—"

Philippe took the nape of Sara's neck in one hand, and his mouth crushed down upon hers, stealing her words, biting and bruising the tender flesh of her lips. Desperate for air, Sara scraped her nails down his cheeks, until he finally relented. She pulled away, panting.

Sara fought to find her feet and reclaim her breath. "You're a bully, Philippe—as wicked as your brother!" she shrieked. Her shoulders slumped and she dissolved in tears, but Philippe just looked stunned. He doubled over as though he'd been knifed.

The bedroom door crashed open. Aurora burst in, followed by a rush of warm, cinnamon-scented air from the kitchen. "What on earth?" Fury darkened her face. "You two are up here snarlin' like hellhounds, throwing each other into walls, and the children are downstairs, scared senseless!" Aurora stepped between them. "Have you lost your minds?"

Philippe sank to the floor, rested his elbows on parted knees and exhaled. Angry red lines streaked his cheeks. His bewildered expression caught Sara by surprise. "I'm sorry, Aurora," he said hoarsely.

Sara dabbed her stinging lip, trying to wipe away the taste of blood. She was too rattled to speak, and she certainly wouldn't apologize for Philippe. Instead, she stormed past Aurora to the other side of the bed, clicked the latch of her suitcase shut, and gripped the handle as if it were her only lifeline in a raging sea. Without a glance, or a word to anyone, Sara walked out.

She was only about a hundred paces north of the house when she heard someone approaching from behind. She felt a tug on her coat and whirled around, ready for battle, nearly sideswiping Aurora with the lantern. "Aurora!" The flicker of the flame illuminated her friend's kind face and perplexed expression.

"Where are you going?" Aurora asked, her tone rife with disapproval. "It's Christmas Eve! The children deserve visions of sugarplums, not two warring parents screaming and clawing at one another." Guilt consumed Sara, but—she reminded herself— this was Philippe's fault, not hers.

"I can't go back, Aurora," Sara whispered. Recalling his anger— and his unwillingness to listen to her—she felt suddenly queasy. "May I please stay with you?"

"Tonight? Or indefinitely?" Aurora countered.

"For tonight"—Sara shrugged—"and then, who knows?" she replied sadly. Aurora linked her arm through Sara's and the two continued, their skirts swishing against the vines, to Aurora's farmhouse.

Aurora ignited a fire in the hearth and put the kettle on. Bone-weary, Sara slipped into a wooden chair at the kitchen table. She rested her chin on threaded fingers. Aurora added a jigger of whiskey, a healthy tablespoon of honey and a dash of ground cloves to a pair of mugs, then lifted the whistling kettle and poured in the boiling water. She slid the hot toddy over to Sara and ordered her to stir.

Sara hung her head over the steaming brew and sighed. "I don't know what to do," she murmured.

Aurora's expression was unreadable, but she clanked the spoon loudly against her mug. "I'll tell you what you're going to do." She slurped the toddy and smacked her lips. "You're going to march yourself back home tomorrow morning and talk to your husband. I don't condone his rough behavior, but for God's sakes, Sara, he made a mistake! Think about what he's endured over the last year. His father shot himself, and his daughter nearly died in a fire that destroyed a year's worth of wine and profit! You both built Eagle's Run—and you're both responsible for its future. Philippe's trying to rebuild his entire *life*, and you're stompin' your little shoe, quibblin' about Saint Martin and the women's vote!" Aurora's palm slapped the table, causing Sara to flinch and flush pink. Aurora, and probably everyone else, had overheard their squabble. Aurora blew a loose strand of auburn hair from her forehead and released a frustrated sigh.

"All I'm saying is that you're not going to find a better man—one who cares more for you and the children—than Philippe Lemieux."

Sara tightened her grip on her warm mug. "You're not married to him."

Aurora's mouth twisted with skepticism. "Did he actually strike you?"

"No," Sara hesitated. "But he hit the wall pretty hard." She couldn't tell her friend about his violent kiss, or explain why she'd scratched him.

"You seem to be in a bit of a muddle, my dear," Aurora said sympathetically. In her usual methodical fashion, she untangled Sara's snarled thoughts. "Marriage isn't fifty-fifty all the time. Sometimes you'll need to put in eighty percent while he can only muster twenty, and vice versa." Sara recalled when she'd lost their baby. She'd drifted for months, barely connected to her body. Philippe had remained quietly by her side, never pressuring her. He'd assumed the burden of her chores and winemaking duties without complaint. That was the Philippe she loved—but she didn't understand why her simple demands had sparked such violence in him tonight.

"Sara." Aurora cocked a suggestive eyebrow. "When's the last time you two, er, you know, took a turn among the cabbages?"

Sara sputtered, choking on her drink. "I've never quite heard it referred to that way . . . but I suppose it's been a while." Maybe once or twice since Johnny had been born?

"I know it's not my business, and I'm not saying it'll fix the rift between you two, but it can't hurt." Aurora winked, a merry glint in her eye. "Sometimes you need a bit of sugar to set things right, no?"

~

An aching stiffness crept into Philippe's bones. He'd lain awake most of the night, staring at the ceiling, caught up in a storm of self-loathing. The sky had lightened almost imperceptibly, and he guessed it was nearly five o'clock. Powerless to undo his conduct from the night before, Philippe sprang out of bed, slipped on his boots and coat, and struck out in search of fresh air.

The early morning cold shocked his senses. Fortunately, the moon glowed full and bright, and he required no lantern. His feet carried him between the vine rows, past the grove of fragrant eucalyptus trees and down the path to Aurora's farm. He didn't know what he would say or do when he found Sara, but he suspected groveling would be involved.

He glimpsed her dark form against the stark white of Aurora's porch. Her breath rose in a steamy mist as she descended the stairs, and her face glowed in the silver moonlight. She glided, always so elegant to him, out into the garden, and raised her head to the night sky. Philippe inhaled sharply. "Damn, woman. You are ripping my guts out," he murmured to himself.

When he at last gathered the courage to approach, Philippe called her name softly, trying not to startle her. She turned slowly, as though she'd been expecting him, and he realized that she was still wearing her red dress from the night before—the one he'd purchased in Tours—though now it was partly concealed by the shawl draped over her shoulders. Her face was an impenetrable mask. Philippe's mind flashed to the night before. Sara had been so lovely in that dress. Although she'd regained her slim figure, her breasts, after months of nursing Johnny, were now subtly larger, fitting like perfectly round apples in his palm. His throat thickened with longing—and disgust for what he'd said and done to her.

Sara lingered several steps away from him. He didn't dare touch her. Instead, he shoved his hands in his pockets. "I'm an ass, Sara."

Her mouth twitched, not quite a smile. "Yes." She leveled him with her piercing green gaze and a sweep of her long lashes.

He paused, wondering how to bridge the distance between them. After a few moments, he extended a hand. "Walk with me?" he asked tenderly.

Sara studied him for a moment. She timidly touched the cheek she'd raked raw the night before to escape his rough embrace. "Does it sting?" she asked, not without sympathy.

"Like the dickens, but I deserved it." He smiled ruefully, enveloping her cold fingers in his. Sensing her hesitancy, Philippe tucked her hand in the crook of his elbow. He guided her down to the creek, where they walked in silence, with only the crunch of dried seagrass underfoot. Sara didn't melt into him as she normally did—instead, she remained rigid by his side. The playful ease that had existed between them had vanished after Johnny was born— supplanted by her stubbornness and his anger, Philippe reckoned.

"I have no excuse for behaving so . . . badly," he gulped, trying to forget how she'd compared him to Bastien. "But will you allow me to explain?" he hastened to add.

Sara nodded. They stopped under a cluster of barren maple saplings. Philippe smoothed his thumb over the fine bones of her hand. If they touched, he might have a better chance of conveying his sincerity.

Words, however, failed him. Instead, he lowered his forehead to hers, hoping she would somehow sense the depth of his regret.

"Sara," he implored.

She slid her palms up his neck and cradled his face. "Tell me," she pressed.

What should he say? He could explain how he loved the earthy scent of her flesh, the regal curve of her neck. He could confess that, as she slept, his fingers traced the loose waves of her chestnut hair—or that he delighted in pleasing her, in surrendering his soul as he made love to every inch of her supple body. After losing nearly everything, he was terrified of losing her, too. Philippe could offer a million reasons why he couldn't part with her, but only one truly mattered. "You're all I want," he declared.

She drew a deep breath. "You hurt me," Sara replied with a steely gaze. She wasn't referring to any physical pain.

"I know, and I'm deeply sorry for it. I'll send the vines to Jacques myself, as soon as possible, and we'll find a way through—"

Her fingertips brushed his lips, temporarily silencing him. She wore a tortured expression, and her eyes brimmed with tears.

"Stay," he whispered urgently.

She squeezed his hands. "You're smothering me."

Sadness lurked behind those blazing green eyes. How could he have been so blind? By trying to tame Sara's enthusiasm for new ideas, by railing against her principled approach to life and family, he was neglecting the very spirit of the girl he adored.

Choked with this realization of his failure, he pleaded, "Spend Christmas morning with us—for the children."

285

Sara paused for a moment, and then cautiously agreed. "And after that?" she asked, unable to meet his eye.

She didn't resist when he pulled her into his embrace and rested his chin in the soft nest of her hair. "After that," he whispered with certainty, "watch me win you back."

Sara awoke at home to the smell of buttermilk pancakes, bacon and black coffee. When she appeared in the kitchen, everyone wished her a happy Christmas, the children's voices muffled by the syrup-sodden cakes in their mouths. Marie was equally cheerful, and made no mention of the night before. After midday Mass at St. John's in Napa, Marie and Sara warmed the leftover turkey and served it with roasted parsnips, mashed potatoes, raspberry jam and, to the children's delight, fruit pudding. Throughout the day, Philippe kept his distance, which only made Sara more aware of him. She admired his strong hands when he poured her wine, the shape of his torso beneath his shirt as he stacked the firewood in the hearth and his impish eagerness to plop down cross-legged on the floor and help Adeline, Luc and Pippa tear the colored wrapping and ribbons from their gifts.

Later that evening, Marie and Adeline chatted amicably as they washed and dried the dishes, while Sara ushered Johnny and Luc upstairs to bed. Pippa, she guessed, was still playing cards downstairs with her papa. When Sara returned to the parlor to retrieve her, she was surprised to find Philippe reclined on the chaise in stocking feet, his long legs crossed at the ankles. His smooth, square jaw rested tenderly on Pippa's head as she nestled in the crook of his arm. Pippa's small hand curled around the stiff cotton of her father's collar. Both were dozing, and looked blissfully content. Sara's heart thudded, remembering the daughter she'd lost. She stroked Pippa's shiny blond hair, saying a silent prayer of gratitude for this girl who was alive, warm and breathing.

Sara sank down on the hassock by the fire, plagued with remorse. Would she have truly left the children last night and traveled all the way to France? In her unsettled state of mind, she very well might have. But it would have been wrong. Her life, and her loyalty, belonged to this family now. And as Philippe had said, they would—they must—find a way through.

When Sara finally peeled Pippa from her father's embrace, Philippe awoke with a start. "What time is it?" He rubbed his face.

Sara signaled for him to hush, and carried Pippa up to bed. After closing Pippa's bedroom door, Sara lingered in the hallway. She felt silly, waiting and hoping that Philippe would come to her, when she knew that after last night, he was likely, and understandably, avoiding her. So she made the decision to act. She brushed out her hair, put on a fresh nightdress and slipped downstairs in search of her husband. Philippe stared into the waning fire, its embers popping and hissing their adieu. As she knelt beside him, Philippe threaded his fingers between Sara's and smiled. "Thank you for today," he offered contritely. "It was a good day." Sara placed her cool hand against his hearth-warmed cheek, but desire soon won over, guiding her fingertips down his neck to the triangular thatch of fair, springy hair peeking through the slit of his open collar.

287

Philippe sat up. "Sara, you don't have to—that is to say . . . ," he stumbled. "What happened between us . . . I know it will take time to—"

Sara drew closer and began to probe his sweet, inviting mouth with her tongue. Philippe's young beard rasped her swollen lip, yet momentary discomfort soon turned to pleasure. She sighed a short, satisfied moan, and he palmed her breast in response, squeezing her nipple gently.

When she started to unbutton his shirt, Philippe abruptly sat back, feigning indignation. "Is this just because I gave in to what you wanted?" He thumbed her chin softly.

"No," she replied earnestly. She couldn't explain why she resented him one minute, and hungered for him the next. Maybe Aurora was right, she thought, blushing.

Philippe studied Sara with intense interest as she continued to undress him. She smoothed a hand down his chest to his navel. He stroked the small of her back. "Here?" he lifted a quizzical brow.

Sara glanced at the dark kitchen. "Marie and Adeline are in their room; everyone else is asleep," she said, slipping his belt from its buckle.

Philippe removed her hand and kissed her wedding band. "No," he said firmly, pulling Sara into his warmth. He whispered, "We need a proper bed for what I have in mind, Mrs. Lemieux." He met her inquiring gaze, smiling. "It's hard work, you know." His eyes gleamed with mischief.

"What is? To win me back?" she asked.

"No," he replied solemnly. "To make you forget why you ever wanted to leave."

# Chapter 27

**W**hile Philippe and Mac shepherded their wines through the aging process at Sumter's winery, Sara spent the winter days managing the vineyard workers, caring for Johnny and Pippa, and planning spring events for the club. Philippe had agreed to turn a blind eye to her activities, as long as she didn't openly lobby for prohibition, which she'd never consider.

With Adeline and Luc at the Las Amigas schoolhouse and the baby napping, Sara had time to teach Pippa. She wrote the letters of the alphabet on her slate with chalk, and Pippa traced each one, twisting her lips to try to make each letter's sound. Sara had until September to prepare Pippa for kindergarten. Luc had adapted easily enough to the schoolroom, but Pippa was a special case. She would be teased and would have trouble making friends because she couldn't really form a smile. Sara wanted Miss Howell, the children's teacher, to see past the child's defect. The best way to impress the teacher was to show her that Pippa could do all the things a normal kindergartener could—and more.

Aurora knocked on the kitchen door a half hour after they began. "Philippe here?" she whispered, as Sara invited her inside.

"No, he's meeting Adeline and Luc at the creek." Adeline was now comfortable taking Luc to school on the family mule, but still needed help crossing Carneros Creek at the ford. "What is it, Aurora?"

"I have something for you both, but I think—well, I think it's best if you give it to him." She handed an envelope to Sara before warming her hands near the firebox. "You'll say no, but I'm insisting, and that's the end of it."

A bank draft slid out of the envelope, made out to Philippe and Sara in the amount of three thousand dollars. Sara's mouth fell open. Aurora explained, "I'm making an investment in your new winery, and I want it finished by summer, in time for the harvest."

Sara knew that this money, when added to the insurance money and their meager savings, would finally enable them to build the winery and purchase new fermenting tanks, a crusher, a press and new cooperage. Aurora smiled, and shrugged. "You're my family. What good is a pile of money if you can't help those you love?"

Sara hugged her tightly. "You and Philippe can pay me a dividend each month out of your profits, until you're able to repay me in full."

"But Philippe—"

"You tell him he's like a son to me," Aurora said, her lips quivering with emotion. "You tell him I said that if he doesn't cash it, I'll hire an architect and start building the winery myself, whether he likes it or not."

Sara read the handwriting on the check again: three thousand dollars. When she looked up, Aurora was gone.

Embarrassed by their last encounter in the operating theater, Marie avoided looking at Matthew Donnelly for an entire week once classes started again. This semester, he was teaching her anatomy class. Even when her hand shot up to answer a question, she kept her eyes on the textbook in front of her. When she challenged another student's comment, she addressed him directly, not her professor. She thought it was an excellent strategy to employ for the balance of the semester—that is, until Donnelly called her up after class.

He sat on his desk, his right leg dangling casually over its edge. "Your name isn't on the list, Miss Chevreau."

"What list?" she asked.

Donnelly pointed to a sign-up sheet posted on the board for a two-week internship at his practice on Nob Hill.

"Write your name down," he commanded, holding out a pencil.

Marie squeezed her books tightly. Something in her bristled at the idea of Matthew Donnelly demanding she work for him in any capacity. Or maybe she worried that she couldn't work so closely with him without losing her concentration.

"I will think about it, Dr. Donnelly."

His lips formed a sly smile. "Please do."

As Marie walked out, she felt him staring. He was so nonchalant. Was it arrogance? His heart couldn't be racing like hers. Why did he want *her* to sign up? Did it satisfy him to criticize her at every turn, or did he truly want to help her?

For the next half hour, Marie paced up and down Webster Street near the side entrance of the college, cooling her heels and contemplating her future. She needed all the professional advantages she could get. She had to talk herself out of this infatuation. Donnelly must have flaws, and to discover them, she'd have to spend more time with him. Marie sighed, ducked back inside and signed up.

Philippe didn't know what to say: a check for three thousand dollars? He couldn't accept it. Sara, as usual, read his mind. "Aurora insisted we use it. We'll repay it over time, with dividends," she suggested.

How could he possibly borrow money from Aurora? But when he looked at Sara's maddeningly beautiful face and emerald eyes, he couldn't refuse. "She's a fine friend," he said roughly. "I'll pay her back by the end of the year, if all goes to plan."

"Picture it, Philippe—a huge stone winery with oak doors and a slate roof. Tasting tables and new barrels. Thirty or forty fermenting tanks, with gardens and a fishpond outside. The children would love a fishpond," she added wistfully.

Philippe laughed, seized with renewed vigor. "You've already spent the money!"

"I had a half hour before you returned with the children," Sara said lightly. "A girl can dream."

The check fluttered in Philippe's hand as his fingers skimmed her cheek. "No gardens or fishpond," he said, smiling crookedly. "In fact, no winery, either."

"No?" Sara was surprised.

"Not before I keep my promise to you." Sara's eyes widened with hope as he drew her close. He waited another moment before uttering the words she had waited four long years to hear.

"Place the order. We'll ship the vine cuttings in March."

# Chapter 28

**M**arie stood outside the three-story Queen Anne–style mansion in Nob Hill. The medical boarding house where Matthew Donnelly worked and lived was beautiful. She'd expected a run-down tenement, similar to the rooming houses she'd visited countless times on Mulberry Street in New York. Instead, this beauty's vast façade was painted pale blue, with ivory-trimmed oriel windows. Marie admired the portico, framed by four ornate columns, then stepped up onto the front porch and shook out her umbrella. The wooden doors reminded Marie of her old home at the Manhattan convent. Their elegant stained glass, however, brought her back to where she was, and she began to shake from top of her head to the soles of her rain-soaked shoes.

At seven in the morning the fog was dense, and the rain pattered softly but steadily. The air had already chilled her bones, causing her to sniffle and her toes to numb. She'd arrived a half-hour early, and although she didn't want to seem overeager, she thought about knocking and begging to warm herself by the fire.

While she deliberated on the doorstep, she saw a shadow behind the stained glass. The door opened and a tall, middle-aged nurse welcomed her in. She wore a blue cotton gown with a wide turned-down collar, a white apron and a matching muslin cap frilled around the face, the same uniform as the nurses at the Lane Hospital. Clearly, Dr. Donnelly was running a first-class operation.

The nurse gave Marie a once-over and her mouth formed a disapproving frown. "You'll catch pneumonia standing out there," she cautioned, ushering Marie into the foyer. "Do you have an appointment?" she asked, lifting Marie's coat from her shoulders and placing it on the nearby coat rack.

"No," Marie replied, "I'm one of Dr. Donnelly's students."

The nurse's face brightened. "You're Marie Chevreau, yes?" she asked excitedly. "I'm so pleased to meet the first female medical student at Cooper." She leaned Marie's umbrella against the cheerful gold-and-blue papered wall. "Never thought I'd live to see the day!" she added.

"Yes, um, thank you." Marie grinned awkwardly, fiddling with her gloves before shoving them in her coat pocket.

"I'm Jane Phillips—just Jane to you. You'll be assigned to me during your rotation. Come, let's warm you up with a strong coffee before the men get here." After handing Marie a cup, Jane excused herself to check on a patient. Sitting in the small parlor just off the foyer, Marie could hear the house coming to life. Matthew Donnelly's voice boomed from the stairwell above, and nurses chirped in answer. Marie's back straightened, and she clasped her china cup, bracing herself for the week's work. Even though she was only here to observe, she hoped to outdo the other three students in knowledge and skill. She had to show Matthew Donnelly just how serious she was about becoming a surgeon.

Marie greeted her fellow students—her rivals—and repeated their names in her head. She'd always had difficulty remembering names and devised a game to identify each by his most remarkable feature. John Redman was easy enough: his eyes were bloodshot either from lack of sleep, Marie thought, or an opium habit. The trim of Larry Deaver's coat looked like the pelt of an unfortunate beaver, and Fitz Greene had a wide, thin smile and drooping eyelids that reminded Marie of a frog. This was an easy lot. Marie had their names committed to memory by noon. Lord only knew what they thought of her.

The first day whizzed by. In the morning, Donnelly performed three surgeries, removing two gallbladders and an inflamed appendix just before it burst. The next day, however, proved more intriguing to Marie. She watched as Donnelly performed a hysterectomy on a twenty-two-year-old ex-prostitute.

The operating room, located in the rear annex off the first floor, contained all the most modern equipment: a steel operating table, bright oil lamps, linoleum floors and clean linen shirts and operating gowns hanging from pegs on the far wall. There was a rhythm to preparing the room before surgery. Donnelly would scrub his arms and hands with antiseptic, put on his operating gown and sterile gloves, then douse and cleanse his instruments with carbolic acid. The smell reminded Marie of Juicy Fruit chewing gum. Meanwhile, the nurses washed the patient's skin and administered chloroform through the mask covering his or her mouth and nose. Marie and the other students stood aside until the preparations were complete and the doctor and nurses closed in around the patient.

Marie found the boarding house a much more exciting venue in which to observe surgery than the Lane Hospital operating amphitheatre. Here she could see everything up close, and pose questions. Donnelly spoke almost the entire time, designating one student to take notes and the others to watch and answer his questions.

At the start of the hysterectomy, Marie's hopes were dashed when Donnelly relegated her to the post of note taker, charging her with the task of inscribing every step of the procedure. Fitz Greene would hand him instruments. None of them were as qualified as she was to assist in this type of surgery. Had they delivered a thousand babies or studied the anatomy of a woman's reproductive organs like she had?

Before the surgery began, Donnelly explained that the young woman suffered from inflammation of the pelvic organs caused by a gonorrheal infection and painful fibroids. After treating her unsuccessfully for several months, he believed surgery was the only option.

Though the woman's pulse weakened during the two-hour surgery, Donnelly worked quickly to remove the uterus, flush the abdomen with a saline solution and close the incision with layer suturing. Donnelly instructed the nurse to monitor her progress—

specifically her respiration, pulse and temperature—every hour following.

After the surgery, the students waited in the parlor for Donnelly to assign them tasks for the afternoon before he left to teach a class. Redman, the Beaver and the Frog chatted with nervous excitement about the possible outcomes of the surgery, and the perils, not to mention scandal, of their patient's former profession.

"How many do you think?" Deaver whispered.

Redman ogled Marie. "Hundreds, thousands, maybe more than one at a time," he suggested lewdly.

"C'mon. There's a lady present," Greene chided them. "Sorry, Miss Chevreau." Marie didn't acknowledge them.

Deaver smacked his lips. "Mmm. There's nothing I like more than a buttered bun, gents." Redman jabbed him with an elbow and the two convulsed in laughter.

If they hoped to shock Marie with their crassness, they would be disappointed. She had worked for years in the Manhattan slums, and to her they sounded like a bunch of naive schoolboys.

Marie remained silent, reviewing the notes she'd taken. A few minutes later, four men pushed through the front door, lugging the inert body of a young man. They shouted for the doctor. Two nurses ran forward with a stretcher, and Donnelly rushed down the stairs.

"What do we have?" he asked, pressing two fingers to the man's neck.

"Knife wound to the heart," Jane answered. Marie watched wide-eyed as small spurts of blood erupted from the man's chest wound. His complexion was ashen and his breathing shallow.

"How long ago?" Donnelly persisted.

"Ten minutes," one of the burly men said. "It happened in the alley."

"Name?"

"Tom Adler." He looked to be twenty-five or so, with a young beard, trim physique and chapped hands.

On bended knee, Donnelly listened to the man's chest, watching its rise and fall. Adler's eyes fluttered open, then shut again. "Tom, can you hear me? This is Dr. Donnelly. Are you in much pain?"

What an absurd question, Marie thought. Tom Adler groaned and nodded in answer. Donnelly placed his hand over the wound. "Tom, the knife went very deep, but we're going to try to repair it," he said loudly.

Adler had drifted back into unconsciousness. Donnelly looked around, asking, "Where's his family? Wife?" Marie knew then that he had decided to operate on Tom Adler's beating heart and wanted to obtain permission.

"Doesn't have any—he's a loner, that one."

"Let's bring him back." Donnelly gestured in the direction of the operating room as he hoisted his end of the stretcher, while another man lifted from behind. Donnelly searched the room before locking eyes with Marie. "I need you for this one," he said, his tone brusque and businesslike. She removed her jacket and followed the men into the operating theater.

Jane ushered everyone out of the room. When Donnelly finished scrubbing his arms and hands, he glanced at Marie. "You won't need that notebook," he said. "I want you to scrub in." She hadn't realized she was going to take part in the surgery. He must be joking! She had no training. But the look on his face told her he was stone-cold serious.

While she concentrated on fastidiously cleaning her hands, Donnelly sterilized his instruments, including a pair of bone nippers, and the nurses administered anesthesia. Once he was out, but still breathing, Donnelly examined the patient's chest.

"Don't worry, Miss Chevreau. Nothing to it," he quipped. Was he trying to put her at ease? Her heart was pounding out of her chest as a nurse fitted her with an oversized operating gown and cap. She took a deep breath to steady her nerves—and her hands.

"This is the second time I've operated on a patient's beating heart, Miss Chevreau. The first was six months ago—a patient with a gunshot wound at the hospital. Bullet went straight through his heart and out his back. There wasn't much to be done in that case. But this here . . ." His voice trailed off as he squatted down, placing himself at eye level with the man's chest. "This might actually work."

Marie stared at the bright red trickle pulsing from the wound just to the right of Adler's left nipple. Donnelly must have read her mind. "With every beat, his pulse grows weaker and his skin grows colder. Knife, Jane."

He made two sideways incisions next to the sternum—one along the third rib, the other along the sixth. He joined the parallel incisions with a vertical cut, creating a three-sided rectangle. Marie couldn't believe it. Donnelly was either a genius or a madman—she hadn't decided which. She held her breath as he lifted the flap of skin, tissue and muscle to expose the three ribs located directly over the heart.

Jane handed Donnelly the bone nippers, and Marie cringed at the *snap-snap-snap* of the three ribs being severed. Once the portions of bone were removed, he startled Marie again. "What do you see?" he asked.

She blinked, trying to regain her focus. "The pericardium."

"Yes, and why is it bulging out?"

Marie hesitated, but then understood what he was asking. "It's filling with blood from the damaged heart?"

Donnelly persisted. "And?"

"And . . ." Marie racked her brain for the answer, but it didn't come. Her face felt hot and prickly.

Donnelly explained, without a hint of irritation, "The heart is trying to pump, but it's battling against the pressure of the pericardium. We must relieve that pressure to allow the heart to pump and circulate blood more effectively." With that, he pierced the pericardium wall with his knife and blood began to pour out. "Jane, sponge. Miss Chevreau, feel his pulse now."

"Miss Chevreau?" When he called her name again, she felt for Adler's carotid artery, but didn't need to press hard. The pulse was strong, beautiful. "His heartbeat is improving every second."

"Now for the tricky part. I need you to slowly and gently cup your hand around his heart," he said, pronouncing each of his words distinctly. Marie was disturbed by the blood that continued to squirt with every beat of Tom Adler's heart.

"Like this," he demonstrated, cupping his palm around hers, shaping it into the form of a bird's nest. "Do it now," he commanded, his turquoise eyes trained on hers. Marie moved her hand under Adler's heart, which was the size of a fist and surprisingly warm. She knew that if she truly thought about what she was doing, she would lose her nerve. She decided to pretend that it was a hatchling fallen from a tree, in need of her care.

This bird was more slippery than she'd ever imagined. She was afraid to ask what was next.

"Hold it firmly, but don't squeeze too hard." To do what he asked was nearly impossible—with each beat, the heart jumped in her hand. "Now"—Donnelly inhaled—"pull it up toward the chest opening, so I can examine it."

She lifted the organ slowly, prepared to stop if she felt any resistance. She didn't want to risk tearing any of the connective tissues. A sheen of moisture had formed on her forehead. She could only hope she didn't look as terrified as she felt.

Donnelly pointed a finger at the laceration on the heart's left ventricle wall. "From this chamber, the oxygen-rich blood exits the heart to move through the body."

Marie understood. "So the blood was pouring out into the pericardium instead?"

"Exactly. Keep holding the heart steady, just like that," he instructed. Before he even asked, Jane handed him the catgut thread and a curved needle. Stitch by delicate stitch, Donnelly repaired the sliced ventricle wall.

The entire time, Marie held Tom Adler's heart in her hand. She expected it to suddenly seize or slow its pulsating, but it never did. On the contrary, his heartbeat grew stronger, and his feet changed color from a mottled purple to a healthier pink. After the last stitch, Donnelly instructed Marie to lower the heart back into its sac. When her hand was finally free, he shot her a knowing glance. "How'd that feel, Miss Chevreau?"

Marie released a sigh, finding it hard to believe what she'd just done. "Like the rush and tumble of a fifty-foot ocean wave." Jane guided her over to the basin, where she washed the blood off her hands, watching it swirl and sink into the drain below.

"Indeed, but the difference is you'll survive this—we all will." Donnelly stitched up the incisions he'd made. "Isn't that right, Mr. Adler?"

Though Adler was still unconscious, Marie believed Donnelly was right—that he would actually survive. When she returned to the table, she saw his fingers and lips were no longer blue, and his breathing was stronger. She placed a sympathetic hand on his shoulder, willing him to heal.

The operating room door opened, and Virginia, another nurse, appeared. "Dr. Donnelly, Miss O'Shea is on the telephone. Should I tell her you'll ring her back?" she asked, frowning.

Donnelly didn't look up. "No, thank you, Virginia. I'll speak with her in a moment." He carefully completed the stitches, placed the needle and thread back on the tray, and began to untie his operating gown. "All yours, Jane," he said pleasantly.

Marie's curiosity was piqued. Who was this Miss O'Shea, and why would Virginia tell Dr. Donnelly about her call in the middle of surgery?

Before he left the room, Donnelly turned and said, "Miss Chevreau, have your notes prepared by tomorrow morning. Tell the others you'll be presenting at seven sharp." Without another word, she was dismissed.

Notes? A comprehensive set of surgical notes would take a week, not an evening. Marie walked toward the front parlor, a bit dazed. Her peers rose hastily from their chairs.

"Well?" The Beaver craned his neck to catch Marie's eye.

The Frog chimed in. "Is your hand cramping from all that writing?" he teased, and they all chuckled.

Marie smiled, unwilling to share her secret. She had held a man's beating heart in her hand and helped save his life. Even their jeering couldn't stop the rush of adrenaline. As they left for the day, she called out, "Seven in the morning sharp, gentlemen. Donnelly's orders."

A few hours later, after she'd written up some preliminary notes, Marie picked up her bag of books and headed up the lapis-carpeted stairs, now covered with specks of lint and dirt from the day's traffic, into the first bedroom on the left. In the second of five beds, Marie came face to face with Tom Adler, just waking from his ordeal.

Jane and another nurse had bandaged the incisions, dressed him in warm woolen socks and covered him with blankets. They took care not to move him, instructing him to lie still and sleep. "You'll need all your strength, Mr. Adler, to make a full recovery. Only water and laudanum—no food until tomorrow."

Jane looked quizzically at Marie, who stood at the foot of the bed. "Oh," Marie said self-consciously, "I've no wish to intrude, Jane. It's just that I have to write up my notes, and I thought it would be easier to collect my thoughts if I sat with him until closing."

Jane winked approvingly. "I told Donnelly you were the best of the lot. You did well today. Others would have fainted dead away if they'd had to hold a man's heart in their hands." With that remark, Adler's eyes flew open and he looked to Jane for an explanation. "Oops," she said. "You're a sly one, Mr. Adler. I thought you were sleeping." Jane hugged an extra blanket to her chest and grinned. "She'll explain the whole procedure to you, won't you, Marie?"

Left alone with the patient, Marie pulled a chair up to his bedside and rested a hand on his arm. "Mr. Adler, the knife penetrated a portion of your heart, and Dr. Donnelly had to repair it. I lifted your heart up, very gently, so he could evaluate the damage and stitch it up right fine."

Adler's eyes flitted down to his chest, back to Marie, then to the open door. He looked like a frightened child. Perhaps he wasn't ready to hear all the details. She added cheerfully, "You were very lucky, Mr. Adler. Most doctors would have turned you away, thinking it was too risky to operate."

"And let me die?" he asked hoarsely.

"Most don't possess Dr. Donnelly's knowledge or skill." Marie poured water into a spoon, lifted Adler's head with her hand, and brought it to his lips. "This will wet your throat a bit."

He swallowed the cool water. "You're a nurse?" He glanced at her—she was wearing her gray walking suit and ivory shirtwaist today.

"No, I'm a medical student, training to be a surgeon."

"Naw, you're far too pretty," he flirted feebly. His dark eyelids closed in fatigue.

Marie placed a hand on his wrist to check his pulse: one hundred beats per minute—too high. "Thank you, Mr. Adler, but I think it's best if you save your compliments for the ladies of your acquaintance who will undoubtedly be thrilled to hear you're back on your feet. Now get some rest—you don't want to disappoint them."

Adler smiled weakly and drifted off to sleep.

Marie blinked at the blank sheet of paper, wondering how to describe the most incredible medical procedure she'd ever witnessed. She must keep her emotions in check, and detail only the diagnosis, treatment and the patient's progress. Yet as her memories of the surgery flooded back and her pencil glided across the page, Marie felt positively euphoric. She was in the right place, doing exactly what she loved. Even though it was late, she decided to stay and keep working. When the night nurse came in, she nudged Marie, who'd fallen asleep in her chair. Marie tucked back a strand of hair that had fallen in her face, thinking she must look ghastly. "I'm so sorry. What time is it?"

"Three in the morning," the nurse whispered, placing a finger to her lips and glancing at the other four patients in the room. "How is he?"

"Pulse was normal an hour ago, down from one hundred earlier."

"Don't pester him with questions when he wakes," the nurse ordered. Marie still had to organize her notes into a report that she could present to Donnelly and her peers in four hours. As she shoved her papers into her bag, her stomach gurgled violently. Marie was ravenous. She would have sold her soul for a croissant and a cup of strong tea.

As she descended the stairs, Marie gazed up at the treads rising to the third floor. Was Donnelly sleeping soundly or reviewing the surgery in his mind, restless from yesterday's excitement like her? Probably sleeping, Marie decided. He'd be used to this kind of thrill by now.

She walked toward the kitchen, which was located next to the operating room, hoping to find something hot to drink or a scrap of leftover food in the icebox. She didn't dare leave the building in the middle of the night. In the larder, Marie found a paper bag containing remnants of day-old bread. She bit in, nearly breaking a tooth on the stale crust. She heated some water and rummaged around until she found a tea bag. Finally, Marie fanned out her notes on the small, square table where the nurses ate their lunches.

Marie hadn't been this tired since Adeline had been awake nights teething. She tried to rub the blurriness from her eyes and focus on what she was going to emphasize when she presented her report in the morning.

"Ahem." Marie lifted her head off her forearm and peeled her eyes open. "Good morning, Miss Chevreau," Donnelly said, standing over her with an amused expression on his face.

Marie started when she saw him and then looked down at her notebook, the cold cup of tea and the sprinkling of breadcrumbs on her napkin. "I thought a mouse had stowed away in the kitchen," he mused. "Imagine my relief to find it's only one of my overworked students." He was dressed in a fresh shirt and suit, and appeared clean-shaven and energetic. In fact, Marie had never seen any man look better.

"I'm so sorry," she muttered as she ran her hands over her matted hair, then down her warm cheeks before folding them in her lap. She must look haggard, she thought, with a wave of embarrassment. Determined to keep the conversation brief, she inquired about the time.

"Six-thirty. Do you like coffee, Miss Chevreau?" he asked as he filled the kettle with water and set it on the stove.

He made coffee? "Ah, yes, thank you," she replied self-consciously.

Donnelly scooped grounds from a tin and emptied them into the filter of an elegant French drip pot. She had noticed the house was filled with many nice things: oriental rugs, top-of-the-line surgical equipment, electric lighting and sparkling faucets with porcelain sinks and running water. His family must be wealthy, she guessed, because surgeons didn't earn much. They were more likely to receive a turkey or a year's worth of free laundry for a surgery than actual payment for their work. Maybe that was another benefit to running your own medical boarding house: you could pick and choose your patients.

Waiting for the kettle to boil, Donnelly leaned against the counter. "How's your report coming along?"

Marie sat up and cleared her throat. What she really needed right now was a toothbrush and some powder. "It's done."

His brow scrunched. "You were here through the night?"

She stacked her papers and books neatly to make room for Donnelly at the table. "I thought it would be easier to determine the patient's progress if I were actually witnessing the patient's progress."

"Good idea. When's the last time you saw him?"

"Three and a half hours ago. How is he now?" She knew Donnelly wouldn't have been able to pass the second floor this morning without checking in on his prize patient.

"Excellent. He's alert, vitals are good and pulse is back to normal. Today we'll start him on some broth and lime-water." Donnelly paused, his sea-green eyes searching hers. "Are you tired?"

Marie shrugged. "I suppose, but I'm used to staying up." She almost slipped and said *when my daughter was a baby*, but caught herself. "As a midwife, my services were often required during the night."

Before he could respond, the kettle began to squeal. Donnelly removed it from the stove and poured water into the drip pot. "I subscribe to the Creoles' assertion that coffee promotes longevity, Miss Chevreau. I simply can't do without." He smiled brightly. Marie found herself admiring his white teeth.

She wondered whether he had a kitchen in his third-floor apartment. She'd rummaged through the cabinets last night and was certain there was nothing to eat here. "Do you eat breakfast?" she asked.

"Of course," Donnelly said, checking his pocket watch. "As a matter of fact, Virginia just ran out to fetch some. Free, fresh beignets are just one of the perks of having relieved the baker of his colitis last month."

Marie narrowed her eyes and tipped her head. "I never thought I'd hear the words 'beignet' and 'colitis' in the same sentence, but thank you for that."

Donnelly's laugh was unexpectedly loud and infectious. Marie found herself trying to puzzle out this enigma of a man, who sliced people open for a living, yet made his own coffee and was always beautifully turned-out, even beneath his linen surgical gown. His wavy brown hair was neatly trimmed, and this morning he wore a navy blue worsted wool suit with a high-collared shirt and gray tie. Not a thread was out of place. On a regular day, Marie knew she was fairly attractive, but this morning her hair was disheveled, her dress creased and her eyes probably lined with dark circles. She couldn't wait to escape to find a looking glass. However, when Donnelly placed a piping hot mug of coffee before her, she couldn't resist. She would stay a few more minutes before excusing herself to freshen up.

Virginia arrived, announcing, "Hot beignets!" When she spied Marie, she seemed surprised. "Miss Chevreau, whatever are you doing here?"

"Oh, well . . ." Marie blushed, but Donnelly interrupted.

"I came upon Miss Chevreau here in the kitchen, hard at work outlining the particulars of yesterday's heart surgery. I'm a bit of a taskmaster, but I'm sure that if Miss Chevreau has any questions, you'd be happy to advise her, wouldn't you, Virginia?"

"Of course," Virginia said as she handed the bag to Donnelly.

The scent of sugared pastry filled the room, and Marie cleared her throat to mask the sound of her stomach rumbling. "Thanks, Virginia," Donnelly said as he sprang up to retrieve two plates from the cabinet. "We'll see you later tonight." The nurse nodded and ducked out.

"I'd like to ask you a favor today," he ventured. "When you're relaying the details of the heart surgery to your classmates, I'd prefer if you didn't mention your role." He threw her a sideways glance. "I doubt the faculty at the college would approve." He bit into a beignet.

Marie was bewildered. "Wouldn't approve because I'm a woman?"

He looked at her strangely while he finished chewing. He dabbed a napkin to his mouth. "No. Wouldn't approve because you're a first-year medical student. It's unorthodox."

Another sip of coffee chased away the mossy sensation in her mouth. "Then why did you ask me to assist?"

Donnelly eyeballed the doorway before his gaze came to rest intently on Marie. He lowered his voice. "Because you have the smallest hands, and you were the most suitable choice at that moment." With that he excused himself from the table, pastry and coffee in hand, and headed for the door. Before leaving, he turned, looked at his pocket watch and announced, "Five minutes, Miss Chevreau." Marie gobbled down her breakfast, piled their plates in the sink and rushed to the powder room.

She finished her presentation of Adler's case without divulging that she'd been the one to hold his heart in her hand. Though Marie was disappointed that her name could not appear in the final record of the surgery, she thrilled in the knowledge that Donnelly had placed his confidence in her.

The following week proved less exhausting than the first. By the time Friday arrived, ten days had passed since Tom Adler's heart surgery and the incisions showed no signs of infection. He'd even taken his first slow steps around the second floor, holding tightly to the railing that surrounded the stairwell. Adler was in high spirits, waving to his fellow patients and pausing to flirt with the nurses. Marie was surprised; the man had been described as a loner, but he was behaving as if he did indeed have a new lease on life. Although she'd probably only ever tell Sara, Philippe and Adeline, she was pleased to have played a small part in Adler's recovery. She was disappointed that her rotation at the boarding house was ending. These two weeks had been the most exciting of her life.

When she walked out the boarding house door on her final day, there was no one in the foyer, no one to wish her luck. All the nurses had scattered, tending to their patients, and Donnelly was nowhere to be found. Marie trailed behind the Beaver, the Frog and Redman, who'd hailed hackneys to deliver them home. She made her way up the steep street toward the cable car, dragging her small suitcase for the weekend. She nearly jumped out of her skin when she heard a *beep-beep* behind her. Marie whirled around to see a shiny black car pull up to the curb. She still found it odd to see a vehicle with no horse. Matthew Donnelly sat behind the wheel of the sporty runabout, with a grin on his face.

"Get in," he called as he stepped out, took Marie's bag from her hands, and secured it in the small trunk of the car next to another case. He offered his hand, but Marie just stared at him.

"You're going to the Ferry Building, aren't you?" Marie nodded, her forehead creased in disbelief. "Me, too. Get in," he ordered, as if it were the most natural thing in the world for her to catch a ride with her professor. Unsure of how to decline politely, she slid onto the red leather seat.

Marie held on to her hat as they charged down California Street, dodging horse-drawn carriages, cable cars and omnibuses. She found herself gripping the armrest and laughing out loud— the sensation felt like flying through the air on a rope swing. When they arrived, less than ten minutes later, Marie was windblown and short of breath.

"Great fun, isn't it?" Donnelly's eyes watered, and his nose was pink from the crisp winter air. Without the white coat, and with his disheveled hair, he seemed almost mortal.

"Yes," Marie agreed.

She dangled a leg out the side of the car, preparing to jump down, when Donnelly placed a hand on her arm. "Please wait. The descent is trickier than it looks." He came to her side to help her down. When he unloaded their cases and carried them up to the ticket window, Marie realized she didn't want to say goodbye. She followed him, waiting to see what would happen next.

When it was their turn at the ticket window, he stood aside, allowing Marie to step up first. "Round trip to Vallejo, returning Sunday," she said, sliding two dollars in change over to the ticket agent.

Donnelly, too tall to look the man in the eye, crouched down to speak through the glass. "Same, sir."

Marie was surprised. Why would he travel to Vallejo? Was he visiting the military hospital there? Before she could ask, he picked up her bag and walked toward the ferryboat. "So, are you staying in Vallejo, Miss Chevreau?" he called out.

Marie quickened her pace to keep up with his long stride. "Ah, no. I'm taking the train to Napa Junction, where a friend is picking me up." She paused, worried that she'd given him too much information. Would he think she was meeting the fictional lover? "They're like family," she clarified.

"Excellent," he replied enthusiastically. "Family support is important when you're trying to advance through medical school." His smile was so genuine that Marie's stomach somersaulted. "A short break from those tedious professors," he teased.

Marie laughed. "Yes, they can drone on. And where are you headed?"

"One stop north of the junction—Napa Depot. I'm staying at a hotel in the city."

She didn't want to pry, but she had taken an interest now. "Do you have a patient there?"

"On the weekend? Heavens, no."

"So you're visiting friends?" Marie persisted.

"Family." He wagged a finger. "You're a bit nosy, aren't you?"

"Maybe"—Marie shrugged—"but I wouldn't make a very good surgeon if I wasn't."

Donnelly chuckled. "Fair enough, Miss Chevreau." He stopped at the gangplank. "After you."

Marie thought they'd part ways aboard the ferry, but he stayed by her side. The fifty-minute journey passed quickly. He shared stories of surgical triumphs and disasters, and she countered with tales of her most harrowing births. He engaged completely with her, asking questions and offering his own ideas for surgical solutions. The professional barrier that separated professor from student seemed to vanish, and they leaned on the railing, elbow to elbow, chatting like old friends.

As they neared Vallejo, he pointed to Mare Island. "Do you know General Vallejo actually named the island himself? When he was moving his livestock across the San Pablo Bay, a strong wind capsized the vessel. His prize white mare swam ashore and was found alone on the island. After he recovered the horse, he dubbed the land Isla de la Yegua, or Island of the Mare."

They spent another hour together during the train ride to Napa Junction, but Marie could have listened to Donnelly all day. They talked about his brother in St. Helena, and her parents' tavern in Tours. The train slowed as it approached the station, and Donnelly looked north toward the sprawling farmland and vineyards beyond. "Do you know why they call this Rancho Rincon de los Carneros?"

"I didn't know that was its full name."

"Indeed. 'Carneros' means sheep. Farmers flocked to the area to raise sheep and cattle here, since it's so fertile." He added apologetically, "I'm a bit of a history buff, if you haven't noticed."

"Do you visit the valley often?"

"Every month or so, I meet up with my brother and sister-in-law in Napa City."

"Oh." Marie wanted to ask more, but the train had stopped. She spied Philippe on the platform, his eyes scanning the train windows for her. Donnelly stood up and took her suitcase down from the luggage rack, following her sight line. "Your friend?"

She couldn't possibly tell him that Philippe was her daughter's uncle. "My friend's husband. They own a vineyard in Carneros," she explained.

"Oh," Donnelly said thoughtfully, "what kind of wine?"

"Cabernet, chardonnay and zinfandel, too, I think. I'm not much of a wine drinker myself, but Eagle's Run has an excellent reputation."

"Eagle's Run . . . you know, I believe I've tasted it." A booming voice announced the Napa Junction stop.

"Let me carry this out for you," Donnelly insisted, lifting her book-filled suitcase as though it weighed no more than a bowl of cream.

Marie couldn't think of anything more awkward than having to introduce Matthew to Philippe, so she held her breath as she stepped off the train onto the wooden platform below. A playful grin tugged on Philippe's lips as he took in the sight of Marie with this strange man. "Philippe Lemieux, this is Dr. Matthew Donnelly," she said offhandedly. "He's one of my professors, traveling to the city this weekend."

"Just Matthew," Donnelly said, shaking Philippe's hand.

"Pleasure," Philippe said, a strange expression on his face.

"I've got to jump back on, but I hope we meet again," Donnelly replied. He tipped his hat to Marie. "Miss Chevreau."

Philippe couldn't wait five minutes before he started ribbing Marie about her traveling companion. It turned out he already knew far more about Matthew Donnelly than Marie did. "You really don't know who he is, do you?"

"Other than a talented surgeon?"

"Ah, yes. He's the youngest son of Rourke Donnelly, the San Francisco iron tycoon. Their foundry is just south of Market."

This was impossible. Or was it? Marie recalled Donnelly's

spacious, well-appointed surgery and boarding house, his impeccably tailored clothes and his apparent knowledge of fine wine. She snapped her eyes shut, a pained look on her face. As if things weren't complicated enough. "Are you certain?"

Philippe raised his eyebrows. "Yes! I've seen his photograph in the *Chronicle*, and I deliver wine to his brother's place in St. Helena every month. Rourke Donnelly owns San Francisco Iron Works. He supplies iron for the navy's cruisers and weapons. He's used the capital from that business to buy up gasworks, railroads, timberlands and real estate. They're one of the wealthiest families in San Francisco."

Marie felt nauseated. Her mind whirled, reviewing every exchange she'd had with Donnelly. Had he ever dropped the slightest hint? Of course not. "If that's true, why wouldn't my classmates have mentioned it? And why wouldn't he have hired a coach to bring him to Napa?" she asked.

"Your classmates already know—heck, everybody knows. As for the coach"—Philippe nudged Marie with his shoulder—"perhaps Dr. Donnelly had a compelling reason to take the train." He snapped the reins, adding cheerfully, "You must have done something to impress him."

# Chapter 29

"Maman, wake up!" Adeline set a breakfast tray on Marie's bedside table in the room they shared.

Marie rubbed her eyes and stretched her arms. She'd stayed up late last night, talking with Sara. "What time is it?"

"Nearly seven-thirty! Luc and I have already milked the cows, and Pippa is helping us with the laundry, so if you have any, just give it to me now. Uncle Philippe is pruning the vines and is driving to town around noon."

"Well, then," Marie said happily, "I'd best get my lazy rump out of bed!" Adeline pecked her mother on the cheek. "How was school this week?" Adeline seemed to like the one-room schoolhouse off Buchli Road. There were thirty students, aged five to twelve, and Miss Howell was a stern disciplinarian. She frightened Marie a bit, but Adeline didn't seem to mind her.

"Miss Howell is teaching the older students about the systems of the body. We learned about the circulatory system. It's amazing." Perhaps Adeline was a kindred spirit after all.

"You know, you could be a nurse or a doctor when you're older," Marie encouraged. "You have just the right mix of brains and compassion." Adeline beamed. Marie hesitated, but then decided to tell Adeline her secret. "Guess what I did two weeks ago? You can't tell a soul."

"What, Maman?" Adeline whispered, closing the door.

"I held a human heart in my hand."

Adeline sucked in a breath. Her eyes filled with wonder. "A live, beating heart?"

"Yes, truly. You know I've been working in a medical boarding house? Well, a patient came in with a stab wound."

Shock registered on Adeline's face. "Was it awfully bloody?"

"Yes, but no more bloody than a baby's birth." Adeline's lips formed a small *O*.

"The doctor sewed the patient's heart up while I held it in my palm, and the man's alive today." Marie felt a new rush of adrenaline.

"That's a miracle, Maman."

"A bit of a miracle, yes, but mostly just a daring and highly skilled surgeon."

Adeline thought about that for a moment. "Can you imagine being able to save someone's life like that? He must have special powers, Maman." Adeline bounced up, heading for the door. Before stepping into the hallway, she whirled around, her soft ponytail swaying, to say, "I'm so glad you're home, Maman!"

~

Marie sat at the kitchen table, books stacked high and papers scattered. If she had to study, she preferred to do it in the company of others, so at least she could pretend she was part of their world for the weekend. Sara stood by the window, bunching small balls of dough in her hands and arranging them in the cast-iron pan. It was four o'clock and they'd already started preparing the evening meal. Sara craned her neck to look outside. "We'd best wash up and change for dinner." She wiped her hands on her apron and flashed Marie a conspiratorial grin. "Philippe's brought a guest."

Marie leapt up as Donnelly came into view through the windowpane, seated in the wagon next to Philippe. They were chatting as though they'd known each other forever. "What on earth?" Marie was horrified. Obviously Philippe had told Sara all about Donnelly. Why would they meddle in her life like this? She drummed her fingers against her lips. Now she'd have to tell Donnelly about Adeline. She wasn't ready to share this part of her life with him. She didn't know if she'd ever be ready.

She gathered her books and hurried down the hall to her bedroom. She felt eighteen again—rejected by Bastien and scared of being judged for bearing a child out of wedlock.

She paced around the room, trying to calm her nerves. She could hear Luc, Adeline and Pippa outside the window. They'd all rushed out to greet the mystery guest, eager to cajole him into playing games with them. Marie heard his voice above all the others, greeting Sara, offering candies to the children. He sounded delighted to be here. Marie contemplated hiding in the closet for the evening.

When she couldn't avoid it any longer, she appeared in the parlor. He was sitting on the floor, eyes blindfolded, while Luc and Pippa ran around him giggling. "What brings you here, Dr. Donnelly?" She tried to sound nonchalant.

His head whipped around, and he jumped up, flipping off his blindfold to greet her. Marie covered her mouth to stifle a laugh. For once, he seemed like the fish out of water. "I hope you don't mind. I met Philippe in town this afternoon and, since I didn't have any plans, he suggested I dine with you all tonight." He was in such high spirits, she could hardly find fault with him.

"Of course." Marie tried to sound pleased.

He moved closer to her, away from the children. "Have I made you uncomfortable?" He searched her eyes.

"No," Marie lied. She rubbed her forehead, wondering if he knew. "Have you met everyone?" she asked, with her emphasis carefully placed on the last word.

Understanding flickered in his eyes. "Yes, I have." His intonation was clear: he was not troubled by the existence of her daughter, and he would keep her secret. His face broke into a smile. "You mean these savages here, who've blindfolded me, roped me up and fed me nothing but worms?"

"Ew!" Pippa and Luc shouted in unison while Adeline watched with delight.

Rose and Sara had soon whipped up a simple but delicious meal of meat pies, potatoes and rolls. Philippe dug out bottles of his 1896 chardonnay and 1897 cabernet from his private cellar. Even Marie enjoyed a couple glasses of wine.

"Your sister-in-law Bridget and her daughter were very kind to me when I first started selling wine at the Napa Junction," Sara said to Donnelly. "Over the past six months, she's introduced our wines to her friends. We sold out of the '99 cabernet months ago, but we still have a small stock of chardonnay and zinfandel we deliver locally."

"That's good news, especially in light of last year's misfortune. Philippe explained to me about the fire." Donnelly shook his head. "What a blow, to work so hard and then to lose it all in one night."

"Would you like a tour of the building site? They've framed it out and started the masonry." Sara sparkled with excitement. "I'm sure Philippe and Marie would love to show you around," she insisted, nudging Marie's leg beneath the table. Marie resisted the urge to respond with a kick.

"I'd love to, but I'd best head back. It's nearly eight and I wouldn't want to intrude any longer." Marie felt instant relief.

Sara spoke up. "Dr. Donnelly, I hope you don't think it's too forward of us, but we have an extra room and we could easily arrange for you to stay the night."

"I'll take you back into the city first thing in the morning," Philippe added. They were definitely in cahoots, Marie realized.

Donnelly nodded appreciatively. "I'd be delighted, thank you." Marie's heart skipped a beat. She should have refused that second glass of chardonnay.

A quilt of darkness had fallen over Eagle's Run. Philippe handed lanterns to Marie and their guest, and they set out for the new winery site. Marie had to agree, the progress they'd made in a month's time was impressive.

"Look here," Philippe said, tugging on the wooden frame. "The building will measure 150 by 100 feet, and between the cellar underneath and the two outlying adobe cellars, we'll be able to store about 250,000 gallons of wine."

"You produce that much?" Donnelly raised his eyebrows.

"We produce about 150,000 gallons now, but I want to expand our capacity and also buy and use grapes from other local growers."

"How many tanks will you need for that, Philippe?" Marie had been surprised to learn that the fermenting tanks they'd had to destroy to extinguish the fire had held 10,000 gallons each and rose up to the ceiling.

"I've ordered forty 5,000-gallon tanks. We should be able to fit them all on the second floor."

"How will you get them up there?" Donnelly looked up.

"We'll have to hoist them up with a crane and drop them onto the second floor, then build the walls and third floor around them."

"Astounding. I had no idea," Donnelly marveled, walking the length of the eastern wall framework. "I'm no expert on wineries, but I know a little about building materials. Have you considered using steel bars inside the walls to fortify the building in case of another earthquake? "

Philippe rattled one of the wood frames, as if to test its strength. "Not a bad idea."

"The foundry's received a lot of orders recently from builders in Napa and Sonoma," Donnelly added. Philippe had been right all along: Donnelly's family had an iron fortune. "You might want to ask your builder."

Just then, Sara called from the house. "Philippe? Can you bring in more wood?" Philippe thanked Donnelly for his idea, excused himself and headed for the woodpile.

Marie could smell the soothing smoke from the chimney from here, but she could barely see the shadowy outline of the house, only its glowing yellow windows, square like postage stamps. The windless air chilled her nose, and revived her wine-dulled senses.

Donnelly took her gloved hand, pulling her over to a nearby maple tree. Marie felt her heart beating in double time. He placed their lanterns on the ground, and leaned his shoulder against the tree. She could hear his breath, and she could smell his spice-scented skin, so enticing that she had to press her back into the tree to support her wobbly knees.

"Marie?" He'd never used her Christian name before, but she loved the way it slipped off his tongue. "May I speak openly?"

"Haven't you already?" she replied, thinking of the many times he'd criticized her, or offered unsolicited advice.

He smiled and linked his fingers with hers. "This is different."

"How?" Marie whispered, distracted by the strength of his hand.

"Why do you think I'm here?" His bowed his face closer to hers.

Marie didn't know if the wine had washed away her reservations, and she didn't really care. He placed a hand firmly on her waist, and she moved closer. Without thinking, she slid one arm around his neck and kissed him, relishing the touch of his lips on hers.

He moaned softly, pressing her small frame against his chest.

After eleven years of self-imposed singlehood, she gave in. Her hands tangled in his hair, and her body twined around his.

Then Marie remembered she was a student and he a professor. She broke away, flustered, unsure of what to say. She focused on the lanterns at their feet, illuminating their shoes. His black ankle boots were shined and spotless, probably custom-made in Paris. She'd bought her worn, brown leather lace-ups at Kinney's. Her heart sank.

Donnelly fell back against the tree, rubbing his forehead, exhaling loudly. "I know what you're thinking, and you're right. We shouldn't do this." He grinned impishly at her. "But I don't care." He pulled her back into his arms and held her there.

Marie finally came to her senses. "But you'll lose your place at the college, and I'll lose my chance to become a surgeon." She shook her head. "It's impossible—for now."

"Not if we hide it. We could meet here, on the weekends."

"And then what?" Marie looked toward the house, hoping the light from their lanterns was too dim for Adeline to see. "I have a ten-year-old daughter, and I'm studying to be a surgeon. I don't have time for a romance."

His fingers skimmed her jawbone. "I understand, but couldn't you carve out a little time for me?" he asked gently.

Marie paused. "Your family will surely object?"

He laughed. "My family objects to everything. They're still reeling from my choice of surgery over steel. Not that they're a bad lot—but wealth often gives people the misguided notion that they know what's best for everyone." He wove his fingers through Marie's chignon and whispered, "I only aim to please myself—and now you." He kissed her forehead. "You're so serious. I like seeing you more . . . relaxed." His hands massaged her rigid shoulders. To Marie, it felt like the most natural thing in the world. She practically melted into him.

"Summer," she proposed. Her first year at the college ended in mid-April.

"What?"

"If you're still interested, we can spend time together over the summer break."

"I can't wait that long," he said earnestly, pressing his forehead to hers. Her heart pounded with desire.

"It's only a month away." She found it hard to believe they'd known each other for only seven months.

He sighed. "Fair enough. But I'm meeting you, with your packed bags, at the ferry on April 19th."

"It's a date," she agreed. She couldn't refuse him. Yet she made a promise to herself. If her relationship with Donnelly ever jeopardized her chances of graduating, she would end it.

The summer months were idyllic. Matthew performed fewer surgeries during the summer, so he visited nearly every weekend. He hired a hackney to drive them into Napa City for dinner and dancing on Saturday nights, introducing her to ragtime music and even teaching her the new four-step. Marie couldn't remember when she'd had more fun.

When Matthew was in town during the week, Marie relished the long stretches she was able to spend with Adeline, who taught her all she'd learned from Sara about grape varietals and wine-making. During June, Marie, Adeline, Luc, Sara and Philippe all helped the vineyard hands prune the young shoots and leaves. After spending the last eight months in classrooms, and the ten years before in crowded Manhattan, Marie delighted in the fresh air and beauty of the vineyard.

The work crews were busy constructing the new winery. Marie watched in awe as the enormous redwood and oak fermenting tanks were lowered onto the second floor and secured. Later the crews worked from morning until night shingling the immense roof. Marie helped Sara and Rose wash the picture windows on the first floor. She even learned to bake bread and made ham sandwiches with Rose to supply Sara's thriving weekend wine wagon business. By nine o'clock each evening, she dropped into bed exhausted. Who would have guessed that farm life could be more taxing than medical school?

"You're quiet tonight," Marie observed, holding Matthew's hand as they strolled down Third Street. "Is anything wrong?"

"Not at all," Matthew flashed a half-grin. "I've just been think-ing about Pippa. Philippe asked my opinion."

"I know. But Sara's nervous about the surgery."

"Which is understandable. It's risky, but it's not uncommon. Dan Richards does ten every month—children and adults."

"Perhaps he'd meet with them and examine Pippa? I think Sara might feel better if she came into the city to visit your clinic. The operating room is neat and clean, and not nearly as intimidating as the hospital. We could explain the entire procedure to them."

Matthew stopped short. "That's a good idea. I'll call Richards on Monday, if he's not on holiday like the rest of San Francisco."

"If he's available, this would be the best time to do the surgery—before the harvest, and before Pippa starts school in early September."

"And you'll persuade Sara to bring her?"

"With Philippe's help, yes."

Matthew seemed satisfied with this, but remained silent until he greeted their driver, who was parked nearby. Once he'd handed Marie up into her seat, he said somberly, "This is your family, Marie. What if something does go wrong, or she has a bad reaction to the anesthesia? She's so tiny."

Marie cupped Matthew's chin in her gloved hand. "From what Sara told me, Pippa's mother wanted her to have the operation, and so does Philippe. Her ear infections are terrible. She has difficulty eating, and other children ridicule her. If it were Adeline, I'd opt for the surgery."

Matthew stepped up, planted his palms on Marie's cheeks, and kissed her tenderly. "I know you would. You're a fine mother, Marie."

Besides Philippe, no one had ever complimented Marie on her parenting before. "Do you think so?" she asked as he settled in his seat and directed the driver toward Eagle's Run.

"Why, don't you believe you are?"

She hesitated. "Yes, but because I've been working all these years, I worry I haven't spent enough time with Adeline."

"Perhaps, but you've taught her perseverance."

"You think?"

"Absolutely. She idolizes you. She's an intelligent and sweet girl, just like her mother."

Marie cringed. "What did you really think of me when we first met?" She knew she must sound riddled with insecurities, but her curiosity trumped her pride.

Matthew smirked. "Honestly? When I first saw you, I thought, 'She is the loveliest young woman I've ever seen, and she'll never survive here.'"

Marie elbowed him in the ribs. "And now? Speaking as my professor, of course."

"Of course," he said with mock seriousness. "I think you have an uncommon intelligence and intuition for medicine. If you keep your head about you, and resist the temptation to fall for your dashing anatomy professor, you may have a chance at graduating."

Marie swatted him with the back of her hand. "You are a devil!"

"You love that I am." He scooped Marie closer to him. They bumped along the road toward Eagle's Run, silt spiraling in their wake.

# Chapter 30

**S**ara stroked Pippa's hair as they sat in the foyer of Dr. Donnelly's boarding house, more to settle her own nerves than the child's. In fact, Pippa had been delighted to take her first trip by ferry into the city. She leaned back on the polished oak bench and swung her legs, humming. Philippe was pacing so steadily, Sara worried he would wear out the carpet beneath his soles.

Marie, who'd arrived earlier, held Pippa's hand and guided the family to the examination room on the other side of the staircase. Sara was so choked with anxiety that she couldn't even string a sentence together. She was relieved when Marie chatted amicably with the child, asking her how big the waves appeared over the ferry railing, and whether she'd been able to see the city skyline through the thick fog. Philippe squeezed Sara's hand, and she pressed her cheek against the curve of his shoulder.

Matthew greeted them with a relaxed smile. To Sara, he appeared capable and confident. He introduced an older man, Dr. Richards, who, he promised, was an expert in repairing cleft lips in children.

Philippe and Sara took seats by the window while Marie eased Pippa onto the table. "Just lay your head down on this pillow," she said soothingly. Her eyes never left Pippa's, and her hand wrapped around Pippa's small fingers. "Dr. Richards is going to fix your lip, so it will be easier for you to eat, drink and speak."

Pippa's eyes widened. "I be pwetty?" she slurred, contorting her lips as she had to in order to form consonant sounds on the right side of her mouth. A lump formed in Sara's throat. Marie rested her hand on Pippa's arm. "Yes, Pippa, you will." Marie nodded to the doctor.

After examining Pippa's face, throat and head, the doctor set out to explain exactly what he was attempting to correct. Sara didn't understand a word, and when she looked to Philippe for reassurance, his expression was blank as well.

Matthew jumped in to clarify. "What Dr. Richards is saying is that fortunately, Pippa has an ordinary cleft lip, which means the center and outer portions of her upper lip have failed to unite. It's not a complicated procedure. Dr. Richards would be able to perform the operation today, if you agree." Matthew looked from Philippe to Sara. Marie quietly ushered Pippa out of the room.

Philippe asked, "How exactly do you plan to correct the problem, Doctor?"

"First, I'll free the lip from the cheek, to ensure there's no tension when we pare the edges of the gap. Then we'll stitch the edges together."

"Won't she choke on all the blood?" Philippe asked.

"She'll be lying on her back, but the nurse will be compressing her coronary artery to control the bleeding. If necessary, we'll turn her on her side, and that will prevent her from swallowing or choking on the blood," Matthew explained.

"She'll be asleep during the operation, so she won't see or feel anything?" Sara asked.

"Indeed. We'll administer chloroform, and after the surgery, when she's awake and alert, we'll give her some pain medication to help reduce her soreness."

"And is there a chance she won't wake up?" Philippe asked, a tremor in his voice.

Matthew glanced momentarily at the floor. A whimper escaped Sara's throat. After a moment, he replied, "That is always a risk, but the nurse will be administering a very small dose, just enough to keep Pippa sedated during the operation. Marie and I will also be in the room, to oversee everything."

Dr. Richards cleared his throat. "Barring anything out of the ordinary, Mr. and Mrs. Lemieux, I expect Pippa to come through the operation with flying colors. She's a strong, healthy little girl, and her life, and yours, will be much easier after today."

Sara's eyes pleaded with Philippe, who was still by her side. "Thank you, Doctors," Philippe said. "May my wife and I have a moment to discuss things?"

"Of course," Matthew replied, as he and Dr. Richards moved toward the door.

Philippe sank down next to Sara. "I think we should do this for Pippa."

"But *are* we doing it for Pippa? Or are we risking her life to please a world that won't accept her the way she is?"

Philippe's tone was firm. "We are doing this to give her the chance to be like every other child." He pointed to the door. "That girl takes life by the horns. She's not even four, and she's already frustrated because people can't understand her." His face crumpled. "She can't even smile, Sara."

Sara wiped her tears. "She's your daughter—it's your decision."

"You know that's not true. I need you with me on this, Sara. One of the greatest gifts you've ever given me is caring for Pippa like she's your own daughter. Pippa and I—we both need you to believe in this."

Sara walked over to the window and gazed out. Mothers pushed their prams down sunlit streets, and a huddle of children played hopscotch. She wondered why she had to make this decision today. But the answer was simple: she was Pippa's mother. She turned back to Philippe. "All right."

His face softened with relief. There was a light rap at the door. Marie stepped in. "May I?"

Philippe waved her in. "Of course."

"I have something that might help." She began to flip through the pages of a book she'd brought in with her. "When I'm studying these tricky surgeries, the drawings are much more helpful than the text." She opened the page and held it out for them to see.

The heading on the right page read: "Congenital Deformity of Lips and Mouth," and below that, two illustrations detailed the ways Pippa's lip could be repaired. Marie pointed to the second one. "Dr. Richards prefers Mirault's method here," she told them. "He'll most likely use this technique."

Philippe looked at the picture intently. "So her scar may be a bit jagged, not a straight line?"

"Most likely. In his experience, the skin tends to fuse together better with this kind of incision."

Sara shuddered. Philippe pulled her close. "This is very helpful, Marie, thank you." He took a deep breath and announced, "We're ready."

The operation lasted longer than Sara expected. As she sat in the parlor, then paced around the stairwell and through the foyer, she was locked in a solitary prison of prayer and panic. Barely aware of Philippe, or the nurses bustling by, her mind kept wandering back to Pippa's last words, their last moment together. Sara had bowed down to kiss her silky blond hair, which smelled of sunshine and soap. Pippa clutched Sara's hand and, whispering words that only Sara understood, declared, "Mama, I bwave."

Sara swam in her daughter's wide, cornflower blue eyes, humbled by the child's spirit. "Yes, you are, *ma petite fée*." She smiled at Pippa, smoothing the hair away from her forehead. Pippa's face grew serene. Philippe had to drag Sara out of the operating room and over to the parlor, where he sat her down and forced her to drink a shot of brandy. With every sip, Sara's tense limbs relaxed. Though her nerves never fully calmed that afternoon, she managed not to crawl out of her skin.

After two excruciating hours, Marie emerged from the operating room, walking slowly toward Sara and Philippe. Sara didn't breathe until Marie broke into a wide grin. "The surgery was a success. Pippa came through beautifully." She reached for Sara and Philippe and hugged them tightly, the three of them shaking with relief.

Donnelly's private hospital would reopen on the second Monday of August. The nurses came and went, helping to organize the stacks of medical records, scrub the rooms clean and make up the beds with fresh linens in anticipation of the new patients who were likely to appear at Donnelly's doorstep next week.

Under the admittedly thin pretext of preparing a special presentation for her upcoming anatomy and physiology class, Marie visited the boarding house three afternoons that week. She sifted through the medical files, jotting down the most memorable cases and their peculiarities. She followed the nurses around, sweeping floors and sterilizing bedpans. She made a point to leave when the nurses did, for she couldn't afford any appearance of impropriety, even if Jane and Virginia did suspect something was going on.

Marie's favorite time of the day was four o'clock, when she knew the nurses would be sorting through the day's deliveries and restocking the kitchen and supply closet just before locking up. Marie would slip into Matthew's office and spend a few quiet minutes with him before she left for the day.

On this particular Thursday, he had a playful spark in his eye. He pulled her down onto his lap and nuzzled her neck. "You know I simply can't stand it anymore."

"Stand what?" Marie asked innocently, but when he kissed her deeply, she knew exactly what he meant. She felt a luscious, tingling sensation. She never wanted him to stop.

"Not having you." She felt his fingers beneath her skirt, meandering up her calf.

She pressed her hand atop his firmly, but kissed him gently. "I can't risk becoming pregnant—not now." Surely he understood? They'd already discussed this. "We'll have to wait."

"Until you finish medical school—until we're finally married?" he asked. "For God's sakes, Marie, I'm a physician. There are ways to prevent these things."

She jumped to her feet. "Are there now? And this is how you court a woman?" They were both Catholic—this would never do.

Matthew looked stunned. He spoke slowly, as though she were a child. "No, it's not," he said without elaborating.

She wondered if Matthew believed the lie that had circulated at the college—about her supposed lover. Even if he'd dismissed that talk, Marie did have an illegitimate child. Oh, yes—now she understood. Her stomach twisted.

She fumed, "You think because I had a child out of wedlock that I'm tainted, that I no longer have morals? That was over eleven years ago, and since then I've worn my fingers to the bone making my own way in this world—keeping my daughter out of the poorhouse—and I'll be damned if I'm going to let *you* ruin my chance to become a surgeon!" Trembling, Marie grasped the doorknob.

Matthew reached for her arms, forcing her to face him. "Come now, Marie, don't talk rot. I think no such thing."

"You don't know what it's like," she retorted. "You'll never know!" She tried to tear herself from him, but he held her so tightly, she could barely breathe.

"You're right, Marie, I don't know," he said calmly. He pulled back to meet her gaze, but held her firmly. "Forgive me. I allowed my emotions to overrule my manners." He smiled tentatively. "And I'd like to make it up to you."

Marie arched a skeptical eyebrow and waited.

"Saturday, my sister-in-law's hosting a party at her home in St. Helena. I'd hate to go alone. Do come with me. She's dying to meet you."

Marie smiled warily. Their affair was intended to be clandestine, but he had told his sister-in-law and brother about her. That had to be a good sign. Then she remembered that his family was one of the wealthiest in San Francisco. She had been raised simply; she didn't know how to behave in that kind of company, and she hated small talk.

"It's a little too early, don't you think?" she asked. "What if word gets out that we were seen together?"

"I doubt any faculty or students will be hiding in my brother's garden in St. Helena, but if it makes you feel better, why don't you come with Sara and Philippe? No one will be suspicious. I'll send a car for all of you."

Send a car? The cost of that alone would pay for a new dress for Adeline. She looked at him blankly. Did he understand how little she had?

"Nonsense, we'll take the train," Marie replied. Perhaps Rose or Aurora could watch the children for the day with Adeline's help. Then something else squelched her optimism. "Will your parents be there?" She tried to sound nonchalant.

"You think I'd feed you to the wolves this early on? No, and that's the whole point. I'd like you to meet my brother and sister-in-law first. They're very modern." Everything about Matthew was modern: his profession, his clothes, his cars and his tastes. He belonged with a rich socialite who would know what to serve at fabulous parties and who would decorate his office in the latest styles. What on earth was he doing with her?

To Marie's disappointment, Sara and Philippe were eager to accompany her to Bridget Donnelly's house party when they discussed it Friday morning. As much as she welcomed their support, she really wasn't looking forward to meeting Matthew's family.

Sara fussed far more than Marie expected at the news, dragging her over to the looking glass. "We only have a day to find you the proper attire," she complained.

"I'll just wear my blue dress," Marie offered.

"Over my dead body," Sara said as she sifted through the hangers in her closet. "Too long, too wide, wrong color." She sighed. "Listen, Marie, I've met Bridget Donnelly and her daughter, and even on the train platform at midday, they were dressed to the nines in silk and lace. They looked like a pair of candied cakes!" Sara laughed. "As nice as they are, I refuse to send you there not looking the part."

Marie had earmarked every last penny of her savings for tuition, books and Adeline's needs. "I can only spare about fifteen dollars," she said, calculating the amount she was saving by not traveling back and forth to the city this summer.

"That will buy you the top half of the dress, and maybe a hat," Sara said, tongue in cheek. "I'll give you the rest."

"You're just getting back on your feet," Marie objected. "I can't take your money."

"That's nonsense, Marie. I made some extra money last weekend. I'll give it to you and, in return, you'll work the wagon next Saturday. Fair enough?" Sara's face beamed with such anticipation that Marie couldn't possibly refuse.

Marie fiddled with the white silk ribbon trimming her lilac cotton dress and then pinned on the fashionable straw hat with matching flowers that Sara had insisted on. Marie inspected her reflection. Her waist was small, bound by an excruciatingly tight whalebone corset. Her hair was dark and lustrous, and her skin was smooth and even. The corners of her mouth hung down now, though, making her appear uptight and grumpy. She forced herself to smile, and the apples of her cheeks brightened with color. Matthew said he liked to see her relax, and Marie couldn't recall ever seeing him tense. The memory of their first kiss in the garden sparked a tingling feeling from her lips down to her curled toes. Marie closed her eyes and sighed.

She was capable of delivering twins singlehandedly, naming every part of the human anatomy and suturing a wound, but for the life of her, she couldn't figure out why Matthew Donnelly had set his sights on her.

When they arrived at the St. Helena train station, they were pleased to find a hackney waiting for them. On their drive, as they neared a bend in the road, Marie heard the string quartet before she could even see the house. The swell of the violins and the deep lament of the cello set her on edge. Sara must have sensed this, for she squeezed Marie's white-gloved hand and smiled. "You're beautiful, Marie. He's going to be bowled over, trust me." Marie managed a weak smile, but as the wheels of their hackney crunched on the driveway gravel, her eyes drifted over Jimmy and Bridget Donnelly's immense house. The three-story Victorian home was one of the largest Marie had seen outside of the city, complete with a turret, stained glass windows, a carpet of clipped green grass and hedges sliced into neat cubes.

She gripped Philippe's hand as she stepped down, but continued to watch for movement from the front door, which hung wide open. Sunlight flooded the hallway, and Marie could see through the house to a lush patch of backyard. The air smelled of sweet honeysuckle, barbecue and freshly baked bread.

As they drew nearer, Matthew appeared at the top of the front steps. His arms opened to welcome them. Marie's breath faltered: he was wearing an ivory linen suit, blue-striped silk tie and a straw boater. His cheeks looked freshly scrubbed and shaved. She linked her arm through Sara's and locked her shaky knees. "Calm down," Sara whispered as Matthew approached and shook Philippe's hand vigorously.

"Welcome," he said, smiling warmly as he looked from Sara to Marie, and ushering them to the side lawn. "Do come around back, and make yourselves at home. I'm so glad you've come."

A white tent, its sides billowing in the light wind, dominated the center of the sprawling back lawn. A beautiful old oak, standing twice the height of the house, shaded a throng of guests who were reclining lazily against its trunk and twirling on the rope swing hitched to its lowest branch. A loud crack sounded from the far side of the yard, capturing Sara's attention. "Matthew, is that croquet they're playing?" She nodded toward a huddle of men striking balls through wickets with short wooden mallets. "We watched croquet at the Olympics during the World's Fair a couple of years ago, didn't we, Philippe?"

"Yes, but this is something different," Philippe replied, squinting at the players on the court.

"The American version—a game called roque," Matthew agreed. "A bit more scientific than croquet."

"I venture it's a vast deal more fun to play than to watch," Sara teased.

"Absolutely. I'd encourage you to try it, except when my brother Jimmy and his friends play, things can get a bit heated. I wouldn't want to injure your delicate ears."

Sara shot Marie a knowing glance. "Believe me, Matthew, after living in New York, Marie and I have heard much worse than you could imagine!"

He laughed. "I have no doubt. May I offer you some punch, or wine perhaps?"

While they waited for Matthew to return with refreshments, Philippe took a look around. "I hate to break it to you, Marie," he whispered, leaning in closer, "but see the couple standing under the oak tree?" He nodded at an older pair sipping champagne.

"They are Mr. and Mrs. Rourke Donnelly, Matthew's parents. You'd best prepare yourself." Philippe winked, patting the small of Marie's back. "You'll be fine, old girl. Just be yourself."

Before long, Matthew strolled back with champagne, a beautiful strawberry-blond woman by his side. He introduced her as his sister-in-law, Bridget. She recognized Sara and Philippe at once, and soon struck up a conversation with Marie. After several minutes of chatter about the weather, Marie's studies at Cooper and the variety of guests, Bridget proposed the unthinkable.

"Marie, dear, you must allow me to introduce you to Matthew's mother," she insisted with a radiant smile, taking Marie's elbow and guiding her in the direction of the oak tree. Mrs. Donnelly, in a wide-brimmed straw hat adorned with yards of white tulle and fresh flowers, was holding court, surrounded by the younger women at the party.

A broad smile lit up Bridget's porcelain complexion. "You know, Jimmy, Matthew and I went on a delightful tour of the Loire countryside in our motorcar two years ago. My favorite châteaux were Chenonceau and Chambord—such grandeur! Matthew disagreed entirely, of course. The Château de Sully-sur-Loire was his favorite. Do you know it?" Marie shook her head, wondering what their châteaux tour had to do with anything. Bridget continued, "The medieval fortress there stands on the edge of the Loire River." She looked across the yard to Matthew, who was sharing a drink with his father. "Anyhow, Matthew loved its elegant exterior: high turrets crowned with pepper-pot roofs, wide moats filled to the brim, and an enormous keep." She paused, shifting toward

Marie. "But he was most captivated by the apartments inside," she added. "The interior was flooded with light, which made the solid stone walls and barrel-vaulted ceilings so beautiful. Matthew insisted that the château's real beauty was in its strength—it had been home to three families over a thousand years. He's always had a knack for discerning the true nature of things." Bridget leaned in confidingly, whispering, "And once he's made up his mind, *no one* has the power to dissuade him."

With that, they approached Mrs. Donnelly. To Marie's chagrin, rather than waiting for a lull in the conversation, Bridget interrupted, blurting, "Mum, you must meet Marie Chevreau." Matthew's mother straightened up like an arrow and peered at Marie through her spectacles. At that moment, Marie could have kissed Sara for insisting she dress up for the occasion.

"You are the midwife studying to become a doctor?" she asked in a faint Irish brogue. Matthew must have inherited his bluntness from his mother.

"Yes, ma'am," Marie replied, forcing a smile. "I'm very fortunate to have witnessed some of Matthew's surgeries. He's very talented."

"Yes, that's what I hear," she said evenly. "And did I also hear that you have a daughter?" she asked in a crackly voice.

The group hushed, except for Bridget. "Mum!" she admonished, resting a hand on her mother-in-law's arm.

Mrs. Donnelly shrugged off Bridget's warning. "Won't you accompany me into the house, Miss Chevreau?" she asked with a civility Marie had not expected.

"Yes, of course," Marie replied. Mrs. Donnelly's gait was slow but steady as they walked down the brick path toward the house. To end the awkward silence, Marie confirmed, "My daughter's name is Adeline and she's eleven."

"So you raised her yourself, while working as a midwife, and now you're studying for your surgical license?" To Marie's surprise, Matthew's mother sounded impressed.

"Yes, ma'am," Marie said quietly. "I did have help along the way, from a convent of French nuns in New York, and from my friends, the Lemieux, who accompanied me here today." Marie gestured toward Sara and Philippe, who were deep in conversation with Matthew's brother, Jimmy.

"And where do you come from?"

"France, ma'am. Tours, to be exact."

"And are your parents still alive, in France? What do they do?"

"Yes, they own a successful business—a tavern in Tours," she added, wondering if this would serve as grounds for instant dismissal from the premises.

Mrs. Donnelly stopped at the end of the brick path, near the back entrance to the house. "What a colorful life you've led, my dear," she replied, her eyes narrowing. She hesitated, but then continued in a hushed voice. "I must say, my son Matthew has also partaken of his share of diversions."

"Yes, Bridget was telling me about their travels in France," Marie recalled carefully.

"Then perhaps she also told you about Matthew's fiancée, Miss Margaret O'Shea of Philadelphia?" Her sea-green eyes widened sympathetically, then darted in Matthew's direction. "I do hope we meet again, my dear," she concluded, before walking into the house.

Marie gripped a nearby newel post and struggled to breathe. Matthew's *fiancée*? Marie thought she'd misheard, but no: *Miss Margaret O'Shea.*

Marie glanced across the crowded lawn. Matthew nodded to her and gave her a wide, charming smile. Marie's mind sifted through every memory she had of him and landed on Virginia's voice, the interruption during Tom Adler's surgery: *Dr. Donnelly, Miss O'Shea is on the telephone.* Marie rounded the side of the house and stumbled toward the front yard, skimming her palm over the smooth clapboards to keep her balance. Perhaps Sara would notice and come find her.

But it was Matthew who rushed to Marie's side. "Was my mother awful?" He sat down beside her on the front steps. "She wasn't supposed to be here."

"Your mother was lovely," she said coldly. "And she is the only one who isn't lying to me."

"Lying? What—"

"Margaret O'Shea. Of Philadelphia?" she said in a deliberate voice.

"Wait a minute . . ." He seemed confounded.

"Your betrothed, or have you forgotten?" Marie replied, suddenly finding the strength to stand and turn on her heel.

He caught her arm and whirled her around.

"Don't touch me!" she cried.

"Listen to me, Marie!" The veins in his neck pulsed wildly. "Our parents arranged the whole thing two years ago. Neither she nor I wanted to go through with it. Yes, we were promised to each other, but—"

"But what? Are you or are you *not* engaged to be married?"

"No, I am not," he replied. "My father dissolved the agreement between our families last month and paid the O'Sheas a healthy sum. Fortunately, Miss O'Shea has already made a new match with an aristocrat's son, so everyone's happy."

"Oh," Marie said bitterly. "So money solves everything, does it, Matthew?"

"No," his eyes glinted like cold steel. "No, it doesn't." He released her, placing his hands on his hips.

"You're a liar," Marie seethed, pointing at him. "You led me to believe you were free!"

"I am free!" He waved his arms in frustration.

"You were engaged when you started courting me in March! You lied to me for months!"

"Yes, but I knew—"

"Everything all right out here?" Philippe asked, gravel crunching beneath his feet as he approached. Sara followed close behind, negotiating the pebble driveway in heels.

"No, it isn't," Marie huffed. "We need to leave," she said to Philippe while holding Matthew's gaze.

"I'll drive you to the station," Matthew offered, shaking his head in bewilderment.

"The hell you will," Marie snapped. "Let's go." She turned and started down the driveway.

"Dash it all, Marie! Will you not listen to reason?" Matthew called, his voice steeped in misery.

Marie set off in the heat toward the station. She didn't dare look back.

# Chapter 31

A little over a week later, Marie pinned up her hair in front of the looking glass, trying to convince herself that today, the first day of the new semester, was no different from any other. After her row with Matthew, and then her refusal to see him when he called at the Lemieux house the following afternoon, she didn't know how to act, or how to *be*. She was humiliated, but she knew she was right. She had a daughter to consider, and she couldn't trust him.

Anatomy was her third class of the day. Marie drew a long breath before walking into the classroom. She chose a desk in the center of the room, hoping to hide behind her classmates. Finally every seat was filled, but Donnelly was missing. Her heart pounded in anticipation of seeing him again.

An unfamiliar professor strolled in and dropped his notebook on the teacher's desk. As the stick of chalk screeched across the blackboard, he announced, "I'll be teaching anatomy this week. Dr. Donnelly has been called away." Marie flushed with shame. Was this true, or had the faculty discovered their liaison and fired him? She swallowed hard, suddenly sick to her stomach. If she excused herself from class now, everyone would be suspicious.

When the bell rang, students and professors flooded the hallway. Marie searched their faces for that familiar turquoise gaze. Maybe she was just imagining things; maybe he'd just switched classes with someone else. Marie found it increasingly difficult to think. Something hard hit her shoulder, knocking her into the nearby wall. Gripping her books tightly, she looked up to see Larry Deaver smirking. He walked on, laughing with his friends, without so much as an apology.

Before she left Friday evening, Marie was desperate to discover Matthew's whereabouts. Her shoes click-clacked down the black linoleum of the second floor hallway. She glanced over her shoulder to make sure the corridor was still vacant. When she arrived at the frosted glass door to his office, her shoulders sank. The room was dark. She turned the brass knob, hoping he'd forgotten to lock it. She longed to feel the leather of his chair sink beneath her weight, to twirl the miniature globe on his desk, to flip through the stacks of papers he'd touched, but the knob stuck. Silly goose, she chastised herself.

"Marie?" She jumped when she heard a man's upbeat voice. Thad stood near the stairwell. He closed the distance between them with a few long strides. "I thought you'd be on the ferry by now."

Marie examined the scuffed toes of her ankle boots, feeling heat creep over her chest and up to her cheeks. How much did Thad suspect? "I'm taking the morning ferry, so I can organize my notes tonight." Her answer was truthful, although she'd also stayed in hopes of seeing Matthew.

Thad moved closer, pointing to the office door. "If you're looking for Donnelly, he'll be back next week." Thad tipped his head to the side, causing a mop of wavy blond hair to flop over his forehead. "Wait . . ." His brows bunched together, then his eyes grew wide with understanding. "Oh," he said, clearly startled. "Oh—I didn't know."

Marie shifted uncomfortably. "It's not like that."

He instantly stepped back. "It's none of my business, Marie," Thad said formally. He gulped, and fixed his stare on the blackboard mounted to the wall. "I'm headed out for the night. Do you need me to escort you home? I mean," he stammered, "if that's where you're going."

"I would, thank you, Thad," Marie said softly, embarrassed about what he might think. He turned tomato-red, causing her to cringe at their mutual discomfort. "Just let me collect my things in the photographic room."

Looking relieved, Thad pulled a cigarette from behind his ear. "Take your time, Marie. I'll be outside. Meet you in ten minutes?"

"Ten minutes." She smiled awkwardly.

The photographic room was located on the floor above, adjacent to the anatomy room. A bellows camera, used by the faculty to record surgeries, dominated one corner. The right wall was lined with wood-and-glass cabinets that held hundreds of specimen jars. The musky odor of formaldehyde stung Marie's eyes and turned her stomach. She moved past the long table of microscopes and microtomes, where she'd stacked her books and her notes, clipped together by subject. Marie used both arms to lift the heavy sash of the enormous window. She was rewarded with a gust of warm air, which instantly freshened the room but scattered her carefully organized papers all over the tiled floor.

As Marie knelt down to collect them, her arms tingled with goose flesh. Her heart thumped wildly when she turned her head to spy a tall figure blocking the doorway. The afternoon light from the hallway cast a shadow over his face, obscuring his identity. "Thad?" Marie asked, but there was no answer. "Matthew?" she whispered quietly. Before she could rise, two men rushed in, slamming the door shut behind them. Marie tried to call out, but the words stuck in her throat. While John Redman propped himself against the wall, staring at her through vacant, bloodshot eyes, Larry Deaver pounced.

"What are you doing?" Marie cried as he charged toward her. Deaver twisted his fingers into her hair, yanked her up and sent them both hurtling into the table with such force that Marie's forehead plowed into a heavy metal microscope, sending it tumbling to the floor. The skin along her hairline split open and blood began to trickle down, forming a crimson haze over one eye and blurring her vision. He pushed her cheek onto the scratchy wood and pressed his thighs against Marie's seat, forcing her stomach into the table's edge. He blew his smoke-and-whiskey breath in her face. "Mathieu? Mathieu?" he mocked. "Don't you mean Dr. Donnelly—your *paramour*?"

Deaver released his grip for a moment, and Marie heard the jangle of his belt buckle. "Don't touch me!" she shrieked, stabbing the heels of her boots into his shins, straightening her arms, trying to push back. Her head throbbed and her vision blurred, but she would not, could not submit.

"Goddamn it, Red!" Deaver shouted. He jabbed an elbow between Marie's shoulder blades, flattening her over the table-top again and causing her arms to flail helplessly. Redman's eyes brightened. He flicked open a small pocketknife and slid it across the table to his friend. Deaver pressed the cold blade to the spot where Marie's carotid artery pulsed with fear. "Don't move, or I'll slice you from ear to throat, whore," he spat. Dazed, and flitting in and out of consciousness, Marie felt his clammy hands beneath her skirt, his hot fingers squeezing her flesh. Marie panicked when she realized that she'd have to endure his assault to stay alive—if only for Adeline's sake.

Shouting erupted in the doorway, and suddenly the wooden legs of the table squealed, scraping against the tile below. Deaver let go, and Marie fell to the floor. Out of her one good eye, she saw Thad wrestling with an outmatched Redman. With one punch, Thad sent him careening into the wall. Deaver thrust the knife at Thad, but Marie's friend ducked, grabbed Deaver's arm and bashed his wrist against the table until he released his weapon. Deaver tackled Thad, driving him into the cabinet and sending specimen jars flying through the air to smash at Marie's feet. The shattering of glass and the sudden sharp formaldehyde smell revived her senses. Unable to find the knife, Marie picked up a microscope and launched it at the back of Deaver's head.

He dropped like a stone. Marie thought her heart would explode. Her knees collapsed and, as she sank, Thad, bleeding and ruffled, caught her up in his embrace. He offered Marie his handkerchief to stem the flow of blood at her scalp and, with one arm locked around her waist, guided her toward the door. Behind them, Deaver stirred and groaned, attempting to rise. Thad gently leaned Marie against the wall. "Wait here," he instructed. He rushed back into the room and kicked Deaver's torso repeatedly, surely cracking ribs. "You piece of shit!" Thad's voice was gruff. Marie's lip trembled and she began to shake, not only for what she'd endured, but because God had blessed her with a brave friend at the very moment she needed one.

Thad tucked in his shirt and then guided Marie down the stairs. He paused only to forage for alcohol and clean bandages in the supply room.

Once they reached her apartment, Thad lowered Marie down on the edge of her bed. She felt as though freezing water was running through her veins, chilling her limbs and causing her to shake. As Thad knelt down before her and dabbed her forehead with alcohol, she winced. "The swelling is worse," he noted, covering the wound with gauze. He pulled some ice from her small oak icebox and pressed it to her head.

"How did you know?" Marie whispered.

He shrugged. "I was standing right below the window. I heard you scream."

She placed a hand on his shoulder. "Thank you, Thad."

He frowned. "Marie, I need to find Donnelly."

"No."

"He can treat your wound better than I can, and we need to report this to the administration."

Marie gripped his forearm. "Please, don't. They'll fire him if they find out about us."

"Is that what you're worried about?" Thad said with disgust. "Who cares? We need to make sure you're protected—that Deaver and Redman don't hurt you again." He sighed deeply, blotting the blood from her hair with a cloth. "God, Marie, look what they've done to you."

She stood up, still wobbly, and peered into the mirror above her sink. Her lip was split, her cheek purple and the smooth skin of her neck stung with red nicks from Deaver's knife. She peeled off the gauze to examine the two-inch gash beneath her matted hair. Though it wasn't a deep cut, it had bled for the last half hour. "Will it need stitches?" Marie wondered aloud.

"Probably not, but it might leave a scar."

Marie spoke to his reflection in the mirror. "Thad, Donnelly and I . . . we only started courting this summer. Just courting—nothing more."

"Even if it was something more, Marie, that doesn't excuse what they did."

"I know." She shuddered and returned to sit on the bed opposite her friend. Marie suddenly wanted Adeline, and Sara. She wanted to feel the Napa sunshine on her face—to flee this dark, dingy apartment.

Thad must have read her mind. "At least allow me to take

you back to your family tomorrow." Marie agreed. He unlaced and removed her boots, but left her to slip off her stockings. She wanted to bathe, but couldn't fight her body's need for sleep.

Marie gently laid her head on the pillow. "Sit with me until then?" she pleaded.

"Of course, Marie," Thad whispered, and covered her with the cool cotton bedsheet.

Philippe took the early ferry into the city Monday morning. He'd been camped outside Donnelly's office for half an hour by the time he arrived.

"Lemieux!" Donnelly exclaimed as he approached Philippe. He looked the part of the stylish physician: fashionable navy suit, gray silk tie, shined shoes and not a stray hair on his head. "I was planning on paying you a visit soon," he said, his expression filled with hope.

Marie's battered face flashed in Philippe's mind. He wanted to throttle the bastard, but knowing how deeply Marie cared for him, he shook Donnelly's extended hand in brooding silence.

Donnelly's expression instantly sobered. "Wait, why are you here? Has something happened?"

"We should speak in private." Philippe glanced down the hallway, now filled with students scurrying to class.

Donnelly's face paled. "Of course. Please, come in." He swung the door open and offered Philippe a seat. "Are you here about Marie? Did she tell you why we argued?" He exhaled loudly, tapping his fingers on the desk blotter. "Is she still upset?"

Philippe waved a hand, halting him in mid-sentence. He didn't want to hear about Margaret O'Shea, or why Donnelly hadn't been with Marie Friday night.

"Matthew, Marie was attacked by two students on Friday. They beat her and, if Thad Holmes hadn't stopped them, they probably would have raped her, too."

Matthew gasped, his face etched with horror. "Is she—does she—"

"She has a gash on her forehead and some cuts and bruises, but our doctor says she'll be fine. She's in Napa now, at the house, with Sara and Thad."

Donnelly's jaw slackened. He stared at Philippe, eyes pink with grief. "Who did this? Why didn't Holmes fetch me?"

"Larry Deaver and John Redman. They discovered your liaison." Donnelly's lower lip quivered and he covered his face with his hands. "Thad wanted to tell you, but she wouldn't let him. And now she won't report the incident because she doesn't want you involved. She doesn't want them to fire you."

"Jesus, Mary and Joseph. That's ridiculous," he said hoarsely. "Can I see her?"

"Tomorrow morning. I've arranged for a meeting with the administration. Sara will bring Marie, and Thad will serve as a witness. We need you there."

"Of course, but I have to be with her—now." Donnelly stood up.

"Give her time, Matthew," Philippe cautioned. "Her spirits have taken a beating, too. She needs another day to regain her strength."

Donnelly stared out the window. "I love her, Philippe," he said quietly.

Philippe understood his pain. His own memory—of Sara's scars from his brother's attack—remained lodged like shrapnel in his gut. "Then fight for her," he urged. Donnelly squeezed Philippe's shoulder in response, his jaw rigid with determination.

Marie couldn't believe what she was hearing.

Matthew leapt out of his seat. "A reprimand?" he exclaimed. "That's it?" He paced around the crowded table, gesturing wildly. "Miss Chevreau was attacked in this very building by two of her fellow students, and you're giving them a slap on the wrist?"

"What else would you suggest?" the elderly, gray-haired provost asked over steepled fingers.

"Expulsion, for starters. You need to make an example out of them!" Marie rarely heard Matthew shout. She watched him thunder away at the college's disciplinary council. He cut a striking figure in his finely tailored dark gray suit, and was wielding his authority as an accomplished surgeon and tenured professor to argue on her behalf. Yet neither he nor any of the men at the table understood what she had endured. Only Sara knew.

The provost cleared his throat, interrupting Marie's thoughts. "Forgive me, Dr. Donnelly, but according to her testimony, Miss Chevreau was not, in fact, raped. The arrest of these students would tarnish this college's reputation. And as for expulsion, well, I suppose we could expel Mr. Redman quietly, but Mr. Deaver's father is on the board of trustees and is this college's most generous benefactor."

Marie bristled. She couldn't bear to listen anymore. Obviously, her safety didn't merit much discussion. Her anxiety heightened until it felt like a thousand needles piercing her hot skin. She sprang to her feet, and her legs nearly gave way. Sara reached out to steady her. "I just need some water," Marie whispered.

The men around the table stood up. Before Sara exited the room with Marie, she addressed the provost. "Do you have a wife, sir? A daughter?" She turned a hard eye on all five administrators, interrogating them one by one. "How would you feel if she were threatened at knifepoint? Beaten? Nearly violated against her will while others watched for sport?" Sara's face was pinched with loathing.

Marie squeezed Sara's trembling arm, grateful for her support. Before Sara closed the door behind them, Marie stole a glance at Matthew. The creases of his face softened. An unreadable emotion hid behind those aqua eyes. Did he pity her, or had he just issued a silent farewell? Either way, Marie felt alone and confused.

In an adjacent meeting room, she ran the tip of her finger around the rim of her water glass. If she focused on the circular motion, she could block out the chatter from the corridor, the sting of her scrapes, even the buzzing in her head. Marie could feel Sara watching her, but said nothing.

The door swung open. Out of the corner of her eye, Marie spied the hem of Matthew's neatly creased trousers, cuffed above his shiny oxfords. Philippe followed.

Matthew knelt down before her, rubbing her hands in his. She couldn't bear to look at him. Her heart was heavy with shame, although she'd done nothing wrong.

"I'm so sorry, Marie," Matthew said. His fingers grazed the wound on her head, which she had deliberately unbandaged for the meeting. "You have my word, I will make this right. You will never fear for your safety again."

Marie lifted her head. "So, they're not going to expel him?"

He shook his head.

She rested her palm on the smooth fabric of his lapel. "Don't do anything to jeopardize your position here," she said weakly.

He flashed Marie a smile. "Don't worry. I'll take care of things here. You need to go home and rest for a few days."

Marie stiffened. "I will not. I'm going to class tomorrow, with no bandages. I want them all to see what he did to me," she insisted.

Matthew pressed a warm hand to her shoulder. "My intrepid Marie," he said with affection. "Whatever you want, but please allow me to see you home safely to your apartment tonight."

Philippe cleared his throat. "I don't think that's a good idea," he said, catching Marie's eye. It was clear that he was concerned that being with Matthew unchaperoned might cause her even more distress.

"Please," said Matthew.


The driving rain pelted Marie and Matthew during their short walk from his runabout to her apartment door. Inside, he hung his coat, rolled up his sleeves and crouched by the wood-burning stove. He stacked kindling and logs and lit the fire. Meanwhile, Marie wrapped her arms around her body for warmth. Gray clouds, bulky with rain, moved sluggishly across the San Francisco skyline.

"Marie, why don't you change into some dry clothing?" he asked, rubbing his hands together. You're shivering." His calm demeanor vexed Marie. It reminded her of their courtship—and how, despite his stately good looks and charm, Matthew had been lying to her the whole time.

She wouldn't allow him to use the attack as an excuse to sweep his deception under the rug. Without facing him, she asked, "If your association with Margaret O'Shea no longer exists, why did your mother tell me that you're still engaged?" Marie watched shiny rivulets of rain run down the glass windowpanes.

After a pause, he replied, "She didn't know. My father and I hadn't told her yet. And I didn't expect my parents to show up at the party."

"Did Bridget and Jimmy know the relationship had ended?"

"Yes."

Seated on the chair beside the stove, he leaned in and spoke straightforwardly. "Marie. I didn't love her."

"Love?" Marie scoffed. "Love has nothing to do with it." A deep ache started at the center of her head and radiated out to her scalp. The wound on her forehead throbbed. An undertow of grief threatened to drag her down. She covered her eyes, but the memories flashed, like frames of a moving picture spliced together. She remembered Adeline's father—Bastien—and the sheer force of his lust. He had seduced her, only to break his promise of marriage and cast her aside. She smelled Larry Deaver's sharp whiskey breath, and felt the prick of his knife against her neck. She flinched, recalling the feeling of his rough nails against her backside. She began to sway and gasp for air.

"Marie!" Matthew cried, reaching out to steady her.

She regained her footing and backed away. "Why are you here?"

"I'm not leaving until we discuss everything that happened." His reply was restrained.

Marie peeled off her sodden jacket and slapped it down on the floor. "Yes, you're right." She tugged frantically at the buttons of her high collar, exposing the lacerations from the knife. "Better yet," she hissed, "let's *see* what happened. This is where Deaver threatened me with his knife."

"Marie—" Matthew took a step forward.

One glance from her stopped him. Marie ripped her shirt-waist open from top to bottom, popping its buttons. She cast the garment aside and unlaced the stays of her corset. As it fell, the thin gauze of Marie's chemise slipped down over one shoulder, revealing the purple and yellow bruises on her chest. Matthew's expression of revulsion pained her, yet somehow spurred her on. She yanked down the chemise. "*This* is what happened when he threw me over the table and slammed my head into the microscope."

Matthew stood stock-still. He looked at her with a mixture of curiosity and dread. Marie wriggled out of her skirts. She stood before him clad only in her chemise and drawers, which she then shimmied down over her hips.

"Marie, enough!" Matthew commanded, but she ignored him. She wanted him to see every indignity she'd suffered. Turning her back to him, she ran her hands up her scratched thighs.

"*This* is what happened!" she shrieked. She didn't know where her angry words were coming from. "Does it excite you? Knowing what he did to me?" she asked viciously.

"No," he choked out. "It makes me sick."

She couldn't contain her self-loathing, but nor could she silence her anguish. "You don't want me now, do you?" Her lip quivered.

"Marie, you're unwell. You look feverish." He held out a hand to touch her forehead.

She batted him away. "Answer the question!" she cried, halfway between a scream and a sob.

Matthew lurched forward and shook her, a wild misery etched on his face. "Stop, Marie, stop!" he yelled.

"What are you waiting for?" she persisted, roping her arms around his neck. He jerked away. Marie screamed, "Take me! Take me, you damned coward!"

She threw herself at him, but Matthew caught her. She squirmed and kicked, but he held her tightly. "Marie . . ." Her hair muffled his words. She clung to him, burying her face in his shoulder, comforted by the familiar scent of his starched shirt. She shook with despair. Only when the tension in her muscles eased, and she could breathe again, did she become aware of his heaving chest.

Fatigue underscored his teary eyes. He looked wretched. "I'm so sorry, Marie," he said hoarsely. The heat of his touch between her bare shoulder blades shocked her senses. Suddenly mortified by her state of undress and her outburst, Marie tried to break away. Matthew held on, reached for the bed quilt, and clumsily draped it over her shoulders.

Gaining control of his voice, he insisted, "Come now. You're burning up and you know you need a bath to break the fever."

"But—"

"Marie, I'm your doctor. And besides, I imagine you're too

sore to properly bathe yourself anyhow." She was too fraught with exhaustion to object.

She eased into the tub, her back facing the door, and hugged her knees to her chest. The water was lukewarm, and not at all soothing. Matthew entered with a bundle of towels. He knelt down, soaped up a wet flannel and gently squeezed the water over Marie's back. He skimmed the cloth over her shoulders, neck and arms. She closed her eyes, concentrating on his careful touch, willing her embarrassment to evaporate. Soon, his fingers were tangled in her wet, sudsy hair, massaging the tension away, but avoiding the stinging wound at her temple. When he rinsed her hair, she shuddered violently as the tepid liquid chased the last vestiges of fever from her body.

It was awhile before Matthew spoke. "Marie?" She didn't dare turn, but he continued, his voice steady now. "I never had any intention of going through with the engagement to Margaret." He lifted Marie's hand and brushed his lips over the split, raw skin of her knuckles. "But you should know—I would have done far worse than lie to keep you."

Marie awoke in her bed during the night, wearing her dressing gown, but wrapped in Matthew's embrace. When she stirred, he mumbled sleepily, "I'm sorry if I woke you. My arm fell asleep." He shifted, and she felt the long, sinewy lines of his body against hers.

The intimacy they had forged over the last few hours had broken through their defenses, and now the unexpected desire was too acute for Marie to ignore. She met his gaze, imploring him, "Please." Her mouth shyly, sweetly tasted his.

He returned her kiss fervently, and his longing was undeniable. Yet, when she began to unbutton his shirt, he pulled away, clasping her hands together. "No, Marie. Not now, not like this." He slipped out of her bed to retrieve his shoes and jacket. He crouched down and stroked Marie's damp hair. She searched his face expectantly. He smiled, explaining, "We'll wait for the right time, my love. After you've walked down the church aisle and we've exchanged our vows. Only then." He kissed her softly, instructed her to lock the door behind him and stepped out into the darkness of Sacramento Street.

# Chapter 32

Although Thad offered to escort Marie to all her classes, she refused. She had to face things herself. Before entering her biology classroom Wednesday morning, she inhaled sharply, scanning the room for Larry Deaver's face. He wasn't there. In fact, he was absent for the next two days. Matthew must have found a way to keep his promise.

She held it together, but by lunchtime on Thursday, Marie found herself distracted by her memories, scattered helter-skelter through her consciousness like sick snapshots of her ordeal. She walked across the street to the hospital, eager for a change of scenery. She passed the surgical theatre, where nurses were sterilizing the operating table and swabbing the floors. She found Matthew alone in the nearby washroom, scrubbing his hands. When she walked in, his smile sent her stomach somersaulting.

He grabbed a towel to dry his hands and glanced over her

shoulder to make sure no one was listening. "How's it going today?" he asked in a hushed tone.

"Better than I expected. Larry Deaver still hasn't shown his face," she reported, her eyes narrowing. "You didn't . . . do anything to him, did you?"

Matthew's eyes widened with surprise. "No, although I wish I had." A look she couldn't read crossed his face, but it was quickly replaced with a relaxed grin. "I told you not to worry, didn't I?" He tossed the towel into the laundry bin. "Are you headed to Napa tomorrow?" he asked.

Marie hesitated. "Maybe. I'm not sure . . ."

He moved closer, resting his hands on her shoulders. She felt a familiar stirring, but she knew that while they were here at the hospital, they could do no more. She closed her eyes, inhaling the scents of soap and antiseptic. His fingers grazed her scalp. "This cut is healing well, but I wish I could have stitched it."

She brushed off his concern. "I want to spend time with Adeline," she blurted. "She'll worry if I don't go this weekend."

"Does she understand what happened?" He squinted with concern.

"Yes, but I want to reassure her that it won't happen again." She hoped Matthew would offer to accompany her to Napa, but he didn't. Marie thought they'd formed a rare bond the other evening, yet he was acting surprisingly aloof. "Are you working on Saturday?" she ventured shyly.

"Ah, yes. Yes, I had something come up," he offered absent-mindedly, before switching gears. "Perhaps I'll go with you next weekend?'

"I'd like that," she replied with deflated spirits.

"Me, too," he replied, and they both turned, suddenly aware of someone watching them.

"Sorry to interrupt, Dr. Donnelly." A nurse stepped forward. "You're needed upstairs to consult with Dr. Meyer," she said, flashing Marie a sympathetic look. Did the whole hospital know about her misfortune?

Matthew squeezed her arm reassuringly, and followed the nurse out of the washroom. Marie stood alone for a few moments, wondering if her behavior the other night had scared him off. Had Matthew changed his mind about her?

Marie had hoped to avoid Larry Deaver for the rest of the week. On Friday morning, however, he appeared in Marie's calculus class just before the bell. He'd suffered a black eye, a broken nose, scrapes along his cheekbones. Matthew must have lied to her—he'd beaten Deaver to a pulp. Marie gripped the edge of her seat, although her natural instinct was to flee the room. To her relief, five of her classmates surrounded Deaver, herding him to a desk in the back of the room. Thad picked up a pig's head, jarred in formaldehyde, and plopped it on Deaver's desk. The professor even nodded his approval, then began the class. Marie sat a little taller that hour.

By her last class of the day, Marie's nerves had unraveled. She hadn't seen Matthew since Wednesday. What if the college had fired him for what he'd done to Deaver? She had to see him before she left for Napa.

"Hey kid," Thad called to Marie just before she exited the building. "How you feeling?"

Marie paused and allowed the swarm of departing students to pass her. "Much better, especially after seeing Deaver's face."

"Oh, so you enjoyed my handiwork?" His expression brightened.

"You did that?" she replied, bewildered.

Thad bowed slightly. "It was one of the year's highlights for me. So where are you headed?"

Marie shifted uneasily.

"Are you worried about Donnelly?"

How did he know?

"Your face shows everything you're thinking, and besides, it's in today's paper."

Dread swelled in Marie's stomach. Had the college fired Matthew?

Thad unfolded the newspaper under his arm and opened it to the society section. All she saw was wedding announcements. Marie's brow bunched with confusion, but then she spotted a headline with a familiar name. The article began, "Margaret O'Shea of Philadelphia married Peter Smithson of Russian Hill in an elegant ceremony . . ."

Thad watched her carefully. "Marie, what are you waiting for?" He handed her the newspaper. "Go find him." She stepped back, stunned by his forwardness.

"Wha—what about you?" she sputtered.

He glanced down, shuffling his feet. When he looked up, his laughing brown eyes met hers. "Aw, I never had a chance. The man's a medical doctor and heir to an iron fortune—who could

compete with that? But it sure was nice to dream for a while."
He winked.

As he started for the door, Marie caught his arm and hugged
him fiercely. She didn't care who saw them or what gossip they'd
stir. She pecked Thad on the cheek and said, "You're a good man."

He flicked his head, his mouth twitching into a smile. "Up to
Nob Hill with you, then. Go on!" Marie's eyes softened with silent
thanks before she stepped out into the sunlight.

She walked down the street, hopped on the next cable car,
and rode it to the top of Nob Hill. She rapped on Donnelly's front
door and rang the bell. Jane answered, and grimaced upon seeing Marie. "Oh, my dear Miss Chevreau! I heard about what happened. What monsters! How are you feeling?" She was so kind,
Marie almost cried. "Please, do come in," Jane offered.

"Is the doctor here?" Marie asked.

"Are you ill?" Jane asked.

"Not exactly. Is he here, Jane?" she whispered, as Virginia
passed them, carrying fresh laundry.

"No," Jane replied, glancing at the clock on the wall. "But I
believe he's coming in on the four o'clock ferry."

"Coming in? From where?" Matthew never traveled out of the
city during the week.

"Vallejo, I believe."

Marie was thoroughly confused. "Thank you, Jane." She hung
her head and stepped out the door. Jane followed her, speaking softly.

"Miss Chevreau, I'm not one to talk out of turn, but if I were
you, I'd skedaddle down to that ferry right now," she advised, a
smile tugging on her lips. She disappeared back into the house.

◠

Marie stepped off the cable car and pushed her way through the Friday afternoon crowds. She would have sprinted, but her heavy bag made it impossible. She scanned the street beneath the ferry terminal's arched windows and clock tower, but there was no sign of Matthew. She entered the terminal, so elegant with its interior arches and bright skylights. She stopped short when she saw Matthew sitting nearby, his outstretched arms resting casually over the back of a wide, polished bench.

Marie dropped her bag. Her feet suddenly felt rooted in place. He smiled broadly, stood up and opened his palms, his gentle eyes never wavering. Overwhelmed with relief, she began to shake, a flood of tears streaming down her cheeks. Scores of people darted by, but they were all a blur. She saw no one but him.

He walked over and drew her close, cupping a warm hand around her neck. "Now, then," he soothed her. "Just breathe." She blinked and blotted her face with his handkerchief.

She sniffled. "Did they fire you?"

He chuckled and shook his head. "I quit," he explained.

"Why? And what were you doing in Vallejo?" Her mind whirled.

"How did you know—?" Matthew looked surprised. "Well, it doesn't matter. I resigned to protest the administration's decision. And I took the ferry because I had an important errand to run. I was hoping to catch you here before you boarded."

"Catch me? Here? But why?" Marie wanted to grip his hands in hers. After they'd spent an evening curled in each other's arms, it seemed ludicrous that people would think them indecent for holding hands here.

"I knew you'd want to hop the ferry to Napa afterwards."

"After what?" she asked, her heart pounding. Hordes of passengers rushed by in both directions, as though she and Matthew were two stones in a raging river.

He reached into his pocket and dug out a small black velvet drawstring bag. He shook it gently, dropping a sparkling ring into his palm. He slid off Marie's glove and slipped the diamond solitaire on her finger. Marie was speechless. She had never seen, let alone worn, anything so lavish.

"Marry me," he insisted. "I was in Napa, asking Philippe, Sara and Adeline for your hand." He smiled. "By the way, they said yes."

His thoughtfulness astonished her. Marie raised an eyebrow, suddenly struck by another, more worrying thought. "What about your mother?"

"I'll have you know my mother offered her highest praise."

"What did she say?" Marie asked skeptically.

Matthew kissed the inside of her wrist. "'She's French, but she's nice.'"

# Chapter 33

Pippa smiled from ear to ear in her new pink frock with tiny yellow flowers hand-sewn into the smocking. Sara could still see the thin, uneven line below her nose from the operation, but that would fade in time. From a few steps away, she looked like any other child, laughed and ate and chattered like any other child. She spoke with only a tiny lisp now.

Philippe, Sara and the children bounced down the road in their wagon, leading the wedding caravan—a string of horses, surreys, runabouts and bicycles—from St. John's in Napa City to Eagle's Run for the celebration of Marie's marriage to Matthew.

Sara waved to the new Mrs. Donnelly, who was radiant in her ivory silk gown trimmed with Brussels lace. When she had walked down the aisle on Philippe's arm, holding a bouquet of peach and white cabbage roses, the scalloped hems of her two-tiered skirt swished elegantly. Elbow-length gloves complemented her gigot sleeves, and her floor-length lace veil was held in place by a crown of tiny silk rosettes that beautifully framed her brown eyes and petite face. Marie waved back. It was truly the most perfect day Sara could recall.

Sara had been thrilled when Marie and Matthew had asked to hold their reception at the new winery. She thought his family would have wanted the wedding to take place at their church in San Francisco, with a big reception at a fancy hotel. But Marie had wanted something small, and comfortable, at home with her family.

Still, the Donnellys had spared no expense. Bridget had helped Marie and Sara plan the reception. It was a sunny, cloudless October day, and the vine leaves were stunning in shades of gold and crimson. China, silver and crystal decorated long white tables in the orchard, protected by the shade of the ripening apple trees. Yesterday, Sara and Marie had spent hours arranging vases of deep pink and yellow dahlias, purchased from the hothouse. The colors burst like fireworks against the linen tablecloths. Philippe had brought out the 1901 Eagle's Run Chardonnay and Saint Martin Chenin Blanc for the occasion, and dinner was to be roasted pig, cooked over a fire pit by George Rogers, Philippe's old friend and chef from the Palace Hotel in Napa.

The guests, an eclectic mix of San Francisco society people, doctors, nurses, medical students and Napa natives, spilled out of their conveyances, and children sprinted toward the orchard, winding through the apple trees, playing tag and plucking fruit from the low branches. Philippe opened the immense oak doors of the stone winery, allowing the afternoon sun to brighten the first-floor tasting room. Sara breathed a sigh of contentment mixed with pride. Despite so many challenges, she and Philippe had worked together to make this day a reality. With a wink, he jumped up on an empty barrel behind the gleaming bottles arranged at the tasting bar, spread his arms and declared, "The Eagle's Run tasting room is officially open!"

The crowd cheered in response, and even the high-society guests seemed in the mood for a good old-fashioned country party. When dinner was ready, Sara had to ring the bell for ten minutes to gather all the guests, who had scattered across the vineyard and farmland.

After dinner everyone crowded around to admire the white cake with its buttercream frosting, adorned with sprigs of lavender from Aurora's garden. As the guests lined up for their slices, Matthew's mother snapped photos of the wedding party with her new camera. For the first time ever, Sara would have a family photo to place on the mantel in the dining room.

As the afternoon wore into evening, Sara and Philippe placed lanterns on the tables and hung them from tree branches. Philippe had even bought a few strands of white electric lights for the tasting room, which now served as the dance floor. He took a turn with Marie, while the string quartet played "Beautiful Erin." Sara swayed to the music as she watched them; they looked like brother and sister, happy to once again be part of each other's lives. Matthew suddenly appeared by Sara's side. "Isn't she lovely?" he marveled.

Sara recognized that hopeless look on his face. She linked her arm through Matthew's. "She is, and you are one lucky man."

"I know," he sighed, extending his arms to offer Sara a dance. In no time, they were spinning circles around Philippe and Marie, who had slowed, locked in deep conversation. When the song ended, Matthew whispered, "May I borrow you and Philippe, and Adeline, too? I'd like you to be with us when I share the news."

Sara knew what he was talking about. "Of course. I'll find Adeline." Sara and Philippe had helped Matthew with all the details, while keeping his secret from Marie.

Matthew guided Marie, Sara, Philippe and Adeline away from the winery and around to the front of the house, never letting go of Marie's hand. Adeline walked close beside them. Matthew put his left arm around her shoulders, pulling her into an affectionate bear hug. "Miss Adeline, I saw you dancing with that Sumter boy . . . What's his name?"

Adeline turned bright pink. "Jess, sir."

"Jess? And how old is this Jess? Isn't eleven a little young for your first dance?"

Adeline shrugged. "He asked," she replied nonchalantly.

Matthew called to Philippe, who walked with Sara a few paces behind. "How are we going to scare off Adeline's suitors, Philippe?" Adeline giggled while Marie rolled her eyes.

Philippe shot Sara a sideways glance and replied, "You won't be needing a rifle. One sharp look from Sara usually scares the devil out of Jess Sumter." Sara jabbed Philippe in the side and smiled apologetically at Adeline.

The front porch was a welcome respite from the crowd of rowdy guests behind the house. Sara shivered in the cool night air, and Philippe drew her close. She melted into his warmth.

Matthew rubbed his palms together. "I have an announcement to make, you two." Marie and Adeline exchanged glances. "With Sara and Philippe's help, I've planned a trip next summer. In June, the three of us leave for France!" Marie clapped a hand over her mouth. Matthew suggested, "Now you can introduce me—and Adeline—to your family." Marie was nearly in tears, thanking Sara and Philippe before throwing her arms around Matthew and Adeline.

Sara and Philippe wandered back toward the winery, allowing the new family some privacy. Philippe squeezed Sara's shoulders. "What a wonderful day."

"Glorious," she agreed, pleased to have a peaceful moment together.

"I hope they'll be as happy as we are."

"The last five years haven't been all hearts and roses, you'll recall."

"No, we've had our share of difficulty, but we're surviving, aren't we?" he said contentedly. A lock of hair fell over his face, and she brushed it off his forehead. His expression was bright and clear, with no trace of the fatigue and suffering that had marked the last few years.

"I'd hoped for more than just surviving," she reminded him.

"Look at all we have now—Pippa, Luc and Johnny, all healthy. The vineyard is back on track, and wine prices are at an all-time high. Who could want more?"

Sara circled her arms around his neck and planted a kiss on his lips. She walked into the orchard, calling to her children. Aurora appeared holding Johnny, who was sleeping soundly on her shoulder. Pippa and Luc darted between the trees, and came bounding up to her, hand-in-hand. Sara's heart filled with a peace she hadn't known for a long time. They had been to hell and back in the last years, but Sara would do it again, if it meant protecting her family.

# Chapter 34

APRIL 17, 1906

Philippe stirred next to Sara. His warm hand slid over her thigh and across her round belly. "Baby awake yet?" he whispered.

She opened one eye, and noting the absence of sunlight, clamped it shut again. "No, and neither am I," she groaned. In her eighth month of pregnancy, Sara craved sleep.

Philippe kissed the soft spot beneath her earlobe. "C'mon, Mrs. Lemieux, you must have big plans today. Don't you have a city hall to picket or a factory to storm?"

"Just laundry," she replied. "But we do have about twenty visitors coming this afternoon for a tour and some wine sampling."

At this point in her pregnancy, Sara found comfort in staying home and managing the flow of visitors through the winery.

"And of course, you'll charm them into buying our entire inventory."

"As much as they can pack into their motorcars and wagons, yes." Sara yawned. Since the opening of the new winery and tasting room four years ago, Eagle's Run was seeing record profits. Prices had increased and demand for wine was so high, Sara and Philippe now purchased grapes from their neighbors to increase their output. They'd cleared and planted twenty new acres of pinot noir grapes, which they would harvest this fall.

Philippe slid out of bed and started dressing. Sara rolled over, admiring his muscular thighs. She felt a twinge of envy when she gazed at his flat stomach. "Are you staying in Nob Hill tonight?" she asked. Marie and Matthew generously insisted Philippe stay with them every time he was in town. Typically they visited the farm every month with Adeline and two-year-old Gemma, born in the fall of 1903, right after Marie started her third year of medical school. Whenever Sara felt overwhelmed with her responsibilities at the winery, she thought of Marie, who was finishing up night shifts at Harbor Hospital and would join Matthew's practice full-time in the fall. Marie was the busiest woman she knew.

"Actually, no," Philippe replied, buttoning his breeches. "Matthew's family is visiting, and I don't want to intrude. Besides, I want to show Luc around the city. We'll stay at the Silverado Hotel on Market, close to the train depot and the ferry."

"I hope you boys have fun," she said. She tried to sound

cheerful, although she didn't really like being on her own, even overnight, when she was pregnant.

Philippe stretched across the bed and pecked Sara's lips. She missed the flare of desire she used to feel when they kissed, but they were happy.

She turned over and dozed off.

When the cock crowed, Luc scrambled out of bed and threw on his knickers, stockings, white shirt and brown leather shoes. He plucked his coat off the hook on the back of the door and bolted for the kitchen. This was the most exciting day of his life so far.

"Good morning, Rose!" he said to their housemaid.

"Hello, Master Luc. You look as delighted as a pig in mud." Luc had always liked Rose. She was round in her housecoat and apron, and bustled between the stove and table with a spring in her step, gripping a spatula. Luc tried to sneak a piece of bacon from the sideboard, but a light swat of her hand stopped him. "You sit yerself right down, young man, and mind your manners," she ordered, waving her spatula like a weapon.

He obeyed, wiggling into a chair. His stomach growled. At dinner last night, Maman had said no pie after he'd rolled his peas under the edge of his plate, one by one, when no one was looking. Luc smiled to himself, recalling Maman's face when she picked up his plate to find a necklace of green peas! She was fit to be tied.

Papa swung the kitchen door open with a bang just as Rose set down their oatmeal, eggs, toast and bacon. "Thank you, Rose," he boomed, ruffling Luc's hair. "I hope you had a good night's sleep."

Luc beamed. "Yes, sir. Ready for our trip." Papa nodded, sipped his coffee and scanned the paper.

Maman soon appeared in the kitchen in her dressing gown and slippers. Luc would never say it out loud, but with the baby coming next month, she looked as though she'd swallowed a leather ball. He thought it would be nice to have another sister— someone else to play with Pippa. He and his four-year-old brother Johnny didn't like playing dolls. If his friends ever found out, they'd call him a sissy for sure. He liked catching the pie pan in spin the platter, shooting marbles, playing blindman's buff and, of course, helping Papa pick and crush grapes.

Papa stood up and pulled out the chair for Maman. He was a gentleman. "G'morning, darling," he said.

She patted his hand with her slender fingers. "You boys all packed? How many deliveries are you making?"

"Twenty or so," Papa replied. He swung around Rose to steal a piece of toast, but she didn't dare slap his hand.

Maman's eyes narrowed. "He's missing a mathematics test," she protested. Luc's shoulders slumped at the thought of having to skip the day's adventure because of a stupid test.

Papa knew just what to say. "Didn't you ever play hooky?" he asked Maman. "Never mind, don't answer that. There's no harm in taking the boy out of school for a day or two to teach him about the business. When he's eighteen and takes over Saint Martin, he'll need to know how to sell and deliver wine—the right way." Papa winked at Luc. "You'll take the test on Thursday, right, Luc?"

"Yes, sir." Luc wiped his mouth and laid his dishes in the sink. "Thanks, Rose, that was dee-licious!"

Rose handed him a paper bag. "You take these sandwiches and jugs and load them up for your father, straight away."

Maman caught him by the waist and squeezed him tightly before he ran out to the wagon. "You help your father, and no sassing, understand?" she called. Even though Maman worried about things like ironed shirts, mathematics tests and clean fingernails, she was soft and warm and always smelled good, like talcum powder and roses.

As they rode to Vallejo to catch the ferry, the moist air began to blow, pushing the fog against the hills like ocean waves rolling over rocks. Luc felt like the luckiest boy alive, with the cool morning wind on his face instead of the dusty air of the classroom.

When the ferry charged from San Pablo Bay into San Francisco Bay, Luc could see the silhouettes of buildings against the sky, shimmering in the glow of the rising sun. Papa unfolded his dog-eared map and moved his finger over the maze of streets. "First we'll pick up the demijohns and bottles at the depot, then we'll head west up to Nob Hill. After we make about seven stops up in that neighborhood, we'll swing back down to the depot, pick up the next load and make our way up Market Street. After we deliver to the Palace Hotel, we'll stay the night at the Silverado. In the morning, we'll make another two or three deliveries and finish in time to catch the ferry home at noon."

"Papa, what's a nob?"

Papa laughed. "It's short for 'nabob.' Years ago, the railroad barons were nicknamed 'nobs' because they built mansions up on the hill to show off their wealth. Ever since, city folks have called the neighborhood Nob Hill."

Luc thought about this. "Does that mean that Tante Marie and Uncle Matthew are nobs, too?" They lived on Taylor Street in a big fancy house, right in the center of the neighborhood.

Papa chortled. "No, they don't put on airs like the other nobs do."

Tante Marie and Uncle Matthew were two of the nicest people he knew. They weren't just doctors, they were surgeons. "Can we stop in to see them?" Luc's mouth watered at the thought of the rainbow-colored candy Tante Marie kept out in a glass bowl in the huge foyer of their home.

"Not this time. They're both working today, and they have guests staying at the house, which is why you and I are bunking at the Silverado. Don't worry, they serve your favorites—pork pie and devil's food cake."

Their wagon climbed the steep slope of California Street from the Ferry Building all the way up to Powell Street. Papa handed Luc the reins as they drove the horses higher and higher up the wide dirt road. Luc stayed to the right, out of the way of the cable cars, runabouts, wagons, carriages and bicycles racing up and down the hill. The whole time, all he could think about was the ride back down. What fun it would be to make a go-cart from a grape crate and the wheels of Johnny's old carriage! He'd start at the crest of Nob Hill, and fly straight down California Street at lightning speed, hair rippling in the wind. He'd have to install a strong brake, so he didn't overshoot the Ferry Building and plunge into the bay.

Luc watched in silence from the wagon while Papa knocked on the back doors of homes as large as the winery building. When a maid or housekeeper came to the door, Papa took off his cap. If a butler answered, he extended his hand. He always smiled, chatted about the weather or the wine, and handed over the bill before stacking the cases of wine or ten-gallon demijohns in the cellar. That way, customers had plenty of time to collect the payment out of the house's safe, Papa said. If he were delivering for a party—typically a large order—Papa would always offer the servants a bottle of wine "with his compliments." What were those? Luc asked. "A gift they don't pay for. Makes them feel special, like the lord or lady of the manor," Papa replied. "Nine times out of ten, the butler or the housekeeper decides which wines to serve at the parties. That bottle of wine I give them might be the reason they choose us over Inglenook or Krug." Luc nodded. Selling wine took more brains than he imagined.

By the time they reached the Silverado Hotel late that afternoon, Luc's neck ached from craning to see the dome of City Hall, the top floor of the eight-story Palace Hotel and the other tall, fancy buildings that lined Market Street. The Silverado was a modest, three-story hotel with a rowdy saloon on its first floor. Papa booked them a room on the third so they wouldn't hear the racket from downstairs. He left Luc to wash up in the room while he fetched the pork pie and devil's food cake he'd promised from the saloon.

They ate on the floor like heathens, licking their fingers, burping and talking with their mouths full—all the things that made Maman frown. Luc taught Papa how to play tiddlywinks on the pine floor. The last thing he remembered that evening was Papa snoring gently beside him on the bed, and feeling happy.

~

Luc awoke with a start. He thought he was dreaming, because the room was dancing a jig. Papa grabbed him around the waist just before another jolt slid them off the bed and hurled them down to the floor, which seemed to be collapsing beneath them. Papa locked Luc tightly to his chest, breaking his fall as they hit a pile of debris.

Cracking noises and the screams of the other guests pierced Luc's ears. He could feel Papa's heart thudding, and his arms wrapped around him. His bare legs stung as wood, brick and glass fell on them. The ground continued to twist like a whirligig and growl like a monstrous train. A hot stream of urine trickled down the inside of his thigh. When the earth quieted, an eternity later, he blinked several times, but all he could see was darkness.

"Papa!" he cried, chest heaving and hands trembling.

Papa placed a big, warm paw on his forehead. "Are you hurt?" he asked gruffly.

Luc felt sore where he'd been struck by debris, but he was more frightened than hurt. He shook his head, but then realized Papa probably couldn't see him either. "No," he answered. "You?"

Papa grunted. "A little." He was breathing heavily. "We have to dig ourselves out." Papa pushed Luc up into a seated position. "Can you see anything?" Luc stretched his arms high. He touched wooden boards, but nothing too scratchy or sharp, above him. Suddenly, he saw a pinprick of dark blue sky. He pushed his hand

up toward the light, hoping to feel the open air. He heard a muffled cry beneath them. A whimpering dog, trapped and scared, he
guessed. "Keep going," Papa shouted over the noise. Before long,
Luc was pushing planks and small metal pieces aside, forming a
hole large enough for them to stand.

When their heads emerged, Luc had to wipe his eyes with
his sleeve to make sure he was seeing straight. They were standing on a pile of rubble—twisted metal, crumbling brick and rock,
and shattered glass—all that remained of their hotel. Clouds of
yellow dust blocked Luc's view of the street. Papa's scratched,
dirt-streaked face contorted into an expression of horror and
bewilderment. He tried to gain a foothold in the wall of debris
surrounding them, but he couldn't. Luc bent over backwards
like a crab, with both feet and hands planted on the ground, and
pressed his thighs together, forming a step. Papa steadied one foot
on Luc's thighs and hoisted himself up and out through the tunnel of rubble. Then he leaned back down, took Luc's hand in his,
and pulled the boy out of the wreckage.

They looked down Market Street. The Ferry Building was not
visible—thick dust filled the air—but thousands of people were
rushing toward it, screaming, in their nightclothes. Panicky horses
zigzagged in the road and a herd of longhorn steers charged, tramp-
ling people beneath their pounding hooves. Luc turned around.
The Palace Hotel, only two blocks up, was a skeleton of its former
self. Its elegant arches and tall walls looked like the bones of an
animal carcass picked over by buzzards. In the distance, black and
white clouds billowed as high as Luc could see, blocking out the
light of the rising sun.

With bare, bloody feet, and wearing only their nightshirts, Philippe and Luc cleared away stones, bricks, metal and furniture, looking for survivors. A heart-wrenching cry rang out. "Over here!" Papa shouted, and grabbed a woman's hand. He kicked away debris with his feet while Luc pulled bricks off her body and threw them aside. She was a young woman, probably a few years older than Adeline, who was fifteen, and she was shouting for her ma. Once free, she pawed at the rubble around her with raw, red hands. In a few minutes, they uncovered her mother's blue, bruised face. Papa placed two fingers on the woman's neck and then shook his head. Luc sucked in a breath. He'd never seen a dead person before. The girl sank to her knees, hunched over her mother, kissing her lifeless face. Her wails cut through the sounds of chaos on the street and sliced Luc through.

Papa held the girl's shoulders as she shook uncontrollably. In a few minutes, she quieted and they continued lifting the bricks and splintered timbers off her mother's body. Papa squatted down, listening for sounds of life from the remains of the hotel. Over the next few hours, dozens of men and women stopped to help them lift fallen timber and pull out survivors. Luc's hands were bleeding, and his arms felt like wet noodles. His throat was parched, and he craved water, but there wasn't any. There was nothing.


This was the end of the world, Philippe thought. Smoke raced down Market Street toward them. The conflagration, fueled by high winds, was devouring what remained of City Hall, the

Donahue Building and the Phelan Building. The heavy smell of creosote permeated the air, leaving a smoky taste in his mouth. His nails bled as he dug for any living creatures. Philippe unearthed a middle-aged man whose legs were trapped under a pile of debris. His nose and mouth made a whistling sound as he strained to breathe. He clenched Philippe's wrist.

"Help me," he begged, writhing in pain.

"What's your name?" Philippe wiped the man's forehead with the corner of his shirt.

"Sam. Sam Freeman." His voice broke. "I can't feel my legs."

"I know." The man's body was crushed from the waist down, and his spine was probably irreparably damaged. "We'll do our best, Sam," Philippe said, swallowing hard, his throat gritty and dry. For half an hour, seven men and women dragged wooden beams and piles of brick off the man until Luc tugged on Philippe's shirt. "Papa, we have to go," he said, his eyes darting to the fire raging only a block away.

Philippe scanned the street. The wind was blowing fiercely, the sky raining ash, and the funnel of fire, fueled by the suction of rising hot air, was growing taller and more menacing every second. He searched the faces around him. One by one, they patted Sam on the head, or whispered words of comfort, and fled the scene. When Luc and Philippe were the only ones who remained, Philippe crouched down next to him and gripped his hand. Sam's eyes flinched. "Wait," he gasped. With a quivering hand, he reached down, pulled the pistol from his belt and placed it in Philippe's hand. Philippe saw the shock on Luc's face. The boy spun away and threw his hands over his ears. He knew.

Philippe's stomach lurched. His scarred hand twitched, reminding him of the searing pain of fire melting flesh. How could he allow this man to suffer burns a thousand times more painful than he'd experienced? But how could he shoot him in front of Luc? Philippe's mind flashed to the memory of his father lying dead on his bedroom rug. He broke into a cold sweat. This was not much different. Both, in their own way, were mercy killings.

"Please," Sam wailed, sobbing like a child now. "I've already forgiven you, and God will, too. Please!" he howled, squeezing his eyes shut, gnashing his teeth.

Philippe felt the fire's heat—only a minute more and their skin would start to blister. He glanced over his shoulder to make sure Luc was still facing away. He held Sam's trembling fingers and whispered, "Godspeed, my friend." The man took one long, last breath. Philippe gently stroked Sam's head, positioned the gun above his heart, looked away and fired. Luc jumped at the sound of the shot. Sam's arm fell lifelessly to the ground. Philippe refused to look at what he'd done. He dropped the gun, grabbed Luc's hand and they ran for their lives.

# Chapter 35

**M**arie sipped her water, looking out over the calm, windless bay. She checked her watch: twelve minutes past five. A pale pink blush swathed the horizon. In another fifteen minutes, the sun would rise in the eastern sky. Marie loved this time of morning at Harbor Emergency Hospital, when drunkards and gunshot victims stopped arriving and the surgeries were complete. Today, she had only a few patients to examine before driving home. She was finishing her surgical internship at the hospital, which stood at the edge of the San Francisco waterfront, not far from the Ferry Building. She thought of Matthew, Adeline and Gemma tucked in their beds, sleeping soundly, and her heart warmed. She couldn't wait to drive the twelve blocks up California Street, quiet and peaceful in the early morning, to their comfortable home on Taylor Street. She'd be home by seven, spend a precious ten minutes with Matthew over a cup of coffee, and then he'd leave for his day of surgery and teaching. She'd spend an hour catching up with the girls before Adeline walked to school and Gemma settled into the nursery with her nanny. Marie would sleep from nine to five and repeat the entire schedule again on Thursday. She'd promised the girls she'd dine with them every evening this summer, once she joined Matthew's practice.

"Marie?" Dr. McMann called from the doorway. Marie spun around. Before she could answer, the ground beneath her swayed violently, and she dropped to the linoleum floor on hands and knees. The supply cupboard doors flew open. Its glass panels shattered, and metal instruments crashed to the ground. The room writhed and convulsed like an injured animal. Marie crawled to the doorway, gripped the doorjamb and pulled herself up with Dr. McMann's help. Then everything stopped.

Shrieks and moans filled the corridor. "Are you hurt?" McMann's face was white.

"No," Marie groaned. She thought of Matthew, Adeline and Gemma. Were they hurt? Then another jolt sent her flying back into the room, reeling and staggering like a drunk. She fell to the floor, hitting her head on the way down. She stayed there, arms crossed protectively over her head, until the rattling ceased.

Marie grabbed a square of gauze and pressed it against her head to stop the bleeding. Dr. McMann ran down the hallway toward the hospital ward. She scrambled into the hall, picked up the telephone and dialed Matthew. No clicks, no operator. Silence.

Dr. McMann's shouts awakened her from her bewilderment. He urgently waved her down the hallway. As the floor lurched again, Marie pushed one shoulder into the wall for balance and slid down the corridor toward the receiving room, packed with hospital beds. She passed a small window and dared to peek out. Tangled telephone wires and fallen, splintered poles blocked half the road. The asphalt-covered streets had buckled and piled up, chimneys had crumbled, and rooming houses had tumbled like dominoes, their walls and timbers in ruins. Marie's hand covered her mouth as she thought of all the people who must be buried beneath the devastation. Then she spied men, women and children emerging from the wreckage. They rushed from their homes, most wearing only gowns and nightshirts, hobbling, limping and swarming toward the hospital.

Marie instantly shifted back into a surgeon's mindset.

By half past ten, the hospital was bursting at the seams, filled with the injured and dead. Patients arrived in droves, and the physicians and uniformed nurses huddled around operating tables. Marie sent orderlies out to the nearby drugstores to fetch as many supplies as they could bring back. Hotel workers carted over hot water and coffee. Crewmen from the destroyer U.S.S. *Preble* arrived with stretchers, ready to transport victims from the Howard Street pier to the naval hospital on Mare Island.

Around two o'clock, Marie finished her eleventh surgery. She untied her apron, scrubbed her hands and leaned on the cast-iron sink for support, staring at the puddle of blood in the clogged drain. She was so weary that she didn't hear her name being called. Someone tugged her sleeve. "Tante Marie?"

"Luc!" she cried, hugging the boy tightly to her. Scanning the room, she spied Philippe sitting on one of the beds, clad only in his nightshirt. He raised a hand and grimaced. The anguish in his eyes told of a nightmarish day. His face, hands and feet were black with grime. She choked down a sob. She'd completely forgotten they were staying in the city overnight. Marie rushed over and, taking his face in her hands, asked anxiously, "Where are you hurt?"

He looked down. He was pressing a bloodied cloth to his thigh. Marie lifted it gingerly, and saw the foot-long gash running vertically down his leg. Philippe winced. "In all the panic, I don't even know when it happened."

"Luckily it didn't go deep enough to sever your femoral artery, but you do need stitches."

"You'll do it?" Philippe asked weakly.

"Of course. Luc?" His face was sooty and tired. "Come with me. We'll find you a place to rest."

Marie fashioned a makeshift bed for Luc beneath one of the supply tables and brought him a cup of water. As Luc curled up on his side, Marie caught sight of his bare feet. They were bruised and caked with blood. She grabbed cotton swabs and disinfectant from the supply table and gently blotted the many tiny cuts. He balked at the sting of the disinfectant on his skin, but he never cried. His eyes were far away, unreachable. "You rest here, and I'll go fix up your father," Marie said soothingly. She wiped sweat from his forehead, trying to comfort the exhausted child. His weary face made her ache for her own girls.

Marie went back to Philippe's side. "We need to do it here, but I'd advise you to look away. I'm going to numb the skin and irrigate the wound with saline before I start stitching." She pricked his skin with the needle and pushed the cocaine anesthetic deep into the flesh. "Lie back and close your eyes. You won't feel anything," she said reassuringly.

Philippe did as she instructed. "Where's Luc?" he asked shakily.

"Sound asleep under a table in one of the supply rooms."

"And Matthew, Adeline and Gemma? And weren't Bridget and Jimmy staying with you, too?"

"I haven't had word. I was here all night. Bridget and Jimmy had to return to Napa earlier than expected, so just Matthew and the girls were at the house this morning."

Philippe's eyes widened with compassion. "They will be safe. The fires started south of Market, near our hotel. They haven't reached Nob Hill yet. I'm sure Matthew left with the girls right away. He wouldn't take chances."

Marie brushed her tears away with the heels of her palms, and stood up. "Let me wash up again, and I'll get to work," she said, smiling weakly.

She stitched slowly, precisely, closing each layer of skin. In a strange way, the repetitive motion was comforting. Philippe told her about the destruction of the rooming houses and Palace Hotel along Market Street, about people beating back the fire with wine-soaked rugs and drapes, about policemen smashing bottles of liquor, carrying out the mayor's orders to destroy all alcohol except beer.

Marie heard explosions in the distance. "What's that?" she said, alarmed.

"Dynamite. They're blasting the perimeter of the fire, hoping to snuff out the flames with the showering debris."

Marie was too fatigued to understand that logic. She finished the last stitch, prepared bandages and tied them over and around Philippe's thigh to cover the wound. "Keep the bandages on for three days, and don't wet them."

"Marie?"

"Hmm?" she asked, tying the last strip.

His blue eyes blazed. "You have to come with us when they ship us over to Vallejo."

"I can't. Not without them. I won't."

"Matthew will know where to find you. If the situation were reversed, I would expect him to take Sara to safety."

Marie stood up, unwilling to argue. "I'm going to check on Luc. You rest."

The boy was snoring lightly beneath the table, undisturbed by the activity around him. Marie staggered outside, hoping for a breath of fresh air, but encountered a shroud of smoke, despite gusts of wind blowing at her back. Thousands of people were streaming toward the Ferry Building and hospital, carrying bundles of bedsheets and family treasures in baby carriages, toy wagons and go-carts. Others dragged trunks or carried limp children on their backs. Every soot-streaked, battered, panicked face chipped away at Marie's heart. Behind them, a gruesome burning tower raged, reddening the sun and blackening the sky.

And it was headed right toward her.

Marie gazed westward. Nob Hill was not yet engulfed in flames, but Marie knew it was only a matter of time. Suddenly, she heard a squeal of delight, and turned around. Gemma. "Mama!" the little girl cried out, running to Marie with her arms extended.

Matthew and Adeline followed behind her, stumbling with relief. Marie's vision blurred through her own tears, but she gathered all three of them in her arms and kissed them.

Matthew wiped her tears with his thumbs. "You look so tired, sweet." He wrapped an arm around her waist and she leaned into him for support.

"You brought the girls—here?"

"Marie, there's looting throughout the city, and the fire will reach the house by dawn tomorrow. What else could I do?"

Of course he was right. Marie rubbed her sore eyes. "What about your patients?"

"That's what took me so long. Some left with their families, others we carried down here." Behind Matthew, Marie saw Virginia, Jane and two other nurses tending to three of the more critical patients, who were lying on stretchers.

"Philippe and Luc are here," Marie said. "Philippe's hurt, but as long as infection doesn't set in, his leg should be fine. They're leaving for Mare Island within the hour."

Matthew squeezed her hand. "You and the girls are going with them. I'll join you in a day or two, after things settle down here."

Marie laughed mirthlessly. "Things aren't settling down, Matthew. The water mains and gas lines have broken, and fireboats are pumping salt water to those fire engines over there, hoping they can save the hospital and Ferry Building. I'm not leaving without you."

Matthew pulled her aside and whispered, "Marie, the girls need you. Philippe and Luc need you. And you've been operating for nearly eighteen hours straight. You need rest. You're boarding that ship with the rest of your family. I'll meet you at Eagle's Run by Friday if I have to swim across the bay. I promise."

Marie was too tired to argue, too tired to stand. Her knees buckled, and Matthew caught her in his arms. "C'mon now, love," he soothed, walking her toward an open area on the ground, next to a row of wounded. "Sit here. I'll get Philippe and Luc. Adeline and Gemma, you take care of your mother. I'll be right back."

Matthew ducked into the hospital and Marie looked up into Adeline's sad eyes. She took her daughter's hands. "What's that?" she asked, her gaze shifting to a small wood-and-leather trunk at Adeline's feet.

"Papa stuffed it with bandages, surgical knives, catgut thread, as much as he could fit." Adeline knelt down and opened the box. "And this." She dug to the bottom, pulled out a small velvet bag and offered it to her mother. Marie recognized it instantly. She shook the bag until her diamond engagement ring fell into her palm. She slipped the ring on her finger and stared at it, sparkling like a ray of sunshine, here in the bowels of hell.

# Chapter 36

APRIL 18, 1906, EAGLE'S RUN

Sara's lower back ached again. She always had trouble sleeping when Philippe was gone, but something about this trip with Luc had worried her. Pregnancy had a strange effect on her. She was hungry all the time, and every emotion she experienced, good or bad, seemed intensified twenty times over. She sat up in bed, stretching and yawning. When she walked downstairs, she held the railing tightly, for the weight of her belly unbalanced her. Upon reaching the kitchen, Sara looked out the picture window at the pink line on the horizon. The sun would rise within half an hour, and Rose would pad down the hallway to make breakfast, but Sara couldn't wait.

She gathered rolls, butter and jam in her arms, and was just about to step out of the larder when the floor beneath her started rattling. Sara's heart was in her throat—another earthquake. The earth rumbled and roared for what seemed like an eternity. She dropped the food and tried to run upstairs to fetch the children, but the shaking intensified, causing the walls to lurch as though they were mounted atop a carousel. Sara was thrown against the wall, and then sank to the floor. She covered her head as glass jars of preserves danced on their shelves and crashed down beside her. The dishes in the cupboard clattered and shattered when they hit the wood floor. Sara heard what sounded like a thunderclap upstairs. The desperate screams of Pippa and Johnny rang through the air.

She had to collect the children before the next shock hit. When the ground finally stopped pulsating, Sara ran to the foot of the stairs, carefully dodging bric-a-brac from the curio cabinet and glass shards from the picture frames that had hung on the wall. Pippa was already rushing down the stairs, holding hands with Johnny, tears streaming down her face.

Before Sara could comfort them, another shock knocked them to the floor. "Stay on your hands and knees! Watch out for the glass!" she cried, as she opened the front door and shepherded the children outside. "Rose!" Sara screamed. Rose appeared from her room at the back of the house, tottering and dazed, a gash on the side of her head. Sara lunged toward her, grabbed her arm, and pulled her outside. The four of them huddled on the front lawn, clear of the danger of falling debris, trembling to their cores.

Sara pressed her children to her chest, trying to cover their eyes. She glanced at the house: windows shattered, timbers splintered, front porch torn in two. She squinted to see the winery behind the house, to the northeast: the ground leading up to its doors had buckled and split, the windows and doors were broken and unhinged, but miraculously, its stone walls stood solidly. Thank God Philippe had listened to Matthew and insisted on steel bars to reinforce the structure. Sara's breath caught in her throat. Philippe, Luc. Matthew, Marie, Adeline and Gemma. Had the quake reached San Francisco, too?

Sara looked over her shoulder, south toward the bay. The morning fog was too thick to see anything yet. She turned to Rose, stood up and pressed the hem of her nightdress to Rose's wound. "What happened, Rose?"

"Oh, missus," she said, placing a quivering hand on her head. "The quake pushed me off the bed, and I hit the corner of the nightstand." She burst into tears.

Sara rubbed her back. "You're all right, Rose. We'll be all right." She wished she felt as calm as she tried to sound. Her stomach churned. How would she discover if Philippe and Luc were safe?

Once the rumbling from the aftershocks had ceased, Mac emerged from the house, carefully lowering himself down over the detached, lopsided porch. He must have run from his room in the barn and through the kitchen door, searching for them. As he approached, Sara noticed he had scratches on his face, and his hair was disheveled, but other than that, he looked unharmed. "Are any of you hurt?" he asked, squatting down beside them, still wearing his nightshirt along with some breeches he must have thrown on.

"Rose has a cut on her head, but the bleeding's slowed. The rest of us were a bit frightened, but we're not hurt." She extended her hand, and he silently pulled her to her feet. She placed a hand on the small of her back for support. "Mac, would you stay with Rose and the children? I need to go check on Aurora."

Mac shook his head. "No, ma'am. Philippe wouldn't like you traipsing over there by your lonesome, with the baby coming and all. I'll go."

Sara was grateful. "I'm most obliged, Mac, thank you. And bring her back here, will you? I don't want her to be alone."

As Mac set out for Aurora's, Sara pressed a hand to her aching head. "Rose, rest here with Pippa and Johnny." Sara stroked the children's heads reassuringly. "I'm going to walk around the property to survey the damage." Noticing Rose's expression of concern, she added, "Don't worry, I won't go far." Rose nodded, hugging the children close.

Pippa, now eight, glanced up at her mother with wide eyes. "What about Papa and Luc?" she whispered. The torment in her face mirrored Sara's emotions. Sara cupped her daughter's chin and said, "Your papa's smart. I'm sure he and Luc are safe and sound, but it may take them a while to return to us." She tried to smile, and then turned away before Pippa could read the fear on her face.

Sara headed north, around the back of the house, to take a look at the barns and winery. The old adobe cellars' walls had caved in; Sara could only pray that the aging barrels of wine were undamaged. She would wait until Mac returned to go inside and find out. Only one mare remained in the stables, and she was unharmed.

The barn where Mac slept was demolished. Sara couldn't fathom how he had only a few scratches. The entire second floor, where he lived, had collapsed onto the first, and was a jumble of splintered wood, nails and crushed glass. As she rounded the western side of the house, she glanced south past the torn-up earth and the acres of rattled vines to the sky, where the blanket of fog was thinning. Sara froze. A cloud of black smoke billowed in the distance.

She glanced at Rose and the children, still sitting where she'd left them on the front lawn. Their eyes flitted to the sky and their jaws fell open. Sara held up her palm, willing them to stay put. She walked slowly through the vines, cradling her stomach with one hand. She tugged the hem of her nightdress up with the other and broke into a run.

By the time she'd sprinted halfway down to Cuttings Wharf, she was panting so hard, she had to stop. She leaned over, hands pressed to her knees, and fought to catch her breath. Looking past the intersection of the creek and the river, past the marshlands and south to the bay, Sara saw a pall of black and gray smoke. San Francisco was burning.

In ten minutes, Mac and Aurora were by her side, half-carrying her back to the house. At Sara's insistence, Mac guided her gently around to the back and through the kitchen door. She looked around. With the exception of the wrecked porch, the bones of the house seemed unbroken. The floor, though, was covered with broken glass, crockery, bric-a-brac and spilled water, all of which

Sara gingerly stepped around on her way upstairs to her bedroom. Mac waited in the hallway while Sara dressed, combed her hair and stuffed all the cash she had hidden behind her hatbox—four hundred dollars—into her bag. She laced up a pair of sturdy shoes, grabbed clothes for the children, some salted ham, cheese and bread, and a jug of water, and returned outside with Mac.

She hugged Pippa and Johnny. "You be brave and good. I'm going to find Papa and Luc. Aurora and Rose will take care of you." Rose, Aurora and Mac all protested at once. "Aurora?" Sara pulled her friend aside.

"What if you die, or lose the baby?" Aurora whispered, scowling. "Philippe will never forgive us." She glanced at Pippa and Johnny. "Your children will never forgive you."

Sara pushed all concern for her own safety out of her head. "If I don't find Philippe and Luc, I will never forgive myself," she said fiercely. "Aurora, please do this for me. *Please.*" Without waiting for an answer, Sara turned.

Aurora grabbed her arm, halting her in her tracks. "Where are you going?"

"There's no time to wait for a train or ferry that may never come. I'll hire a skiff out of Cuttings Wharf to take me," Sara said.

"You'll do no such thing!" Aurora's grip tightened. They both looked up as Mac approached.

"I'll go with her. I know the route and the waters."

Aurora's face reddened. "You two are insane." She poked Mac's chest. "You'd better bring her back alive, you hear?" He nodded. "Bring your gun, and turn back if it's too rough out there."

After Mac had collected his firearm, a bag of food and two

lanterns, he took Sara down to the dock. Across the southern sloughs, Sara could see San Pablo Bay, littered with scows, skiffs, barges and huge iron-sided naval ships. Mac walked up to a short, scruffy man he seemed to know. A few minutes later, he was back.

He jerked a thumb at a flat-bottomed boat loaded with wine and produce. "This scow's leaving in ten minutes for one of the piers near the ferry depot," he said. Sara searched her mind, trying to recall Philippe's delivery route. He usually ended at Nob Hill and stayed overnight at Marie and Matthew's, but this time, he'd booked a hotel on Market Street. He would have been just blocks away from the wharf when the earthquake hit. The ferry would be his fastest route out of the burning city.

"Yes, let's go."

Mac held up a hand. "He says he can't take civilians. Too dangerous. Doesn't want to risk it." He looked back at his friend, who was watching them intently. "But as you see, I think he can be persuaded."

"Offer him a hundred."

"You sure?"

"Do I look anything but?" Sara reached into her bag, pulled out the cash and handed it to Mac.

Mac returned to offer the money, but the man just glowered, shaking his head. When Mac came back, Sara couldn't believe her ears. "He says he needs more because you're pregnant. More of a risk." Mac stuffed his hands in his pockets. "Maybe we should just head home and wait for Philippe and Luc," he suggested.

Sara pulled out another fifty. "For the baby's passage."

She scowled at the boatman as Mac helped her aboard. They navigated the cluttered Napa River slowly until they reached San Pablo Bay. When they reached San Francisco Bay an hour later, Sara could only stare at the tower of fire rising above the city's skyline. The heated air created a powerful suction, pulling winds from the east, west, north and south into the burning ruins. Shockingly, the bay waters were calm, but black smoke blocked out the sun and settled over the bay, raining ash on their scow. The creosote tasted bitter on Sara's tongue, and she covered her mouth and nose with a hanky.

When they reached the coast, they saw fireboats and naval boats surrounding the Ferry Building, showering the shore and buildings with salt water in an effort to halt the fire. Sara knew then that she'd made a grave mistake: she should never have come.

They docked at the end of Howard Street, near a huge navy destroyer. Sara climbed the wooden ladder up to the pier, with Mac right behind her. When they reached the top, they just stared at the hordes of people, many injured on stretchers or using crutches, being loaded onto the destroyer. Salt water pooled around her feet, soaking her shoes. And then she remembered. Marie worked near here, at Harbor Hospital. Sara had visited once last year. She waved to Mac to follow her as she walked briskly against the stream of refugees, searching everywhere for Philippe's face. From Market Street to Sacramento, fire engines lined the street, pointing their hoses at the inferno, only blocks away now. Sara pushed through the crowds until she finally spied the small wooden building through the haze of gray smoke. Above the double doors, Sara read, in block letters, *Harbor Emergency Hospital.*

She rushed inside, unprepared for the sight before her. Patients were everywhere, two to a bed or strewn about the linoleum floor, moaning, retching and bleeding. Some were missing limbs, and others were bandaged around their heads, arms and legs. Sara stood motionless. She looked everywhere, hoping to see Philippe or Luc, but found only strangers' expressions of fear and resignation.

She whirled around, determined to scour every inch of the building, when she ran straight into Matthew. He held her arm. "Sara?"

"Matthew? Oh, Matthew!" She hugged him tightly.

His face registered shock. "Did you come here looking for Philippe and Luc?"

"You've seen them?" Sara exclaimed, as Matthew frowned at Mac over her head.

"Yes, come with me. We've got to get you out of here. We've started to evacuate the rest of the patients. This place will be overrun by fire within the hour."

He took her by the elbow and guided her into the street. "Listen, Philippe, Luc, Marie and the children are all on that destroyer." He pointed at the Howard Street pier, where Sara and Mac's scow had just berthed. "It's headed for Mare Island."

"Are they—?"

"They'll be fine, but the ship's about to leave and you two need to get on it. Now go!"

"But you'll come soon?"

"I'll be right behind you, on the next ship out. Tell Marie. Go, Sara. Run!"

Mac pulled Sara by the hand, and they stumbled over the debris and lifeless bodies in the street. Sara kept her eyes fixed on the long steel boat and its four smokestacks, willing it to stay put until they reached the pier. By the time they reached the gangplank, Sara was huffing, trying to catch her breath. Sharp pains stabbed her back, and her stomach twisted with nausea. As they fell into line behind a hundred injured people, Sara leaned over, cradling her belly. Mac rested a hand on her back. "What's wrong, ma'am?"

Sara exhaled loudly. "Nothing, Mac. I'll be fine." The truth was that she'd just felt her first contraction. She had to get on that ship and find Marie.

When they reached the gangway, a cavalryman stopped them. "Only the wounded and their physicians, ma'am." Sara looked at him dumbfounded.

He just barked, "Pregnant ain't injured, ma'am. Please step aside." He shot Mac a withering look.

Sara wouldn't budge. "My family's on that ship. One of them is a physician, and I'm in labor. Either you let me on this ship, or I'm going to birth this baby right here in the street, and you'll have an even bigger problem on your hands." She bent over again, bracing for another contraction. She gulped air and gripped Mac's arm until it passed.

High atop his horse, the cavalryman looked unimpressed. "Desperate people will say anything," he told them. Just then, Sara felt a burst of water whoosh down her legs. Mac jumped back. Sara's heart hammered. This baby was coming now, and nothing—no one—was going to stop her from finding Marie. Sara looked the soldier in the eye, and then pushed straight past him onto the ship.

Marie leaned back against a stack of crates, feeling the sharp wind on her face. They'd just cleared the harbor and were charging toward the Mare Island naval shipyard, where they'd dock and, God willing, find a conveyance to Eagle's Run. Luc, Adeline and Gemma were sleeping, propped up against crates or each other for comfort. Marie scanned the harbor, packed with boats of all shapes and sizes. When she glanced at the city skyline, she saw a tall, spiraling chimney of black smoke engulfing Nob Hill, no doubt gutting their home, and advancing toward the hospital and piers. Her heart sank when she thought of Matthew. How would he escape the burning city? Would he leave in time? She signed the cross, laced her fingers and prayed.

Wounded people were packed like sardines on the long, narrow deck of the ship. A few physicians and uniformed nurses hovered over patients, checking vitals and reapplying bandages. Sara and Mac wove through the bodies, examining every face. Sharp labor pains stabbed her belly, slowing her progress and breaking her concentration. When she next raised her head, a vivid blue gaze instantly caught her eye.

Across the ship's stern, Philippe's worried face softened, and his eyes brimmed with affection. Then Sara knew: their passion might have temporarily ebbed, but everything Philippe had done since their marriage was out of love for his family. He'd only ever wanted to protect them—the best way he knew how.

Luc ran up to Sara, burying his face in her embrace and sobbing. "You came for us?" A lump formed in her throat.

"Always," she replied, grasping Luc's hand while holding Philippe's gaze.

When she reached him, she collapsed beside his cot. Philippe clasped her face in his hands. "What were you thinking?" he whispered, his expression shattering.

"I had to come," she replied breathlessly.

"You ran into a fire—pregnant! And Pippa and Johnny—they're unharmed?" he asked anxiously.

"Everyone's fine. Aurora and Rose are with them," she answered. Just then a strange, sickly feeling crept over her. Sara doubled over, writhing with pain. Marie knelt down beside her. "Sara, how far apart? Five minutes?" Sara nodded, gasping.

"Now? You're not due until next month!" Philippe wrapped his fingers around Sara's as she gasped for air. With the contraction, she gripped his hand so hard she worried she might break his fingers.

Marie rubbed her back, gently kneading away the tension in her shoulders and lower back. "Philippe, move slowly to the floor, and don't rip those stitches! Mac, will you help him?" When Philippe had vacated the cot, Marie laid Sara down on her left side. "Mac, Adeline—fetch some hot water and clean towels if you can find them." Marie sifted through a small leather bag. She pulled out scissors and rubber gloves, and doused them with disinfectant. She placed them on thin layers of gauze. "Sorry, Sara, but we have to do this here. Everyone move over there," Marie ordered. She lifted Sara's skirts. "You're fully dilated and the baby's crowning." Without a moment's hesitation, Marie dug under her own skirts to untie her double-ruffle petticoat.

Sara bore down. After three pushes, she finally felt the release, and within seconds, Marie caught the baby in a cocoon of petticoats. A girl! Marie clipped and tied the cord, cleaned the girl's mouth and pinched her bottom. The baby let out a high-pitched, vibrating wail. Marie swaddled her tightly and handed her to a stunned Philippe. "Your daughter," Marie said, smiling.

Philippe cupped one hand under the baby's neck and nestled her gently in the crook of his arm. The child was bright-eyed, with a wet tangle of dark hair. Philippe flashed Sara a tender look, and she summoned just enough strength to stroke her new daughter's pink cheek.

When Adeline and Mac appeared with water and clean sheets, Marie cleaned the baby's soft, wrinkled skin and swaddled her in a sheet. She handed her to Sara, sat back against her wooden crate, and sighed.

The U.S.S. *Preble* steamed into San Pablo Bay toward the Mare Island naval shipyard. None of them would ever forget the day San Francisco died—and the day Lydia Marguerite Lemieux was born from its ashes.

# Chapter 37

**M**arie was losing faith. They'd arrived at Eagle's Run Thursday afternoon and slept for twelve hours, with the exception of Sara, who rose every few hours to nurse baby Lydia. It was now Friday afternoon, and there was still no word from Matthew.

Marie was determined to keep busy. Philippe saddled their one remaining horse, and they rode into downtown Napa. She tightened her arms around his waist, keeping a close eye on his injured leg. She knew he probably wouldn't pay any mind to his doctor's orders to be careful.

When they arrived in town, Marie was surprised to see so many people crowding the streets, wearing tattered and soiled clothing—refugees from the city. The National Guard patrolled the area with billy clubs and rifles, even at the church, where Marie and Philippe dropped off used clothing to the ladies of the Red Cross. When they finally reached the central telegraph office, they were turned away. The brick façade of Newman's store had fallen into Main Street, knocking out the telegraph, telephone and power lines on the south side of town.

They rode up Main Street to the northern Napa telegraph office. The south wall of the Opera House had fallen into the Napa Hotel annex, and Revere House, where Matthew and Marie had once dined, was demolished. Chimneys had toppled, and dry goods had blown through shattered storefronts into the street. Their mare slowed to a walk, stepping carefully among the scraps of wreckage and avoiding the wagons, buggies and motorcars surrounding them. Marie sneezed and coughed from the thick dust, but at least here there was less evidence of singed flesh and decay. Few lives had been lost in Napa, she guessed.

They waited in line for hours to send telegrams to Matthew's parents, who were visiting Los Angeles, to his brother and sister-in-law in St. Helena, and to Marie's parents. Philippe sent news of their safety to his grandparents in Tours and Sara's mother in Vouvray.

They left Napa at twilight. Marie held the lantern high over Philippe's shoulder, trying to light the dirt road before them. An hour later, she caught sight of the house. She could see the children's shadows bobbing in the yellow light of the few undamaged windows. Matthew's face appeared in her mind. Her longing for

411

him pressed against her chest, smothering whatever courage she'd mustered over these last bleak days.

When she lifted her head again, she caught sight of a tree silhouetted against the indigo sky. A single lantern floated in the air beneath the sprawling maple where Marie had first kissed Matthew. She squinted, and the glow brightened, revealing the form of a man. He was leaning against the trunk, one hand tucked casually in his trouser pocket. Marie's skin tingled with relief, and a sob escaped her throat. "Stop! Stop the horse, Philippe!" she cried.

He tugged on the reins, and the horse halted abruptly. Marie handed Philippe the lantern. She slid off the horse, hiked up her skirt and ran into the widespread arms of her husband.

# Chapter 38

Sara lit the thick birthday candle she'd bought for Luc when he was three years old. Today, she would keep the flame burning until the wax melted from the number nine down to ten. The candle would serve as a blessing, according to the superstitions, and would ward off any evil spirits bold enough to enter their home.

August twentieth was always bittersweet for Sara. It marked Luc's entrance into the world, but also her sister Lydia's departure from it. Though the sadness of that day would never leave Sara, the sharpness of her pain had eased with the passing of time.

After everything they'd endured in April, Sara was determined to make this the best birthday Luc had ever celebrated. She'd even written Maman and Jacques, as well as Philippe's grandparents, to ask them to send notes and trinkets for him on his special day. As Rose finished swirling the mile-high frosting on the chocolate cake, everyone settled into chairs around the dining room table. Sara piled Luc's gifts and letters on the table in front of him. He beamed with excitement, rubbing his hands together with delight.

"Go ahead, we're all waiting," Sara urged.

Luc smiled, and pulled a letter from the stack. Instead of ripping it open, as Sara expected, his hand fell to the table. He lifted his head, and said, in a voice far too serious for a ten-year-old, "Thank you so much for being here."

The family burst into applause, pressing him to open his gifts. The first was a letter from Maman and Jacques. They sent a photograph of themselves, standing in the flourishing replanted vineyard of Saint Martin. Sara glanced at the photo over the boy's shoulder, happy to see Maman and Jacques looking so healthy and content.

The second envelope came from François and Jacqueline LeBlanc, Philippe's grandparents. Two letters fell into Luc's hand when he opened it: one for him, and one for his father. While Luc read his letter aloud, Sara watched her husband, quietly studying his in the corner. His expression was unreadable, but when he slipped out into the kitchen, she followed.

"What is it?" she asked.

"Nothing to worry about now, but . . ." Philippe handed it to Sara. "Read it."

Sara scanned the elegant handwriting. "The kaiser is building a navy to wage war? Do you really think it's a serious threat?"

414

"I don't know." Philippe shrugged. "My grandfather reads the international papers, and keeps up with all the political news. He's seen a lot in his seventy-seven years."

A cheer erupting from the dining room tugged on Sara's heartstrings. "Perhaps, but I'm sure he'll alert us to any real danger." She slid her arms through Philippe's. "In the meantime, let's worry about our ten-year-old, who needs your help cutting his birthday cake." Sara kissed him enticingly, coaxing a smile from his lips.

After the party, Sara and Philippe took their customary evening walk in the vineyard. They strolled into the pear grove, pausing to murmur goodnight to the child who hadn't survived. Sara found this nightly ritual soothing. She picked up a stray stone, wiped it clean of moss and dirt, and placed it back into the circle of smooth, white rocks marking the little girl's grave. They continued on, past the winery. The spotless windows glistened in the waning sunlight, for they had just finished cleaning every inch of the building—and scrubbing and hosing down the equipment—in anticipation of the upcoming harvest.

As they moved deeper between the vines, Sara's skirts swished against the broad cabernet leaves. She felt for the medium-sized, tightly knit clusters and plucked several small blue-black grapes to sample. She playfully popped one in Philippe's mouth. He chewed, closing his eyes in concentration. "Nearly ready, I'd say."

Sara bit into the grape's thick skin. "Mmm," she agreed, her mind drifting back to the day they started their life together. "Do you remember what you said on our wedding night—to calm me down when I was nervous?" They fell into step together, meandering west toward the creek.

Philippe squinted at the gold and blue sky, streaked with wide, thin clouds. "Didn't I quote Genesis? 'And the two shall become one flesh,'" he recalled, threading his fingers between hers.

"That's right." She squeezed his hand. "But I've been wondering," she began searchingly, "if the two become one flesh, then what about the spirit?"

"The spirit?" He laughed softly, sliding his arms around her and resting his chin on her shoulder. "I think it's fair to say that we'll *never* be fully joined in spirit, my love—you're far too stubborn." She elbowed his ribs and tried to wriggle from his arms, but he tightened his grip. "Perhaps the most we can hope for," he whispered tantalizingly, "is a satisfying roll in the hay." He pinched her derrière, and Sara squealed, jumping from his grasp. He reached for her, but she sprinted down the slope and ducked into a cluster of scrub pines by the creek's edge. As she waited in the shadows, shiny green needles rustled in the evening breeze, tickling her skin. Out of nowhere he sprang, catching her waist. She shrieked with laughter, until his fingers twined through her hair and he quietly, insistently, parted her lips.

Sara had never been this sure of anything. Her spirit would always return home—not to Saint Martin, or to Eagle's Run—but home to Philippe.

# Author's Note

*The California Wife* was a pleasure to research and create. The main characters and storylines leapt from my imagination onto the page, but in order to lend historical credibility to the novel, I've included real historical figures, places and events.

For example, I mention several influential winemaking pioneers of the nineteenth century, such as Gustave Niebaum, Charles Krug, Agoston Haraszthy, George Husmann, Henry J. Crocker, H.W. Crabb, W. J. Hotchkiss, and Jacob and Frederick Beringer. The fête at the Italian Swiss Colony in Asti—featuring the gigantic wine cistern—and the meeting between the Napa winemakers and the California Wine Makers' Corporation in St. Helena are actual events that transpired during 1898. The conversation between W. J. Hotchkiss and the Napa winemakers is based on the transcript from the meeting ("Wine Men at St. Helena," *Pacific Wine & Spirit Review*, February 24, 1898, p. 22). To explore Napa's history in more detail, I recommend William Heintz's *California's Napa*

*Valley* (Scottwall Associates, 1999) and Lauren Coodley's *Napa: The Transformation of an American Town* (Arcadia Publishing, 2007).

The Paris Exposition of 1900, and the controversy over the decision to exclude American wines from the competition, dominated the wine trade papers of the day. I recommend Richard Mandell's *Paris 1900: The Great World's Fair* (University of Toronto Press, 1967) for more details about the exposition and its exhibits.

The Women's Medical College of the New York Infirmary, founded by Elizabeth Blackwell, America's first female medical doctor, boasted cutting-edge obstetrics and clinical midwifery programs in the late 1800s. Dr. Levi Cooper Lane founded San Francisco's Cooper Medical College in 1882, and built its medical school on the corner of Sacramento and Webster streets with his own funds. It became the second medical school in California to admit women in the late nineteenth century. The two-hundred-bed Lane Hospital was established in 1895, adjacent to the medical school. In 1908, Stanford University acquired Cooper Medical College, which became the cornerstone of what is now the Stanford University School of Medicine. To learn more about Dr. Levi Cooper Lane and the rich history of Stanford University's School of Medicine, see www.lane.stanford.edu/med-history/.

The Harbor Emergency Hospital was located on the San Francisco waterfront and received many of the injured during the Great Earthquake and Fire of 1906. This earthquake, which measured close to 8.0 on the Richter scale, was one of the most significant natural disasters of the century. Along with the fires that raged from April 18 to 23, it killed thousands of people and destroyed nearly eighty percent of the city. For more information, I recommend reading Gladys Hansen and Emmett Condon's *Denial of Disaster: The Untold Story and Photographs of the San Francisco Earthquake of 1906* (Cameron & Company, 1989) or visiting the virtual museum of the City of San Francisco at www.sfmuseum.org.

For more information on my research and writing process, please visit my website at www.kristenharnisch.com.

# Acknowledgments

*The California Wife* was a labor of love and would not exist without the advice and enthusiasm of these generous people:

My agent, April Eberhardt, who champions my work with such energy and positivity.

My She Writes Press publisher Brooke Warner and author liaison Caitlyn Levin, and BookSparks CEO Crystal Patriarche, for their boundless encouragement and guidance.

My amazing editor, Lorissa Sengara, who artfully guided me through several revisions.

The HarperCollins Canada team—Iris Tupholme, Jane Warren, and Noelle Zitzer—for their gracious collaboration with She Writes Press.

Sarah Wight for her crackerjack copyediting, and Lisa Bettencourt for the gorgeous cover design.

Nancy Levenberg and Alexandria Brown of the Napa County Historical Society, for reviewing the manuscript and providing the photos, eyewitness accounts and other research materials I needed to craft accurate descriptions of historical Napa.

Tina Vierra, associate publisher of *Wines and Vines,* for her careful review of the manuscript's grape-growing and winemaking scenes.

Patrick Cahill, DO, for sharing his obstetrical expertise, and Kevin Miller, MD, for reviewing the medical and surgical scenes with such precision.

Greg Gauthier, Susan Falcon and Thalia Balderas of Bouchaine Vineyards; Paul Torre and Tim Stel of Beringer Vineyards; Kim Ilsley, a real-life vintner's daughter; Steve Stone of Napa Valley Bike Tours; and Max Roher of Max Napa Tours for their hospitality and for sharing their vast knowledge about winemaking and Napa history.

My publicist, Caitlin Hamilton Summie, for her tireless efforts to make *The Vintner's Daughter* and this series a success.

The entire staff of the Darien Library for the superb research materials they provided along the way.

My first readers, Maryellen Lacroix, Frank Lacroix and S. Taylor Harnisch, for their thoughtful and constructive critiques of my early drafts.

Janel Silva, who first introduced me to the great city of San Francisco and its fascinating history.

Kathy Murphy and the Pulpwood Queens for their wonderful southern hospitality and support.

The Donelan, Lacroix and Harnisch families and all the devoted friends, readers, book clubs, bloggers, booksellers and libraries who have contributed to the success of this series. I am deeply indebted to them.

And last, but never least, a heartfelt thank you to my four biggest fans: David, Ellen, Ryan and Julia.

# Selected Titles From She Writes Press

She Writes Press is an independent publishing company founded to serve women writers everywhere. Visit us at www.shewritespress.com.

*The Vintner's Daughter* by Kristen Harnisch. $16.95, 978-163152-929-0. Set against the sweeping canvas of French and California vineyard life in the late 1890s, this is the compelling tale of one woman's struggle to reclaim her family's Loire Valley vineyard—and her life.

*A Cup of Redemption* by Carole Bumpus. $16.95, 978-1-938314-90-2. Three women, each with their own secrets and shames, seek to make peace with their pasts and carve out new identities for themselves.

*The Island of Worthy Boys* by Connie Hertzberg Mayo. $16.95, 978-1-63152-001-3. In early-19th-century Boston, two adolescent boys escape arrest after accidentally killing a man by conning their way into an island school for boys—a perfect place to hide, as long as they can keep their web of lies from unraveling.

*The Black Velvet Coat by Jill G. Hall. $16.95,* 978-1-63152-009-9. When the current owner of a black velvet coat—a San Francisco artist in search of inspiration—and the original owner, a 1960s heiress who fled her affluent life fifty years earlier, cross paths, their lives are forever changed . . . for the better.

*Little Woman in Blue: A Novel of May Alcott by Jeannine Atkins. $16.95,* 978-1-63152-987-0. Based on May Alcott's letters and diaries, as well as memoirs written by her neighbors, *Little Woman in Blue* puts May at the center of the story *she* might have told about sisterhood and rivalry in her extraordinary family.

*Faint Promise of Rain* by Anjali Mitter Duva. $16.95, 978-1-938314-97-1. Adhira, a young girl born to a family of Hindu temple dancers, is raised to be dutiful—but ultimately, as the world around her changes, it is her own bold choice that will determine the fate of her family and of their tradition.